Penguin Books

The Disinherited

Matt Cohen was born in Kingston, Ontario in 1942 and educated at the University of Toronto. He taught religious studies at McMaster University before becoming a full time writer.

His first novel was published in 1969. Since then, he has received critical acclaim for many books, notably ''The Salem Novels'' — *The Disinherited, The Colours of War, The Sweet Second Summer of Kitty Malone* and *Flowers of Darkness. Café le Dog*, his most recent collection of stories, was published in the Penguin Short Fiction series, and *The Spanish Doctor*, a novel, is also available in a Penguin edition. Cohen has contributed articles and stories to a wide variety of magazines including *The Malahat Review, The Sewanee Review* and *Saturday Night*.

Matt Cohen now lives in Toronto, Ontario.

MATT COHEN

The Disinherited

Penguin Books

Penguin Books Canada Limited, 2801 John Street, Markham, Ontario, Canada L3R 1B4
Penguin Books Ltd., Harmondsworth, Middlesex, England
Penguin Books, 40 West 23rd Street, New York, New York 10010 U.S.A.
Penguin Books Australia Ltd., Ringwood, Victoria, Australia
Penguin Books (N.Z.) Ltd., Private Bag, Takapuna, Auckland 9, New Zealand

Published in Penguin Books, 1986

Copyright © Matt Cohen, 1974

First published by McClelland and Stewart Limited, 1974

All rights reserved

Manufactured in Canada by Gagne Printing Limited

Canadian Cataloguing in Publication Data

Cohen, Matt, 1942-
  The disinherited

ISBN 0-14-009303-6

I. Title.

PS8555.038D57 1986   C813'.54   C86-093617-1
PR9199.3.C63D57 1986

for my parents

The
Disinherited

ONE

Richard Thomas woke up, aware of a slight feeling of nausea, an acid line that stretched from the base of his throat to his stomach. He swallowed and rolled over, but the feeling persisted until finally, drowsy and resentful, he pushed and worked himself into a sitting position. He adjusted the blanket over his knees and rubbed his eyes. Outside the air was dark blue with the pre-dawn light. But the room itself was still uncertain and composed of shadows. Through the window he could see the silhouette of the maple tree that stood beside the house, shading the summer kitchen. The tree was old and brittle: two of its limbs had been sheared off by lightning and Richard Thomas was always saying that he should take it down before the rest of it fell over and caved in the roof. Sitting up, he felt better. He remembered that he had intended to sleep in. He thought of his son Erik, in the city, in his glass cage. He should be at home, to help with the haying in the summer. It wasn't right to have to hire people. Richard Thomas's shoulder was sore, and when he moved it he became aware of his stomach again. It hadn't relaxed; it was just simmering. He had thought it was an ulcer, but the doctor had said it was diabetes and gave him a special diet. Miranda moved in her sleep, pushing into him for comfort. He slid his hand under the blanket and let it rest on her back. Her skin was smooth and hot. He considered waking her up; it had been more than a week, but then decided against it. The impulse was fading already.

He could see the brass handles on the dresser now, and folds in the blanket. He slid carefully out of bed, took his clothes off the chair, and walked slowly downstairs to the kitchen. Standing in front of the mirror, brushing his teeth, he looked old, even to himself. There were tiny red veins in the whites of his eyes and his flesh, beneath the surface of the sunburn, seemed pale and distant. He spat into the drain. He still had his own teeth, anyway. All the Thomases had good teeth. Not like Brian, half his age, who had false teeth already. He splashed water over his face, making sure to wash the sleep out of the corners of his eyes, and went back into the kitchen to make his tea. His stomach still wasn't quite right. He poured the tea and sat down at the table. Automatically he reached out for the bottle of saccharine, rejected it, and took a spoon and a half of sugar.

He wrapped his hands around the teacup. It always amazed him to see Erik's hands, the fingers slender and defined. His own were like battered sausages, covered with calluses and scars. "Like an old bull," he said to himself. A few months ago, in the middle of winter, he and Miranda had driven into town to go to a movie. There had been a short about bullfighting. It had pleased him to see how many people it took to weaken the bull enough for the matador. The matador himself, making his fancy passes over a half-dead animal, hadn't impressed him at all. He finished his tea and went outside.

It was still too early to do anything, Brian and Nancy wouldn't be up for an hour. He walked past their trailer and through the barnyard towards the fields. His stomach was uneasy, but the movement distracted him, made it feel possible that he wouldn't have to bring up. There was a place where he used to stand with Miranda when they were first married. She liked to walk with him there, after supper, and talk about what they would do with the farm. "Don't you ever cry?" she had screamed at him one time. That was when he had gone there, angry over something, he couldn't remember now, and sat for an hour, waiting for her. She came to him and they had started fighting again, shouting at each other. His parents had never argued, but he and Miranda, the first few years, fought over everything. Some nights he had stormed out of the house and gone down to drink with Pat Frank and his twin brother Mark. He would never say why he was there, just sit in the kitchen and drink with the two men until dawn. Then, dazed and contrite, he would make his way home.

If she was still angry, she would be wearing her nightgown and sleeping in the spare room. Otherwise, she would be in their bed, naked and patient.

When he and Miranda came back to the farm, his father had moved to a house in town. The house was long gone now, there was a supermarket there instead. Every Sunday his father would come out to the farm and eat dinner with them. Then, when it got dark, he would drive back. He had a housekeeper who lived in but he never brought her with him. When he came to dinner he seemed entirely disinterested in the farm. At first he asked polite questions about what Richard was doing, but eventually he didn't even do that. After the funeral, Richard Thomas had cried. He had lain on his bed, shaking with grief and rage at his father's withdrawal. Miranda had kissed the tears from his cheeks. "It's good to cry," she had said. Her lips had been moist and cool. With the tips of her fingers she had traced patterns on his skin.

The sun spread a narrow yellow band along the horizon. Richard Thomas, a slow-moving, stocky man in his mid-sixties, worked his way down the hill, away from the barnyard and the house and the trailer. His stomach felt worse; with each step it bounced uneasily, precariously, but he thought that the motion might help. He wanted to go back to the lake and watch the sun rise there. They had told him to sell his waterfront for cottages, had said that his taxes would go up, that he would be better off without it. The man from the real estate company, sure of himself in his striped shirt and tie, had sat across the kitchen table from him and pulled out the forms from his briefcase, already filled out and just waiting for Richard Thomas's signature. "Fifty thousand dollars," the man had said. "We'll give you fifty thousand dollars for the waterfront and the island." He said it in a low voice, as if the mention of so much money might scare Richard Thomas to death and prevent him from signing the deed. "I was brought up on a farm myself," the man had said. "I know how it is." He helped himself to some of Richard's tobacco and expertly rolled himself a cigarette, backwards, the way the farmers do it. He pulled out a cigarette lighter, one of the ones that hold their fluid in clear plastic. It had a naked woman etched onto the plastic. He saw Richard Thomas looking at it and held it out to him. "Ever seen one of these?"

Miranda, sitting on the couch, spoke for the first time. "I gave him one for Christmas," she said. "Five years ago."

The man put the lighter back in his pocket. He picked one of the wooden matches out of the glass on the table and struck it with his thumbnail. He took a map of the farm out of his briefcase and spread it out in front of him on the table. "We'll put a road in here," he said. "You won't even see it from the house."

The hay fields, freshly cut, looked smooth and manicured in the early morning light. The toes of his boots were black with dew. He stopped at the gate to the maple bush, deliberating whether to lift it open or climb over it. He leaned on the gate, decided against a cigarette, tried to remember when the thing with his stomach had started. Sometimes he reassured himself by saying that he had always had a weak stomach, that nothing had changed; but he knew better. He felt dizzy and sat down in the grass. He leaned his back against the gatepost and lit a cigarette. There was nothing wrong with sitting down, not when he hadn't slept properly. The doctor had given him some pills for dizziness; but he had left them in the house, in the bathroom cabinet where they had been put the day he got them. They were right beside the vitamin pills that Miranda had bought him after he complained about not having enough energy. He had watched them chase the bull on horses, tearing into its hide and slashing it with their strange spears. The bull, bleeding from its flanks and exhausted and disoriented, had finally turned on one of its tormentors, pinning horse and rider against the wall of the ring. Richard Thomas squeezed the cigarette out between his thumb and forefinger, put it in his shirt pocket, and got to his feet. He opened the gate and then closed it behind him. It was easy, he had done it thousands of times, he couldn't imagine why he had hesitated. He started to walk quickly, enjoying the feeling of the blood pumping through his body, the full green smell of the trees and ferns. They had managed to pull the rider up over the wall but the horse had been gored.

He stopped to look in the sugar house. It hadn't been used for over ten years, since Erik left. The arch had caved in but the building was still solid. Light came in through the cracks of the roof and stood in the air like thin white sheets. He lit his cigarette again and blew smoke towards the roof, watching it appear and disappear in the strips of light. He always did that, every time he came there. His father had shown it to him one spring, fifty years ago. "Here," Simon Thomas had said, handing Richard his cigar, "you try it." That, Richard realized, was the time when the problem had begun, the first time he could remember the feeling of ripe discontent in his stomach.

Walking slowly, it took longer than he had planned, and when he finally got to the beach the sun was already up. It hovered, just above the horizon, gradually cutting through the mist on the lake. He had always thought that after Erik was married he would let him build a summer cabin on the island. He had mentioned that once, before Erik left for college. It had been understood. But he wasn't married and he didn't want to come back to the farm. Erik had even once said to Brian, as if it was for him to say, that *he* should build a cottage there. "It must be hot in the trailer," Erik had said. That was at Christmas, the only time he ever came home now.

Richard Thomas searched on the beach for flat stones and skipped them out across the water. When he threw the stones there were flashes of pain across his chest and left shoulder. He swung his arms around to loosen up but it just made him dizzy again. He sat down and lit another cigarette. The doctor had told him to quit smoking. He bent over to stub out the cigarette. As his hand moved towards the ground, the morning jolted and stopped. He pressed his left elbow against his ribs and tried to get a breath. He knew in the very centre of it there would be a place where he could gather himself and survive. It was as if some giant hand had wrapped around his ribs and was locking him into that one particular moment.

When he came back to consciousness, he was lying in the sand. He pushed himself up and wiped his face clean. He felt better, purged of whatever it had been. He stood up, wobbled briefly, and then started walking back towards the house. The sun was much higher, he thought it must be eight o'clock. They would be wondering where he was. His arm was a bit numb, as if it were asleep, but he knew that the danger had passed.

He wished he had woken Miranda up, made love one last time. "Don't be stupid," he said aloud. The sound of his voice startled him, as if he had thought he might be dead already. He felt unfinished, unready to die. A man was supposed to be prepared when his time came. He noticed his left arm was almost without feeling, was swinging vacantly at his side. He forced his hand into his pocket. He tried to imagine Brian running the farm. Brian and Nancy living in the house, making Miranda stay in the trailer. No, that wasn't fair: they wouldn't do that. Nancy, who was slow and sullen, sometimes left dishes for days on end. She was taking pills, she had told Miranda, so that they wouldn't have a baby. She wanted to wait until they had saved some money.

"Why don't you pay Brian a decent wage?" she had asked him. It was one day when she was hanging up her clothes on the line that stretched from the house to the trailer, the trailer he had bought for Brian when he said he was getting married. They had eaten together the first few months but after that Nancy had said something to Miranda. Every afternoon Nancy would come to the house and take things from the freezer and the shelves for supper. But at noon they all had dinner in the house. Nancy always seemed to be dragging herself around, as if she couldn't wait to get out.

"She's just like that," Miranda said. She hadn't gotten fat. She refused to eat potatoes and sometimes did exercises in the morning. At the sugar house again, he paused to rest. His shirt and pants were soaked with sweat. His face was wet too. He felt caught out; he had been crying the whole time, like a little boy who had cut his knee and was hobbling home to be kissed.

He had accepted death only once. A few years ago, when he was ploughing, the tractor had hit a rock and started to tip. There was no time to do anything, he could feel the centre of gravity swinging wildly away; he hoped it wouldn't hurt too much. Then the plough caught again, and the tractor righted itself. His brother had been killed the same way.

He had started moving again, slowly, keeping his head down and picking his way along the path that should have been familiar. The moisture in his eyes threw everything out of focus. The grass looked disembodied, closer than it should have been, the stalks bending and swaying above the green fallen maple leaves so his shoes, black and soaked through now, seemed up too high, near where his knees should be, moving slowly along the path like a young boy's shoes, carefully assessing each separate unit of space, considering and deciding exactly what should be crushed and what should be allowed to remain. One of his toes encountered a log, dug into the soft bark and stood still while the rest of him swayed, threatened to pitch over and finally ended up half kneeling, supported by a hand that had found a branch. He pushed against the branch, freed his foot and sat down on the log. That was a mistake, he thought, shouldn't have sat down. No it was all right; it had been necessary. His vision seemed better, even better than it normally was. The crying had loosened and relaxed the muscles in his face. There was a noise beside him. A partridge emerged from the underbrush. It stopped, looked at him, moved closer, cocked its head. "Come here," Richard said. The bird stepped forward then stopped again. It flexed its tail feathers and a shudder ran through its wings. Then, almost spastically, it flapped its wings again, twice, and landed on Richard Thomas's lap. They were both so surprised that they froze. Then it moved again. Its foot landed on Richard Thomas's hand and the feel of it, damp cold and spiny, startled him and he drew his hand away. Then the bird was gone, leaving more strange sensations where the feathers had brushed across his face.

"And you know it," Miranda had always concluded her arguments, appealing to the Greater Rationality within him, the part of him she had so painstakingly constructed over the years of their marriage. She was still slim, but she had been taut, suggesting columns and electricity. All her movements fascinated him then: he wanted to know how she could remain and live inside herself. In the early part of her pregnancy, her belly and breasts resisted swelling. For months she was like an intimate stranger, always in heat. When they made love, colour flushed her skin in slow waves, rising through her throat and turning her face a bright red. When it was finished, she receded, rolled over on her side and drew up her knees. Constantly now he was checking his body, the state of his stiffened arm and hand, the relative measures of pain.

The bush was in constant motion, greens and browns flowed into each other, washed across the surface of his vision. Images of Miranda, wearing that blue dress: arms holding Erik high in the air. The bull, panting and sweating, not yet convinced that this was an interesting way to die. "Catch," Miranda said, and threw him the baby, laughing at the feet kicking out of the diapers and Richard's outrage. When they used to laugh together it was like sex, without ownership of voice or body. When he wanted her after dinner, he would sit in a particular way, his chair shoved back and his feet up on the table. She was more direct and came to him in the fields and in the mornings. He could still feel the imprint of the bird's foot on his hand. Toes, partially webbed. Upper surfaces black and corrugated but smooth and cold underneath. He realized that he had misplaced himself, that the log he was sitting on was not supposed to be there, that he had changed direction without knowing it and had circled back towards the lake. It would be impossible to get up. Different currents were moving through his body, claiming the rhythms of his bones and nerves. It would be impossible to get up.

"Don't be stupid," he said to himself. The sound of his own voice startled him: it seemed to have broken apart. He closed his eyes and saw himself lying, without a coffin, in an open grave. He pushed and wriggled, making himself comfortable in the soft earth.

"Doesn't he look nice," Miranda said.

"Don't be stupid," Richard said again, this time more loudly so that his voice sounded stronger. He opened his eyes and looked up to the tops of the trees where the light was filtering through unevenly. He was reminded of the sugar house, his stomach, his father's cheap cigars. He had tried to take Erik for walks the same way but knew that it wasn't working.

"A man can't die before his time," his father used to say—a statement not of hope, but of duty. It was uttered in only one context; it was an alternative, when he was tired, to taking Richard to the woodshed. Miranda had tried to prohibit that too.

She was crying but it was contained. "It was better this way," she said. "He would have hated to go in a hospital." Beside her stood Nancy. She was piously clasping a bible in her hands. Erik and Brian peered over the grave, to make sure he was dead, and then drifted away, with Nancy, so only Miranda was left. "Well," she said, "what are you waiting for?"

He could feel the moisture between his toes. He took out a cigarette and lit it, promising not to inhale. He looked at the log carefully. There were still marks from the chains. He stood up.

He noticed he was hunched forward and he straightened himself, pushing his head and neck until his spine felt centred. His left hand was still in his pocket. He corrected his direction and began walking again. When he came to the path, he dropped the cigarette and pushed it with his foot until the tip was covered with dirt. He kept his eyes up, looking ahead, calculating the distance to the next rise. It had once been a road, but it was ten years since he had driven a tractor or a team over it, and now the alders and aspen were pushing in on it, outgrowing the young maples and being threatened themselves only by juniper bushes. There was no wind but the trees seemed to be swaying, almost fluid. He found that he was holding his arm over his face, to protect himself from snapping branches. To make the kill the matador had plunged the knife into the bull's neck; a long red antenna had sprung forward, hung over the forehead like a third eye, one that perceived the universe as a punctured spine and a sudden spurt of blood. Richard Thomas stopped. He thought he had heard someone calling his name. He heard it again. He wanted to shout back but could barely raise his voice above a whisper. The bull had slowed down. It wavered past the matador and then sank to its knees. The matador waited until the bull stopped trembling and then walked up to it and cut off one of its ears. He presented it to a black-haired woman who was sitting in the front row. She smiled at him and put her arm on his shoulder.

The real estate man had marked the hydro right-of-way on his map too. It cut from the invisible road, through a stand of basswood, to the waterfront. "They give you seventy dollars for every pole they put up," he said. "And they'll saw your trees into five-foot lengths for firewood." He pushed the map around, so Richard could see it.

"We got an oil furnace," Miranda said. "Right after we learned how to read. It was advertised in the newspaper, you know."

"We're honest," the real estate man said. He pulled a brown paper bag out of his briefcase and dumped its contents on the table. There were, held together by blue elastics, twenty bundles, each composed of ten one-hundred-dollar bills. "I didn't come here to waste your time," he said. He spread the bundles in a neat row across the kitchen table. When Brian came in for dinner, the real estate man was still there. He had put away his money and his maps and was working on a bottle of rye and a package of cigars. "Pleased to know you," he said, when Brian was introduced to him. After dinner, when he had persuaded Brian to take a cigar, he handed him the lighter with the naked lady. "Ever see one of these?"

He turned towards the camera and Richard Thomas saw him for the first time. He was very young, just beginning to grow a moustache, and with sideburns that lightened at the tips. His face was tanned and oval and his eyes were shining like those of a newly ascended angel. The last scene showed the crowd singing and drinking at an outdoor café. The young matador was seated at the best table, surrounded by admirers. Beside him, but completely removed from everything, the black-haired woman waited.

Each step separated into its components: a survey of the ground for rocks and branches; a motion through the pain and back down again; a new beginning. He was certain that he would make it if he didn't fall; it was only necessary to repeat the cycle over and over. Then he was propped against the gate to the hayfield; his muscles had collapsed and the wood pressed into the bones of his arm. He heard the voice clearly now. He looked up and saw Brian running through the field towards him, waving and shouting. He waved back at him. Brian seemed upset. His face was all red and he was running so fast that he was tripping all over himself. Richard Thomas wiped his face and took out a cigarette. It was a beautiful morning. He was glad the hay was all in and he didn't have to work today. He waved at Brian again. It was too hot to run. Brian slowed down. When he got to the gate, his face was flushed and sweating. He looked embarrassed. Richard remembered the time he had walked into the barn and caught Brian with Katherine Malone's youngest daughter. "What's wrong?"

"Nothing," Brian said. "Miranda was worried about you."

"I decided to go for a walk. I woke up early." They were leaning on the gate. Everything was normal. "Did you do the chores?"

Brian nodded. Richard noticed that he was still smoking the cigarette. His left arm was stiff and he had the hand stuck into his pocket. He put his cigarette in his mouth and with his right hand he reached into his shirt, to offer Brian the package. "Cigarette?" he asked. As he spoke, his own cigarette fell out of his mouth onto the ground. He put his foot over it casually.

"No thanks," Brian said. He saw the sand on the side of Richard's face.

"I went to sleep down by the lake," Richard said. "I haven't been sleeping well." He stepped back from the gate, so Brian could open it. Brian was staring at him. "I was just on my way home. I thought we'd take down that old maple tree today." Now Brian was looking down at the ground. "It's all right," Richard said. He noticed that he had dropped the package of cigarettes too. He stood, waiting for Brian to do something. Brian seemed oblivious to everything. "Open the gate," Richard Thomas said. Brian lifted the gate open and Richard walked through. "I dropped my cigarettes."

"Yes," Brian said. He retrieved the package and then closed the gate. They stood in the hayfield.

"It has to be ploughed in the fall," Richard said. "We'll plant corn. We should have built a new silo years ago." He looked around the freshly cut field, imagining it was August and the corn was ripe. "What do you think?"

"The barn roof needs fixing," Brian said. "The beams are starting to rot." He began walking across the field. After a few steps he turned around. Richard hadn't moved. "Do you want me to get the truck?"

"No rush," Richard said. "It's a beautiful day." He looked up at the sky. It was almost noon. "After lunch we'll measure up the roof and then tomorrow we can drive to town and get the materials." The long sentence left him winded. The motion was disturbing his stomach but he knew he could make it home. He would tell Miranda that he had the flu and would go to sleep. In the middle of the field he stopped again. He felt dizzy. "I think I'll sit down," he said. He used Brian's arm for support and lowered himself carefully to the ground. "It's a beautiful day. No point rushing to work." He gestured vaguely, indicating that Brian should sit down. "How about a cigarette?" he asked.

Brian crouched down beside him and started to take the package out of his pocket. He hesitated and looked at Richard Thomas again. "Jesus," he whispered, "you fooled me. I thought you were drunk." He got up and started running across the field, towards the house. "Don't move," he shouted back.

Richard Thomas lay down on his back and closed his eyes. He felt cold. He should have brought his jacket. He wondered what it would be like to be dead. He could feel a bug crawling up his leg. He reached out to slap it. When he moved it happened again, fast and harsh. He could feel something inside resisting and being torn apart.

He didn't hear the truck at all, but he opened his eyes and tried to help as Brian dragged him into the front seat. They were afraid to move him, so they left him in the truck while they waited for the doctor. He was aware of Miranda sitting beside him, sponging his face and holding his hand. She tried to make him take one of his pills but he couldn't swallow properly. She put a cushion under his head. "Don't try to talk," she said. "Everything is going to be fine." She rolled up his sleeve. Another pair of hands reached into the truck. He tensed up for the needle and then passed out again.

TWO

There was the time, in the October of his nineteenth year, his second year at university, that Erik came home from Toronto to visit. It was fall already, not quite that stage of the season that is simply a prelude to winter, but a fall that was connected to late summer, and the leaves, still sparsely scattered along the sides of the roads and in the ditches, seemed less a kind of death than an unnamed late harvest, a not necessarily final moment through which the summer would pass before relinquishing its fertility. He had tried to swallow the city whole but it still lay undigested in him, so that being home was uncomfortable for him and he was resentful of the feeling of familiarity, of relief almost, of the way Richard and Miranda and Brian still claimed him for their own, as easily and thoughtlessly as the land. When it was finally afternoon and it was possible for him to leave for a few hours, he went for a drive in Richard's car, aimlessly following the back roads, watching the leaves change from yellow elm and poplar to the redder maple of the higher land and then back again to yellows and browns and even just greens where he wound around the edges of swamps. He had driven like that, aimlessly and without any real sense of where he was, the first summer Richard let him use the car. His drives then took place in some vaguely indistinct geography; he never knew the exact location of what he found except in terms of the mythology he constructed on those hazy afternoons when he wanted only to get away from everything, to have time pass quickly so that he would be away from home finally, somewhere where he was not known. Sometimes he would come to an abandoned farm or overgrown road that he had not seen before; then he would get out of his car and walk around, enjoying just walking in a way, he didn't know why, that he never did at home. On one of those drives he had come to an old empty house. The wood, never painted, was weathered grey and the roof was sagged and missing patches of shingles. There was an apple tree beside the house, so close that one of its branches was pushed right through a broken window in the downstairs. For some reason he hadn't gone inside but instead had climbed up on the roof of the house and sat there in the sun, smoking cigarettes and dropping the butts down the chimney.

In his mythology of escape the old house had endured in his memory as the place where he had most clearly known his own desire to leave the farm. That, and his curiosity about whether he could find it again, were in his mind this particular October afternoon. A few miles north of the farm there was a large section of country that seemed very homogeneous to him. The farms were poorer than his father's. Much of the land had never even been divided into farms: it had been logged and now supported only rocks and second-growth brush that crowded in on itself and the road. He remembered that the house was shielded from view by an orchard and he drove slowly, not wanting to miss it even though he wasn't sure whether, in fact, he was on the right road.

He noticed her as he was turning and, because it was so unexpected, he saw her only in passing, a snapshot that had to register to be real: there were no details, only angles and colours framed by the now open door of the school house. When he looked again, the confusion of movement gradually resolved into a small child and the way that the woman walked, a strange swaying stride that should have been a limp, picking her way carefully down the broken steps and then, lifting the child down after her, walking out towards the road. The grass around the house was long and wild but the fence had been fixed and the mailbox was freshly painted. When she came up to the fence, she stood without speaking, looking at him, the jacked-up car, and the tools and wheel as if they all fitted together in some impossible happening, an apparition from outer space, as if, in fact, the entire occurrence of him and his dissembled machine had struck her speechless.

The child too was silent. It was of indeterminate sex, wore diapers and a faded sweatshirt, and stood with one hand in its mother's and the other rubbing contemplatively against its mouth.

The fence was fixed but there was no gate, only an old set of hinges and a rope strung between two nails. She lifted off the rope and came and sat in the grass beside his spare tire, cross-legged, with the child still at her side, holding to her but staring at him gravely as if, perhaps, he might be the answer to the unnamed problem. He wanted to say hello, or make some comment about the weather, or at least have something come out of his mouth that would acknowledge their presence and distract from the crippled machine with its excess parts, but everything about the woman was somehow so uncertain and unexpected that he could only turn his back on them and resume work on his car. The woman let the child go; it wandered about him as he worked, trying to pick things up, dropping them when it succeeded, and sticking its fingers in the holes of the wheel.

It was October, cold enough so that the nightly frosts were beginning to cut down the grass and all but the hardiest flowers. In the morning the mist had been so heavy that he couldn't even see the barn, but then the sun had burned it away, leaving the day warm and lazy. When he was finished, he stood up and turned around. She was still sitting, her eyes closed against the sun and her hands folded into each other. Unwilling to go home yet and unsure what to do, he sat down beside her. It was impossible to tell her age, he thought she must be a bit older than him but not much. Her hair was blonde and wispy, and enclosed her face in a way he found not attractive but, as with everything else about her, vaguely alienating. "You can come in if you want," she said. She picked up the baby and led him inside. The school house's exterior had not been altered but inside the ceiling had been lowered to keep in the heat and the far end had been partitioned off. There was a loom against one wall and, in the very centre of the building, a huge black cookstove. "Sit down if you like," she said, gesturing towards the kitchen table. "Would you like a beer?" Her voice was high and pure, like the voice of a young girl, and when she spoke her face also seemed younger than it had.

"Is it your baby?"

"It's a girl. I didn't mean to scare you but I haven't talked with anyone for a few days. It's just a habit."

"That's all right," Erik said. The bottle of beer was wet from the well. She hadn't offered him a glass. There was a tea towel draped over the back of his chair; he used it to dry his glass and then put it back. It was the kind of towel that used to come in boxes of laundry detergent and had "Home Sweet Home" stamped on both sides, in red, surrounded by a red outline of a heart with a green vine twined around it. Clusters of grapes hung from the vine. While he drank his beer she moved about the kitchen, cooking dinner for the girl who was now seated in a highchair beside the table.

"Do you want anything to eat?"

"No thanks," Erik said. There were a man's hunting jacket and boots near the door, an empty rifle rack on the wall. The partitioned-off section of the school house had two doors in it; one of them was ajar and the other closed with a padlock.

Later, they unlocked the door and stood naked and shivering in the room, holding up a kerosene lantern. The room was filled with an elaborate construction of long hollow joined tubes which were interconnected to each other and slid along tracks which had been bolted to the ceiling. On one wall was a series of jars filled with different colours of paint, and in a corner was a small motor and something that resembled the control panel of a gigantic electric train. "It's a mechanical painter," she said. "He spent all last winter building it. He sits in the corner and plays with the controls; the painting comes out on a piece of canvas put in the centre of the floor."

"I see."

"No, you don't. This year he wants to get an automatic pilot." She locked the door and led him back into the bedroom. "He wouldn't mind about this, but he'd kill me if he knew I'd shown someone his machine."

"He shouldn't have left you a key to the room."

"He trusts me," she said. "I only ask him for money." In the light he had seen how her body had been marked by the child. There was even a scar where the baby had been removed. He had been afraid to look at it closely, but now, in the dark, he traced it with his finger. "Don't be afraid," she said. "It doesn't hurt anymore." She pinched him suddenly, startling him so much he rolled off the bed. The quilt and then the weight of her body followed; before he could catch his breath, she had wrapped the quilt around his head and was sitting astride him, pounding his chest and shouting. When she stopped, she just let him go and climbed back up onto the bed. "I'm sorry," she said. "Was it your first time?"

"I guess so."

"I didn't mean to scare you."

"You didn't." Erik briefly saw himself as he must appear to her: sitting on the floor, with his knees drawn protectively into his chest, hugging the quilt around his shoulders, rocking back and forth and shivering.

"Do you want me to say that I love you?"

"No," Erik said.

"But you'd feel better."

"I don't care," Erik said. "I think I'd better go home." She had felt strange, her skin loose and pliable as if it might pull away from her body.

"But you'd feel better," she said. "It wouldn't be right if I had just walked outside and accosted you for no reason at all except, say, that my husband was away."

"Anyone can get lonely."

"I wasn't lonely." When they went outside, the dew on their feet was wet and cold. They walked around the old school house, peering in the windows, sliding along the grass, looking for ghosts and other clues. "Before we bought it, an old man lived here. It was the school he used to go to, and all his friends who were still alive would come and visit him so they could sit in their old school house and drink. He was really small, about five feet tall and thin too. He told us that he had been brought up by a family down the road. They let him live there as long as he liked but they never paid him a cent. He couldn't ever afford to move out until he started getting the pension."

"My brother is adopted."

"It can be different now. The only chance this man ever had was to go to war. He would have been all right if he'd gone to the war. If he'd come back. Then he would have had some money saved. At least he would have known there was something else."

They were standing still, on the front steps of the school house. Erik was getting cold again. "I'm sorry," she said. "I guess I just don't like sex. I need it but I don't like it."

"Forget it."

"My husband got to know him somehow; they were distant relatives. We used to come and see him sometimes. Then he died and we bought the place."

"What a depressing story," Erik said.

"Yes," she said. "I guess I'm like that." She held the door open for Erik. "It's funny, you know, you hardly talk at all for a while and then once you get going it's really important. Sometimes when I haven't seen anyone for a few weeks I start talking to myself. Late at night, after she's in bed, I walk round and round the school house, explaining things to myself or telling stories or even, what's best of all, having conversations with people. Sometimes, say, with my parents or Jim, but then I get bored with them, maybe I was already bored with them, and I talk to people I haven't seen for years, like someone I was in public school with and hardly ever knew or the guy that took me to my first drive-in movie, I couldn't stand him, he had bad breath and he kept wanting to kiss me, or to this girl I used to know in high school but then she moved away and I never found out her new address, anyway I talk to her, as if I was writing a long letter. After talking to her, I always have this warm feeling, as if we'd just seen each other and been really close. I guess it's easy in a way, getting that kind of satisfaction from people without them even being there, it's like dreaming about someone without their permission, and sometimes I think the world would be a lot better if everyone knew how to do that though, for all I know, everyone does it all the time. Maybe that's even the problem: everyone's so busy having all these imaginary conversations, they don't ever, you know, consult each other. Like even right now, here I am talking to you, I hardly know you, well, we slept together but that wasn't very important, we both just did it because we were supposed to in some way, telling you these things which make no sense to you at all. The funny thing is I don't even care if you're listening, I mean I hope you are but I'm not worried about it, not in the way I used to be with my husband. I guess that was because I was afraid he would listen; that was the only thing that really bothered me about him, that he might kill me. He always looked at me, not like you are now but with his eyes pushed round and open, like they were made out of glass and he was *blind*; he didn't do it to be mean or anything, it was just his idea of a joke. What he liked best was having a wife, someone to take care of him and cook and help fill up the space when he felt empty. Once I gave him an inflatable doll for his birthday. The only time he could feel anything for me was when I was asleep. He was always asking me if I was tired yet. Just to please him sometimes I would pretend I was and go to bed. He would sit up for a while, playing solitaire and having a few drinks, maybe cleaning one of his guns or working on his machine. Then he would turn off all the lights and come to bed. He would get under the blankets very carefully, he didn't want to wake me up, and then he'd try to have me. At first I didn't mind, I guess I felt sorry for him and anyway, I wanted it too, even if I had to pretend I didn't, but after a few months I just learned to sleep with my legs crossed. Anyway, it's over. Some people would even say that because it's gone I shouldn't talk about it, as if nothing had ever happened and each second was altogether new and cut off."

He was suddenly conscious of his hands on the tablecloth, of the expensive restaurant and the sputtering candle that was sending explosions of light and darkness against Valerie's face. He tried to compose himself. He shifted his legs under the table and moved back in his chair. Then he leaned forward. No, it wasn't right: he could feel his body tense against the awkward angle.

"Do you want me to read your palm?"

"Sure," Erik said. He held out his hand to Valerie. If he was going to propose to her it should be something more elaborate, a moonlight ceremony with music and a diamond ring. There should be staging, a prepared speech, a series of declarations leading up to the final flashing moment of betrothal when he slipped the ring on her finger and fell to his knees. Or something entirely casual: a joke in bed about the colour of the curtains or the name of their third child. Or nothing at all. Simply this last dinner in honour of his new job and an ironic farewell at the airport.

"I'll miss Toronto," he would say.

"Yes."

"Well then, good-bye." He would board the airplane. He

would drink scotch and look out the window. A few hours later he would arrive at the University of Alberta. A taxi would take him directly to the office of the chairman.

"I can't see your hand," Valerie said. Erik moved it closer to the candle. "I'm sorry," Valerie said, "I've forgotten the book already." A waiter appeared with a tray of pastries and they both chose the same kind: chocolate icing with a lemon centre.

Erik ate his with his fingers. When he was finished, he wiped his face with his napkin and looked across at Valerie. She had her pastry on a small plate and was cutting it up with a knife and fork. When she opened her mouth her teeth showed, but just a little. That was something he admired about her, her mouth and teeth. They seemed dainty and lady-like to him. He didn't like people with sloppy faces. He wondered if she could grow herbs: his mother had always lined the bottom of the garden with bursts of parsley and chives.

"What are you thinking about?"

"My mother's garden," Erik said. The waiter brought their coffee. Soon they would be able to go back to his apartment and take off their clothes. Valerie was wearing a new dress and would want to hang it up carefully. He felt he only met her at certain moments while she, unaware, went about the business of cycling blood through her anterior regions, breathing, walking from the bed to the window. As he reached into his pocket for cigarettes, the unfamiliar cloth of the suit scratched against his skin. He offered the pack to her. They had eaten quickly, hardly talking, not really enjoying the food. They had discussed marriage a few times but only theoretically, as if it was something that couldn't possibly happen to them. Some of their friends had children. Their houses seemed to be filled with broken toys and empty beer bottles. "I don't know how they can live like that," Erik would say afterwards, meaning not just the mess but the constant harassment.

"Let's go," Valerie said. The waiter had put their bill in a little plastic tray. "Don't forget to leave a tip." Outside they walked quickly. It was warm and humid and the streets were filled with cars and people.

"We could go to a movie," Erik said.

"No. We'll go back to my place."

Her apartment was the third floor of a large run-down house near the centre of the city. Although the house, from the outside, seemed almost like a mansion, the apartment itself was small and closed in by slanted ceilings. She had painted the walls white and then filled them with posters, and it looked like thousands of similar apartments in Toronto, speaking distantly of trips to Europe and movies very old and very new. There was a back door leading to a fire escape. It and all the windows were open for the breeze. They sat on the floor, drinking beer. Erik looked at the posters on the wall and tried to imagine the apartment transferred, whole, to Edmonton. "I'll miss Toronto," Erik said.

"Yes."

"I don't know why," he said.

"There was never anything here I wanted." He picked at the label of his beer bottle. "I wonder, you know, if you ever get through things by thinking. I wonder if you ever get through anything at all. Anyway." He didn't want the job but he didn't know what else to do. "Maybe I should go back to the farm for a year. Do physical work. You know."

Valerie laughed. "You never do any work at all," she said. "I've never known anyone as lazy as you." She moved over so she was sitting beside Erik. "You don't have to marry me."

"It's not that."

"We could just say good-bye and send letters to each other. People do it all the time. We could plan a vacation, but at the last minute it would be impossible."

"Something would come up."

"Yes," Valerie said. "Something like that."

He was looking at one of her posters, a brass church spire. That was the way he felt it should have been: a hot summer day on a terrace somewhere, red wine, overlooking the Mediterranean and laced through with the sounds of sand and water.

"I would have liked to have seen your farm," she said.

"My father's farm."

"Yes," she said. She had edged away from him again, so that they were facing each other over the beer bottles and the ashtray. "I'm sorry," she said. "I didn't mean to make it so difficult."

"It's not your fault."

"Decisions are stupid anyway. It's better just to let things happen." She stood up and walked to the hall. Erik followed her. The hall was the only place in the apartment where it was possible to move around freely, without being conscious of the eaves. The house had once belonged to someone wealthy enough to have had servants. The kitchen, only half the size of the bathroom, was a made-over cupboard. "Well," Valerie said. They were standing in the hall, looking at the stairs. She went into the bedroom. "Help me undo my dress," she said. Her skin was soft, almost like velvet. He wanted to be swallowed up by her and to be free of her. He slid his tongue between her teeth, sharp and even. She enclosed him. He forgot the dinner. He was left finally with the image of himself flopping on top of her like a fish out of water.

"I love you," she said. She twisted away from him so that he would be forced to look at her. He wanted to answer her in some way but didn't know how. He could feel his mouth twitching vaguely. "It's not important," she said. The urge to laughter was cramping his stomach and sprayed across the muscles of his face. "What's so funny?"

"I don't know." He reached over her to the night-table and picked up the package of cigarettes. He rotated it so it would open towards him. She took the package from his hand and skimmed it across the room. "I feel I should be able to respond," Erik said.

"Yes," Valerie said. "I guess you should."

They slept and when they woke up it was dark. It was cooler outside and they walked slowly to Erik's place, stopping on the way to buy an ice cream cone. "This is what I like about the city," Erik said. "You can always walk around at night."

"Can't you do that in the country? I think it would be nicer."

"You can walk but there's nowhere to go."

They had come to his apartment building. As they went into the lobby, Valerie pointed at the furniture, chained to the floor. "I like the way they do that," she said. "You know it's going to be there in the morning." The padded walls of the elevator had been slashed open so often that they appeared to be a collage of masking tape. Even as they were approaching his door they could hear the ringing of the telephone.

"Erik?" As always, Brian shouted into the phone. Erik could hear the familiar buzzing of the rural party line behind his brother's voice. "Richard had a heart attack," Brian said. "Take the night train. Pat or I will meet you." That was all. Valerie drove down to the station with him and kissed him under the big clock.

"I'll come with you, if you want."

"You don't have to come."

"I'd like to."

He looked up at the clock and then kissed her again. "Hurry," she said. "You'll miss your train." She took his arm and started him moving in the direction of the departure gate.

"I'll call you in a couple of days, when things are calmer." As he said it he imagined himself getting onto the train and never seeing her again. "Don't worry," he said.

"It's a fast train between stations but it stops a lot." The conductor pronounced this to Erik, in practiced cadence, and then, pleased with his own wit, continued on his way down the near-empty car. The train moved in fits and starts, pausing at every town between Toronto and Montreal to exchange grey canvas mailbags. The trip took eight hours: perfect for those who had berths and were travelling the whole way. Erik was only going half the distance, to Kingston, and he sat up the whole time.

He had his feet propped against the seat in front of him. More like Miranda than his father, he gave the impression of being vaguely ethereal, of being cautiously balanced in his movements—as if he didn't quite trust the reality of his body and was carefully shepherding it through the necessary obstacles. He was large-boned but not heavy. Unmarked by his years on the farm, he had entirely taken on the appearance and smoothness of a city person—one for whom the outdoors was a park where one might seek diversion or renewal but not the place where survival was decided. He was tall with wide-set blue eyes, thick brown hair, and Richard Thomas's strong features. While the train was stopped at Belleville he went and got some coffee and a hamburger that was heated in a micro-wave oven. It tasted of cardboard and stale tomato paste.

When he was home at Christmas, he went to visit her again. All traces of the leaves and fall colours were completely erased. The trees were stripped bare and metallic, grey-black in the late afternoon sun that glared off the ice on the road, the banks of snow on either side that already, only Christmas, pushed up over some of the fences. An old pick-up truck was parked in the front yard of the school house and wood was stacked high against its southern wall. She opened the door for him as he knocked, not seeming at all surprised to see him. The boots and coat were still near the door but there were no toys scattered about and the highchair had been pushed into the corner. The room was hot and filled with the steam of cooking. She brought him soup and then stood at the table, slicing cheese into thin yellow squares. She put the slices on top of pieces of bread and then slid them into the oven of the cookstove that now, in winter, dominated the room even more than it had in the fall. "I had to trade," she said, "the kid for the truck. He has a new woman now and she made him take it all to court so he could have visiting rights at Christmas and during the summer." As she moved about the kitchen, he noticed again, as he had when he first saw her, the stiffness in the centre of her walk that made her sway slightly, as if she ought to limp. And remembered too the hard, almost corded muscles that wrapped round from her belly to her back, the triangle at the base of her spine that curved wildly to one side. "I knew you'd come back," she said. She was wearing sweaters, three sweaters, and a heavy tweed skirt. On the back of one of her hands were two long scratches; they might have been made by a cat. "I didn't dream about you very much," she said. "Did you dream about me?"

"Once," Erik said. All he could remember was that it had been in the afternoon and that someone, pounding on his door wanting a book, had woken him up in the middle. Her fingers were bony and strong: now she was back at the table, waiting for him to tell his dream, tearing open a fresh package of cigarettes. The first time they met, in the summer, he had not even asked her name. But this time she had told him, Rose. And he had wanted to say it was the perfect name for her because he found her as dangerous as she was beautiful, to be looked at without touching, but of course said nothing because it would have sounded so appallingly sincere. She still had the loom. It stood in the shadows, but even in that partial light he was struck by the bright colours of the wool. "How did you know I would come back?" he asked.

"I guess I just wanted you too," she said. She was smoking her cigarette now, nervously, tapping off the ashes before they had a chance to form. The sight of her agitation only increased his own; he pushed his chair back, it squeaked and bumped across the floor. He wondered if the husband still came to have her in the middle of the night, driving from wherever he lived and then sneaking in the door with a flashlight, sliding into bed with her. He had forgotten his soup and now discovered he was holding a spoon in his hand; he bent his head towards the bowl and moved his hands, but the spoon slipped, dropping out of his fingers onto the table.

"Nerves," he said.

"Do you want me to feed you?"

"It's all right," Erik said. The soup was thick with vegetables—carrots and celery and potatoes. He loaded the spoon up carefully, making sure it wasn't too full, and brought it to his mouth.

"Do you like college?"

"It's all right," Erik said. The room seemed to be getting warmer. He took off his coat. He wondered how she could be wearing so many sweaters. The room was permeated with the odour of woodsmoke, cedar and maple, but through that he could smell his sandwich. As quickly as he thought of it she was on her feet, standing over the stove and opening the oven.

"It's not burnt at all," she said. There was a pile of split wood beside the stove and she re-filled the firebox before bringing his food to the table. "It's hopeless," she said. "Soon you'll have lines on your forehead and smoke cigarettes. What you need is a hat." She went back to the stove and got herself some soup. "The Chinese tell each other their dreams every morning. Anyway, how are you?"

"I'm fine," Erik said. The question pushed him away from her. He felt suddenly depressed and disinterested in words.

"It snowed so much," she said. "I didn't want her to go but they just took her. His stupid machine is still here though; I bet she won't ever let him get that in the house. All the oil froze anyway and some of the tubes split open." Her face was still tanned but her hair had darkened without the summer sun. It was streaked and wispy. "You can finish your dream if you want," she said. "What happened to the giraffe?" With the child gone she seemed different: more present in a way because that part of her which had been constantly attentive to the child was now integrated into her and asking something from him. It was there not so much in her voice as in the movements of her arms and hands which swam around as she talked, shaping the space between them in a way which was unclear but somehow threatening. "I went to the city and saw a play," she said. "It was about two paralytics who had only one wheelchair between them."

"That's good," Erik said. He wondered if by coming to see her he had somehow refused her the possibility of privacy.

"They could take turns pushing it," she said, "but they didn't know if they could leave it behind. They had to spend all their time taking care of the wheelchair and arguing about whether they were afraid."

"What happened?"

"They got married," she said. She had woven a shawl for herself and now she was enclosed in it, wearing it as an exotic cowl, as if winter had revealed her to be an exotic creature who could survive out of season. While Erik ate his sandwich, she picked at the cellophane of the cigarette package, tearing it off in strips and wadding it up into tiny balls which she flicked absently about the room, sometimes at Erik, sometimes in no direction at all. He felt she was trying to make some sort of web about him, that his fear of her was irrational, that there must somewhere be a long intricate answer for this long intricate puzzle. When she finally came round the table and touched him, he jumped, startled, as if she had moved straight through the protective layer of flesh and made direct contact with nerves and bones.

He was the only passenger to get off at Kingston. Pat Frank was waiting for him, leaning against the wall of the station. "I hardly knew you," Pat said. "You look like a preacher." He led Erik towards the car. "Your mother's at home. You can go to the hospital in the morning. They say he just needs some rest."

"I was out," Erik said. "I didn't get home until almost midnight. I just made the train."

Pat nodded. He drove casually, in the middle of the road, as if anyone with any sense knew better than to squeeze himself over to one side. There was no traffic. "You want a drink?"

"No." He had been to Edmonton only once, for the interview. He had almost no impression at all: a flat, neatly-made city with a river running through its centre. On the train he had known exactly what it would be like to introduce Valerie to his father. He would look her over point by point, pretending to inspect her as if she were a cow he was considering at a sale. Maybe he would pinch her to make sure that the flesh was firm, not just layered fat. Then he would slap Erik on the shoulder.

"Looks good," he would say. "Better get her while she's still young."

The sky was showing signs of dawn. Erik adjusted himself in his seat, lit a cigarette. He couldn't seem to focus on what was happening. He felt he should be back in Toronto, in bed with Valerie, building castles. He let himself doze but was woken when the cigarette started to burn into his fingers. His last real conversation with Richard had been eight years ago, the night he drove home from the school house in the snow. It was after midnight when he got home and he found Richard in his arm-chair, waiting for him and drinking the sherry that Erik had brought him for Christmas. Sitting down, Erik felt a curious unease, a resentment springing from the feeling that he was known and transparent to this man who happened to be his father. He was conscious that he was sitting very still, preserving the feeling of warmth against his skin, the details of her body that had stayed so close to him. This time too they had gone outside afterwards, stood away from the building and watched the snow falling slowly in its light. He rested the glass on his knee, twisting the stem back and forth so that the liquid rode up to the rim of the glass, bored and polite, watching the corners of the room float through the sherry.

"I spoke to a lawyer," Richard said. "He told me it would be best if the land for your house was surveyed and put into a separate deed."

"What house?" Erik had asked, stupidly, then realized what Richard had meant.

"You could live here if you wanted," Richard said, "but I thought it would be better, if you get married, to have a place of your own." Erik, even when he was with her, had known that what made it possible for them was the knowledge that he would leave. He felt like a fool, peering timidly over the sherry glass at his father. Nothing had ever been said about Erik returning to the farm and each knew exactly what the conflict was. "I have a map here," Richard said. "You just have to mark on it whatever you want."

"I don't want anything," Erik said. "You know that."

"And what are you going to do?" Richard had asked. "Buy a house in the city and keep a cow in your shed?" He looked towards the window that faced Brian's trailer, as if he was afraid Brian might be outside, eavesdropping. It had been Christmas night; everyone else was alseep. "And what do you think I'll do with the farm? Turn it into a fishing camp?"

"It's your farm," Erik had said. "And there's Brian."

"You're my son. I made it for you." When he said that, Richard's face turned red, embarrassed that he had had to state the obvious.

"You made it for yourself." Erik stood up, to go to bed. Richard stayed in his chair for a moment, fiddling with his glass. Then he too stood up, the glass in his hand. He looked down at it, turned it slowly in his palm, and then threw the glass into the wall. It broke with a sharp crack, showering fragments all over the room.

"Clean it up," Richard had said. He turned off the light above his chair and stomped upstairs. Erik left early the next day. Miranda wrote and apologized for Richard, saying that he hadn't been feeling well. Since then, Erik had come home once a year, at Christmas. He and Richard confined their discussions to the weather and local politics.

"Funny thing is that your father won't say anything about what happened. Didn't even want to go to the hospital." The car lurched as Pat swerved to avoid a groundhog. "Brian said that when he met your father he looked real strange. Said he was too weak to lift the gate."

"How is he?"

"They say he'll be home in a couple of weeks. Just needs some rest." Pat coughed and cleared his throat. "Guess you didn't hear about the strange lady."

"No."

"Madame something. She lives in Kingston. Your mother's been going every week for almost a year, ever since she got the car. The madame reads tea leaves. Your father almost had a fit when he found out. Came over and got drunk, just like he used to. And he said she charges two dollars a visit. Didn't do him any good though, she still goes, every single week."

THREE

Erik took an orange from the windowsill. It was warm from the sun and he rolled it in his hands. Earlier, he had helped with the chores, picking his way through the barn and the yard, trying to keep his shoes clean. "It's just cowshit," Brian had said, pleased to see Erik uncomfortable. Now Brian was sitting at the kitchen table, with Nancy, eating his breakfast, slowly. He had always done that, Erik remembered, just like Richard Thomas, chewed each mouthful slowly and methodically until it was reduced to liquid. Brian's arms were thick and tanned, the old scars barely visible, as if time and his flesh had found this collaboration easy enough, each year washing away the record of fire and death.

From the window he could see Brian and Nancy's trailer. They had painted it metallic green and white and it was set on a foundation of concrete blocks. The clothesline, stretched from the trailer to the house, sagged like a broken toy telephone. They used to take turns punching each other on the shoulder until one of them gave in. As they got older, their strength had grown faster than their ability to absorb pain. He wondered how bad it was with his father, if they would have him connected up to bottles and machines. He had never liked to see people with too many tubes coming out of them; he had never even given blood. From the upstairs came the sounds of Miranda's preparations: water being turned on and off, the opening and closing of bureau drawers, the high heels clicking paths from room to room as she assembled her supplies. When she was ready, the noises stopped and she paused at the head of the stairs—her warning—and then came down into the kitchen.

She was still slim, and her black hair had very little grey. In a way that was particularly her own she always seemed slightly off-balanced and nervous, keyed to move in the least predictable direction. The lines on her face were carved deep and symmetrical. They ran from her nose to her mouth, bisected her cheeks, exploded away from her eyes. Her forehead was short and vertical, creased not with frown marks but from eyebrows perpetually raised. When Erik was younger, Miranda had told him that her face was like that because it had to express everything she was not allowed to put into words. "But you talk all the time," he had said.

"It doesn't matter," she replied. "It's just skimmed right off the top." Now she was holding her handbag, stuffed with extra pyjamas and reading material for Richard, and looking about the kitchen, automatically checking what had been eaten, making sure each had fed enough to endure the day. When they got to the hospital and were waiting beside the nursing station, she stood exactly the same way, her head and shoulders moving about as she inspected and blinked—once for each detail.

It was nine o'clock. Breakfast was over and an orderly was wheeling a large aluminum cart from door to door, picking up the trays of dirty dishes. Some patients were out of bed already, walking the halls in their housecoats and slippers, stopping occasionally at a neighbour's to visit. Those who were waiting for their operations moved briskly. They avoided the others, the ones who shuffled slowly up and down wearing, beneath their housecoats, the regulation blue hospital pyjamas because they were still unable, or unwilling, to change into their own. Two or three of these, Erik noticed, carried in their hands, pressed close to their bodies, transparent plastic bags. Beside the elevator, waiting to go downstairs for surgery, were two people lying on stretchers. Each was attended by a nurse and lay calm and sedated, staring quietly at the ceiling.

Opposite the nursing station, blocking an open doorway marked FIRE EXIT, sat an old woman in a wheelchair. She was wearing a bright tartan robe. Her eyelids, her lips, her hair and even her fingernails had blended together with her skin to form a thick colourless grey surface. The resilience was gone and everywhere a bone or a ligament protruded, it was layered by creases and folds. Her head was lolled to one side but her hands moved ceaselessly, drumming the arms of her chair in one last urgent and incomprehensible message.

"Are you all right?" Erik asked. The sight of her made his own skin feel thick and separate from the rest of his body.

The woman kept moving her fingers. Almost convulsively, she jerked her head so that it lay nearer Erik. She opened her eyes and stared at him. The whites were completely bloodshot but the pupils seemed hazy and diffused. He wondered if she saw anything at all. She grunted something he couldn't understand and then waited for him to reply.

"Do you want anything?" She nodded her head slowly up and down and made another noise. Then, apparently satisfied or resigned, she closed her eyes again. Her jaws worked but no words came out. She lifted her hands to her head and began running her fingers through her hair. It was still long and each time her hands emerged from it she clenched her fists. Finally she gave up. Her hands were lowered back to the chipped varnish of her wheelchair, and resumed their task.

When he looked up, Brian and Nancy were already going down the hall, towards Richard Thomas's room. Miranda was waiting for him. As they walked, Erik looked in the open doors of the rooms. Most of them were the same size but the number of beds in each room ranged from one to four. Some of the rooms still had their curtains drawn and there were a couple with closed doors and NO ENTRY signs. "She was there yesterday too," Miranda said. "The nurse says that she just likes to sit there, to watch the people coming and going."

His father's room had two beds, Miranda had paid the extra for semi-private, and one of them, though it looked slept in, was empty. Richard Thomas was half-sitting; the back of the bed was at an angle and there were pillows propping him up further. There were no visible tubes or wires extruding from his body. In the corner, beside his bed, was an oxygen tank. The face mask and other apparatus were sloppily draped over top of it. Brian and Nancy had gotten up from their chairs and were in the process of settling down on the other bed.

"I thought you were supposed to be sick," Erik said. He sat

down in one of the chairs while Miranda arranged herself, kissed Richard, took out extra pyjamas for him and then his reading glasses and a thick file folder. His father looked better than he had expected, but the sight of Richard in bed jolted him, reminded him that his past would eventually be reduced to remembered deaths. Richard's palm was cool and strong; he would survive for a while. The glasses had frames of black lacquered plastic, and with them on Richard Thomas looked like an aging square-faced businessman set to an unpleasant task.

"You needn't worry about me," Richard said. His voice surprised Erik. It was almost mellifluous and lacked the harmonics of illness. But his left arm was motionless, seemed to have been placed carefully into position and left there. He scanned the papers and then put a magazine under them and signed them, each one carefully, along the dotted line at the bottom. His face was slightly flushed, but he was washed and shaven and his hair was combed. "It says here," Richard pointed at the papers, "I can have two hundred dollars a month for not working." His voice was almost challenging. He looked at Erik, bland and direct. "If you can run the farm without me telling you what to do."

"He can turn a switch," Brian said, "but he doesn't like to get his feet dirty." Erik got up and went towards the window so he could light a cigarette. There were only a few cars parked in the courtyard, as if to say that no one got sick in the summer. The building across from him was a laboratory and he could see white-coated figures sitting bent over their microscopes.

Remembered deaths and unwanted gifts, Erik thought, observing the way his father was working around the subject of the farm, unsure what the terms were or who must be betrayed. The four of them were all talking at once, meaningless chatter about weather and cows. Miranda, sitting up straight in the chair beside Richard's bed, directed traffic, keeping the noise flows muted and overlapping, washing over Richard a magical and gaudy quilt. The past would collapse into these deaths and Erik wondered if Richard, lying in his bed and trying to force them to accept his will about the farm, had also turned his back on life at every moment, had denied Miranda and withheld himself from her the way he was now excising Valerie: long smooth death-strokes where the blood never showed. Through and across the overlay of the four voices he could hear shouting and slamming in the corridor and, as he went to the door to investigate, he could hear a drumming sound, a sound of flesh against hollow metal.

Near the nursing station several doctors were standing closed and white around a metal filing cabinet: one doctor, the one who had been shouting, was pounding on top of the cabinet in rhythm with the points of his argument, building up his innocence like an incontrovertible debate. They were standing opposite the first room, one of the rooms that had had its door closed, with a NO ENTRY sign on it. Now the door was open. A stretcher emerged from the room. A sheet, long and bulging, covered the stretcher entirely and hung unevenly over the edges, its hem ruined and made crooked by the body's erratic profile. An orderly pushed the stretcher rapidly to the elevator: the doors were open and ready. The doctor who had been so vociferous calmed down as soon as the stretcher was out of sight. He shrugged his shoulders philosophically, with the ease of a politician, and resumed talking in whispers. A new file was pulled out and after a brief consultation the doctors closed the door of the first room and went into the room across the hall. A few doors down from his father's room, at the opposite end of the hall from the nursing station, was a large brightly-lit lounge for the patients. Some of those who had been walking around earlier were now crowded at the glass doors separating the lounge from the hall. From there, none of them had been willing to go any closer, they stood watching the same scene as Erik.

"Must have been a mistake," one of them said.

"They say he got an infection. There wasn't anything wrong with him when he came here. He was just having a lung taken out."

"Not supposed to die during the day."

Erik went back to his father's room and sat beside the bed. Richard Thomas had finished with his insurance documents and was reading a magazine. Brian and Nancy were still sitting on the vacated bed. Nancy was holding a piece of paper on her knees and making a shopping list. A nurse came into the room and stuck a thermometer into Richard's mouth. She smiled at everyone. She was very young, not even twenty, and pinned to her uniform was a plastic-covered *Nursing Assistant* badge. "How are you today?" she asked and smiled again. She took his wrist away from the magazine and started measuring his pulse.

"Pretty good," Richard Thomas said. She finished with his wrist and put the magazine back in his hand. Then she got a glass of water from the bathroom and gave him three different coloured pills.

"And your breathing?" she asked. "Are you breathing any better?" There was nowhere to sit so she crouched at the end of the bed with her elbows resting along the horizontal metal tubing. Miranda had put down her magazine and was watching her intently, as if all officials had the same information and might betray it by flaws in their deportment and other accidental human moments.

"Pretty good," Richard Thomas said.

The nurse stood up and flexed her knees. She smiled around the room. She had a little notebook out but wasn't writing anything down. "He never tells me anything," she said and slid her face through the necessary gesture. She smiled again and looked towards the bed where Brian and Nancy were sitting. "I guess he'll be back soon," she said.

"He's a hockey player," Miranda explained to Erik. "He broke his foot and it didn't set right so they're breaking it again for him."

"That's nice," Erik said. He had lost the feeling of active discomfort and now was just lethargic and tired. His watch said only ten o'clock. Richard lay still in the bed, the sheet folded over him exactly and his right hand draped carelessly on the back of his left. Erik wondered how long it would take his father to die, whether it would happen easily and passively one night in his sleep or whether he would have to be prolonged by esoteric mutilations. Or possibly this was just a temporary setback for the body and it would endure finally, without reason or shape, like the woman in the hall or the cars scattered carelessly like wheelchairs in the empty courtyard.

The girl in the school house had told him that death was nothing special.

"When you're young, life is too much for you and you try to push it away."

"And?"

"When you're old, there's less to push away." They were

standing in the middle of the room, fitting the tubes of paint to the machine as it was necessary. They had covered the walls and the floor of the room with paper and were running the machine at full speed. "His idea was to perfect the machine and then to go around to institutions offering to do murals. You could do a gymnasium in a few hours and even something like an office building in a couple of weeks." The arms of the machine wheeled about the room, spraying thin stripes of paint in long curved arcs. "You see here," she said, grabbing one of the arms and switching off its connection to the motor. "You can set it any way you want." She turned the nozzle and let it go again. It sputtered paints in small round dots. Now that they had made love and were covered with paint, he had lost his fear of her. They were wearing long, knee-length laboratory coats, and with the yellow and red paint splattered finely over her, she looked more like a field of wildflowers than a rose, harmless and transient. She was smoking a cigarette and demonstrating the details of the invention. "Of course there were still a few problems to be worked out," she said. "He hated being young. He always said that he was just waiting for time to pass, to be sixty years old, or even older, like the man we used to visit here, so old there was only enough energy to cut wood and go for a walk every day."

"People don't know what to do with themselves," Erik said. He sprayed a white circle on her chest.

"You'd think it would be hard to clean," she said. "But it isn't. All the tubes connect to one central place with plastic piping and you just hook them up to a bottle of turpentine."

"You can't drink it."

"Some people do."

"Pat Frank drank some turpentine once. He was sick for a week."

His watch said only ten o'clock. Richard was going through his magazine, turning each page slowly. Like the people on the stretcher he seemed under control, pleased to slide easily and gratefully though his last time. In the car Miranda had summarized the available information, diabetes and a heart condition; they didn't know exactly what had happened in the field. It was serious but not hopeless. They would drive to the hospital and sit, unobtrusive and cheerful, in a room and wait for him to live or die. Then they would go home. Richard Thomas would not be allowed to smoke cigarettes.

"We're going to do the shopping," Brian announced. "We'll be back by noon."

"You can have a box of chocolates," Nancy said. Her short-cropped hair and slightly snubbed features made her seem turned-in and sullen, like a self-explanatory cartoon. Her fingers were short and stubby and her nails were bitten down to the quick so her hands looked like they must belong to a nervous child.

"No chocolates for him," Miranda said. "Nothing with sugar. You could get him some of those special candy bars though, they're marked."

"We'll be back by noon," Brian said again. Miranda looked at him, raised her eyebrows in protest of the repetition, and then picked up a magazine. Richard had leaned back and closed his eyes. Erik went into the patient's lounge. The windows looked out over Lake Ontario. It was a clear day, but windy, and the lake was spotted with whitecaps. One of the patients came and stood beside him. He was wearing a blue terrycloth robe and smoking a pipe. His hair was carefully cut and brushed. It was silver-tipped and curled at his collar. His hands were fine and delicate. He gripped the wooden sill of the window, not supporting his weight but tense, looking out at the water, as if he had spent time at sea and the sight of the lake returned him to it.

"Big boat went by an hour ago," the man said. "Just before they took that fellow out."

"I missed it," Erik said.

"Can't have people dying here," the man said. He looked at Erik as he spoke and Erik felt that he was being somehow measured, appraised. "My wife made me come here," the man said. "I've got little tumours all over my bladder. Most likely it's cancer." He spoke, still looking directly at Erik without taking the pipe from his mouth. "Caused by smoking, couldn't have been anything else."

"I'm sorry," Erik said. He found it difficult to maintain this conversation.

"People die," the man said. He was small and fine and the tone of his voice implied other languages. "They're going to give me radiation treatments," he said. He looked perfectly calm. He might have been discussing the weather. "What are they going to do for you?"

"I'm not sick."

"But all too human," the man said. He laughed and looked out the window. His pipe had gone out and now he withdrew it from his mouth and held it in his hand. "It's easier to have something," the man said. "Until you get it." He re-lit his pipe. "They're going to let me out for the weekend. I could sure use a drink." The doctors had progressed down the hall and were now standing outside his father's room, discussing the case in whispers. Erik strained to hear, but couldn't. They decided on their strategy and marched into the room. A few seconds later Miranda came out of the room and into the lounge. Her eyes were red and she looked like she was about to cry.

"What happened?"

"Nothing. I guess I'm just tired."

"What are they doing?"

"Just what they always do. They take his pulse and listen to his chest. Then they ask him a few questions and leave."

"I'll go talk to them," Erik said. He went and stood outside the door. They had drawn a curtain around the bed but it wasn't opaque. He could see the doctors standing above the bed, leaning down, their shadows brushing against the curtain. One of them was asking Richard what kind of cows he kept. Richard began to explain the operation of the farm. In the middle of a sentence one of the doctors opened the curtain and they all left the room. "Excuse me," Erik said. He positioned himself in front of the one in the most expensive clothes. "I wanted to ask you about my father."

"Yes?"

Erik took the doctor by the arm and led him away from the door and down the hall a bit. "I want to know what's wrong with him, and whether his arm will get better."

"There's some damage," the doctor said. "But not much."

"He can hardly move his arm."

"Yes, we're going to try physiotherapy."

"And?"

"We're hopeful it will respond to treatment." All the time the doctor spoke, he looked down at his feet as if it was some kind of error that he was not at least two feet taller than Erik. The doctor was wearing sandals.

"He's a farmer," Erik said. "It's important to know whether he'll be able to work again."

"Yes," the doctor said. "I see. Well, it's possible but very unlikely." He looked directly at Erik for the first time. "I'm sorry," he said. He shrugged his shoulders. He was the same doctor who had been so angry earlier in the morning. "If he loses fifty pounds, stops smoking and takes things easy, if, that is, he survives the next two weeks, then he could live very comfortably for five years. Even ten or more." He patted Erik on the arm and then left him, to join his colleagues and begin discussion of the next case.

Erik went back into the lounge. His mother was talking to the man with the tumours. "What did he say?"

"Nothing much," Erik said. "We'd better go back in; he'll be wondering what's keeping us."

At noon, Brian and Nancy came back and Erik and Miranda went out to get some lunch. The old woman was still sitting by the fire exit, her hands in perpetual motion.

"Oh God," Miranda said. "Sometimes you two are so predictable." At the hospital Richard had finally brought up the subject of the farm, asking Erik if he would stay there for a few months, until he was better.

"I didn't know what to say."

"You spend the whole day sitting on the window sill, just waiting to pick a fight with him. Pass me the sherry. I don't know why there's never anything but cheap sherry in this house." She took the bottle from Erik and re-filled her glass. "I remember when they first got electricity here," she said. "Every light in the township was on all night. House and barn. Do you remember? Of course Richard had to do something special; the next day he drove into Kingston and bought a refrigerator. Everyone came to see it. You would have thought it was the Queen. My grandfather used to keep his playing cards in it. In Winnipeg. Made them snap, he said."

Erik lit a cigarette. Her father had been killed in the war. Or had just died in the trenches, no one was sure. He pictured the First World War as an endurance contest, set in a bog in France. He had never met any of his grandparents except through photographs and odd bits of stories. In their pictures they all wore high collars and stiff, set faces; they might have been anyone at all. "The trouble is," Erik said, "I don't even know if he really cares about who gets the farm."

"That's not it at all. You know he cares."

"And you?"

"It is all determined," Miranda said. "We can only bow to our fates." She nodded her head vaguely and then sipped at her sherry. "Madame says that we cannot escape our destinies."

"You believe this stuff?"

"No," Miranda said. "But life without faith is like an empty egg."

"Oh."

"You should meet her," Miranda said. "You'd like her." She reached down to the floor and picked up her purse. She put her hand inside it and drew out a card. "Here," she said. "You can go see her when we're in town tomorrow."

Rose Garnett
12 pm—4 pm
Weekdays Only

"I've taken a job at the University of Alberta."

"That's wonderful."

"You don't sound very enthusiastic."

"It's so far," she said. "When will we see you?"

For the past five years he had been coming home once a year, at Christmas. He stubbed out his cigarette. "You can come and visit me," he said. "We could meet in Winnipeg and you could show me the house where you grew up."

"It's gone."

"I feel like I don't know you anymore," he said.

"Tomorrow, I'll bake you some cookies." She smiled at him and twisted her glass in her hand. He imagined her after Richard was dead: drinking a little every day and not having too much housework to do. "Your father went to the city, to university. He could have stayed but he decided to come back. It was the right thing for him to do." Richard had told him once about his own father, Simon Thomas who had mourned his wife by forgetting her, and, as soon as he could, moved into town and lived common-law with a woman who couldn't cook.

"But she let him drink," Richard had said. "And though she couldn't cook, he never went hungry."

"Forty years ago," said Erik. "In a few years only rich city people will be able to afford to live on this kind of farm. All the food will be grown on huge farms run by businessmen. Or made in factories." He had heard the story of Richard's return to the farm dozens of times. The story had evolved and lengthened with the years, but was always climaxed with a romantic epiphany on a streetcar. The exact place had never been stated, but after he moved to Toronto Erik had decided that the streetcar had been moving west along Queen Street. The sun had been setting between the rows of tenements and shops, and the red glow of the sunset had been caught by the rails and reflected down the long corridor of the streetcar like a brief scene from an old movie that had been burnt at the edges. "I was on my way to visit Miranda," Richard would say, "to ask her to marry me. I was wearing my suit and my shoes were shined. It came upon me suddenly. I felt out of place in those crazy clothes, sitting in a metal machine running down a piece of pavement. We were being shuttled along like cardboard boxes...." The image of his father, young and dressed in a suit, always overwhelmed the rest. "In a few years this kind of farm won't even exist," Erik said again. "Less families live here than did ten years ago."

"You sound like one of those government experts," Miranda said. "I bet you don't even remember how to milk a cow."

"Everything's run down here. You should be spending more on the farm. I'm surprised the barn is still standing."

"You can fix it tomorrow." She crossed the room and took one of Erik's cigarettes. He was still surprised at how easily she had absorbed this death, forgiven it before it had happened. It was impossible to believe in illumination by streetcar. Richard had also once told him that if he stared into the lake long enough it would turn into a fish. Their first central heating was a wood furnace; maple burned the best but they mostly used elm. It never lasted all night and sometimes, if someone was sick, Richard

Thomas would stumble downstairs in the middle of the night to keep the fire going. By February, it seemed that winter had existed forever, that it was always late at night, already dark for hours and twenty below zero. And even in March the nights were still cold and frozen. That was the month he learned to tap the trees, pushing the brace with his chest and turning out long spiral worms of white maple. As it grew warmer, the black and grey bark took on shades of green and brown, soaking in the rain that turned the fields and hills into sheets of ice and, later, the roads a foot deep with mud and impassable. Even after the tops of the hills were bare and dried there was still snow three feet deep in the bush. Soft snow with a porous ice crust that broke easily and slid in cold fragments between boot and pantleg. In the spring too the creeks swelled with the melting snow and were triple their summer width, rushing down miniature waterfalls and fallen logs on the way to the lake, with cold still pockets where suckers and pickerel bred. At first with Richard and later alone they would come to the creek at night with an old potato sack, spears and a flashlight. They would stand for a while in the late twilight, watching the colours of the sun through the boughs of the cedar and still bare elm trees. That was the part Erik liked best, that and the feeling of the water tugging at his boots, in the promise, he used to think, that if he could just find the hidden code he would be carried down the stream into the lake, and along the length of the lake to the sandy narrows where it was joined to another bigger lake that in turn was joined to a system of lakes and canals that could finally lead him to the St. Lawrence River and then to the Atlantic Ocean. But it was Brian who caught the most fish, spearing them quickly and tearing them, flapping and gleaming blood, off the barbed hook and depositing them first into the potato sack and later, when the sack was full, just piling them along the banks of the creek, sometimes not even bothering to snap their spines. When they got the fish home and cut them open the eggs would spill out by the thousands onto the newspaper, tiny black yolks encased in mucus and streaked with blood. And by the time they were finished cleaning the fish, the eggs and the blood and the water and the ink from the newspaper were all smeared and run together on the floor. Erik standing back while Brian knelt over the fish with his sleeves rolled up, his hand plunged into one stomach after another, the scars from the fire still new and inflamed, running from his wrists to his elbows.

"Yes," Miranda said, dismissing Erik's whole conversation about the farm, as if he couldn't possibly know what rules were operating here.

At noon, when Brian and Nancy came back from their shopping, Miranda had stood up and said that she and Erik would go to lunch. When they got to the car she stopped outside the door on the driver's side, opened her purse and gave two dollars to Erik. "Meet me downstairs in an hour," she said. She looked at Erik and flushed guiltily. "There are some things which are too important to talk about." Then she climbed in the car and closed the door, hardly waiting for Erik to get out of the way before backing out of the parking space.

The second day, the old woman was still stationed beside the fire exit. She was wearing the same bright robe but her hair had been pinned up and contained in a blue net. She beckoned to Erik as he passed, and then reached one hand up and leaned it against his chest. She looked at him closely, this time her pupils seemed tiny and sharply focused, then turned her head and pushed him away. "I'm sorry," Erik said. The hockey player was back. He lay on the bed, his foot encased in a white cast which was placed in a sling hung from the ceiling. There wasn't enough room for everyone to sit around Richard's bed, so Brian and Nancy sat beside the hockey player and talked about cars. Richard seemed better. There was only a temporary inconvenience. He spoke of hiring the Frank brothers after he got home, to help out for a few weeks. His arm was still motionless but he could use his hand to hold the corner of the magazine.

At noon Erik went outside. The morning, warm and still at the farm with the first shadows lying long and transparent across the fields, had been destroyed by the city, turned into a hot and dusty day that couldn't be absorbed by the lake and now eddied about the brick and limestone towers of the city's buildings—hospitals and prisons. He followed the directions Miranda had given him, walking to Rose Garnett's past a playground that had been turned into a daycamp, and a factory where he could see loaves of processed bread passing by an open window. The house was on a corner near the lake: cold sharp limestone that had faced down the water and the cold winter winds without yielding or even softening its edges in the time that had passed since it was built, his mother reported to him, by a retired British army colonel who had been attracted to Kingston by its peace and propriety. The lot was closed in by a thin wrought-iron fence, which appeared as much an unnecessary afterthought as the few rosebushes that bloomed unconvincingly in the shadows of the house.

He had not imagined how she would look, but expected her to have become a hazy replication of his mother, a middle-aged woman fortified by money and religion. Instead she was as she had been, a plain light-haired woman who moved and spoke without ceremony, as if she were an assistant in someone's office and knew nothing of any God or the glib magics that can be dispensed in the afternoon. "What can I do for you?" she wanted to know, as if it wasn't obvious that he must want something more dramatic than could be named, everything or nothing. She brought him tea and sat down beside him on the couch, her legs crossed under the long dress, the bones of her hands and arms slender and quick, fine like the tips of her hair and the shadows that defined her face. She looked at him again and he saw that she hadn't really aged, only become polished and taut, living removed from the background of long grass and unpainted wood.

FOUR

Her flashlight was hooded with green plastic so that she came to him as a cyclops swimming through his dreamless sleep. He left his eyes open for her, knowing she would see he was awake and stop by his bed. It was only his second night, but already she was familiar to him, a part of his new world.

"Are you awake, Mr. Thomas?"

"Yes." Her hands were pushing up the sleeve of his pyjamas, wrapping his arm in the soft rubber. She inserted a thermometer in his mouth: he had learned to sense the closeness of her hand and lift his tongue. The rubber tightened round his arm. Then the pressure held and was slowly released. The rubber was unwound. It left his arm feeling cold and exposed. She pulled down the pyjama sleeve and held his hand. Everything was simple and known. She took her hand away and withdrew the thermometer from his mouth. The light shone again as she wrote down his blood pressure in her notebook.

"Does your chest hurt, Mr. Thomas?"

"Just a bit," he said. He didn't know if he was lying. It wasn't so bad that he wanted to scream. When it was that bad he asked for a pill. But he couldn't imagine moving. He had become accustomed to it already, along with everything else. He remembered reading that intelligence is the ability to adapt to new situations. The boy in the next bed groaned and rolled over in his sleep. The nurse swung her flashlight. Then, satisfied that he was asleep, she sat down in the chair beside Richard Thomas's bed. Casually, as if he was not supposed to know that she was measuring his pulse, she took his wrist in her hand. "It's still going," Richard Thomas said.

"You're doing very well," the nurse said. She put his arm back on the covers and wrote down more figures. Then she took his hand again. The first night he had been awake the whole time, unable to sleep in this strange place, unsure whether this was all just a brief prelude to dying. The drugs and the illness combined to make him feel old and doting, foolish already. The nurse kept asking him questions, sitting by the bed and trying to make him talk. Now she was asking him about his children, his two sons. She said she had seen them when they were visiting that night. "Look alike too," she had said, as if there could possibly be much resemblance between Erik, tall, thin and awkward, and Brian, stockier and dark, looking more like Richard Thomas than Erik did even though it was Brian who was adopted.

"They were always playing tricks on me," Richard Thomas said, searching for whatever she would expect, trying as soon as he had said that to think of something they had never done together. "When they got old enough to pitch hay I used to work the farm on shares with them during the summer. One month, I got the bill for tractor gas and it was a hundred and seventy-six dollars. You couldn't burn that much gas if you ran the tractor twenty-four hours a day. A hundred and seventy-six dollars. I even bought a lock for the gas drums. What happened was that every night, while I was doing the milking, the boys would fill up my car so they could spend the night driving around the county. I was paying them too, good wages. Their mother knew the whole time but she didn't say a thing. Carried the key around in my pocket after that. Those little buggers. They should have known I'd catch up with them." He was running short of breath and he stopped. He had left out the most important part, but he didn't know how to put it into words. It had something to do with the look on their faces the night they found he had locked the drums. The nurse had her fingers on his wrist again.

"You should try to sleep," she said.

He couldn't imagine moving. Pain had made everything false and instantly fitted him into a new history.

"It's the sleeping pills," the nurse said.

"Nothing else," he said. The sentence dissolved his present, and left him standing on a Toronto street corner with Miranda, declaiming with a sweeping gesture that included the whole city, the lake which had brought it into being as a one-night stop-over for weary canoeists. Miranda took his outstretched hand and held it to her mouth. She ran her tongue along the tips of his fingers and nibbled gently at his veins.

"It's the sleeping pills," the nurse said. "It takes a while to get used to them. Sometimes, when I change shifts, I take one the first night."

"The day my father died I was in town, visiting him. He asked me to go to the store, to get some soup. When I came back he was dead. The doctor said he'd had a heart attack. It wouldn't have mattered if he'd been there, he said. There was nothing to be done. Ripped his chest right apart."

"My mother died the same way," the nurse said. "She was eighty-six years old and had gone senile. She wouldn't walk to the bathroom anymore. She did it on the bed and then crawled around in it, on all fours, playing with it. I have some pills at home and if I ever start to get like that I'll know what to do. I guess she was happy though."

"They were always trying to sneak one over on me," said Richard. "One time we planted two acres of tomatoes, one for me and one for them. The night before we picked them, it rained so they were all nice and clean. Worked all day putting them into wooden crates to take to the cannery. At the end of the day, we'd picked it all, and I noticed they had more crates than I did. Little buggers, when I wasn't looking they were stealing my tomatoes. I didn't say anything though, until I'd made them load their share into the truck."

"You see?" Erik had said. He was standing beside the truck and had just passed the last crate up to Brian. "I told you he'd figure it out if we took too many." For his answer Brian jumped onto Erik from the tailgate and they both went sprawling in the dust. There was a moment: they were rolling over on the ground wrestling when suddenly Erik was on top of Brian with his hands around his neck. "I could kill you," Erik whispered. He was thirteen and Brian was fourteen. They had long ago traded their toy pistols for real .22's and boxes of brass bullets.

"I dare you," Brian said. He stopped resisting, stretched his long scarred arms out on the ground, and smiled confidently up at Erik. Erik hesitated; this was unexpected. The scars on Brian's arms showed pink through the dust. Three scars: one on each arm and one on his left cheek, a pink triangle. He could remember when they had brought Brian home, his arms bandaged and the burn on his face bright red, like fire. "Chickenshit," Brian shouted, clapping his hands into Erik's face.

"I had a patient," the nurse was saying, "who thought he was a monkey. That was when I was working out. You wouldn't believe who his family was, they lived in one of those big stone houses on King Street, and kept him locked up on the third floor. He wouldn't eat anything except bananas and red river cereal. It was all one big room and he had it done up like a zoo, with wooden huts and sawdust on the floor. He was very clean; he didn't shave of course but he kept his nails short. His favourite place was a little stool in the corner. He'd crouch on it all day, making funny noises. There wasn't anything wrong with him either. I guess he made them nervous and they wanted someone to keep him company. I wouldn't work at night though and that's the worst when you're alone." She rubbed his hand sympathetically. "My husband was a baker at the penitentiary. He had to get up in the middle of the night to go there and start the bread. Then he'd come home at noon and sleep. After a while he started going earlier, playing poker with the guards I guess, so for the last five years I hardly ever saw him. I moved to my mother's: it was a week before he even knew I was gone. One Sunday he asked me to come back but I wouldn't. Said I'd rather be alone in my *own* bed if it came to that. I never saw such a man for eating doughnuts."

Richard had gone to Toronto to visit Erik once. He hardly recognized the city, it had over-run its old perimeters and gutted itself of most of its trees. The house he had lived in, a three story redbrick house with an always freshly-painted verandah, had been torn down to make way for a zoology building. When Richard Thomas went to university he was older than most of the other students. There had been two winters when it snowed too much for him to be able to get to school. He had spent them with his father, Simon Thomas, on the other end of a bucksaw, taking firewood out of the elm swamp. And the year after he finished high school his mother had been very sick, so he had stayed home that year too. He was to be a lawyer but first, Simon said, knowing but not knowing what it meant, he was to become a gentleman. They studied the university calendar with the same care as the Eaton's catalogue, trying to familiarize themselves with the whole thing before making a selection: finally history and philosophy were selected as those subjects most conducive to gentility.

"It's different when you're young," the nurse said. "It hurts but you know it's going to go away. My mother used to say that the grass comes up green every spring. That was before she went strange. She didn't want me to go back to him, either. She said he was playing around up at the hotel. And here I'd thought he was just playing cards." She put her hand around Richard Thomas's wrist again. He could feel her fingers sliding around, dissatisfied with his pulse. "I guess most men are just animals. Even with the monkey-man I didn't dare turn my back: he was so *fast*, I don't think there was anything wrong with him at all."

He imagined his body was divided into zones, like a butcher's diagram of a cow. But there were only two kinds of zones, pain and numbness, and gradually the pain was migrating through the dotted lines, occupying new territory. His chest was still sore: from shoulder to shoulder and down to the bowl of his stomach. His rib-cage felt like it had been shaken and rattled by a steam drill. His left hip, for no reason at all, seared every time he moved. Perhaps he had been limping on the way home, had somehow irritated a nerve. His legs and arms hardly seemed to exist. He felt the nurse's touch but from a great distance: he might have been watching it on television. As always when he had a fever, he was strangely aware of the points of connection between his hair and his scalp. The movement seemed to be downwards. The pain would infiltrate his right hip and then continue down into his genitals and legs. The only place finally exempt would be his left arm. He had tried to move it earlier, for the doctor, and had barely been able to lift it off the bed.

She was speaking again but he couldn't hear individual words. Her voice jumped and faded, turned harsh and grating, then was just a thin background noise. She was holding a glass of water to his mouth. He could feel the rim cold against his lip. He stuck out his tongue for the pill, dry and chalky, then let his jaw relax so it could be poured down him. He opened his eyes and saw earth banked up on either side of him. There was a slit of light at the top and as he watched it widened into a rectangle of sky with bodies stretching far away from the line where the earth met the air.

"Doesn't he look nice," a voice said. Other voices murmured; they bent down to examine him and dark round patches blocked the grey light. They had folded his hands across his stomach, stretching his fingers wide apart so they could be meshed together like a child in prayer.

"Doesn't he look nice," Miranda said again. She was dressed in a dark blue suit and stood almost leaning against Richard, her gloved hand squeezing his elbow, supporting herself as they stood at the end of the grave, facing the minister who was mumbling out his words, loud but unarticulated, across the open grave towards them. The sky was grey-yellow, so thick with cloud that none stood out singly.

Richard and Miranda had been placed at the head of the grave as if they were the honoured guests at a dinner, though, as Richard's father had bitterly pointed out, he had already provided his tithes to God. It was a constant thing with him after his wife died, and when he came to eat he always insisted on saying Grace.

"Oh Lord," Simon would intone in his dry voice, "accept the homage of us Your humble servants for You have given us this earth that we may feed and love You." He would laugh self-consciously and rub his palms together, looking at Richard and Miranda to see if they might have guessed that everything was not as it should be. Then he would draw his lips back from his teeth—those that remained, since he refused to go to a dentist or get false teeth having said he was done with vanity and pride—and waggle his tongue in anticipation of Miranda's cooking which, though he never would have admitted it, was the bribe necessary to bring him out to the farm.

The first person to cry at Simon Thomas's funeral was the housekeeper he had lived with after he moved to town. No one dared say anything against her while he was alive, but now she regarded those at the funeral with pure terror and was down on her knees weeping hysterically. All else stood dry and bored, staring down into the blank grave. They were in that corner of the cemetery reserved for their own family. There was a story that his father's father, the first Richard Thomas, had not wanted to use the cemetery at all, but had wanted to be buried in the apple orchard behind the house. But his wife had been religious, so he had finally agreed to be buried in the church's cemetery on the condition that he could plant an apple tree near where his grave was to be. This was what happened, despite the objections that the roots might eventually disturb some insensible skeleton.

Simon Thomas had died in early December, before there was much snow, but after the ground was frozen too hard to dig. So they had saved his body until spring. The grass was thin and lemon green, and the tree, though crippled, turned in on itself and dense with wild grape vines and bittersweet, still produced a few new leaves in spring, each one small and slick-surfaced, new leaves of an old tree. Because of the age of the corpse, they had immediately covered the coffin with a layer of dirt and stones. But the imagined odour made its presence felt. All faced the grave with hypocritical solemnity as the minister worked himself towards the ultimate peroration, the consecration yeast that would make the soul levitate from what remained and begin its long journey in whatever direction God saw fit. The presence of the house-keeper made it apparent that the odds were long, but the minister, perhaps inspired by the difficulty of the case, or perhaps simply remembering certain transgressions that were known to several of those clustered about this sunken altar, gave it his valiant best. His jaw was long and scarred with cuts where the skin between razor and bone had been too thin to resist his mirrorless efforts, and his eyes, sunk into deep-boned sockets, were so large, they appeared to bulge out of his face like those of an underwater animal.

It was a warm and almost balmy day, though the cemetery made the air seem still. Running along one edge of it was the old unused railway track that had been constructed at the turn of the century to take out white pine and bring in dry goods and tourists. The line had run south to a small town twenty miles east of Kingston, and Simon Thomas had gone on the train, once a year, to visit his half-brother Frederick. In those days the roads had not been very good. But as they were improved and the area was logged out, the train became smaller and emptier with each yearly visit to the hospital. Frederick had died long before the run was discontinued.

Miranda's hand was tight and damp against Richard's arm. He looked down and saw that she was crying. She and now everyone else were snuffling and crying over old Simon Thomas who had ended his overlong life living common-law with a woman who couldn't cook. The minister's voice had risen and cracked open. He had given up all pretence of words and now moaned and howled, his bulbous eyes wide open and vacant, swaying back and forth at the head of the grave. His throat shook with muscle spasms. He had thrown the book in the grave and had his arms stretched wide, his great scarecrow hands fluttering against the yellow-grey sky, calling for the day of judgment to begin, right now, that the measure of this man's sins might be taken and forgiven. All had joined the widowed housekeeper and were on their knees, scraping dirt and stones into the grave, the cemetery closing in behind and threatening to enclose them all. Only Richard stood. And as he watched, cold and dispassionate, he could feel the weight of the earth on his body, the moist granules lying on him like a cool and porous blanket that surrounded him but also flowed through him, a medium he could move in if he wanted by sifting and swallowing, using his body to create space like a worm. "Yes, swallow," Simon Thomas had told him, "the earth can swallow you like no woman." And went on to tell about a relative who had come to live on the farm of the first Richard Thomas, to help with the work and escape the damp British winters. "He was a poet," Simon Thomas told him, showing the book that had been privately printed in England, the leather binding still supple but the sonnets stiff and dead on the pages, birds and flowers shot down in full flight. "They say he was all right the first winter. They kept him inside mostly, trying to get him used to the cold.

"Even when he came he wasn't too young, in his thirties, and they say he was thin and stooped too; looked the part. In the spring they started him off easy, working in the garden and other woman's chores. They say he was always walking about with a notebook, writing things down and making lists. And of course he had read something about the science of agriculture because he always had lots of good advice for my father. It seems he had thought we would have an estate, with servants and riding stables, and whatever he might like. Ten kinds of wine and a fancy cook. So that's the way he lived anyway. In the winter, every night after he helped with the supper dishes, he would put on a red jacket, the only decent piece of cloth that he had, and sit by the stove, smoking a pipe and reading aloud. And in the summer he would go for a walk or maybe write a letter home to someone saying what a good life he was living."

The story about the poet had been one of Simon's axioms of universal behaviour. He told it only a few times, each time in righteous detail. After that he referred to it when necessary, the point already having been made.

The farm had first been settled by Richard Thomas's grandfather, Richard S. Thomas, the middle initial standing for Simon. That is what he called his first son: Simon. This first Richard Thomas had built the house, married, built three barns, cleared some fields. When he was too old to work, he passed the farm to Simon, who, in turn, married and had children. The first child was male and named Richard, after the grandfather.

"The farm was different then than now," Simon Thomas would say—it was important to know that this physical universe was not a constant but an artifact that could only be bought with time and blood—"and near the crest of the hayfield behind the barn was an old willow tree." Despite the story about the poet, Simon Thomas also smoked a pipe. He refused to carry one on his person but had them scattered all over the house and barns. In his front pocket there was always a package of cigars, but if he was inside or even near any of his outside hiding places for them, a pipe would materialize as he talked, accompanied by a yellow oilcloth pouch and a box of wooden matches. After mentioning the willow tree, he would take his pipe and slide the stem back and forth in his mouth, lean away on one foot, and look carefully at Richard: "Willow trees are pretty but they don't last long." When Richard had come back from the store that day he found that his father had died clutching his pipe. He had pried it out of Simon's fingers, afraid they might snap, and carried it with him from that time until the day of the funeral, undecided whether to keep it or throw it into the grave after him.

"When the poet first came here he was afraid of almost everything that was alive. He would come running from the garden because he had been bitten by a few mosquitoes. And he never wanted to go swimming or even walk in his bare feet for fear of the snakes. He showed us a book he had gotten in England that had a picture of a ten-foot water snake swimming in a lake, its neck three feet out of the water and a head like a heron."

And it was on the day of Simon's funeral that Katherine Malone, pushing away the time that had grown between them in layers first soft but then impenetrable and marbled with the ways they had turned from each other so that their memories had become mazes wound and exploded to conceal everything but the nods and false annual jokes, came to stand with him. Her hand, as it always had, remembering ten years by touch, curved within and around his, the fingers long and seeking. While Peter Malone, her husband, was bent down far over the grave, his head gone from sight and his coat slid up past his waist carrying his white shirt with it and showing a wide curved roll of fat where his belt bit into his back. "It took me by surprise," she said. "Even though. It doesn't seem so long since he came to see me." Not riding in a car, which he didn't have, or even with a team and cutter, though he went near there every day with the milk, but walking because, Simon said, it was too late for the horses, walking three miles to the big old house where she lived alone that winter and climbing the steep unploughed drive that was several feet deep in snow and had no marks except the soft shallow dents where Richard had walked hours before and then, even though the lights were out, hammering on the door without stopping until finally Katherine, knowing who it was, had gotten out of bed and lit a lamp. At first he refused to speak and just paced about the kitchen belligerently as if he expected to find the evidence in traces of food. "Mostly he liked to have a secret place to come to. He used to bring me presents of food and sometimes cloth. The other thing was so fast. His skin was pure white and dry, crinkled like parchment. He used to sit in the wicker chair near the stove and tell me how he'd thought of me since the last time he came, it wasn't very often, and you could see it meant so much to him. It was only because I was young, having me was that for him and I didn't mind it so, I guess I let it go too long, until that night."

The sounds of Simon's hard-soled boots against the maple floor of the kitchen and then his father sinking down into the wicker chair beside the stove. "You'll want some tea," Katherine said. It had been snowing earlier in the evening and Richard knew it was not too cold. He could hear his father groaning and rubbing his hands together.

"It's good to see you Katherine," Simon said. He always spoke, but especially in certain situations, with a dry complacency, like a church deacon. "I've been worried about you lately."

"Excuse me a moment," Katherine said. "I'm freezing." She went upstairs, her bedroom that winter was directly above the kitchen, and knelt beside Richard on the bed. "I'll just give him a cup of tea," she said. "He must be half-dead from cold. You stay here." She took a sweater from the floor and put it on. On her way downstairs she closed the door softly.

"I didn't interrupt you, did I?" Richard's father said. "A person doesn't always know."

She said nothing but moved back and forth in the kitchen, preparing tea and cutting a piece of bread. Her slippers rasped as she walked, a thin layer of sand between leather and wood. There were rugs on the bedroom floor but the voices were carried up by the stovepipe.

"I like to trust my friends," Richard's father said. "If a man can't trust his own family and friends, well. People can't always be checking up on each other. A person should know what honour is."

"And snooping," Katherine said.

"You gave me your word," Richard's father said. "You gave me your word and I trusted you. Were you not worthy of my trust?"

"Don't be stupid," Katherine said. "Now here, drink your tea. You mustn't be so difficult. Here, I'll sit beside you." Their voices grew lower. Richard was alternately afraid and outraged. The wicker creaked.

"Thank God," his father said a couple of minutes later. "You're a generous woman Katherine. If it weren't for you I'd have dried up years ago." He stood up and composed his clothing. "And it's a beautiful night tonight. Trouble with my children is that they always want to stay inside."

"Yes."

"There's nothing like exercise. I'm a man who believes in keeping the circulation going. My father did too."

"Yes."

"You can't get too much exercise," Simon Thomas said. He was fully dressed to go outside but was still standing beside the stove. He had the kettle in his hand and was picking it up and setting it down as he talked. "You see the kettle here," Simon said. "When it boils dry it burns the pot."

"Yes," Katherine said.

"A man's mind is a very complex thing. I don't know if anyone really understands how a man thinks."

"No," Katherine said. "I don't suppose they do."

"According to the Greeks now, a man didn't think at all. He just remembered everything that he knew, because he used to know everything before he was born."

"It's getting late," Katherine said.

"Now just the other night," Simon said, "I was reading a book that said there is a mind in your head that you don't even know of. It has a will of its own and remembers everything you forget. It's the same idea the Greeks had, only about the lower things in life."

"I don't know anything about the Greeks," Katherine said. "My mother told me that Queen Victoria used to have men come up the back stairs and visit her and when she was finished with them, she would tell them to leave and they would or else she would chop off their heads."

"It's a fine life being a queen. While it lasts."

"Yes."

"Now this man said there exists in every man's head the desire to kill his own father."

"Now."

"A man brings up his children to honour their parents, not to kill them. And he expects people to honour that enterprise and not to make it difficult."

"Yes."

"Well Katherine, you're a wonderful woman and God knows why I'm saying all of this to you." He kissed her noisily on the lips. "Thank you for the tea."

"Say hello to Mrs. Thomas."

"When he first came," said Simon Thomas, "he told people he was a poet and because of that and his fancy accent he felt out of place. So the second winter he decided that he would learn how to chew tobacco. Even while he was smoking his pipe, he always had a wad sticking out his cheek or even pushed under his lower lip. People used to like to see how far they could spit their juice. This fellow never learned how; he would just lean over and dribble it out in a thin yellow stream." The different incidents strung together, beads on a necklace of the poet's disintegration.

"Now my father, though he could outwork any man in the county, was not in all ways a strong man. Especially as regards my mother whom you never met." And the poet, alone and trying to fit his forms and language to a landscape they could not contain, began to turn his attention elsewhere.

Richard's father, when he told these stories, would be working his hands the whole time: playing with his pipe, rubbing his palms together or sliding them up and down his pant leg, delighting in the inevitable comparison. "And Frederick, of course, in no way resembled me, except for my mother's ears. Now." When they visited the hospital, they would have to wait downstairs for Frederick to be brought to them. The lobby had a tile floor, and placed about the walls were long wooden benches, in the style of church pews. In the centre of the lobby was a desk where a woman sat, always the same woman for all the years they visited him, waiting for requests. When someone came to see a patient she would write down the name on a slip of paper and then walk slowly across the room to a door that was latched from the outside. She would open the door and hand the slip of paper to a uniformed person standing waiting on the other side. Then she would return to her desk, her duty accomplished. A few minutes later, Frederick, wearing a shabby double-breasted suit and carrying a rubber-tipped cane, would be led into the lobby. His flesh was white and raw, as if he was never outside, and he seldom spoke except in response to his brother Simon's questions. Sometimes it was unclear whether he recognized them. Then he would sit obediently on the bench, trying to sense what was expected of him.

"They say my father caught them in the barn," said Simon, referring to his mother and the poet. "The next time he went to the store he bought a box of rat poison. A couple of weeks later, at dinner, the poet took the box from the shelf, ripped it open and poured it on top of his food. Then he looked at my father, who was watching my mother, and began to eat. Nothing happened. The second summer he was outside all the time. He even slept in the barn and he used to spend the whole morning walking around with his notebook. Even then he still pretended he was going to write an epic poem about the farm and was always asking questions. I never saw his poem but found some old notebooks that must have been hid."

Richard could feel the nurse again, the rubber tight around his arm. Maybe I don't want to die, he thought, and wondered then what would be required to take him out of this hospital, whether there was some disease he had which could be labelled and cured so that he would be restored to some younger self, or whether his body had just somehow derailed and would be placed back on the track, that much further along. The nurse was leaning over and talking to him, her voice so low he couldn't hear her, only feel her breath, a warm funnel by his ear. This sickness had made his body too large to deal with, so now Richard stripped away the edges, cut whole zones out of consciousness, reducing himself small enough to cup in his own mind. "You don't ever feel anything," Miranda would say. But the night of Simon's funeral Richard cried like a baby, crying and shaking until Miranda started to cry too and both their bodies were covered with sweat and tears and like a baby Richard licked the salt water from her belly, tongue and skin and water, bodies groaning and slapping together like young whales.

He could feel the nurse's fingers on his wrist again. Like a growth, he thought, demanding life that could be measured, rivers of cells passing by the counting point. That first winter with Miranda was in Toronto and they would walk in the Don Valley, its shoulders open and swollen with snow, lined with makeshift tin-roofed houses and shacks, their windows protected by cloth and cardboard, tin chimneys perched at crazy angles in the cold air, wired onto the walls and eaves. Some were deserted summer cottages and once they went into one with a bottle of wine and a blanket. There were ovals of ice on the windows, orange in the twilight. The floor was covered with old sacking and the blanket stolen from the boarding house. Lit a fire and drank the wine, waiting. She moved first, when it was so late Richard was tired and only wanted to have it over with and marked up–a beginning. The sacking never even unfroze and afterwards he remembered feeling like a goat with scraped red knees and drippings. Then she wanted him again, soft a one-time expert coming over the trenches.

Inserted in the book of poems was a photograph of the author. He was standing tall and thin, wearing a baggy suit and carrying a walking stick. He had been posed in front of a large hedge and above him curved a flowering tree. The book was in the same case, hand-made by Simon Thomas, as was the encyclopaedia he had purchased for his children, the family bible, and various historical romances. In the telling of the story the book would inevitably be flourished. The poet had brought the book for his cousin to see. But the diaries were found only by chance: Simon had discovered them hidden in the loft of the old milkhouse. For a long time he wouldn't show these, but only made references to them, saying they were even worse than the poems. Even when he finally moved to town Simon only let Richard look at them, not read them, saying that he could have them, and the curious ring that was tied to one of their place ribbons, when he died.

May 21: The snow all went three weeks ago & now the land & forest demands all or would drown me. What a vast infertile wilderness. Panorama of attack & flowers. God has betrayed man here & he will betray Him also.

May 25: I saw myself in the glass today & have become plain & weak. My cousin's wife knows what is in me & constantly finds excuse to talk to me & even stand against me when we are in the garden & in the house. Sometimes she is bolder & once when I was washing outside remarked upon my skin. Most of my past remains unknown to them & they are content to believe what I say. Her attentions to me are proof of His care.

May 26: It rained all day His Presence. Even the rocks swarm with traces of His being. The gap from flesh to land is too great. Only iron & machines can break it. I beg my cousin to discard his plough & trust God's Mercy.

May 27: Rain again & the trees & ground are stained with it. Went & sat with the cattle. Their eyes show how they have lived with the fear of the forest & wolves. They are the cattle of my ocean dreams & in their midst I am safe.

May 30: A night of fire. It has been written that only death can bring us into the garden. My cousin believes in this life & is wrong. He is a pagan yet lives inside his body like a snail. I say again that I have lived outside my flesh & He has shown me His Way. Earth's blood will drown them & be like the sea is to a teardrop & in that garden we will partake of everything & mutilate nothing & He will forgive us at last. When I was in the street & they took me because my wounds were impure they denied the truth to St. John who also went into the desert & suffered many things. & God watched them cover me from His face & in their jails too I wished to take the skin from my body to show the beauty of His works.

June 1: My cousin's wife grows closer & we spoke today about the need to be eaten & assimilated & passed through the blood of another. That is what Death is, being purified by God & she wanted to know if He had a liver. Yes, I answered, it is men's corpses & that is why they are Holy. After dinner I went outside again. The men work at nights pushing back the edge of the forest to create their new wilderness & come in their arms & faces swollen & red with bites.

June 2: I say to her that the soul is free of the body & can walk in the green fields without bending the grass & whereas the body cannot live without killing & that is the cause of its death. & I show her how to press her hand against the earth & feel the life that is in it & even in rocks & all the ground & water & that is why the fishes can live in water because it is alive & that is why a man & a woman can live inside each other because they are alive in God who is the air & I told her that it is Profane to kill & she wept & begged me to help her.

June 5: I dreamed we must go outside & lie beneath the tree & she will receive me & then the truth will be known to her as it was to me so we may make each other stronger & show others the way to God. He is with me at all moments & I will bring her to Him.

June 6: I explained my dream to her & we went into the field as was instructed being careful we were not seen. She does not understand how wild & pagan this country is. My cousin is evil & does not trust me & God will punish him. Insects constantly swarmed about us & we had to go back to the house before it was done.

June 7: I am a slave & prisoner here. My cousin would like to be a gentleman but he cannot even succeed in pretence. There is violence in his house & he cares for nothing but money. His body has been removed from God & it makes his wife suffer.

June 8: We are His instruments only & today it was done.

In his picture the poet's face was narrow and sunken, the hair slicked back, parted down the middle and long enough to cover his ears. The author, the poet, claimed to be a relation of the grandfather Richard Thomas, had the same last name himself, Thomas. The Reverend William C. Thomas he had announced to be his name, saying he was not of the ordinary clergy, but one of those who had chosen God of his own free will. And though Simon discovered the diaries shortly after the poet died, he kept them to himself for almost fifty years.

FIVE

Brian was dreaming about the fairgrounds, hoping that he might
find some trace of the boy there, someone who might have seen
him or heard of him. He was dreaming of the fairgrounds and in
his sleep he was pressed against the wall of the trailer, hemmed
in by the plastic wooden panelling on one side and Nancy's
imagined touch on the other. He slept with one arm outstretched
along the wall. There was a map of the world pinned up beside
the bed and his fingers rested vacantly on South America, sliding
up and down the coastline as he breathed. He was dreaming that
he was on a ferris wheel with Nancy, swinging high above the
fairgrounds at night, eating an ice cream cone. Every time they
came round to the top the wheel paused so he could get a good
look at the lights and the people below. Nancy, frightened for
some reason, was clinging to him. He kept trying to push her
away, say something to her so he could concentrate on the view.
Finally she stopped bothering him. She sat quietly in the corner
of the seat. When he wasn't looking she jumped. She never actually landed but only floated endlessly downwards, pointing at
him accusingly. Sirens began to whine; their sound sped through
the hollow tubes of the ferris wheel, through his bones which
now seemed to exist independent of him, like the stand-up skeleton he and the boy had constructed. He was still eating his ice
cream, eating it faster and faster so that it would be finished
before they got to him. The sirens blended in with shouts and
together they deepened and took on the intonations of a foghorn,
of a cow bawling. He was out of bed right away. He put his

clothes on in the living-room of the trailer and took the flashlight from beside the door, where he had left it.

When he got to the barn, the cow was lying down in her stall. Seeing him, she got to her feet. With each contraction she sank down again. Brian rubbed her neck and talked to her. In between contractions he got two pails: one full of hot water and one to use for milking the cow when the calf was born. She had stopped bawling and was just grunting now, circling restlessly in the stall. Periodically, in a mysterious manoeuvre, she would twitch her skin and shudder. As her skin moved the flies would draw back, and hover momentarily before settling again. The cow's grunts elongated into moans, not loud but wavering and reedy. Some of the other cows, woken up by the activity and curious, began to push into the barn to see what was going on. Brian rolled a cigarette and, still half asleep, leaned against a post and waited. The cement floor, he noticed, was pocked and cracked. The government inspector hadn't said anything on his last visit, but soon. The cows were all Holsteins, white with irregular black splotches. They were big-boned cows, with wide-flared hips and long skinny legs. The cow in the stall was having its first calf. Unsure of what was going on, she was still moving around, making her strange singing noises and scratching at the straw. Brian thought of going to wake Erik but decided against it—he would see enough calves being born when Richard Thomas left him the farm. One more stroke and he would be gone for sure, the doctor had said. Yesterday's had almost killed him. They had stood beside him all afternoon, watching him through the oxygen tent. But in the evening he had been better, even eaten some supper and joked with them. Five thousand dollars in the will and half the cattle and machinery. Erik wouldn't take the farm anyway, and wouldn't dare sell it from under him. The cow grew more agitated. It lay down on its side. First the hooves emerged, bright yellow, and then the front legs. "Push," Brian said, "push you little sucker." The cow groaned and the head, purple-blue, came out. The calf's eyes were closed tightly and it had tiny white eyelashes. Brian waved the other cows out of the barn and closed the door. When he turned back to the stall the calf was totally out. Its colour had started to lighten already. While the cow struggled to her feet Brian inspected the calf: a heifer, good. He stepped into the stall with the hot water and washed down the calf. The cow kept getting in his way, wanting to lick her. When Brian left the stall the calf was wavering around on its feet, poking at the cow's udder and then falling over. The cow was more concerned with cleaning the calf than feeding it, so every time the calf got near her teats she turned around, knocking it down. Brian came back with the other pail and drew some milk from the cow. Then he picked up the calf and carried it to the adjoining stall. He poured some of the milk, it was colourless and very viscous, into a baby bottle. He stuck the nipple into the calf's mouth. The calf seemed puzzled, so Brian, cradling its head and neck in his arm, squirted the milk down its throat. The calf, startled, made its first noise: it sounded like a toy duck. The cow seemed to have already forgotten everything. Even though the afterbirth was still hanging out of her in a red triangle, she was munching at the straw in her stall and swishing flies away with her tail. Brian threw her some hay and went outside.

His first memories were not of Richard and Miranda but of Ann Cameron. The car door had opened, freckled arms with silver bracelets had reached out for him, hands wrapped around his arms, pulling him up into the air; and then the car was moving again, accelerating down the dirt road. She had him on her lap, her hand pressed over his mouth. Her breath was sweet and minty but her hand tasted sour. "There," she said. She took her hand away and stroked his hair. She was much younger than Miranda. The man was young too; he looked like pictures in magazines with his wet combed hair and clean white shirt. Brian grabbed her hand and bit it as hard as he could. "Joe," she screamed, "the little bugger bit me." The hand flicked out from the wheel, knocking Brian off her lap and into the door. As Brian tried to get the door open the hand reached out again, grabbed him by the hair and forced his face down into the woman's lap. He wanted to yell but the hand was wrapped tight in his hair: every time he opened his mouth it was pushed down, pressed tight against her thigh. Even biting was impossible because his mouth was so wide open he couldn't get a good grip; the woman was leaning over him, whispering in his ear. "Don't be afraid," she was saying, "I'm your real mother." When they came to the highway, the man stopped the car.

"Do you promise to sit quiet?" He still had Brian by the hair but had pulled him up so that his face was just a few inches away. For years afterwards Brian saw the face in nightmares: pasty white, huge nose and eyes, the tip of the nose covered with tiny black hairs. Brian spat. The hand let go, flicked twice, and he was on the floor. Bodies leaning over, pulling him up onto the woman's lap again, she was crying too, had her arms around him and was rocking back and forth. "Bitch," the man said, "just like you." His scalp and face were on fire; she rocked him and hummed as the car sped down the highway. He let her touch him, curled into her body. Her hands were constantly moving, stroking and consoling him. He opened his eyes. On the front of the car was an eagle, silver like the woman's bracelets, slicing open the air so they could pass through.

They woke him up when they got to the house. "You'll have your own room here," the woman said. It had bright painted shelves filled with stuffed toys and children's books. On his bed, folded neatly, were a pair of pyjamas, a housecoat, and slippers. "You have to brush your teeth before you go to sleep."

The next day, after breakfast, she explained to him that she was going to work. She put a plate of sandwiches and some paper and crayons on the kitchen table. Then she and the man left, locking him in the house. When they came back he was in his bed crying.

"I thought you said you didn't cry."

"I want to go home."

"This is your home." She caressed his shoulder. He pushed her hand away.

"I want to go home."

"You'll like it here," she said. "You're my child. I carried you for nine months." She brushed the hair back from his forehead and stroked his face. "Joe." The man came running upstairs and into the room. She held out her hand. The toothmarks were visible.

"All right," Joe said, "go downstairs and make supper." He sat down on the bed beside Brian. "Why did you bite your mother?"

"She's not my mother."

"Yes she is," Joe said. He pulled out his wallet and showed

Brian a picture. A woman was holding a baby. "After you were born your mother had to go away," Joe said. "Mr. and Mrs. Thomas said they would take care of you until she came back. But when she did they didn't want you to go away so we had to come and get you. Children have to live with their parents."

His scalp was still sore and the inside of his mouth was cut and swollen. "I want to go home," he said.

"You are home." Brian considered this. He didn't like Joe being near him, his smell. He wanted to get away from him, to go downstairs, but knew that if he moved Joe would hit him. Joe put his hand on his shoulder. Brian sat perfectly still. "We can be friends," Joe said. Brian forced himself to smile. Joe squeezed Brian's shoulder.

"I want to go outside."

"After supper. And in a few weeks we'll go on a camping trip and live in a tent." Joe took his hand away. "You've got to respect your mother," he said. "She went to a lot of trouble to find you."

The next day after they left, Brian played with his colouring crayons and paper. He drew pictures of everyone he knew, especially Erik, whom he missed. He drew him in different colours and with long winding tails and floppy hats. He drew pictures of himself too, with his head sticking out of car windows. He ate his sandwiches and searched through the house, exploring the contents of cupboards and drawers. He found some cigarettes and matches in Joe's suit pockets: those he hid in the basement, in a special place he had discovered. He noticed that the kitchen window could be pushed open. He climbed out the window into the backyard. The woman next door was hanging up her clothes and, instinctively, he hid from her, running down the narrow alleyway between the two houses. He came out onto a wide street. All the houses looked the same except that they had different coloured doors. His own house had a red door and a fire hydrant in front of it. At the end of the street was the park where Joe had taken him. He found a stone fountain and sat on the different wooden benches. When they got home they were pleased with him. They gave him more crayons and paper.

Every day after they left he drew pictures. Then he went outside. When someone talked to him, he pretended that he couldn't hear and walked quickly ahead as if he knew where he was going.

One day, when he had strayed further than usual, he came across a boy his own age. He was standing on a bridge, dropping pebbles onto the road below. Brian gathered a handful of stones and stood beside him. "What are you doing?"

"Nothing." The boy was thinner than Brian and his clothes were torn and dirty. Brian looked down at himself. Every night Ann Cameron gave him a bath and every morning he put on fresh clean clothes. Brian waited until he saw a truck coming. Then he bounced a stone off of its roof as it went under the bridge. The boy threw a stone at the next car. Soon a car came by with its top down. It was full of people waving and laughing. They looked up and saw the two boys leaning over. Brian dumped all his pebbles on them and then ran. "Come on," the boy said, "we've got to hide." They ran down the street and into a house. "Upstairs," the boy said.

They were in an attic, filled with bones and skulls. One of them had a horn sticking out of it. "That's a rhinoceros," the boy said. Some of the bones were partially reconstructed into skeletons. The rest of them were simply piled in heaps around the walls of the room. Skulls lined all the window sills. The floor was covered with fur and stray parts. The boy turned on a radio and cleared a space to sit in. "Where do you live?" Brian started to tell him about the farm and then stopped. He described the street that Joe and Ann lived on. "That's close," the boy said. "I can take you home after."

They spent their afternoons in the attic. The boy had a book with pictures of animal skeletons and they were wiring and gluing the bones together into a mammoth elephant. "Sometimes they find them under the ground," the boy said. "My father found one last summer." Brian asked the boy why he wasn't in school. "I have to stay home for a while," the boy explained. "I tried to set the school on fire." He paused. "I didn't mean to hurt anyone, I just wanted to see if it would burn."

She always wore her silver bracelets. He got used to the feel of them on his skin, trailing after her hands as she soaped him in the bath or held him on her lap and read him stories. While she bathed him she would lean over him and he would look down her dress. "What are you looking for?" she would say, and laugh, hugging him even when he was soaking wet. "My little baby," she would say and laugh again. He was eight years old. The man was distant. He sat in his chair and read the newspaper. Sometimes they would walk to the park. After supper the man always helped with the dishes. One night he noticed the window in the kitchen, the marks on the sill.

"Look," he said to Brian, pointing at the window, "where have you been going?"

"Nowhere." The hand moved quickly, snapping out the dish-towel and knocking Brian against a chair. He crashed to the floor and then rolled under the table. He could see the man's trousers, rising up from his leather shoes. The woman's legs were thin and bony and her feet, bare, were covered with blue veins. She got down to the floor and slid under the table. The man left the room. "I want to go home," Brian said.

The next morning the window was locked. He went down to the basement, there was another window there that could be pushed open, and climbed out. He took the cigarettes and matches with him. The elephant had been completed. It took up the whole centre of the room. When Brian got there the boy was sitting in front of the elephant, staring at it. They had put socks on its feet and covered it with fur rugs. Brian sat down beside the boy. "Today we have to hunt the elephant," the boy said. "Are you scared?"

"No."

"It's dangerous. My father was killed hunting an elephant."

"But—"

"It didn't hurt though. He was brought to life again, like Jesus."

"Lazarus woke from the dead. He went back home."

"That was different," the boy said. "He was all covered with scabs and everything." He stood up and went to the window. He selected a skull and handed it to Brian. "You throw first," he said. The skull was large, with a depression in the top. Some of its teeth were broken off. He stuck his fingers in the eye sockets; the rims were sharp against his skin. "It's a lion," the boy said. Brian turned the skull and examined it.

"It's a cow," he said. He had found a skull like that with Richard, down near the creek. It had been half-buried in the moist earth and grass was growing out of it. They took it home and set it outside to dry. The next day it was gone. Brian took his fingers out of the eyes and hoisted the skull in his hand. He threw it at the elephant. It bounced off, onto the floor. Its lower jaw had broken and the top was caved in.

"That won't work," the boy said. He selected two long curved bones and gave one to Brian. They stalked the elephant. The elephant was not exactly as it had been pictured in the book. It rose uncertainly from the floor in the shape of a vague hemisphere, a sloppy fur-covered adobe or igloo. The socks located feet without defining them. The tusks were supported at one end by a chair and the tail resembled that of a racoon. The trunk was a long snakeskin with a tennis ball squeezed into it. "It's a boa constrictor," the boy explained. "Elephant trunks don't have bones." He poked at the elephant with his club. One of the furs slid off, revealing two bones knotted together with string. "This is stupid," the boy said. He sat down. Brian had brought some of his stolen cigarettes and matches. They tried to smoke the cigarettes but gave up, coughing. Then they attacked the elephant again, jumping on it and trampling it until it was broken into pieces and spread across the room. "I guess it's dead," the boy said. "Let's go to your house."

They let themselves in the basement window and then went up to the kitchen. Scotch-taped to the walls of the kitchen and hall were Brian's drawings. "I guess I'll go home soon," the boy said. Brian lit a match and held it to one of his drawings. At first nothing happened. Then the drawing began to curl and blacken, sending flames and smoke towards the ceiling. When it had burned he started on the next one. Soon all the drawings in the kitchen were gone. Remnants were still stuck to the walls and the walls and ceiling were scorched. They went into the hall.

"Here," Brian said, "you do it." He gave the matches to the boy.

"It's your house," the boy said.

"I don't mind."

The boy chose the biggest drawing. He tore it at the bottom corners so that it was partly rolled up. When he set the flame to it he ran it carefully along the bottom, licking it with the burning match. "The wallpaper's caught," Brian said. The boy had already moved on to the next drawing, without even waiting for the first one to finish.

"That's good," he said. When he had all the drawings going he stepped back to watch. Brian ran into the kitchen and came back with a pot of water. He threw the water on the wall. It made a loud hissing noise. Part of the wall turned brown and steamy. Surfaces took on a new texture. They were red and alive, the flames sending out messages to each other, biting deeper into the wall and sporadically shooting long, curling tendrils towards the ceiling. There was so much smoke on the ceiling that it took them a while to realize that it too was on fire. Then it began to seethe and bubble, sending down bits of plaster and glowing chips of wood. The heat forced the boys into the front vestibule. The fire had travelled across the stairway; the bannister posts, carved wooden spirals, wreathed themselves in flames. "Come on," the boy whispered. He ran up the stairs to the first landing. There was a window: he tore off the curtain and threw it down into the fire. Then he disappeared into the upstairs. He came back, his arms loaded with sheets and blankets. He dumped them down into the hall and went back for more. "Come on," he shouted to Brian but the stairs were barred by heat and smoke. The books and toys from Brian's room came tumbling down into the hall. Brian could see the boy, dancing up and down the stairs, veiled by the fire, his arms waving wildly. "Open the door," the boy shouted, "open the door." Brian fumbled with the lock, the metal was hot to the touch, and finally forced it back. Then the door burst open; Brian was sucked into the hall as the fire rushed up the stairwell. The boy didn't move. He stood on the stairs, his arms outstretched and swaying vaguely to the beat of the flames. "It's too hot," he said. His voice was quite ordinary. There was an explosion.

Brian drove with the visor down, the light reduced to a long wide slit with the sun burning out the edges. Like a robot in a space suit, he could see almost nothing at all through the glare except the vague outlines of the paved road and the more intense reflections of metal roofs. He had his foot to the floor and the radio on so loud that the buzz of the bass notes in the speakers competed with the music. As he drove, he tapped his fingers on the wheel, keeping time. Nancy was half-lying on the seat, her head against his shoulder and her feet sticking out the open window. She was smoking a cigarette and singing along with the chorus, shaping the smoke as she mouthed the words. When the song ended, the announcer came on with the news. Brian reached down and turned off the radio. Nancy shifted around so she was sitting normally and turned the radio back on, looking for a station that was playing music.

"It's all news," Brian said. He had his hair cut short on the sides and long in the front, so periodically he had to push his hair back from his face, either with his hand or, more often, a quick movement with his neck that he could remember practising and mastering. They were coming to a junction in the road; the pavement was covered with gravel and Brian jammed on the brakes, locking the rear wheels and then letting them spring loose into a fishtail. He waved the steering wheel from side to side, gradually straightening out the car as it slowed down. Nancy had slid away from him and was leaning against the door, smoking a cigarette and looking at him intently.

"I don't want to go to the hospital tonight," she said. Brian nodded. He flicked the butt of the cigarette out of the window, watching it spark against the road. Then he turned onto the gravel road, driving north and away from Kingston. He pushed the visor up and lit another cigarette.

"They don't own us," Brian said. "Pat Frank told me that Richard is going to give the farm to Erik."

"He doesn't know anything."

"They could have given us the house. But they didn't do that; they put us in the trailer like hired help."

"They make me nervous," Nancy said. "Sometimes Miranda won't even talk to me."

"That's what they say about the Thomases," Brian said. "When they need you they can't do enough for you, but then when they're finished with you they just forget you. Remember when Mark Frank came back, Richard hired him for the summer, but then he let him go again when winter came, even though he knew it was too late for him to get taken on somewhere else."

"They say Katherine Malone's children look more like the Thomas family than anyone else. The first one was buried before she had even laid eyes on Peter Malone. And it wasn't Richard either but Simon Thomas who was its father."

"Old Peter was always bragging he couldn't get it on to save his life, but they caught him with the wife of the manager of the hardware store. They were up in the loft of the old blacksmith's shop and they say you could hear her right across town. When he got home Katherine sent him down to the basement for some pickles. Then she locked him in. Wouldn't let him out for a week, even to do the chores." She called one of her children Richard— whether after some relative or Richard Thomas was unknown. But there was a spring when she told everyone she was going to marry Richard Thomas; the next fall he went away to college and Peter Malone, Simon Thomas's new hired hand, began to visit her every evening. Richard Malone had been the same age as Brian, and Brian remembered him as thin and always sick; he died of pneumonia the same winter they built the new school.

"Well," Nancy said. "What are you going to do when the old man dies and Erik tells us to leave?"

"I don't know," Brian said. His voice sounded like it was whining inside his head. Every day she seemed to ask the same questions, to push him that much further. He slowed the car and went onto a narrow dirt road. The road wound between cedar trees, gradually losing height until finally it ended on a massive slab of rock that jutted out over a lake.

Nancy took a blanket from the back seat and spread it out on the rock. "We could have gone to a movie," she said. "It's still early."

Lying flat on his stomach, feeling the rock against the V of his ribs and his elbows, Brian narrowed his eyes again. This time there was no road but only the tiny ripples of water and the shadows of surrounding trees. He had lit a cigarette and was half-absently puffing on it, sending the smoke out across the lake, breaking apart in the light and then coming together again in large hazy swirls. He lay with his chin propped up by his hands, the cords of muscle in his neck standing out thick and round. Sun and cold had already permanently weathered his skin, turned it brown and tough so that the scar tissue on his face and arms was barely noticeable, appeared only as a subtle indentation that ran full-length along both forearms and, on his face, a smoothness as if worn by tears beneath one eye.

The lake buzzed with the sounds of feeding and hunting, the

sharp splashes of fish coming to the surface for the insects that skimmed across the water. Occasionally, making everything else seem silent, the staccato scream of a loon crossed the lake; the sound bounced and twisted off the steeply rising shores, rising into the hazy sky and filling everything like a light. Brian liked to watch the loons fly. Huge and unwieldy, they seemed almost too awkward to overcome gravity, as if the earth's atmosphere was not exactly what they had been bred for and they were meant to glide through space as, the boy insisted, they once had, carrying the spores of dinosaurs and certain mushrooms: a series of underwater corals and plants that are still undiscovered at the bottom of the Indian Ocean. He had told Richard about the loons once, when they had walked down to the lake and back through the maple bush, and Richard had shown him how some of the fallen trees were decomposing into the ground, how eventually they would be covered by other trees and vegetation, compressed and aged so that the whole bewildering array of what was not green and moist would eventually be hard and black, pure carbon like a piece of wood that has been heated without burning.

Now the loons were diving again. There were two of them and they seemed to take turns. In between dives they floated across the water, appearing as weightless on its surface as they seemed cumbersome in the air. They never seemed to look down before they dove, but moved suddenly, unpredictably toppling over and knifing soundlessly into the water. They seemed to stay under for a long time, emerging far away from where they had begun. Richard had told him that they travelled so far underwater because they expended no effort—just floated with the currents that ran along the bottom of the lake.

Brian lay flat on his stomach, feeling the rock against his bones and the soft glare of light from the water trying to pry open his eyes, like the fire had sought to enter and possess him, making him follow the boy up the stairs. The mist was beginning to roll over the lake. Later it would settle like transparent jelly into the hollow pockets of the road, absorbing and diffusing the light from the car so that the car and the mist were part of one unified machine, floating slow and crab-like through some imaginary ether. The boy had told him that the dinosaurs' planet was spotted with trees and ponds, connected by shallow canals etched into the benevolent desert. They had found no trace of the boy after the fire, not even bones to be rebuilt by future explorers. They had found no trace of him, so it was vaguely possible, Brian thought, though he knew better, that somehow the boy had been blown free by the explosion and had run away. For years after the fire he would dream of it, waking up hot and with the flames before his eyes. There would be no panic or even desire to move: an awareness of lying in bed in the midst of the fire, that soon it would consume him and the dream would be over. But while he waited, the flames would recede, leaving him with only whatever light the night could offer. Sometimes in those dreams he would see the boy framed in the doorway or outlined against the wall, moving towards him in that slow way he had had, seeming dreamy and disconnected even in the dream, possessed of whatever knowledge would reduce the world to being that simple. In school he would often think about the boy, hoping that he might have found his address and be at home waiting for him after school. Sometimes he considered hitch-hiking to see the house, to see if he still lived there. Then he thought that they wouldn't meet until later, years after. The boy would appear one day at the door of the farm, wearing old dusty clothes and a wide-brimmed hat to shade what the fire had done to him. He would be half-crazy, only his sight would be whole and he would move in his own dreamy and unreal way through the world, dispensing death and justice, just as Richard decided which animals would live and which would be slaughtered, which would be bred and which would be sold, which would be allowed indoors and which would have to fend for themselves, expendable and ignored, too unimportant to be worth the effort of killing.

When they took him back to the farm, Brian had trusted neither Erik nor Miranda, but had wanted to be with Richard all the time, as if he was somehow part of the boy's world. And, when he had been in the attic with the boy, it was only Richard he remembered, the boy having replaced Erik. The boy would tell him of his father and the way he searched for traces of ancient times beneath the surface of the earth (like the orange inside the orange peel the boy once said) and in return Brian had spoken of Richard who seemed to share something with the boy's father, and who, Brian felt, would somehow be at home in the roomful of bones and discarded furs. They brought him back from the hospital and he lay in bed, his arms bandaged still and the burn on his face like a flame, for two weeks in what he knew was punishment for the murder of the boy, punishment for his murder and the destruction of the house; and also a sign that he would always carry with him so that what he had done would be publicly visible. He was willing to play with Erik and accept food from Miranda, but it was Richard he needed; he told him everything that he had learned from the boy because his message had been intended for Richard too. For Richard had shown him the cow's skull in the old creek bed and had taken him outside one night to watch the meteors: all night he and Richard and Erik had lain on the blankets, head to head, watching for falling stars. They were made out of an old disintegrated planet, Richard had told them. Another time he showed them a bit of white fuzz in the sky, long and elongated, like a pod. While they were watching it, they saw more shooting stars, and Richard explained to them that what they saw was a comet making its centennial visit to the sun and that the shooting stars were stray bits from its tail which, like a huge gaping net, was sifting planets through it as it travelled.

And so every night after supper Richard would come up and sit with him in a special chair they put beside his bed. They would talk of the boy and the fire and planets and dinosaurs, but of the city Richard had nothing at all to say. It seemed, Brian thought— then and later—a subject even more closed than death or sex, as if the centre of the meaning of the city was so horrible that no one should be exposed to it, as if, in fact, he was saying to him that he had already gone through what the city had to offer and he would be foolish to enquire further.

"And what will you do when Richard dies and Erik sells the farm?" When she spoke it was always the sound of her voice that startled him, the words demanding that everything else be pushed back because it was thought but not noise.

If the boy had lived the question never would have been asked. He would have come to the door with his wide-brimmed hat and crazy scarred mouth and they would have left the farm, hitchhiked south to Mexico or Peru.

"We could go to Peru," Brian said.

"What are you talking about?"

"Peru," Brian said. "It's a big country with sheep farms and mountains."

"I'm not going to Peru," Nancy said. Brian looked at her and saw that she was lighting a cigarette and looking disgustedly at him. He would have moved in an abrupt way, his legs thin and hard and possessed by the spirit of some dismembered desert prophet. Sometimes Ann Cameron had read to him from the Bible. Her voice would move light and silver over all the images, lying about them by the way she spoke them. But he and the boy had discussed it one day in the attic: the Bible, the boy had said, was created by a group of escaped Roman slaves thousands of years ago. They had broken out of prison and had found a series of old cave dwellings high in the mountains of Northern Italy. They spent years in the caves; they married and had children and grew food on the high mountain plateaus. Except for the occasional hunting, the women did all the work; the men had made themselves a huge meeting-hall in the back of one of the caves and they spent most of their time there, making up the Bible and memorizing it. After it was all done, they taught it to their children and, it had taken twenty years, even to their grandchildren. Then they all went in different directions, hiding every trace of the time they had spent in the caves, spreading the word as they went, passing it on as if it were something everyone knew. They said it was an old religion, some of it so old that it was beyond memory, and that those who practised parts of it were persecuted and put in prison. In the telling, the boy said, was the only true meaning of God; and only God (as he acted through men) could write and re-write history either by words or by deeds. And the sign of the scars he would carry with him was not, he knew, any sign of holiness but a sign that he had tried too much to interfere with the world, that in doing that he had caused the death of the boy—the only one who could have led him to any kind of truth— and in some way his own death. Even Richard had told him, when he was sick, that though every man was mortal it was still true that every man caused his own death—usually not, like the boy, in one movement, but in bits and pieces scattered through his life. He himself, Richard said, had already caused parts of his own death, just as Miranda and Erik and everyone he knew had.

And even the earth would eventually die, Richard told him, and when he was better, took him outside and showed him how the earth had scraped and scarred its own skin with ice, the ice that had pushed huge boulders into impossible places, made long twisted scars in the bedrock and stripped it of its covering of soil so that in places now, even millions of years later, the rock showed or, worse, was only a few inches beneath the surface waiting to greet the person who was stupid enough to try and plough it or shape it to his needs. Everything causes its own death and dies of being itself, Richard had said, like the dinosaurs who died because they succeeded in growing huge or even the sun that would die because it was consuming itself. The scar beneath his eye burned for months, imposing itself on every moment, on everything it saw. When it finally stopped, it seemed that something in him had been exhausted.

"They say," Nancy said—as she spoke she flicked her half-smoked cigarette into the lake and Brian realized that a certain amount of time had passed since she last spoke and he had said nothing, could not even remember what he had been thinking about and could only remember lying with his eyes closed, a child in bed with Richard sitting beside him—"or maybe *you* should see a doctor." She looked at him, retreated, changed the subject. "Peru," she said, pronouncing the alien word as if it might mean molasses, rain in March, anything at all. She had bought him an atlas one Christmas and then watched Brian spend half the afternoon leafing through it, taking everything slowly, in his own literal way. "He treats you like a slave," Nancy said. She spoke to him carefully, like she would speak to a horse, her hand on his back so she could sense his reactions by the tensings of muscle and spine. "You live on the farm and you work there every day for twenty years. When he passes you in the yard or sits beside you at the table or asks you to pass the salt, he never recognizes you are anything more than a dog. And now that he's dying he doesn't even think of you, he only wants to make sure his precious son gets the farm, Erik, the fool who doesn't even know his own mind."

He knew what she was doing, but couldn't find the words to speak about it. She had done it different ways different times and he had not spoken about it then either, knowing that each time it went unanswered ensured the next time. "They hypnotize you," the boy had explained to him. "People try to hypnotize you into believing that what they say is real. They talk about things like walls and tables and you know there are walls and tables and so then they talk about other things and you think that because there are walls and tables there are other things too, that everything they say is as true as one thing they say. They tried to do that to me in school," the boy said. "They tried to do that to me, so I set fire to the school. Now they leave me alone."

"And don't you ever get angry with him?"

"Sometimes I could kill him," Brian said. But the sound of the words was unconvincing. "I don't know," he said.

"He's afraid of you," Nancy said. "And anyway, you look more like Richard than Erik does."

"Sure." Even Miranda had remarked on it once, watching them come across the field for a drink, both of them square and stocky though Richard was heavier. He had asked them about Ann Cameron on the way home from the fire. They had picked him up at the hospital. His arms were wrapped in gauze and they drove him home that same night. There was salve on his cheek too; every time he blinked his eyes it would stick to his lashes. But they had said only that they had adopted him from an agency, knowing nothing about his background.

"Anyway," Brian said, "he's sick but he's not dead." He was still lying on the rock, but the sun was completely gone now, the lake lit only by a faint red rim that circled the horizon and a few clouds that still caught the last bits of reflected light. "I'm already tired of going to the hospital," Brian said. "He's only been there a week now. The doctor said it could take six months or more."

"He could live for twenty years," Nancy said. "Lots of people are invalids for that long. They would let him come back to the farm and you would have to run the farm and Miranda would have to take care of him like a baby." She could feel the muscles in his back jumping nervously, making long deep ridges on either side of his spine. "Even now he can't get out of bed," Nancy said. "He tried to once and it almost killed him. The doctor said he might be able to walk in a few days but you know they always say things like that. And his arm. I haven't seen him move that arm since he went to the hospital."

"You would have liked that, wouldn't you?" Brian said. "You would have liked me to have left him lie in the fields and die without me going back to the house." He stood up and spat into the lake.

"God you're disgusting," Nancy said. Sometimes he would wake up in the morning hating her. Every movement she made, every place their bodies touched, would make his stomach jump. He would slide out of bed slowly, careful to keep his face turned away from her so it would not betray him. Outside or sometimes even in the next room the feeling would pass. But then it might come back to him in the evenings, when they went from their house to the trailer for the night. The trailer was too small: a bedroom, a living-room, and a small kitchen that was hardly used. He had meant to build a house, Richard had said he could wherever he wanted, but he had promised him no deed. He put his arms clumsily around her shoulders, unsure of how they had arrived at a standing position already. It seemed to him that he hardly ever wanted her lately, and then only in brief and sudden sparks that passed too quickly for her. But still, sometimes late at night or early in the morning, she would turn to him, her mouth buried in his shoulder and asking only the essentials. "I should have pushed you in after it," she said. They were standing on the lip of the rock. There was a crescent moon, so diffused in the misty sky that its reflection was only a careless arced smudge on the surface of the water.

"I'm sorry." In the car he switched on the motor and then sat there, letting it idle, while he smoked a cigarette. "He wouldn't let that happen, spend twenty years in bed, making other people take care of him."

"That's what old people do," Nancy said.

"Not always. Sometimes they die." Death, Richard told him, trying again to console him about the fire and the boy, was also an act that people could will.

"Like animals," Richard had said. "Animals die for their own reasons and always at the right time. Unless someone shoots them."

"People don't like to die," Nancy said. "I'd be afraid to die."

Brian turned the car around in the dark and began driving out towards the road. All his feelings seemed to be trapped inside his body and his body was trapped in the car with Nancy, in the trailer with her every night, in the routine of going back and forth to the hospital every day. "He hasn't even decided yet," Brian said, "whether to live or die." He opened the window and turned on the radio, driving slowly, drifting through the fog, turned the radio up louder so finally Nancy, as if by automatic reflex cuddled up against him and put her head on his shoulder.

"Drive faster," she said, "and maybe we'll have time to stop at Pat Frank's for a drink." She had her head on his shoulder and her hand on his leg, rubbing up and down from his thigh to his knee. "We should go to bed early," she said.

"Sure."

"Do you like this?"

"Sure," Brian said. But her hand made him fidget, blocked the connection he felt with the car and the road. He reached for a cigarette and then, while he was pushing in the cigarette lighter, he brushed her hand off his leg, casually, as if it was accidental.

"Jesus," she said. "Maybe you *should* see a doctor."

"Jesus," Brian shouted. "Jesus Christ." The car was skidding along the gravel; he had one hand on the wheel and the other at Nancy's throat, gathering her sweater and pushing her against the door. When the car stopped it was sideways across the road, its lights pointed into a swamp. He held her at arm's length, letting her gouge her nails into his arm. "Just stop it," was all he could say. "Just stop it." He took his arm away. The blood was flowing freely down his forearm. "Jesus," he said. "You sure know how to scratch." He looked at Nancy and saw that she hadn't softened at all: she was leaning against the car door with her mouth open.

"Don't tell me." She got out of the car and then slammed the door behind her.

"Stupid bitch," Brian said. She was running down the road. He straightened out the car so that the lights were aimed towards her. He noticed that she ran like a man, her heels coming up straight behind her legs, not kicking out like a woman's. Then he gunned the accelerator, pinpointing her in the highbeams before swerving to one side.

SIX

From his bed Richard could see the empty courtyard. It was lit by a single street lamp and the windows that faced inwards. The hockey player had been cured already; now Richard had the bed by the window. They said they would leave the other empty for a while, that business was slow in the summer, that, without words, it wasn't nice to make a new patient share a room with someone who might actually die without warning. His body had completely betrayed him and become a battlefield of competing pains. With his eyes closed, he could make his retreat from the edges, find places to rest and curl about his fear, like a small child with a summer illness. Other times it seemed that each incision was fresh and new; the nerves retained every memory and could live now only on the edge of initial feeling. He would wake up shaken with them all at once, unsure whether he was trapped in his own flesh or forced back forty years into Katherine's bed, her shadow wavering above him as she performed her own rites of exorcism. Miranda only held him in the present. He felt obliged to stay awake while she visited. "Are you afraid," she asked once, when the others were out. He said no; but the question disturbed him, made him aware that he could be forced to choose.

His fear came and went. Sometimes it fluttered within him, spurting through his nerves like a caged bird. Or he would see something move out of the corner of his vision: a chair suddenly placed differently, a small animal darting through the room.

Katherine had believed in ghosts. Both her parents died within a year, leaving her alone and still unmarried in the big unpainted frame house her grandfather had built. "It doesn't matter when someone dies," she explained. "It feels the same to them except it's easier without a body. After all, most people are sick when they die. They don't want their body any more so they just float away and leave it behind. It takes a long time for them to leave their houses though; that's because without a body a person doesn't have very much to do so they like to stick near the familiar." When Richard came to see her, she would often be pacing through the big house, talking aloud. "Of course you don't have to talk loud like that; they can hear you without sound and even without words. They don't speak to me at all in words, but I feel their presence all the time, like a wind." She was in her early twenties then; there was nothing acutely wrong with her and it was unusual to be unmarried at that age. But her parents had been invalids and she had stayed in, taking care of them, never (as Simon Thomas pointed out to Richard in his unctuous way) having a chance to become a woman and left alone for two whole winters with no one to help except, of course, Simon Thomas. "The best way to do it," Simon Thomas told Richard, in the only advice he ever gave on the subject, "depends on whether it's during the day or during the night."

Later, when he died, Pat Frank and his brother would be asked to carry his coffin from the wagon to the graveyard, to lay him in the ground as if his body still existed and it was finally most important that Richard Thomas be placed in this perspective:

Richard S. Thomas 1832-1915
Simon Thomas 1866-1936
Richard Thomas 1904-1970

They would carry him to the grave just as automatically as the ground carries dead leaves, or, slaves their master. Richard Thomas would be the last name on that list. Even for his grave they would have to cut away the roots of the apple tree, Miranda would be squeezed in beside him and the plot would be full, ready to have everything about it forgotten except the names and numbers–statistics to tell how many years each had achieved. "The old ones always go to heaven," Simon Thomas used to say. Every week after dinner he would lean back in his chair and smoke a cigar with his coffee. He had acquired a striped vest and a pocket watch and, with the thumb of one hand hooked into the watch-pocket and the other busy with the cigar, he would recite his banalities—purposely whistling through the gaps in his teeth Miranda pointed out—knowing that Richard was silent by habit and Miranda frozen by duty. "The old ones go to heaven because sinners all die young, drained by their excesses." He had told Miranda the story of the poet, and often when he came to supper he would bring one of the diaries with him, reading from it to verify his points as he talked. And what the diary left untold, Simon filled in with an inseparable mixture of his own fabrications and those told to him by his father or, more likely, Frederick Thomas, his half-brother. "After the birth of Frederick," Simon Thomas said, "the poet began to fall apart. He wanted to follow his son around all the time, because he thought that he must be holy in some way and was waiting for a sign. Frederick was much older then me, but they say that he was strange as a baby, never speaking or crying but only looking out the window as if he too were waiting. The poet was less patient than the child. One day he ran away, taking the child with him. He was two years old then and they didn't come back for a full year." And because of a certain incident involving the poet, it was a custom that no member of the Thomas family would touch the coffin of one of their deceased.

These nights in the hospital, Richard Thomas's sleep was always transparent. The nurse would come into the room and sit with him, his wrist in her hand, her fingers resting lightly like a toll-gate on his blood. And when she was sitting there, she talked, talked without stopping, talked endless careless rivers of disorganized words, her voice always at that soft and pulling level that could penetrate his sleep but wouldn't wake him, long flat stories about people who died and people who refused to die, stories that went nowhere but hung with him on the edge, making him feel at times that she was allied with Miranda, forcing him to make a choice where there was none, telling him there was something where he thought there was nothing, or just talking and talking endlessly because he was lying still and helpless and she had him as a perfect audience, a living breathing immoveable being whose every brain cell could store and record her perfect story, and, if she could make him survive (what kind of audience is it that dies half-way through the performance?) it would somehow justify not only her words, which even she knew were beyond any possible redemption or even forgiveness, but all the ridiculous deaths and near-drownings, misunderstandings and terrible jokes, long horrible nights and sunless days, all the events and years that made up the currency of what she was telling him and, it began to occur to him, made up the inner lives of the people who had passed through her hands. Sometimes it seemed that she was aware of this, of the way she had presented two generations of citizenry as a mass of fears and diseases, last nights and hypochondria, and then she would tell of someone else, someone who, as she put it, came back from the sickbed, like a football player with two broken wrists or the broken-footed hockey player whose father came to visit him every day when he was there and inspired him with true-life tales of athletes who had recovered from off-season surgery, athletes who had survived divorces, car crashes, cancer, broken limbs, arthritis, temporary paralysis, fear of airplanes, almost every affliction and handicap known to man, including even jail sentences, only to come back, like the deaf pianist Beethoven, twice as loud and twice as good as ever.

"Sure," the hockey player's father said, "it hurts. I know it hurts. I broke my arm once and it hurt for two weeks." And he told his son about a basketball player who had lost his wife and two children in a car accident, (as well as breaking his own back and not being able to collect on his insurance policy) and yet, despite everything, this basketball player had come out of his coma and struggled for three years until finally he made it back on the team, married the coach's wife, and won the league scoring championship. "Of course, you understand," the father said, "he wasn't as fast as he used to be."

The fear came and went but it was already a permanent presence, like the sudden obscure shadows or the feeling, as he drifted to sleep at night, that there was something about the quality of the sleep, about the way he was being pulled, that had to do with being tired but not with any cycle. And although it seemed that he slept because he was tired, the sleeping left him tired too, not because of the nurse who talked to him all the nights or even the drugs, but because somewhere he had been cut off from the sources of renewal. He shaved now with an electric razor that Miranda had given him, a day nurse holding the mirror for him, and when he looked at his face in the glass he kept seeing it as he had seen it that morning, the tired face of an old man. Now even the veneer of sunburn had gone and he was simply pale and veined, his eyes red-rimmed and bloodshot. But looking at his face, finding it old, he could never quite see death in it, or the need for death. On that subject it still seemed to be maintaining a curious neutrality, wondering with the rest of him how he had survived the walk back from the lake, curious to know if there had been some inner reason for all that struggle or whether it was just the instinctive flapping of a body already severed from life.

Sometimes, when he was lying curled into himself in the bed with the lights out, feeling large and fat in this hospital bed which was too narrow for him and had no other body to slide into for warmth so that he was made to know they had placed him on the bed like a large lump on a high ledge, always in danger of sliding off if he kicked or jumped in his sleep, sometimes when he had finally accomodated his mind to his body's precarious position, it would strike him that the darkness when he closed his eyes would one time be the darkness of death, that it would come over him as a veil and he would never see anything again. And knew that even if behind that veil he was still struggling to see and live, his countenance and body would still be those of a dead man; the nurse would stop talking and they would take him away, embalm him, bury him, cry over him, forget him, all while he was frantically trying to escape. The fear. He envied Simon his all-at-once death, quick and easy in the rocking chair. Of his family only Frederick had died in a hospital, like him, and his death had occurred before his body stopped functioning, when they had started to give him so many drugs that he was always in a stupor, couldn't hear and could hardly talk. In the dark he could draw the sheet over his head; like thus it would be. So. Catching himself at what he was doing, coddling himself like a senile old man, such a baby, only sixty-seven years old and already out of juice; or afraid to live. He could remember his grandfather Richard Thomas who, at eighty, still walked stiff and straight, carrying his two years in the army with him all his life because, as he told

Richard, "A man can't believe in himself if he can't believe in the Queen." He had lived to be eighty-three years old and, Simon Thomas said, *his* grandfather, Richard Thomas's father, had lived to be an equal age.

"Any Thomas can live for a long time," Simon said, "as long as he stays away from tobacco and women." He himself, of course, had chosen the other route, and in addition to living with his housekeeper, he had been known to make a nuisance of himself at every opportunity. Simon Thomas and his father had been wiry men, and, as he lay in bed comparing his own longevity with theirs, Richard tried to imagine what it would be like to weigh fifty pounds less. The doctors had him on a diet now, but it wasn't the same, lying in bed, imagining the muscles being starved while the fat remained, as it might have been to lose the weight while he was working. The association of fat with age was so complete it was impossible to conceive of being old and still thin; the matador, he thought, would age like that, staying thin and becoming sinewy and pot-bellied as he grew older, his stomach sticking out as his chest collapsed, like the dessicated history professor he had had, a gentle old man who wore a yellow-checkered waistcoat beneath his pinstripe. Men like the matador, the professor and Simon Thomas (who, though he said he was beyond vanity, was disgusting to behold eating, always having to reach into his mouth with his fingers and poke the food so that it could be reached by all his best teeth simultaneously) seemed to Richard to be almost a different species, having concentrated bulk in some areas of their lives but never on their own actual persons, of their own actual flesh; and so he would say, when Miranda teased him about getting fat, that he was not afraid to be a man of substance. In fact, he felt himself, by not having limited his size, to have somehow experienced motherhood, the unlimited rule of flesh which had nothing to do with diapers or training but was strictly a quantitative problem and could be measured by the bulk that was fed and cared for, that had to be moved if anything was to move. Of the thin men he knew, only Pat Frank seemed to have any idea of what it was like for him, and he, he admitted himself, experienced the world's transportation problems through his liver which had been constantly maligned for most of his life.

He pushed himself up into a sitting position. With his eyes closed he might be back at the farm, sitting in his own bed. From there, if the outside light were on, he would be able to see the maple tree and the tin roof of the summer kitchen. And he would be able to hear the wind threatening the leaves and branches, sweeping through the long grass of the spring pasture. The hospital was entirely surrounded by concrete. Though the lake was visible from the lounge, he was, in his room, cut off from all outside noises except the sounds of wet car tires when it was raining and the nightly uncertain movements of wind through the courtyard. When he opened his eyes, these nights, there was often nothing at all; the whole world disappeared into the dark, a mistake, stopped in a trance, the way Simon used to sometimes find him, sitting in the barn or on the ground somewhere, staring off into space. And when he came across him like that, Simon would shake him awake, accuse him of being a slug, feeling sorry for himself. Miranda too: she would come up behind him and kiss him on the neck. "It's not so bad," she would say.

"No," Richard would agree, "it's not. I'm just thinking."

As Simon described his own activity when he sat on his porch in town, he in his armchair and Richard in an old straight-backed wooden chair wired together, drinking the strange berry wine that old Mark Frank used to bring to Simon Thomas every week as payment for some old forgotten favour.

"You know," Simon said, about to divulge the product of all this cogitation, "I remember every woman I've ever had." He spoke in his usual self-righteous way, as if he was proudly reciting his prayers. "And in my opinion," he smacked his lips, "the best time to have a woman is in the morning, in winter, before or after the milking, it doesn't matter." Richard's mother hadn't died until the winter before he went to university, but for the decade leading up to that she had been sick most of the time. During those years it had been necessary to have a woman at the farm to help with the cooking and the chores and, in the winters, when there were no city relations or schoolgirls to spare, Simon had an arrangement with Katherine's parents, Henry and Elizabeth Beckwith who were first generation Scots and ran the school from the time Simon got married to the day it burned down during spelling. In the morning, in winter, the floors would be so cold that they would snap instead of creak, sounding like frozen branches underfoot when Simon got up to tend the fire, or go from Katherine's room back to his wife. "The first woman I ever had," Simon said, "or perhaps she had me—a gentleman must know the meaning of the difference—with the exception of your mother, God rest her soul for she was more interested in His world even when she was alive—was not in the barn like so many of the rabble that populate these parts, but in the carriage house of a bishop." Although it was not the local custom to boast of chastity, Simon Thomas was considered to be somewhat exceptionally descriptive in his talk, especially at community gatherings where many of the apparent subjects of his anecdotes were present, along with their husbands. But no one ever got angry or even believed him, except for Peter Malone who threatened to set fire to Simon Thomas's house if he was ever caught talking to Katherine again. Katherine Malone, born Katherine Beckwith. Who entered their life when Leah Thomas, Simon's wife, got sick. And stayed between Richard and Simon like a fulcrum, the currents between them to be measured in her terms, balanced thin as Simon's knife.

Brian came almost every day. "How's the farm?" Richard would demand. Or ask after a particular cow that was due. Brian would talk to him in monosyllables, answering questions, asking questions. And when Erik and Brian were there together Richard could see how they were defeated by each other, nothing between them except automatic and sterile violence.

"It's not so bad," Miranda said.

"No."

"The doctor says that in another week or two you should be able to come home. We'll put the bed downstairs, in the living-room, so you'll be able to walk to the bathroom."

And later, the nurse prepared him too. "When you go home," she said, "it's important to remember that there are people taking care of you, so you should try to make it as easy as possible for them. Now the monkey-man I was telling you about, for instance. You would have thought he would be just a terrible problem, what with hardly any toilet training and he wouldn't even speak most of the time. But somehow he seemed to know what a nuisance he was and made it easy on me. Whenever he wanted something to eat he had a way of signalling to me, he was so cute, he liked to get on his knees and wave his arse, like a dog begging I guess, though I never saw a dog beg like that, and if he wanted to be changed or to have something else, he always had a way of telling me—and not at a time when I was busy. I mean sick people often get selfish you know and they forget that other people have a problem looking after them. My husband when he was sick was absolutely impossible; all he wanted to do all day was eat and get me in bed with him, you would have thought it was some kind of special holiday him bothering me like that. Better than when he was working anyway. But don't you believe that a sick person is just a burden, because they're not. You take my cousin, her youngest has cerebral palsy and can't hardly walk or do anything but he's happy all the time and never complains and I'll tell you that it's a lesson to everyone else just to see that child. It even started them going to church again and I didn't think anything would ever start that, especially after Carrie found out, she's my cousin, that Herbert the old bugger had been going to the same prostitute every week for four years and, what really made her angry, meeting her in front of the Dominion store every time so all her friends had known it right from the beginning and never said a thing. Not that Carrie couldn't make it uncomfortable for *them*.

"Now the best thing would be to put the bed on the same floor as the bathroom. At first you'll be able to go to the bathroom by yourself and there's no use in falling down the stairs if you don't have to. I guess the most important thing is to have the right attitude. Now my mother didn't have the right attitude at all. Once she started making her mess in her own bed, well, I guess she was senile or didn't have anything else to play with though, to tell the truth, I've never told this to anyone and it sounds dumb but especially after everything else I've said, but, anyway, this is the one thing I'd rather you never told anyone, cross your heart, anyway my mother got so I didn't know what to do and one day I started to go out and buy her toys, like a baby. I mean if a person is just going to act like a baby then that's the way to treat them. Just like the monkey-man who acted like a monkey. Anyway, I went to the five and dime and I bought my mother some rattles with polka dots on them and some of those toy cars with little steering wheels and even, it was what she liked best, a plastic boat for the bathtub that had a little hole in it so that when you squeezed it, water squirted out. I used to put her in the bath and let her play there for hours, she never seemed to get tired of it. There were some who said she would have been easier to handle if I had given her tranquilizers but Lord knows I robbed the hospital blind for drugs as it was, I mean her at home and me being away so much the best thing was to let her sleep while I wasn't there otherwise it would just get her upset.

"I guess I complain about it a lot but we really had good times together too. I'd make us a picnic supper and spread it out on the floor on a blanket and we'd both sit there and eat and pretend it was summer. I'd turn on the radio too so we could hear the concerts; my mother loved listening to the Sunday opera and she always liked to sing right along, she had such a good voice and said she was always the best singer in the convent though I'm sure she lied about that just like everything else, and then maybe we'd have a drink or two, and go to sleep early. She got so cute when she was drunk, I'll say that for her, she even wanted to dance while she was singing but of course I didn't let her, that wouldn't have been responsible, I mean she could have broken a hip or something and then I would have had to put her in hospital and, you know, they didn't even have insurance in those days; even with keeping her at home and stealing everything I could from the hospital it was costing me a fortune."

In the fall and winter, while school was on and it was cold, Simon officially shared his wife's room, keeping her warm, as he would say, but really just keeping himself warm by being that much closer to Katherine's bed. But in the spring and summer, when Katherine lived at her own house, Simon would sleep downstairs on the sofa. In those seasons Richard remembered his mother's room as surpassing the kitchen as a source of odours, strange pseudo-alcoholic vapours and camphors being exuded from the rows of bottles she kept on the floor by her bed, each bottle different, each one with its own long list of benefits and testimonials, pictures of frock-coated doctors or relieved patients framed and brown-toned on each label, the entire collection telling its own separate story of sickness converted to money. And in the summer, once the roads were passable, Simon would go into town every afternoon that it rained. He would take, alternatively, Richard or Richard's brother Steven, one being left at home to be with his wife, Leah Thomas, *Lee-aah* all the neighbours called her when they enquired after her health—seldom visiting her, as if her stint of teaching school had set her apart from the rest of the community and now, in punishment for having corrected the grammar and manners of those she taught, she deserved to be left alone to suffer in her particular grammarian's purgatory.

When it was his turn to stay at home, Richard would help his father and brother hitch the horses to the wagon and, dreading those afternoons which seemed to have an existence entirely apart from any other aspect of his life, ride with them from the barnyard to the end of the driveway, always looking up and down the road as they came to it, in the impossible hope that some neighbour would just chance along, in the rain, wanting to visit his mother so that he would be sprung free for the afternoon. When they came to the road, he would jump off the wagon and walk back slowly, protected from the rain by the huge maple trees that the poet and his grandfather Richard Thomas had planted together, lining the drive on either side as a suitable prelude to the mansion that was supposed to have replaced the original house, which, with its limestone walls and winecellars, marked the prosperity of this farm. But the original house still stood, buttressed and augmented, and the maple trees were themselves the main attraction, growing huge and healthy in the clay loam soil and more renowned for their yearly run of sap than for the farm which they announced. The two rows of trees had stretched and touched in the middle, so he could walk back along this protected line, following the small streams and ponds that were eroded into the drive, trying to fit his feet into the sand so the varying textures of wet and dry would match his soles exactly, looking for places where the waters had been diverted by the imprints of the horses' hooves or the long deep cuts of the wagon wheels, which he followed in turn, squeezing and narrowing his feet so he could walk in the cold water like a tight-rope artist. And when he came to the end of the trees he would run past the house into the yard and then the barn, always with the excuse to himself that there was a bridle or harness that had been dropped and must be returned to its nail, that it was time for him to shovel the shit out of the horsebarn. Knowing that his mother was already aware of this avoidance, that he would have to list his rainy-day duties for her when he finally went upstairs. So he would hang up the harness and throw a few shovelfulls out into the hayfield, through the tiny window sized for a small pitchfork that was deemed to be the ultimate weapon for sheepshit in 1914 and then, in what seemed to be the most horrible moment of those wet afternoons, go to the door of the barn and stand there, leaning on the shovel and looking towards the house, imagining that Simon and his father would never come back and that somehow the farm would be suddenly his to take care of, all the details and the work suddenly bequeathed to him along with his mother. With the rain protecting him in long beaded chains he could see her window, and hear again Simon speaking to him when he had first stood there, resting after helping with the horses; his back snugged into the frame and his eyes blinking in the new outside light, everything re-seen after working with Simon in the half-darkness: Simon, talking while he worked, telling him of the poet who had helped to build the barn and then decided to live in it, all one winter with his child, for the child was holy and Jesus too had walked among sheep.

The barn had belonged to the poet because he had helped Richard S. Thomas to build it and then he had lived in it. And it belonged to his child Frederick Thomas because the child too had lived in it and the poet wanted to share it with him. And after it belonged to the poet, William Thomas, and his son, Frederick Thomas, it belonged to Simon Thomas. He kept it for himself and then he tore out the staunchions and pens that had been placed there for sheep and took out the old box stove and chimney that the poet had put there for himself—and the sheep and the ducks and chickens and rabbits and sick birds and snakes and foxes and even groundhogs that he had befriended and taken into the barn with him for the education of the imbecile Frederick Thomas—and then for two years left it empty. At the end of that two years, an old barn near the maple bush that had been used for storing the horse-drawn grain harvester (which still existed like a huge and rusted side-saddle windmill in another barn that was built long after but now itself threatened to collapse) was burned down during threshing and Simon decided to convert half the poet's barn into a machine shed. So he put a wall down the middle and tore out half the west side of the barn and then, in the remaining closed-in half, constructed stalls and put in a cement floor so that the horses and their machines could be housed together in an absolutely modern manner. Because the poet and Richard Thomas had perhaps more than a few points of conflict, they had taken their time constructing this barn, each attempting to outdo the other in care and permanence, so this barn that was once the poet's house and was later the first building that Simon dared to change to his own needs, still stood, supported vertically and horizontally by long hand-squared beams which were fastened together with wooden pegs, having survived generations of other barns without any sign of crack or rot.

In this way it became known that the barn was the wedge to ownership of the farm just as once the cleared field had been that wedge. And it was therefore understood that Simon intended that the farm be passed to Richard because that particular barn was Richard's responsibility: every night in the winter he would have to go out and feed the horses and put down fresh straw for them, and in the summer he was made to stand in the loft of the barn and supervise the storing of the hay. And after the hay was in the barn, Simon would make him go up to the loft every day and rummage in the hay, checking for dampness and heat, poking in a drugstore thermometer tied to a long stick. In the rain, the barn was almost black: the windows were always dirty with bits of straw and manure, and the doors, swollen with moisture, refused to open more than part way. But after the first winter the barn was his, the proportions and sense of space entirely familiar and he could move in it equally adept in light or dark.

Standing in the doorway with his hand on the wooden latch, he could see his mother's window through the curtain of rain and know that she would be sitting up in her bed, her back supported by two red satin cushions which she had been given when she retired from teaching to marry Simon, sensing his presence and waiting for him. Then, feeling like a puppet on the end of a string, he would move slowly towards the house, dragging himself through the rain, his stomach in revolt against the fact that it was possible to grow old and sick. And Richard, now in his hospital bed and looking out into the courtyard with its wet cement surfaces and lights, given haloes by the rain, was reminded again that he could be forced to choose—or see himself in that same bed, the lifeline to the trailer reversed, the days spent listening to Miranda's footsteps in the house, the minutes of presence that would be calculated as what was necessary until she too got sick, and they could be moved into a home, like Frederick Thomas, a place where they would be issued a permanent dressing gown and given a few flowers to tend, man become boy again. And even when Richard Thomas had gotten to the house, he had stayed outside in the rain, standing under the maple tree that was then sixty years younger and straighter, barely reaching over the summer kitchen to the top of the house, its leaves coming out each spring before any other of the older trees that lined the drive, snapping out of their buds like rifle shots green and turgid, bursting with eagerness to get on with the summer but still unable to match or even evoke the massive spreads that the older trees would finally achieve, their leaves and branches spread in ponderous arches vulnerable to August storms so that each year they would lose limbs to lightning and wind. He would stay outside in the rain, leaning against the wall of the summer kitchen or sitting on the steps of the old milking platform that had been converted to a laundry stoop, rather than go inside and face his mother alone, the look she could give him of absolute need and longing as if she knew the power that her sickness had over him, the way she possessed him entirely by her total plea.

In her presence he felt her need enter his veins and arteries like a foreign army. Then she would speak, and her voice, soft and not asking anything but only suggesting by its every intonation and nuance, by its silences and the way it moved through the vowels like a general inspecting the dead in the field, that it had exactly surrounded what it didn't do, avoided asking anything at all but only laid siege to the enemy in this honourable and gaudy silence that was strewn between them in broken and evoked colours; her voice terrified him so that he was routed—disorganized, broken apart and stampeded into an unruly retreat to the past which was, between them, a long chain of unconnected resentments and needs, all of them to his mind trivial and insufficient to explain the way she could move her voice within him at will.

It was one of the rules that once visiting her he wasn't allowed to leave until she dismissed him and she, knowing that she held that power over him, would play it subtly, mentioning that perhaps there would be something he could bring her, or something which needed to be done elsewhere in the house, or that soon it would be time for him to go outside and help his father with the chores (as if she ran the house and the farm from her throne, did all the essential work except for a few unavoidable and undesirable tasks which she relegated to the men—who weren't suited to anything else anyway—in the vain hope that they might be able to do something *this* simple). The only one who didn't fear her was Richard's brother, Steven. What this meant was understood without being spoken. Simon taught it by the way he behaved towards this second son, erased him by ignoring him until finally, when it was evidently incurable, he treated him gently but at a distance, like a giant dog that was a children's favourite but couldn't be taught to do anything useful. When the rain came down hard it slid off the young tree in long corded sheets, whipping against the house like movement and voices, the sounds of his mother getting up from her bed and calling to him for help. But if he became convinced and went to check on her, he would find her as always, leaning back against the brass bedstead with her hands moving like puppetmasters beneath her knitting and her eyes staring straight forwards, towards the door, absolutely unbowed by whatever had forced her body to the bed (an illness that never seemed to be named) and planning further strategies in her war against Simon. "Your father," she would say. "No one understands a thing about your father except for myself." She would chew at her tongue before continuing, leaving out all the unknown evils he had perpetrated for the sake of Richard's youth and all their souls. "They say he is a gentle man." She would repeat that several times, each time pausing at the end of the sentence, giving each vowel its proper hint of British reflection as if she were still teaching school or standing up in front of the parents in one more hopeless attempt to persuade them that the culture of the Empire could not be perpetuated in the fields but had to be brought to the pagans in the class-room, where the monarch's framed picture could oversee the task, order it, make the glove fit even the most recalcitrant colonials. And when she paused, she would reach over to the bedside table and pick up a linen handkerchief from on top of one of the small bound volumes she kept there (never the poet's diary, for Simon kept that to himself his whole life and would only recite snatches from it at his leisure) of consumptive verse and cough lightly into it. "Would you light the lamp please, Richard," she would say; and then she would wait silently while he cleaned the globe. He would give it to her and she would hold it up against the light to make sure that there were no streaks. While he prepared her room for the night, she didn't speak, but waited until he was finished to resume her discussion of his father. "They say that Simon Thomas is a gentle man," she would say, "because he has never killed or beaten anyone." Here she would cough again, the rhetorical comment of the trained speaker. "The little runt never went to war because he was a coward." And then, speaking without stopping until she heard the sound of the wagon bringing Simon and Steven home, she would tell the story of how her father, who had named her Leah because she was his first daughter, had forced her and Simon together, against their will. And while she talked, sounding at least half-convinced of the truth herself, Richard listened not to the words, which seemed to be the least essential part of the story, but to the chorus that made up her voice, the army on the move which one day would set out from her bedroom, strike Simon dead, and make things right, once and for all, meting justice and revenge throughout the whole township, this vocal army that was like the lead soldiers he had, their paint still bright over the grey and brittle lead as if this surface should be enough to convince any child. Her family had emigrated from the United States to the area north of Belleville, United Empire Loyalists she said but they had waited until after the revolution. And then, because of some obscure family quarrel to which she would allude but never explain, her own father and his wife had moved away from the family estate and started a new farm, clearing the less hospitable land that was available sixty miles to the east. When she was seventeen, the money appeared to send her to Toronto, to normal school. And when she was there, unmarried and with no further choices, she taught in the school that was, though in the next township, only six miles by good road from her own house. Her family had sent the toy soldiers for Richard, a reminder of the armies of her past: the Colonel who drank tea, had a handlebar moustache, and took his men—all Boston gentry—bear hunting in the Florida swamps to gain his mastery over them; and the army of British culture which, she said, was the foremost civilization in the world and had conquered the French by sheer manners and a superior command of the English language, and which now, she didn't need to say specifically, existed in her own being, in the manner of her speech and hands, in the way she had sacrificed her legs for empires so that she might be, as she put it, "a person of dignity and not the common slut your ignorant father would prefer." And this last in a rising voice, because while the grandfather Richard Thomas had lived, she had been forced to moderate her talk of armies and ignorance, had not, in fact, even been able properly to take to her bed because the old man, walking about the house and the barnyard with his cane and stiff back, as if he had indeed succeeded in creating life in this barren colony and was required now, like God, only to oversee his purvey and punish insects and acts which offended even his benevolence, had never liked her—had taken to wearing his old moth-eaten uniform after he heard her stories about the American colonel, challenging her syntax on obscure grammatical points which he claimed to have learned from a church deacon when he was a child in England, walked every morning from room to room in this old house which he had built, but had now given over to his son and family, and inspected them for cleanliness and order, came into her room, when after one of her fights with Simon she had decided not to get up, and poked the covers off her with his cane—that and every time thereafter so that it was not until he was buried that she could spend even one sick day in bed.

"Your mother was never meant to put up with this world," Simon said. He had his thumb hooked into his watchpocket and was sucking noisily on his pipe. For once he wanted to go outside and see the farm so Richard, feeling foolish and suddenly an intruder, put on the hat he always wore, a black felt hat to keep away the bugs, and took Simon Thomas back to see the new hayfield he had made out of two smaller ones, clearing and draining the swampy ground that lay between them so that there was now at least one field on the farm larger than ten acres, large enough even, with its sudden rolls and dips, that there were places in the field where you could stand and not be able to see the fences. And there was a place in that field, a knoll at the beginning of the old swampy section, where they could stand and see the small valley that bisected the field and then, at its edge, ran into a section of second growth bush and continued through the bush and some pasture to a country road that led to Katherine Malone's. "It's none of your business," Simon said, "but your mother would only do it outside." And he re-lit his pipe, his hand passing quickly over the scar on his jawbone, now pale and almost enclosed by wrinkles, where Richard had cut him the night they had both come home from Katherine's. The field, newly seeded that spring, was thick with its second growth of clover, dark green and reaching almost to their knees, the thin stems winding about their ankles and shins as they walked. "You'll watch the cows don't get in here," Simon said, in that manner he had always used for giving orders. And again, as he spoke, the hand moved over the scar. A true man with a knife, Simon Thomas, and when a cow bloated they would always call him to cut open its stomach. And when he was finished, he would wipe the blade on his pantleg and slip it back into its sheath, another vanity, that he had sewn for himself out of calf leather. And he still carried that same knife, though the handle had been replaced once, and now pulled it out of its sheath to ream his pipe, spitting the juice into the clover and then detaching the stem from the bowl so he could blow it clear. "A father would not kill his own son," Simon said. "Not even for a woman would he do that." And then, the pipe cleaned, he stuck it in his pocket and took out a cigar, splitting open the cellophane with his teeth. "A man would not kill his own son," Simon said, "but a person might kill his brother for nothing at all, out of carelessness." A true man with a knife, Simon Thomas, and the support beams of the barn were marked with thousands of tiny little nicks where Simon Thomas, pacing up and down, had thrown his knife, aiming at real and imaginary flies. Before the hayfield was enlarged, the swampy section iced over in the winter and was the best place to skate. After the first snows, but before it got really cold, there would often be deer tracks to the place, because there was a small spring there that ran most of the year. And if it thawed in January the bears would come too; leaving their marks all about the spring and crisscrossed through the field. As always now, as always since the day when his brother had been killed, Richard let Simon say what he pleased. On the knoll they were still warmed by the sun. And the wind too came off the field warm, warm and slow so they were almost overwhelmed by the scent of clover; and Richard had a sudden desire to let himself be taken over completely by the land, absorbed as if buried, his will tenuous and snapping as the poet had said it must, and could feel it ebbing from him that quickly, as if in one moment of doubt all the energy that kept him able to impose the farm on the land might be dissipated and the land return to its own chaotic intentions, as if the farm was only a thin transparency laid on it like a decal that could be blown off easily by wind and time so that the bodies and the hours and the effort that were buried in the immense fertility of this field would finally be nothing but a brief digression in its existence as a forest and swamp; and the swamp he had spent a month surrounding with ditches so it would drain would reassert itself and then, in its own time, fill in and become part of a meadow which would be no pasture but ground fit only for juniper seeds and sumac trees. And even from where he stood he could see bush where there had once been a field, a field cleared by a cousin of his grandfather's who had bought the adjoining farm and lived there for twenty years before selling the lot to Richard Thomas for enough money to take his family back to England. And in the centre of that bush, which was over fifty years old and now contained elm trees which rose almost a full hundred feet into the air and maple trees which could give three gallons a day of sap during the first spring run, there was no trace that it had once grown hay and even grain except for several huge piles of stones, scattered like the cairns of dinosaurs through the fields, and an old foundation which no one who did not know its location would ever be able to find, already surrounded and covered by trees that had died and rotted over it. And standing there with Simon on this knoll that now centered his new field, he could not say whether the new field was a sign that soon there would be more fields, that one day the entire bush would be cleared and all the land that was flat enough and suitable would be part of some unimaginably prosperous farm of which he and Simon and his grandfather, all by then long dead, would be remembered as the founders, or whether the field was just another chapter in the insane struggle to dominate this land in a way which had nothing to do with it, and that the three generations of Thomases would have accomplished nothing except to scar and chop up enough land for their own survival, like any other race too weak or lazy to live by roaming or hunting, like any other race that lived on this patchwork of forest and surface rock that periodically burst forth like a tide to erase all struggles, plots and fornications of the creatures who wrestled with it and then subsided, leaving them their tenuous stage once more so that they could again convince themselves that this time it would be within their power, that they would shape the land to their needs and it would be a once and for all victory after which it would be necessary only to sow and to harvest in some unknown and paradisiacal god-assisted rhythm.

And Simon, again passing his hand by the scar in that strange gesture of his, as if a movement of renunciation that would let him swallow time whole, without resisting, swallow it as he had said the earth had swallowed him so that they might all, as he had quoted the poet too who he now claimed as his father along with Richard Thomas, be part of one belly, for God had made man with a mouth, passing his hand by his scar and then reaching into his own mouth for some forgotten piece of food, flicking it into the grass, spitting out the amalgam of saliva and tobacco juice that had been disturbed by his hand and then putting the same hand with a quick motion onto Richard's arm, claiming him and drawing the line between them as a trajectory of inherited flesh: coded movements and unexpected intersections: the fast movement hissing of a blade through the air and then while it is still vibrating in the wall the feeling of wood rapping against the muscles of the thighs—the table overturned and he is moving forward, the knife already out of the wall and in his hand, Simon's chair upset and him helpless on his back, pinned by the table as Richard moves in with the knife

Swinging

above his father's head like the executioner's pendulum.

Like Katherine
Beckwith coming slowly up the stairs after Simon had left, her
slippers sharp files against the cold wooden stairs, then padding
across the rug, sinking into the bed and under the covers wrapping herself around Richard before he can speak, surrounding
him with his own unanswered question, her hands now on Richard's skin move like tiny scalpels and he knows that it is cut
open in sharp curving flaps, these witches' rites she has learned
and practised with her ghosts, her hands moving on him like tiny
scalpels exorcising as they kill, springing open cells and floating
them in this river of blood he has become, his body has gone and
now he has become her, woven into her darkness that is stamped
in silhouette against the window, he knows that he is absolutely
with her and they are both ecstatically fucking his absence

Exorcising as they kill

Swinging
their bodies above his father's body.

Simon Thomas sent home
walking on the old county road he and Henry Beckwith made,
with township money, cutting down thin elms and cedar to fill
out the wet spots and then dragging wagonloads of sand and
gravel from the old mineshaft that still stood open on the Beckwith place.

Simon Thomas standing with his son in his son's new
field and the newness of it has cut the valley open, exposed it,
they can see down its trough from belly to neck. Simon Thomas
spits and turns around. The last time he will see this farm.

SEVEN

For the first time since he is in the hospital he feels sick: not dying
or gothic sick but just an ordinary flu that travels mostly in the
skeleton, generating aches and pains and dizziness every time he
turns or moves. They are letting him walk a bit now but this fever
has addled his sense of balance and when he stands beside his
bed, one hand on the rail to steady himself and, with the other,
trying to put on his housecoat, he feels like a huge upright walrus,
swaying uncertainly in this unnatural two-footed heat. It is already August and the bed beside him is still empty, waiting for
him to decide. August: the heat of that month has always been
useless to him: less fertile than July it is something inevitable but
unnecessary—to be endured in the hope that it will spread into the
future and delay the first September frost. He stands beside the
bed, one hand on the rail. It feels cold despite the heat. His
calluses are beginning to disappear and now he begins to feel
things on his palms: temperatures and textures. Last night Pat
Frank had come and brought a bottle of wine: while he was
raising it up he had noticed a sharp line in his hand, almost like
a thin wire. But when he put down the bottle it had turned out
to be just the edge of the label, cheap Niagara sherry that even
Pat Frank admitted was too sweet to drink. A nurse sees him
standing uncertainly by the bed and comes into the room.

"How are we today, Mr. Thomas." "Would you like to lie
down, Mr. Thomas." "All right, Mr. Thomas, I'll just shut the
door for you here and come back to check on you in a few
minutes." "Don't forget, Mr. Thomas, you don't have to strain."

And in fact she needn't have said that because his night nurse had told him a long and disgusting story about a patient of hers who had had a stroke while on the toilet, arresting her bowels at the crucial moment so they were paralyzed open (only temporarily of course—the nurse was always careful about his morale) and for several weeks thereafter things just dropped out.

"I hope you don't mind me talking to you like this," the nurse would say from time to time, her hand always on him, wrapped about his wrist to check his pulse, holding his hand, moving over his chest and shoulders to apply liniments that would loosen his breathing, stroking his forehead and loosening the muscles of his neck when he couldn't turn over.

A new point of time had come into existence. Despite all his sluggish efforts to make it his own, it never existed in the present but appeared only in retrospect, like a vehicle moving up quickly in a rear-view mirror: the knowledge that he was going to die in this hospital, that the choice had already been made. Richard Thomas stood beside the bed, the aluminum rail cold and alien in his palm, dizzy with an irrelevant flu and wondering if it would be possible for him to die or if death was just going to happen to him, like everything else. And beneath that, still unsure because they thought otherwise, thought that they were winning against the death (which they too placed in the past, but in a different way). Despite the empty bed and the refusal to say anything definite, they thought he would be going home. They were helping him to walk. They made measurements and graphs of his heartbeat showing the wild skip that had developed—a train racing out of control, but still, the tracks were there. And so he did it all at once: the checking and signing of the will and all the little bits and pieces of paper that Miranda kept bringing to him and the preparations to go home as, hopefully, more than an invalid, a walking, talking perfect imitation of himself who would be allowed to be a spectator at his farm if he controlled his diet and ingested certain quantities of pills on a program that they were now getting ready, a spectator at his farm who could do anything except work and, of course, the doctor had for some reason blushed while saying this, as though age made it obscene and ideally it would be done only by China dolls at night when the lights were off in the store, sexual relations would have to be curtailed for at least six months; saying this so emphatically that Richard wondered if there was in this doctor's past some unknown legion of almost-saved patients who had died in each others embraces, in unspeakable orgies, in just a quiet goodnight kiss when the wife was least expecting it, scores lost one night in a senior citizens' drive-in double bill. The nurse came into the room. "Did you go, Mr. Thomas?" She went to check that he had flushed. Then she helped him up into the bed. He could see that she didn't mind his age and bulk, accepted the challenge and the necessity the same way he did when dealing with a cow that was down and needed to be rolled over and, if it was in the barn and possible, ropes passed beneath its belly so that it could be lifted to its feet again. "Now a horse," Simon used to say. "Once a horse is down they'll never get up. You might as well shoot it and save the feed." The movement and sudden sinking into the mattress had made him dizzy. He knew his eyes were open but he could hardly see her face: it swam distant and out of focus–separated from him by a translucent film that now broke apart into tiny red dots. He knew she was speaking but couldn't hear her. She was leaning towards him, unaware that anything was different, sliding the thermometer into his mouth and marking down his trip to the bathroom on her chart. The moment was already passed and he couldn't remember the lesson, whether the mind had survived the failure of the body or whether it had all gone at once. With Simon Thomas, it had all been in his hands, the fingers always restless and moving, long sinewy fingers that could balance a knife or a needle with equal ease, sure and nervous. The same hands as Erik, Richard thought, but Erik seemed to live only through words and his head so that his body was already vestigial, threatening to grow old before it was ever claimed by this world.

The nurse brought him a fresh pitcher of water, straightened the sheet and blanket over him, opened the window. The day staff thought that he would live; they had their charts and their figures to prove it. They treated him with a combination of deference and good cheer now, the shared good fellowship of those who have been to the wall together. The night nurse knew better. She spoke to him in urgent whispers, telling him increasingly outrageous stories of survival. "You can live," she said over and over again, "you can live if you only want to." And when she insisted on that Richard would get a picture of her patients, thousands of half-broken metal toys, the paint scraped off and rusted but still recognizable to the trained eye, deciding whether or not to wind themselves up for one more run.

Simon Thomas had never hesitated. He was always busy, connected by those nervous hands and the sound of his own misplaced church deacon's voice unctuously mouthing his own particular hypocrisies. After he had moved into town he even took up a new trade and began to bind books specially for the town's historical society library, replacing the broken cloth covers with handsewn calf's leather, the names of the books and their authors stamped in gold along the spines. He had bound the poet's diaries the same way, numbering the volumes and embossing the full name, Reverend William C. Thomas, on the spine of each of the three volumes; but refusing to let the diaries be copied or reproduced in any way but preferring only to attend occasional meetings of the historical society and shock the wives of the doctor and minister by reading out choice excerpts from what Simon considered the poet's special interest to have been, which was the genealogy of the area seen as a manifestation of God's Will working its way through those of his creatures who knew it best.

The nurse stood back and inspected her tableau, looking at Richard Thomas in that particular way he had come to associate with the day staff, all of whom had part-time jobs arranging window displays in the shopping centre, then stepped up the aisle between the beds and pulled him forward so she could puff up the pillows, there, and then back to crank up the bed to its mid-morning angle, leaving his good arm in the perfect position to reach for the grey metal night-table with its single drawer and oversize compartment for the bedpan; on the top of the table Miranda had spread a cloth, red and blue threads needlepointed into Irish linen, a farmhouse and surrounding trees. Every morning when he was well enough Richard Thomas stuffed it in the drawer of the table and every afternoon, before Miranda came, one of the nurses took it out, so the wife of the ingrate sickman wouldn't be disturbed.

The morning before Simon Thomas's funeral Richard had unpacked some of the boxes left from Simon's house in town, finding, among the old pipes and empty tobacco tins, the bound volumes of the poet's diaries that, despite his habit of reading from them, Simon had refused to show Richard, saying that he would get them in his turn. So, before the funeral, sitting in the living-room and reading these diaries, Miranda scurrying about, getting things ready, telling him the details of the bath he was supposed to take, the shirt he could iron for himself if he didn't get moving, the dogs that hadn't been fed for two days. And at the funeral, displaced into the poet's chain of flesh, Katherine coming to be with him, standing with him over the open grave, swaying,

   swinging like the executioner's pendulum,

              Katherine

Malone, born Katherine Beckwith. The parents had died and left her to the care of Simon Thomas, Henry Beckwith's only true friend in the community, the only man who dared stand up for him. Even at the time of Simon Thomas's funeral she was still a young woman but her body had grown shapeless from child-bearing and her face, following, had lost its shape too, as a signal, now almost a rounded pudding with only the movements of eyes and mouth to indicate otherwise; sliding her hand into Richard's arm for support and he, not thinking, putting his hand over hers briefly, knowing and not considering, so now, the day after the funeral, wondering what she would do, went back to the field where he had stood that last time with Simon Thomas and then on down the valley and through the bush to the old country road that led to Katherine Malone's. It was a slow spring, soft and wet, this day the warmest it had been, melting the snow that was still deep in the shaded places, moats of it across the hollows of the old road, never ploughed to meet Katherine Malone,

   barelegged in long skirts and rubber boots, sinking in past the top of the boots in some places, the fields now almost unfamiliar to her, then, when she got to a rock that had melted warm or even a hummock of dry mud and grass, she would take off her boots and shake out the snow and bits of ice. With the sun out it was warm, almost hot. She had taken off her woollen mitts and walked bareheaded on this old road where no one ever travelled any more and she could walk without fear of being seen.

Mitts off and the coat too short for her, her arms suddenly appearing to her beyond the soaked frayed cuffs of the coat as they had thirty years ago, the arms of a girl; and remembered that in Kingston she would see women of her age and they were still young, with their one or two children and their new clothes and maybe even a car to drive from home to downtown. And even her cousin who lived in a limestone house in Kingston with its carefully drawn curtains and carpeted rooms, her cousin was her own age and still dressed up Saturday nights, wearing gowns that showed her neck and shoulders and even jewellery to draw attention to the skin which was still smooth like it had always been, only now creamy, as if that husband of hers with his major's uniform and his money had managed to upgrade her breeding; no, it was true, she was still a young woman. The spring air in her lungs—she could swallow it so it would be in the belly too, rejuvenating; only Henry Beckwith had paid any attention to the old Indian habit of drinking the maple sap straight, without boiling, as a tonic, even fed it to the cows, fifty gallons every morning he drew for them from the bush behind the house. Now she stepped to the side of the road, to a maple that stood there and ran her finger in the cracks of the bark, finding a place where the tree bled naturally out of an old wound, the sap warm and sticky. She laughed and slurped it off her finger as she had always done; she would go home after seeing Richard and go on a diet, move to Kingston and wear fancy clothes, laughed again at the thought of Peter Malone, skipped and bowed, he was inflicted on her body like any other season, could this be love? clapped her hands. Richard would be coming soon. Not their first spring either but they used to meet here in the spring but only quickly, would do it standing up when the ground was too wet. He would hold her in the air, his weight pressing her against a tree. Simon so thin and white. Or when there was time they would go to the barn. Simon Thomas thin and white. Could this be love? Clapped her hands and hummed, her feet doing a miniature waltz in the rubber boots, she could feel the felt scrunching up beneath her toes. The Beckwiths, because they were near the other township and the school, had gotten hydro ten years before everyone else so Richard used to come over to listen to their radio and then, later, come and sit with her in the parlour, the radio on and she would light the kerosene lamp and she showed him how to waltz in the living-room, one two three, one two three, like an older sister she had been, the same older sister as she had been for him when she stayed at the house for the winter, with Simon always wanting to sneak into her room just to tease her, one step forward and two steps back, she'd let him lead her as soon as he knew the basic step and so he did, his hair watered back and down and his arm out straight, holding her away from him as if his father had stamped her, holding her away from him but curving his own belly towards her, like a child. Katherine Malone took off her mitts and clapped her hands, scooped up some snow and rubbed it into her hands and wrists—spring snow, red hands, red wrists, her arms pink and still too long for her coats, she always had long arms and while they danced she could rest her hand on the back of his neck and caress his hairs there: sexy, Peter Malone called that habit, used to. Found herself giggling and giggled more, sinking down into the snow and laughing out loud at that dumb Peter Malone who thought he knew it all with his city magazines and his two serge suits, set up by Simon she knew but didn't care, Peter Malone bowing and scraping manure off his boots even while he stood there, a bouquet of flowers in his hand, the only man who ever even knew you were supposed to bring flowers, and while one part of him was responding to Simon's invitation to this easy township lay, the other stood hesitant and soft with these flowers that were already dying in his hand, the kind of man ghosts would approve of, crazy and soft but so hopeless in bed, one step forward and two steps back, made her at times even go to Simon just to have it easy and simple though he was not the bull that he thought himself, just easy; not like the gentle Peter Malone whose sex was never quite decided but when it was over he was still with her, still. She stood up and shook the snow out of her coat, shook, feeling the way her flesh lagged behind her bones, whole fields of grain and potatoes trailing on her body. In the winter, the evergreens were dark and layered with snow; but now they were bare and wet, the tamarack, the spruce and the cedar all fighting for space along the fences and the road, their roots rising out of the snow already, melting themselves clean for the summer, digging deeper around the rocks for more soil; they had never struck her, these trees, until she had children and two of her children died; then she began to notice them, hanging tenaciously from impossibly eroded cliffs, growing up strong and healthy from ground too swampy to support anything except useless wet grasses and bullrushes, clumps of them standing nonchalant and accomplished in the midst of rocky mounds, never starved or drowned or dying from pure stubborness. Snapped off a bit of cedar and crushed it in her mouth to release the smell, good luck to smell cedar in the spring, then reached into her pocket and rummaged around for a package of cigarettes, came to the place where the pocket was torn and pulled her coat up so she could continue the search in the lining of the coat. Found a promising lump and drew it up, yes, and they were wet but not broken, matches stuck into the cellophane, Peter Malone would have a fit if he saw her smoking outside. Could this be love? she sang out the words in her best contralto, rounding her lips and trying to sing from that place in the throat, the music teacher had put her finger there, love, and said sing again, relax and you can feel where it should be coming from, stopped and took a drag from her cigarette, sang again softly letting the smoke trail out with the words, stopped. On a higher section of the road now, the mud unfrozen and soft, unfrozen like the cemetery which they chose because it thawed first, a necessity for such a place because the bodies, once frozen by winter and encased in their pine box should not thaw before burial, though it was said to the children that cemeteries were thawed not by nature but by the devil who had to create new individual hells in the new world because it was too far to stretch the old one under the ocean, stopped, took her feet out of her boots—red and chafed from the rubber—let them sink into the mud. The tiny surface puddles were hot from the sun, already filmed over with heat and bacteria; lifted her foot and slowly lowered it down onto the mud, slowly and deliberate, like a press, watching it squeeze in slow motion over the sides of her foot and between her toes, crouched down on the road and lowered her hands slowly too, the palms and fingers arched apart, leaving their print in the mud; an instant fossil that made a sharp sucking sound as she drew her hands away, then moved them back, the pores drawn by the mud, pushed her hands deep into the road, letting the mud surround them completely, the cigarette hanging unaided in her mouth so finally she had to take out one hand and wipe it on her coat, waste not want not–Peter Malone with his kitchen table aphorisms to explain everything in this world in the same manner as his own limp fertility, Peter's Peter, the other hand coming out of the mud, palm towards the sun and flattening out, the liquid breaking apart into thousands of tiny fertile bubbles. Looked up and saw a rabbit haunched up at the side of the road, looking at her, nose twitching like a cartoon and jerking back and forth, one step forward and two steps back, stops entirely so only the hairs on its nose are quivering: the fur is not absolutely white but is spotted with pink and brown, as if it might be shedding its winter coat or is just a particularly mangy specimen. Its eyes jerk back and forth in its head, its head begins its strange dance again, surface body ripples; together they can listen to the water which now seems to roar in the ditch beside the road. She wants to go inspect it for carp and suckers but the rabbit is fighting her off, she looks towards the ditch again and then the rabbit is gone, like an ignored sign arrowed into the cedar bush. Katherine stands up and now there is so much mud along the hem of her skirt that it weights it down, she bends over and squeezes it out in rolls, so when she is finished it is arranged about her in a vaguely symmetrical ring of twists. Bun in the oven, Simon called it, riding over everything in his own way, but already old beneath it, thin and white like a ghost he would slip into her room and pull the covers over them like a tent so he could whisper without being heard, whisper to her and then come inside her where he would, the first winter, lie without moving, lie it seemed for hours without moving because the moon would come back and it would be visible through the window and then it would pass by and the whole time of the moon passing by the window would be only one small part of the time that he would lie there, sometimes talking to her or asking her questions always in those small white whispers under the tent, the quilted tent that Katherine had brought with her to sleep with and had been made all one winter by herself and her mother. Bun in the oven Simon called it, meaning at first himself and then, years later, the child they conceived the same way, him lying inside her so endlessly that maybe it was only boredom that began to convulse their bodies until finally, out of control but soundless, they could regain themselves. Thin and white just like winter, Simon was always old to her, not middle-age but old, his body without any signs of beauty or even the decay of beauty but the skin already ancient, like winter too and it was only that first winter and the one other time that he was anything but thin and fast, like an injection he needed to dispose of for some forgotten reason, his duty done to her, he said, all that silent winter, he had earned the right to do it as he pleased, an old man leaving God's message at every available station. The cigarette is now caked with mud too, dried brown along the seam and mud mixed in with the tobacco where she has wiped her mouth with the back of her hand. Holds it up in front of her eyes, lets it bisect the sun, sees that it is torn too, laughs and throws it in the air, clapping her hands as it passed through them, watches it land finally on its side in a puddle where it splits open and the tobacco begins to ooze out of the paper like miniature intestines. In India, Simon told her, they take them out and wash them in the river, in the river, inside out, with a long soft rag and handfuls of sand.

Richard would come over on Simon's errands and stay to listen to the radio, sent, Simon said, because he wanted to be sure that she wasn't entertaining anyone else. But he must have known what would happen with Richard, uncomfortable at first and even refusing to dance but only wanting to sit in the kitchen until enough time had gone by—seventeen already and already she could see the outlines of the life he would have: square and durable but not too heavy, muscled and strong like any farmer but his mouth and lips uncertain, like a baby who has been kept too close to his mother and now refuses her, to spite himself. His lips and eyes betray the body and with Simon's challenge she cannot help herself, feels suddenly older than him, a babysitter, tells him all the ghost stories she half believes. All the time he would sit in the kitchen until finally one afternoon she just moved the radio into the living-room and made him dance with her when he came, one two three, dance his own awkward way but she said he would need to know this for college and that she would teach him to be a gentleman so they wouldn't laugh at him in Toronto. He combed his hair with water before setting out but by the time he got there it was always dried along the sides. With her hand starting at the back of his neck she would have to ruffle it out so in the kerosene light it was finally thick and soft like the coat of an animal and to her he smelled more like the outdoors than the outdoors itself, spending all the day in the sun and wind before coming to her each night. And he came every night that summer, every night for six weeks until he finally admitted that he was frightened of her and didn't want to come back.

"Surely," she said, "a Thomas man could not be frightened of a woman." They were sitting across from each other at the kitchen table and she, six years older than him and unmarried put out her foot under the table so that it rested, instep curved on his knee. Saw Richard lower his head then raise it again, looking helplessly across at her, not even knowing the question. Then he pushed himself up from the table and was gone, swinging out the screen door of the summer kitchen and running down the drive, she could hear his boots' slow rhythm on the hard-packed mud. And then the whole night and the next day she was sorry for what she had done, holding the father over the son that way, as if he would have any strength at all with his mother in bed and a father like Simon Thomas, so jealous of his sons he boxed them in one way after another, trimming them at the edges the same (thoughtless) way he pared his nails at the table. The next night he was back. Stood casually in the kitchen and then as she was walking by grabbed her without any excuse or preamble, grabbed her and dragged her into the living-room and put her on the couch where he lay on top of her without even taking his clothes off, lay on top of her and then with one arm around her neck tried with the other to reach under his own weight and her skirt to pull off her panties until finally, unable to restrain herself and catching her breath, Katherine started to laugh and pushed him onto the floor. Up came his two arms and he pulled her down to the floor with him, her still laughing but his own face grim and solemn, laid her down on the floor beside him and undid her skirt, started to pull it off and she could remember lying on her back, not even thinking about what he might be doing and then felt him tugging again at her skirt, as if this one remark of hers was supposed to have given him ownership, kicked up and pushed at his chest with her feet but he just swept them aside and began tugging again, not knowing how to unfasten it properly and afraid to tear it, kicked him again so he rolled on top of her, stalemated. Then again, the whole time they hadn't spoken, reached under her skirt to work on her panties, this time figured out to push up his own weight on his elbow so he could have room to work, got them down, then still supporting himself on one elbow, his face red with effort and refusing to look at her, he undid his own pants and pushed them down so that finally he had all the right pieces pressed against each other and could take a rest. Nothing happened.

"Now what?" Richard Thomas said.

"You're too heavy. Use your elbows, you idiot."

He rolled off her and stood up. Turning his back to her in the half-light, he did up his pants and tucked in his shirt. Standing at the window, smoking one of her cigarettes, his features shadowed by the dusk, he might have been a modern Casanova, posing for an advertisement between conquests. She smoothed her skirt out and kicked her panties under the couch, an old horsehair monstrosity covered in scarlet brocade that Henry Beckwith and his wife had bought themselves for their twentieth wedding anniversary from a catalogue. Then she got up and went to stand beside Richard at the window. They went outside to the porch that Henry Beckwith had built, the porch that surrounded the house on three sides, and sat on the steps. "I'm sorry," she said.

"It doesn't matter."

She reached over to him and undid the top button of his pants. "You take everything so seriously," she said. "A gentleman never takes anything seriously."

"I thought, you know, that all you had to do was get things started."

They got up again and walked down to the road, and then back up to the house again, up and down the long driveway that Henry Beckwith had so admired about the house originally, a log house when he came there that stood at the top of the hill and looked down on the road as if this was possibly a real house overlooking a boulevard teeming with carriages and parasols, the Champs Élysées of Eastern Ontario that required only the density of time to manicure all the details and bring it to life so that one morning finally, in six months or a thousand years, Henry Beckwith would step out of his house wearing his red satin smoking jacket and carrying one of the special leatherbound books that Simon Thomas had made him and go sit beneath the willow tree on a stone bench and watch the young people, former pupils become Prime Ministers and explorers, school girls out for a ride between lessons, men of his own age already dressed for the day and tapping their way along with silver-tipped canes, silver on stone. The moon was almost full and she could see him well, re-seeing him because where once he had seemed helpless there was now the question of restraint. Now in the driveway she could believe her own ghost stories. And half-see her mother bending over the well, the pump handle worn and split, held together with baling wire, hear their voices which came to her now not in words but disguised in smells; each tree and bush and flower seemed to have its own distinct odour, sweeping across her in sequence, each one total and distinct, each entirely erasing the last and urging her to bond herself to this man as she was to this place so that every moment would be veiled by the other's presence. The skin on his back was smooth, smooth like Simon's but deeper and newer, and the muscles too were different than Simon's, fluid and alive where his were pocked and knotted, permanently strained. His back and his eyes were all she could remember from that first time: his eyes because she noticed that their colour was still steady and deep, not yet burned out and lightened from the sun, like those of the older men, like his own later became, changing from blue with green flecks at the edges to a grey-green that at times could be shallow as cats' eyes.

The sun is hotter, higher now and spring is here, not just signalled. Katherine crouching by the side of the road, leaning forward to see into the stream that now runs full tilt in the ditch, snow still along the shaded bank but the water is cutting it away from underneath so that now it is beginning to fall into the stream, drowning of its own weight and the water still so cold it doesn't melt instantly but is carried down the stream a few feet where each small snow boat then smashes apart on a curve. Kneels by the side of the stream and lumps up small balls of snow and tosses them in to watch them be swept to the curve, wondering if she can make a snow-jam there, then leaning at different angles to see if the sun can illuminate more of the bottom of this stream which is shaped not only by the ditch but by all the branches and rocks which have been pushed or have fallen into it. Simon thin and white. Simon white and dead. Simon one winter night coming to the house. Stream cold and silver she cups her hands and puts them into the water, leaves them watching the water turn her skin transparent, webbed bones draw the water to her mouth. Simon white and dead, on his knees, half-mocking; his hands surround hers like a large dry bird with a ring in its craw. The same ring, he says, that the poet took back from the body of Elizabeth Thomas. Simon white and dead kneels and asks her to marry him and when she won't answer tries to cry but can't. Warm winter night then and it had begun to snow, would snow for one day and two nights in the exact same large sloppy flakes falling slowly to the ground, gradually piling up and drifting slowly in the slow warm wind. On the first night Simon came and asked her. Finally they went into the living-room and she gave him what was possible. He left the ring on the table. Not a wedding ring at all but a strange gold ring that had a small green stone set into its crown, a ring that must have belonged to some forgotten secret society, the inside worn smooth and silvery but the outside finework tiny miniatures of tangled snakes and tongues on either side of the stone, still pure in colour with very thin green lines in the crevices where Simon's hand had not been steady enough to follow with the needle. The next day too it snowed, so slow and each flake so large and far apart that it seemed the ground and sky were in some conspiracy of grey light, and that evening Richard came to see her, saying his mother was sick again. Sees the ring on the table and picks it up, barely able to even slip it over the first knuckle of his little finger where it sticks briefly, looking as if it belonged there.

Kneeling by the stream, splashes water on her face, cold water in the pockets of her eyes, on her forehead, cold fingers pushing channels through her hair, takes off her coat and splashes the water on her neck and shoulders, everywhere the water touches is stunned by the cold, falling through lake ice once they took her home and she was actually blue, her skin taut and rough turned blue-purple with cold. Simon thin and white. Simon lived and died. Simon lived on four hours sleep all the first winter her parents were dead, coming to her house late at night or just after dawn, stomping through it like a skinny bull outraged at death and ghosts, covering the floors with snow and mud, sawing wood for her and leaving it stacked outside the door, the big elm logs on top with the sharpened axe for her to split them with, starting fights and then when he had sucked her in and got her angry at him laughing at her anger, gleefully jumping up and down and pushing her about the kitchen forcing her to admit she was alive, bringing her kittens and puppies to be saved, a cow that was in calf, chickens that demanded more work than the eggs were worth and then so pleased with his plan to save her life that in the spring he brought her a goat and left it downstairs early one morning before the sun came up and she woke up to the sound of the goat going crazy in the kitchen, trotting back and forth chopping at the floor with its sharp hooves, knocking down the butter and the lard, leaving plates shattered on the kitchen floor, so much noise she thought it must be Simon drunk and then after calling and getting no answer for once really believed in her dumb ghosts and finally working up her courage and going downstairs to see this monster, boarded in from the living-room so that it was only the kitchen floor, the hardwood maple floor that was covered in broken dishes, grease and goatshit.

Searching in her coat again for a cigarette and this time finds a better one, her hands dry now and clean, puckered white at the fingertips, along the edges of the tiny blisters she always got on her fingers when she was nervous; Richard's blisters this time, his touch at the funeral. She finds the box of matches and fumbles with it momentarily, decides to open it upside down

Canada's longest covered
bridge is in New Brunswick

reads the motto, the blue ink threatening to run on the cardboard. Three matches before one lights. Leaves them on the road, letting them roll into the mud, too removed from the stream now to bother floating them. He could have taken her there, to New Brunswick. She knew nothing about it: forest and railway tracks. But she could remember Ottawa, where the match company was, the match company that ate the logs they floated down the river every spring and at night sent its sulphur fumes rolling across the river, so sharp it made you gasp and when you did you could feel the acid scissor into the lungs. Mustard gas, Henry Beckwith used to say. Seven brothers dead of it in the war. Simon would come up to visit him and they would sit on the porch steps telling each other their favourite lies. Wine and tobacco. Exhales the smoke, blue-grey and in the perfect circle learned from Henry Beckwith's pipe, her coat wrapped around her now, cold from the water and the snow, walking faster, arms swinging in time to the sucking sounds of the boots in the mud, looks up the road to see Richard Thomas standing there, in the middle of the road with his hands in his pockets and his wide floppy pants too long for his legs and rooted straight to the ground, his hands in his pockets and a blue and red checked flannel shirt twice as wide as his father, now begins walking towards her too, begins in a way that makes her think he has been standing there half the afternoon, watching her skip and stumble all over the road. Looks down and sees her skirt still standing out in little spiked twists, mud all over her boots and coat, her arms raw and too long, swinging out of the frayed cuffs, stops.

"I didn't think you'd come," Richard Thomas said. His voice is thin and formal. They are standing face to face, stopped six feet apart on the road. Simon white and dead. Lived his exact seventy-year span. He is wearing the black felt hat she gave him ten years ago. Now it is crumpled and water stained. His face is thicker and redder than it was. Flesh has begun to gather along the lines of his jaws. He had shaved for the funeral and there are still tiny cuts on his throat. This isn't how it was supposed to be. She smiles and starts again. Curtsies to show off her muddy skirt and boots. As she flexes her knees and bows, her mittens, soaked and crumpled into wads, fall out of her coat pocket into the mud.

"We could go to the old barn," Katherine said. "I'd like to sit down." So they walk down the road without touching to a place where there is an old gate and a cowpath to the barn where they used to meet in the late summer and fall. Now that she is with him she wishes she'd not noticed the way he'd touched her at the funeral. She sees as she walks that he has come to her this way, by way of the barn, walking fast, bootheels sinking deep into the mud. The land here is higher, there is hardly any snow and on the tops of the knolls there are places where the grass is a different, lighter green, small shoots that are too soon and will be frozen. The barn is warm and seems moist with hay. She pushes her way through the loose bales to a place where the sun comes in, a long wide stripe where there was supposed to be a board. Then crawls to the gap and looks out at the trees that surround the barn, crowding in towards it, beginning to cover a field that was cleared but then abandoned because the soil was too thin and dry, frosting easy in the spring and fall and burning in the summer. Even ten years ago it had been pasture. She would meet Richard there and the cows would be grazing outside, moving slow and indifferent to the frantic humans in the barn. Her hand touched a bottle and she looked up, surprised, seeing the row of bottles there that she and Richard had drunk, all shapes and sizes, the insides filmed with dirt, all the tops still on. And Richard, touching her arm, offering her another of these unmarked bottles that the old Frank farm seemed to collect so old man Frank could fill them with half-distilled liquor made from anything that once grew:

"It's one of his better," Richard said.

"I can't go home drunk."

"Old Peter Malone wouldn't notice if a horse ran over him."

"If you wanted to have your say," Katherine said. She took the bottle without looking at him, had forgotten what it was like to run into this Thomas meanness unaware, sudden and unpleasant like, she realized, this terrible wine which was so bad that she spit it out without swallowing, coughing and handing the bottle back to Richard.

"I'm sorry," Richard said. "I think it froze and then started to ferment again." They were sitting side by side, facing each other, their legs stretched out flat on the hay. Richard reached down and put his hand on her knee. Something, the way he did it, made her feel like a huge slab of meat. He took his hand away. Her feet felt cold and numb now. She took them out of her boots and rubbed them with her hands, hardly conscious of Richard's presence, wondering why she could have been so foolish as to walk like this, thirty-nine years old; she didn't even want him to see her now, veins blue in her belly and thighs, rolls of fat, started to cry and the tears made her face and the inside of her head feel warm, kept crying for the warmth not knowing if she was upset or just cold, not caring, letting her body cry too, warming her, knowing he would use her crying as a way to get by her, not caring that he would or that it was the wrong time of the month and she would have to go home and do it with Peter Malone, one two three, just the way Simon Thomas told her to once, making his calculations, ordering her body in his universe, Simon Thomas thin and white, making her so angry she swung and almost took his head off with the axe, Simon Thomas, came to her the second night with the snow still falling wet and slow, came to her again as she knew he would, Richard in the bedroom and the ring sitting on the kitchen table, in the middle of the table beside a cutglass ashtray, just inside the circle of lamplight so that he could see it as he pleased, on his knees again with his large palms on her knees, began to speak to her in a low liquid voice, could this be love? Clasped his hands and bowed his head, saying that he would not offer up a prayer to the good Lord that He would see fit to help him in this evening, to help this woman to know that it was His wish that she replace Leah Thomas when He called her, yes, to end this suffered Life on Earth. And then looking mournfully at her and at the ring on the table Simon stood and walked to the wicker chair where he sat down, always the signal that he wanted some tea, took out his knife, the point long and curved just slightly, Damascus steel, cleaned his nails.

"Some stranger leaving footprints in your drive," Simon said. When he spoke Katherine could see the broken rows of his teeth, the way they had worn for some reason, short and thick with a brown line along the tops and bottoms, teeth short and thick like ancient ruined castles. And his nose now, the bone worn clean, still straight and thin on top but the nostrils puffy and broken-veined with age, moving in and out with his moods like bellows, a family habit he said, descended from a count who droned in his port. "It's a strange time for a person to be roaming about," Simon said. "You could never hear him in this snow, he would sneak up to the house and be inside before you knew a thing." The knife moving in his hand, and eyebrows jiggling as he talked, lines cut into his forehead from all those decades of sleight-of-face and lies.

Katherine moving neutral in the kitchen, building up the fire and preparing the teapot. And Simon, sitting in the wicker chair near the stove, the bits of fire flashing through the grate, the light working up and down his body, slow fire on a windless night, elm fibres hissing out their moisture, crackling in their own heat. "I'm cold, Simon," Katherine said and, before he could use it as an excuse was on her way up the stairs, beginning to panic, imagining that Richard would jump out at her and force her into screaming but then she was in the bedroom and he was curled under the covers like a baby, scared to death of his own old father, so she came to him and sat beside him, her hand on his forehead like he was sick and took a sweater from the floor. And down quickly again to Simon, afraid suddenly he would be the one to force it, to come up and find Richard like this, afraid. And when she was downstairs again and poured the tea for Simon and gave him cream and sugar to go with the tea and a spoon to stir it with, Simon put the cup on the table and picked up the ring, balancing it in his palm, and asked her if she would come to live with him when Leah Thomas died. And when she said no he asked her again, talking in a voice that was very unusual for him, low and humble, and insinuating voice that had the gall to say she could believe the lie because she was a woman and had no choice. And when she said no a second time he got up and lifted the kettle from the stove so the fire leaped up, the flames on his red face and white hair making him look like an ageless skinny devil, and with his free hand tossed the ring into the fire. Then sat down again and began to drink his tea, moving the cup up and down quick and nervous, drinking it so hot he had to blow away the steam before each sip. And then two rapid steps to where she was sitting and pulled her, lifting her by the waist and sitting her down again, on his lap in the wicker chair, his arms wrapped round her like steel cords, cutting off her breath and squeezing her ribs. And when he finally left and she went upstairs Richard was still in bed, undressed, waiting. She had the lantern with her and set it down near the door, sits down beside him but he has retreated, wraps the quilt around him and sits up in bed to smoke, his mouth pouting, his body closed in on itself. Younger then, hair long and thick she liked to bend her head, break up the light in the veiled fall of her hair, leaning over Richard and hugging him, forcing him to open so she can lie on him and feel him against her, a bath to wash away Simon Thomas, his bony ancient body with its pockets of stain and decay, parchment skin like dry paper, Simon Thomas thin and white, forcing him to open so she can lie on him and feel him against her, a bath to wash away the winter, Peter Malone one two three, could this be love?

Opens her eyes and sees that she has covered Richard's face with tears, licks them off, her eyes still crying and her nose running but she can feel herself unclenched and licks his eyelids, the corners of his eyes, lets the point of her tongue trail salt along his eyebrows, along his new hairline, further back than she has seen it and thinner, along the red mark left by the hatband, testing out to see if he has washed his ears and then sliding her hands up into his shirt, one step forward and two steps back, Henry Beckwith and his pipedreams left his own and only daughter to his best friend, God rest his soul, God rest their souls, Richard's beard in her neck, his chin rasps, flipping her up and over so he is on top, bits of straw forced through her skirt and coat, sewing skin to bone, hard and bumpy not like Peter Malone, Peter pillowman, propping her up so he can fall in effortlessly, still. Ten years of Peter Malone and his impossible litters. Waking up some mornings with Richard's image fixed before her eyes, stuck to the day like a transparency, twisting everything into the ten-year gap. One two three, now the back of his neck is barbered too and bristly, shaved fresh for the funeral, unbuttons her blouse and pushes it back, exposing a line from neck to shoulder, runs his teeth along the flesh, flesh to bone, do corpses fuck? she wonders as he pushes himself inside her, and she, afraid at first but then curious again, to know what it might feel like to be filled this way helps him, her arms around his back, pulling him towards her, her fingers hooked in his belt-loops, one for the dead. And loosened later by the wine, two for the living.

His back propped against the bales and his hand on her knee. The bottle is only half-empty but she is asleep and he puts the cap back on the bottle and sticks it up on the beam with the others, this one new style, dark green translucent, and he can put his eye to the bottle and see the sun dead level through it, the trees still naked in the spring. Stands up slowly, careful not to disturb Katherine and pulls his pants up to his knees, bends over to pick the straw away from his underclothes and skin, so many million sperm to be discharged in secret from Miranda, whole populations and races passed through in an afternoon, leaving no trace but a few bits of dead grass stuck to him and to each other. His pants on, he lowers himself down the ladder of the barn, his muscles pulled out of shape and exhausted, wondering why a strange body takes such a greater toll than the familiar, wondering why he didn't marry Katherine and move to the Beckwith place where the fields were flat and deep-soiled and ran in long well-drained slopes towards the road. Three silos, Peter Malone had; three silos and three bank accounts. Standing outside he can see where the ice and wind have worked away the sheathing at one corner leaving the post exposed, now dark brown with water soaked into it. The air is still warm, even warmer than it was in the afternoon when the sun was higher, a slow breeze moving across the hollows from the west. Near the barn is a small pond, and he goes and sits beside it, letting the sun tip and reflect into his face. No splashes or fish in this pond though later, briefly, there will be frogs and bullrushes before it dries up for the summer and grows its useless marsh grass. Moored to a tree at its edge is an old rowboat, its bottom resting on the bottom of the pond, waterlogged twenty years almost exactly, twenty years since he and his brother built it from scrap lumber for the barn and stuck it in the water where it sank immediately. They tied it with a rope to the tree, Richard explaining that the wood needed water to swell it and press it together. When the rope rotted, Richard had thrown a chain around the boat, securing it more permanently to the tree so it could not, should it finally achieve its watertight destiny, drift away and become hopelessly lost on this quarter-acre pond that was up to three feet deep in its centre channels. Katherine Malone, née Katherine Beckwith, bearing children easily, all shapes and sizes, while he and Miranda were still waiting for their first. Peter Malone who always bragged he couldn't get it up but rushed home whenever someone told him that Simon's black Ford was parked in front of the old Beckwith place. Half the time to find Simon just sitting in the car, smoking his pipe and reading a book. "A man gets moved from his own ancestral home," Simon liked to say, "and he needs to be able to go out and visit." For his house in the town Simon did what was necessary: in the winter he would shovel out the drive every day, snow or not, and stack his bought wood neatly in the front yard.

And in the summer, every Tuesday and Friday evening, he would mow his lawn, wearing a special peaked cap he had purchased for these occasions and taking exactly the length of a cigar to do it.

Richard stretched, looked back in the barn to see if Katherine was stirring, walked a bit on the path near the barn. He felt drowsy and lethargic, wished it were possible to sleep before walking Katherine home and then going home himself. Ten miles: Miranda would be wondering where he was. The path wound between hickory and aspen, young maples seeded from the sugar bush and a few pine trees that still stood. Eventually it widened from a cowtrack to two wagon wheelruts—now gouged so deep that they were useless for everything except frogs, who bred in them every spring, leaving their eggs in tangled silver strands. Then the ruts turned into an old dirt road that led to the big field he had cleared and the valley that cut right through it. The first summer he started seeing her he liked to walk to her place the long way, this way, preferring the anticipation to the event. But after that, in the winter, he always went as quickly as possible, going right to the old road, keeping a path between the two farms.

Richard saw Katherine standing by the barn, watching him as he moved indecisively up and down the path, inspecting to see if summer was really about to happen, poking aside bushes with a long stick he had picked up, then, in between, using it as a cane, the black felt hat pushed back on his head. Walked down towards her, seeing the barn and imagining near it, up on the knoll that overlooked the spring pond, a house that was made out of field-stone but resembled an English cottage with its elaborate patios and leaded windows. And although the house wasn't there, his grandfather, Richard S. Thomas, as part of some elaborate forgotten scheme, had made sketches of the hybrid, planned the garden and the apple trees which would have honeysuckle and bitter-sweet wrapped round them—had even planted those trees, on the knoll and near the barn, and dug a foundation and well for the house, both lined with stone, so now it looked as if it had all existed and burned away, the foundation overgrown and falling in from the top rows and the trees already long past their prime, twisted together with other, younger generations of apple trees or even attempting spectacular miscegenations with cedar and spruce. Katherine coming up to meet him, barefoot and her skirt covered with mud and hay: so much less ordered than Miranda, good-natured body that let itself be pulled out of shape by circumstance. And stands facing her, she is almost as tall as he is, her hand inside his arm, carrying herself unprotected from things, the opposite of Miranda who will go into the garden when it is warmer with her bright kerchief wrapped around her hair and her tennis shoes, lotion on to keep away the bugs and cotton gloves to save her hands from blisters—Miranda knowing which side is which and gradually taking the city to the country with lilac bushes in the front yard and sneaking flowers in among the vegetables.

She can see the sun, deep yellow and changing colour through the bare branches of the trees as they walk back to the road, keeping touch with his body, her hand on his back as they walk, or hooked into his pants, or wrapped round the inside of his arm, fingers feeling the play of ligament and muscle. Richard walking with his hands in his pockets so she slides her hand down on his arm, into his pocket, palm against palm, remembering measuring palms that first summer, her own only slightly narrower than his and her fingers longer and thinner, folding over the tops of his nails like a roof sliding over a wall. Richard talking to her about Miranda, already patching things up, everything to return to normal, certainly, they will meet at the church and smile distantly, Richard stepping outside after with the men, what do they ever do, go to the back of the church all of them and drink and piss against the wall, dance at the summer social, one two three, maybe she will be pregnant, and Peter Malone so sure of the accuracy of his failed weapon she could call the child Richard and no one would more than suspect, Richard so solemn beside her, doing his duty seeing her home, God, all those years and he never moved at all, never. Richard saying that they are thinking of adopting a child and went to see some social workers in Kingston, in confidence of course, you understand, never moved, because she must have been a whore to give herself to Simon, not like Miranda, always on her toes, who would never do a thing like that, oh no, too proper, in Toronto they never fuck on Sundays, no sloppity sounds or other vulgarities from the ladies, oh no, one two three bang, tea service is what you get, yes. "And biscuits too," her cousin would say, her lace shawl drawn over her bare shoulders: taking lovers when her husband was on his rotation but not, you understand, being foolish, but only taking them in the Spanish style–breeding idiot kings strained through silk panties–"you have to get your blood up; Katherine look at you. And besides its good for the liver you know." Richard had stopped talking and was quickening the pace, keeping his eye on the horizon, could this be love? she sang, startling Richard who drew away from her, but she chased after him, pushing him to the side of the road, hugging him and kicking at his shins with her rubber boots, fat already, he hadn't even seen her belly, still doing it in secret. "Look," she said, stopping and holding open her coat, pulling up her blouse so he could see the scar from the caesarian. Richard bending over, twilight already, the sky winding pink and blue behind them on the road, her scar blue too, and puckered up: small gaps where the flesh had healed right across and at the top, still, needle holes that refused to go away. Took his hand and pressed it into her stomach, so deep now it looked like he could be kneading it. "God," she said, "I am getting fat." And hungry too. Knowing Peter would have decided it was his duty to cook supper and prepared his specialty, pork chops and boiled potatoes, the pork chops fried in lard and covered with dollops of brown sugar and applesauce. And Richard, the pig, saying nothing at all in consolation, probably thinking of Miranda, always turned her nose up at the little cakes. The gentleman and his lady will be out this evening. Turned and curtsied to Richard who was still waiting for her to put away her stomach and continue walking, please excuse. Again walking in silence, quicker in the cold, until they came to the place where they had met that afternoon, stopped. In the dark Richard was close again; she could feel his hand exploring her back and neck–they were both looking forward down the road, side by side, as if this inconvenience was only to be temporary.

"It was nice to see you again," Richard said.

"Yes."

"The wine wasn't that bad."

"It was passable," Katherine said, waiting for him to stiffen. "Well."

"Maybe you'd better go back," she said. "It's getting dark."

"You won't get lost."

"No," Katherine said. "I think I know the way." Taking his hand from her back, kissing it, a little bite, then turning him around and moving on her way, why not, quickly, another springtime afternoon, around the first curve and feeling lighter already, not tired at all, it would be good to run, springtime Simon dead and white, Peter Malone.

Richard swinging his legs

Swinging down to the floor

Waiting for the skin on wool: friction skin grip stands and stretches on the braided rug. Hearing her tell about Simon Thomas's proposal. And asking him to say nothing. As if this night is only a minor misunderstanding, traffic confusion, something that will be forgotten. Outside the snow is still falling slow and warm. A full moon, diffuse, casts an indefinite grey light and now there are three paths, each pressing down the other, one of his and two of Simon Thomas. Five miles and he knows that Simon will be sitting up and waiting for him, sitting in the identical wicker chair in his own kitchen, (he and Henry Beckwith bought them together in Kingston, spent half their winters together, those two and old Mark Frank, drinking and planning their nonsense trips), rocking back and forth, drinking tea and playing with his knife, waiting. Standing with Simon in the barn and Simon telling him that there are, in each man's life, only a few crucial moments and that these must be recognized, that a man who fails to rise to them will never forgive himself and will be marked, fork thrust forward sheepshit flying off the cold tines, ricocheting and falling out the special wooden manure hatch. Following the path, down the centre of the road and then through the bush, black, branches layered with wet snow swaying sluggishly when hit, dumping their loads behind him. So warm it threatens to rain; Richard took off his toque and stuffed it in his pocket, letting the branches comb across his wet hair and his ears, still feeling wooldamp and hot. The path came out of the bush and into the valley that led down the centre of the fields, interrupted by a marshy spot where they skated earlier in the winter, snowed over now and going to be ruined by the wet snow which would freeze in a thick crust over the rink, too much work to clear. Here Simon had stopped too, most way home, and tromped about the rink, stamping down the snow, maybe considered waiting here or even going back, no, Simon would fight on his own grounds. Coming to the house finally and seeing that the lights were on, upstairs and down, two o'clock in the morning. Richard had a sudden premonition that all this time he had been mistaken, that his mother had been dying and that Simon had come over to get him, fornicating with the Beckwith girl while his own mother died. And Katherine had said nothing, even told Simon to go away, that greedy for him. Then came upstairs with her story, why not. Remembered how his mother had resented Katherine Beckwith's presence in the house, said it was unnecessary and that while everyone else was out the girl tormented her, refused to bring her anything in bed and got in her way when she tried to go to the kitchen herself. Stopping in the barnyard, looking at the path carefully to see if Simon had branched off, was hiding in one of the buildings. Then followed the path the rest of the way, to the house, unsure of what Simon was going to force him to, not wanting to have to do it, so tired now, his body hollow and exhausted. His brother's huge shadow against the upstairs window, his mother's window, any bigger and they could send him to a circus Simon would say, puzzled at the size of this prodigal offspring who threatened to outweigh both his parents at once. And as he swung open the door and began to kick the snow off his heels he could see through the kitchen window, made wavy by condensation, Simon rocking in his wicker chair, back and forth, his head turning round to meet the noise, waiting. Richard pushed off his boots and came into the house, stripping off his coat, soaked with melted snow, and his sweater, plunging the dipper into the bucket of cold well water that stood by the kitchen sink, feeling the flares shooting off in his stomach, barely interrupted by the water, keeping his eyes on Simon who now had piled up on his lap the framed photographs of his parents, Richard's grandparents, the poet William C. Thomas, other assorted relatives, and was going through them ostentatiously, as if to say to Richard that this was the absolute all-time greatest betrayal of history, a case of Brutus stabbing his own father in the lowest possible place, seducing his own father's bride-to-be while his mother, fatally weakened bearing this ungrateful son, died of neglect.

"Your mother is asleep," Simon said. "And your brother Steven is upstairs with her, doing his duty." On the stove, still hot, was a thick soup left over from supper. Richard ladled some into a bowl for himself, sat down at the table to eat. Simon pulled his chair forward so he was sitting opposite Richard, spread the pictures on the table in front of him. Included was a picture of Simon and Leah Thomas, taken at their wedding: Simon in a striped suit and a high starched collar that pushed up his chin, standing straight and thin, a cane hooked over one arm and Leah's gloved hand resting on the other. Beside him she looked short and squat, durable. She wasn't smiling at all but held on to her bouquet grimly, as if afraid that the camera might release invisible dangerous rays. "So," Simon said, "I hope you had an enjoyable evening." He had picked up a piece of kindling and was carving it, as was his habit, not making anything but just reducing it to a pile of shavings, the knife sharp and quick in his hands. Richard got up and sliced himself a piece of bread, buttered it and brought it back to the table, dipping it into the remainder of his soup as he ate it.

"I thought I should tell you," Simon said, "that tonight I asked Katherine to move in here again, to help take care of your mother." He licked his lips and put down the piece of wood and his knife, took a cigar out of his shirt pocket, wet it, cut off the tip, put it in his mouth and lit it. When it was going he picked up the knife again, flipped it from hand to hand. "She said she would come, Richard, but she asked me to make you promise that you would leave her alone."

"Fuck you," Richard shouted. Then nonsensically turned back to his soup. Simon's hands, back and forth; Richard saw the flash of metal, could hear it moving by his head, whistling like a slow train, jerked spastically, upsetting the soup and then breaking the bowl as his hand came down, turning and drawing the knife from the wall with one hand, the other sweeping the table clean, claiming one half of the bowl, springing forward, the table pressed against his thighs and then yielding, into Simon Thomas, Simon Thomas going down, one leg taking the full weight of the thick elm table and Richard Thomas, the sound of bone snapped; and Richard moving in with the knife in one hand and in the other, swinging forward and above his father's head a broken cup, down into Simon's face and now the knife follows, arcing down to where Simon's hands already cover his face. A sudden noose on his wrist and Richard's shoulder feels like it is being torn from its socket, his knife arm thrown high in the air and then his body finally follows, slumped into the wall and slides to the floor. Richard sees Steven looking back and forth, Richard to Simon. Steven lifts up the table like a feather in his giant hand, lifts up Simon too and sets him in the chair. Steven looking back and forth. Face large and bulging. Shrugs. The knife in his hand and he gives it to Simon. Simon's face beet red, a small jagged cut on his head already white and thin, his scalp showing red through his hair, the blood falling from his cut in long slow drops, breathing hard, flipping the knife in his nervous hands, back and forth, looking at Richard who moves his arm and feels it with his good hand, nothing torn or broken. Back and forth, they are all looking back and forth and waiting, watching the knife's reflection flash in Simon's nervous fingers, flashing back and forth like a magician's coin, Leah Thomas's voice has been shouting from upstairs and now they hear it coming closer and she is in the doorway, standing with her arms folded across her chest and her hair sprung out at the sides, black and wiry still, her hands buried under her arms so she is standing unaided, barefoot and flushed in this winter kitchen. "Simon Thomas," she says, "Simon Thomas you old fool. Get upstairs, and wash your face." And Simon doesn't answer or indicate even that he has seen her. The knife moves in his fingers and then is gone again, the point buried in the wall, right beside Richard's head. "Simon Thomas," she says again, "Simon Thomas you're just a jealous old man." And she looks at Richard's brother, Steven, the second son. And he takes the knife from the wall and hands it again to his father.

"You do as mother says."

"Get out of the way," Simon Thomas said. Then the knife flashes one more time, sinking into the wood in the exact same place, just above Richard's ear and he can feel his skin tingling so it is impossible for him to know at first if he has been startled or cut. Steven takes the knife again. This time he slides it in his belt, making the knife look like a child's toy next to his massive body, some kind of freak Simon Thomas always said, descended from his wife's family, but with his disjointed walk and gentle manner resembling no one at all but Frederick Thomas, the poet's son.

He stood in the middle of the room, circling this centre uncertainly, the knife in his belt, waiting for instructions from Leah Thomas. "It's time to go to sleep," he finally said.

"Simon first," Leah Thomas ordered, pointing up the stairs. Simon sat still, waiting. "Take him," Leah Thomas said. Looked from Leah to Simon, back to Leah again. Standing in the doorway with her arms folded over her chest, wearing her stained and faded pink housecoat, a wedding present, barefoot and coughing lightly every few seconds, her hand moving by reflex to her mouth, always anticipating the cough by a slight movement of the shoulders, a last-second concession that never worked, stepped back from the doorway and nodded her head to her son. Who lifted the table away from Simon, placed it at the side of the room, and then stepped towards him, to pick him up, stopped, looked at his mother again, then bent over to lift him, chair and all. Simon out of the chair and his hand snapped like a snake, the knife red in the kerosene light, pirouettes noiselessly in the cloth of his son's shirt.

"That's all," Simon said. His voice is dry and rasping again, the knife wiped clean on his pants and returned to its handsewn calfskin sheath. And he is hopping about on his good leg with one hand on the counter, lithe and almost dancing. Leah Thomas coughs deeper, puts her hand to her head, begins to slide down the door jamb, one hand extended towards Richard so that he will not forget to catch her.

In bed again she can't stop coughing. Blood at the corner of her mouth, light pink flecks coughed up from her lungs. Simon sits in his chair in the corner of the room. Richard standing by the door, his shoulder still sore and strained again from the effort of carrying Leah Thomas upstairs. His brother kneeling by the bed, one hand on his chest, it too stained with blood, this blood dark and thick, seeping out the shirt, the exact triangular hole carved by Simon Thomas. And when Richard goes outside to hitch up the horses and get the doctor, he can see the snow is still falling, soft and large, binding earth to sky with slow wet chains.

Returning with the doctor in the early winter morning and finding Simon and Steven upstairs, in the bedroom of Leah

Thomas. Steven still holding his hand to his side, shirt and pants soaked in blood, the doctor prying his hand away and seeing the excised section of cloth and flesh, cut right through to the bone. Simon Thomas now unable to walk, his broken leg swollen to three times its size. Leah Thomas propped up in the bed just as Richard left her: died from natural causes, the doctor wrote down.

EIGHT

The bedspread beneath his palms; all those threads, twisted cotton fibres loomed and interwoven, pulled tight, kept in shape by
habit, discipline, should have a school for bedspreads. Using the
tips of his fingers as pivots, Richard can lift his hands enough to
break the suction between sweat and thread and flesh, let the air
move in along the cross-hatched pores. One hand hurts. The back
feels swollen and sore. The other is enclosed from the top, extended indefinitely, something moving on it. Richard turns his
head and opens his eyes slowly, realizes he has been sleeping for
a long time, the fever is gone now, sees Erik's hand on top of his,
moving in slow circles, vulture, opens his eyes wider and sees Erik
looking back, doesn't move his hand, circles. Turns his head the
other way and tries to lift his left arm. Now it does respond; but
the back of his hand is swollen and sore, looks, sees a plastic tube
coming out of it, sight and pain, leans back and twists up–a bottle
suspended above the bed, dripping into him. Erik smiles. Richard
looks past him and sees the oxygen tank is beside the bed, beside
the window. A nurse sitting at the end of the bed, smiles in turn
as she sees him looking at her. He realizes they are happy. No.
He realizes this is more than they expected. Closes his eyes.
Richard can hear a clock ticking somewhere in the room. Then he
thinks that he might only be imagining this. He listens closely
and it is still there. The more he concentrates, the louder it gets,
each tick with its own half-stated ring, as if it were something
that time could be created by a spring, measured out, paced, like
his heart, compulsory time that he must live through, no, this

wasn't supposed to happen. It could be worse, he thinks, already hating himself for this further betrayal of mind: would it be necessary for them to have him entirely connected to machines, great coiled protuberances growing out of his body and ears before they would finally give up on him and pull out the plug? A man gets sick and gets better. You have to share your body. Spades digging into the flesh, taking it out for raw material, recycled protoplasm to be used in further incarnations. Opens his eyes again. Miranda is standing in the doorway, now coming towards the bed, smiling too, they are all smiling, all having the time of their lives.

Later in the day he is sitting up, feeling better. His left arm is beginning to work again and they took the tube out so now there is only a bandage on his hand. He can use it too; holds his coffee cup with his right hand and uses the left to spoon it out, practising, coffee and chocolate custard. Bruises, blue tinged with yellow, spread out from beneath the bandage, and the small bones of his hand feel violated, as if it were them that had been punctured, marrow injected into the failing passages that keep hollow bones alive. They are all there, watching him, Brian and Nancy on the empty bed and Erik and Miranda in chairs: prize exhibit, number one father rises again; the matador however has not been gored, only stepped to the side for a drink of red wine, wipes his sword clean, describes the coming kill in rhyming couplets to the ladies in the box: parts of the body are assigned as trophies. His arm, moving again, the first time since the walk, feels like it has been asleep. All the somnolent nerves tingle now, go off in tiny clustered explosions just beneath his skin, up and down his arm, never where he expects it, sometimes echoes in other areas of his body, so as he eats he feels continually jerked about, these electric currents re-establishing their equilibrium, not caring who they inhabit. Miranda pulls her chair up closer, waiting to be noticed. But only the food interests him. She sees that he is still hungry and goes out into the hall and gets some more dessert and orange juice from the cart. She sets them in front of him and he begins to eat them too, having sudden fantasies of how he will eat until he is better and then go home, a changed man, ruling the house as Simon did, voracious and demanding, having afternoon banquets out on the lawn and then huge midnight snacks, eating endlessly, eating the entire produce of the farm, annexed farms, insatiable as a palm-wine drunkard eating a cow a day, whole gardens served heaped up on wooden plates made by cross-sectioning the largest trees, feasts of mushrooms gathered from the paths near the lakes, all washed down by bottle after bottle of Pat Frank's worst home-made wine, wine brewed after the exact recipe of his father and his father's father, both of whom died from it, wine made from every fruit and berry that grew in the area, strengthened by distilled alcohol and all the garbage that was carelessly allowed to fall in, wine to be served not in goblets but in its original bottles, only to be drunk two-thirds empty because of the sediment that could poison you even more quickly, wine to wash down the beef and the fowl and the omelettes which Miranda could cook so well, and as he sat and he ate he would toss the salads with his hands and throw the leftovers to the dogs who surrounded him, waiting all their lives to go hunting but now grown so fat from leftovers they could hardly move, staggering once a day to the other side of the driveway to relieve themselves and then back to surround their master, swishing off flies with their tails and looking up at the table with great brown gorged eyes. There was a tray swung over the bed and he had stopped eating, resting his hand on the tray, then picked up the spoon again. Miranda is still watching him and Richard is perplexed, wondering what he will say to her, how long it has been since he has said anything at all. The tan has faded from his hands and arms, the hair getting darker while the skin returns to its normal colour, but Miranda looks healthy and brown, her eyes bright and concerned. Now he remembers: before supper they were talking about the farm, getting the cows bred in the fall. He looks at the tray and sees the remains: a squeezed lemon with shredded pale fibres still hanging from the skin; bits of bone and fried crumbs from the fish; carrot cubes mixed with some sort of sauce; a small corner of instant mashed potatoes.

"You must have been hungry," Miranda said. Her voice seemed dry and removed. "Do you want anything else?"

Richard shrugged his shoulders. The movement jogged his stomach and he could feel his bowels announcing that, despite everything, illness and inconvenience taken into account for as long as possible, a rapid accommodation would be necessary.

Richard put the palms of his hands on the bed, tried shifting his weight, realized that he really was much better. He pushed away the tray and then, with Miranda holding his arm, stood up. It felt good, not dizzy at all, but his back was stiff and rigid from lying still so he walked bent over, his shoulders bent so low that his housecoat trailed on the floor. Miranda helped him sit down and then left him hunched over on the toilet, stared at the tiny grey curled hairs that grew sparsely on his thighs, relics.

Then leaning forward over the sink and looking at his face in the mirror, he could see the marks of this battle: oases of stubble where the nurse had had trouble shaving him; red blotches on his skin which seemed to have fallen away from the bones, gathering along the lines of his jaw which had gone from square to round. His nose, cheekbones and forehead were all slightly shiny, as if the bones themselves were becoming luminous and would glow through the skin, burn it off, burn it all off when he was dead, creating itself as skeleton by its own energy. His eyes were reduced to pinpoints in the bright light–flesh purple and bagged below them, puffed blue eyelids. Miranda came in and stood beside him. In the fluorescent light her face looked different too, jaundiced. "God," Richard said, pointing to their heads, side by side in the mirror like two matched trophies, "soon they'll be taking us away in a wheelbarrow." But with Miranda supporting his arm he could walk past the bed, to the window overlooking the courtyard, back to the door, and then to the bed again.

Propped up again on the pillows, looking out. At some point in the afternoon, before supper, he must have been feeling well too, when they took the tube out of his arm and let him eat. But he can't remember the afternoon or how long he was sick. Only Erik in the morning, waiting, and the very beginning, when the nurse took his temperature. Talking seemed like too much work and Richard was now just waiting for them to go so he could relax, be well, read the newspaper and let the nurse rub his back. Miranda leaned forward to tell him something, putting her hand on the bed and he is suddenly reminded of Katherine Malone, wonders if she would come to the hospital to visit him. The fear again, a movement traversing his nerves, quick like something moving in the corner of his eye and then gone, traceless. Miranda has just finished saying something, he can see by the way her mouth is closing and she is moving away, waiting for him to reply. "I'm sorry," Richard said, "I didn't hear you."

"The doctor wants you to make your will."

"Well of course," Richard said. It was remarkable how easy this was going to be. He would get a bit better, learn to walk again so he could sit in the lounge for a few days. Perhaps they would let him smoke cigarettes. He would settle his affairs in a dignified way and then, on the last evening, telling no one at all, he would simply go to sleep permanently. There was absolutely nothing to fear. He didn't even feel curious.

"Richard," Miranda said, "you're going to have to decide about the farm." She was leaning forward again, it seemed she was always leaning forward. He wondered if she was beginning to have difficulty with her eyes. Yes, the farm. The others had left the room and had gone to the lounge. With his eyes closed, he could see them sitting there, their legs crossed, chatting about the cows, selling the island so Erik could buy himself a house in the city. "If you don't decide about the farm ... " Miranda was saying, speaking very slowly and shaping her lips carefully, as if she thought he had suddenly become retarded, at his age, God, they wouldn't even let him into school. She was waiting expectantly again.

"I'm sorry," Richard said embarrassed. "I didn't hear that last sentence. Just the last few words."

"You have to decide about the farm," Miranda said, this time in a loud whisper, almost hissing. "If you don't, then I do."

"Oh death," Richard said. He was surprised at the resonance and tone of his voice. "Oh death," he repeated. "How do I fear thy sting. Yes." He stopped. Miranda was crying. Bitch. Too bad. "Oh death," he began again, this time trying to make his voice vibrate, "how do I fear thy sting, where fortune's end doth ring and little birdies sing." Miranda was still crying but now looked at him, her mouth open, as if he had slipped over the edge. "Beware the quick brown fox," Richard said. "I always told you." He had too, when they were in Toronto and Miranda was taking typing lessons. "Now that I'm dying, I can do anything I want, right?" And to answer his question he swept out his arm, his left arm which now seemed to be working perfectly again, swept it across the tray so the chocolate custard dishes and the coffee cups were pushed onto the adjacent bed. "Damned kids," Richard said. "Shouldn't be allowed in places like this." Miranda had stopped crying and was staring at him, puzzled, as if she was hoping she could hypnotize him into shutting up. "Nope," Richard said. "It won't work. Look at your eyebrows, the dimples on your knees, God damn. You won't believe this but I feel pretty good. What was I saying? Yes. Maybe I'll just fall out of my bed and, splat, die." His voice didn't sound so good there. He tried to remember exactly what it *had* sounded like, repeating the words over in his head, but then forgot them and found he was repeating nothing at all. "Did they get the hay in?"

"Yes," Miranda said. "And they say if the weather keeps up there'll be a good second crop."

"Clover," Richard said. "Should've switched over to corn ten years ago."

"The farm."

"Yes, that lollipop of land. God. For did He not make us to go out into the fields?"

"Richard."

"Listen." He reached over to the bedside table and took one of the diaries that were stacked there, notebooks of thick yellowing paper, bound three at a time in calf-skin and stamped in gold on the outside by Simon Thomas, the gold now mostly worn off, but the impression still clear: *The Diaries of the Reverend William C. Thomas (Volumes I–III)*; flourished it in the air the way Simon Thomas used to during his Sunday evening preamble, as if this time, without any hesitation, doubt or further recalcitrance, he was absolutely bound and committed to make the ultimate revelation, the swallowing of the seventh veil that had been promised from the very beginning but never delivered, the dissemination and clarification that would finally make sense of all that had preceded it in a way that could not possibly have been anticipated, yet once experienced would necessarily be recognized as the absolute only root reality that could ever have existed, supported the whole structure, pierced through the confusion like a needle, his own needle. His Own Needle, in brief The Word that would join man to woman and present to past to future in one last instant and eternal matrimonial victory of the aether over its obsolete and confused constituents, flourished it in the air and then with the absolute certainty of the man who knows that this moment is, for once in his life, the occasion for which has been rehearsing, opened the book at a marked place and began to read:

God has said that the land is His
and can belong to no man and therefore
how can one man give what is not
his to another man who cannot possess it.

The poet had had a strange hand, his letters standing straight up and square, sailing across the page like a stubby ship. But the ink was beginning to fade, had turned from blue to brown, and without his reading glasses Richard Thomas could hardly make out the words, preferred to let his eyes relax and see it all as nicely patterned wallpaper, old colours burnt into old paper.

"You have to decide about the farm," Miranda said. Erik came into the room and pushed a chair over so he could sit beside Miranda. His head seemed big and bird-like, bent forward on his long neck. And his body thin and unbroken, cut off from anything that grew, his sleeves rolled up carelessly, floating about his elbows, virginal bony arms that could belong to a senile old priest, rattling in their sockets, denying everything. Now his head bobbed back and forth, like a puppet's head with half the strings cut, taking in Richard, Miranda, the dishes overturned on the other bed. His mouth seemed to be moving slightly; he was forming his lips to speak. In fact it was possible, Richard realized, that his son was talking already, but that he had failed to make his words sound. Erik: Miranda's son. Always unco-ordinated, but now every year in the city seemed to remove him further from his body, every motion and action preceded by that slight hesitation, the time it took to send the signal from wherever he had decided to locate the control centre, as if this was the way it should be done, in full retreat from the front lines, burnishing his mind—an old maid with her tea service. Erik now lit a cigarette. He held the ashtray in the palm of his hand, tipping it back and forth, sliding the match around the inside, turning his head away from him, Richard noticed, blowing the smoke towards the open window. They had taken the stand and the bottle away, but the oxygen tank and mask were still in the corner of the room, determined to keep him alive until he had gone through all the necessary motions and made the gestures, rites of passage, a separate section in the pale blue hospital booklet outlining the rules and regulations application to patients desiring the privilege to die without prior notice, preserving to the last gasp the myth that somewhere in the hospital, in the county at least, there might be one person who would actually take upon themselves the entire responsibility of mopping up the details of their own existence.

"This afternoon, just before supper, you got angry at Erik," Miranda said. Erik was still sitting there, his head bowed innocently. "Do you remember?"

"No," Richard said. He bowed his head too, feeling contrite even though he didn't seem to be able to remember anything at all before the chocolate custard, wondering if this was part of it, some sort of instant senility brought on by the stroke and the flu that would progressively shorten his memory span from hours to minutes to seconds to nothing at all so that his body would then not remember how to function or even stick itself together. He looked up at Miranda again. She was just finishing another sentence, one that he had missed entirely. "Anyway," Richard said, "I feel all right."

"They gave you two tranquillizers before supper," Miranda said. "You'll probably want to go to sleep soon. We'll be back in the morning." She smiled at him. He smiled back. He liked the way she was talking slowly and carefully again, as if a person in a good mood must be removed from normal humanity. She leaned over and kissed him. He could taste her lipstick, feel the roughness of her lips. She had tiny black hairs now growing around the corners of her mouth and on her cheeks, like an old woman. He had a sudden image of the two of them, the air let out in random places so they were spotted with holes, working their way up the steps of a rooming house. She was standing up now and looking down at him, her hands folded in front of her, crossing the shiny white handbag to her stomach. Her lips opened and closed and he could hear the clicking sound, tongue tapping on the roof of her mouth, her signal that she was going to soon lose her vast and uncountable patience, despite everything, if the world didn't line up right away, the same sound she had made the night he came home from seeing Katherine Malone in the back barn. He took her wrist and pulled her back towards him, so she sat beside him on the bed. She had already started again, the tears small and delicate this time, making him feel that he had deserted her. The same twinge he had had after separating from Katherine on the old township road; and then going home slowly, feeling he had betrayed Miranda, but at the same time there was something else too, a kind of physical sensation in his mind that he couldn't identify. And on the way, when he was almost home, he had stopped at the creek and lain down on the high slanted bank, staring up at the sky through what seemed to be an arched cathedral window of branches, the same view he was suddenly sure that his grandfather Richard Thomas had seen, the same view and the same feeling of his back springing out of the earth like the trees, his spine like the wooden tree spines with their wooden nerve arms spoking out for the sun. Orion was visible through the gap in the branches, a winter constellation setting early in the spring: Orion with its sword like his grandfather's sword. And lying on the high slanted bank of the creek, Richard Thomas could still feel the warmth of Katherine Malone, the impress of her thighs and belly, the fertility that demanded him, even against her own will, leaving him warm and empty, his mind cut loose and cow-like roaming this whole five hundred acres of forest and swamp and pasture, cut loose and filled with pity for its own death, pity for these strange forest creatures condemned to destroy their own home and place the substitute on the wreckage, new exercises for the new world. But even knowing that he had betrayed Miranda and conceived a child with Katherine Malone, there was still that physical presence in his mind which excused it, something he had known but couldn't say, that lodged in him even while he was thinking of his grandfather Richard Thomas, and that stayed with him when he got up to go home, stayed with him all night and the next day too as he got up early after lying awake half the night beside Miranda and went out to the barn with the cows, muttering to them, not even bothering to make words, but just uttering strings of sounds, his mind still fastened on it, holding it, not knowing what it was, but holding it. Finally giving up in the middle of the morning and going in for breakfast, not caring anymore, enough blind loyalty, and now, without trying, it was coming to him again and again in the hospital, coming up from behind, and it was nothing, not worth knowing, only the knowledge of his own death; and even that night going home from Katherine Malone he had come upon it, tripped over it, a groundhog that had been killed by a dog when it stuck its head out of its hole, dumb fable mortality. Click, click, Miranda's tongue, sputtering its morse code signals, unable to say more because now they were all in the room, Brian and Nancy crowding in the doorway just as Erik was trying to get out, Miranda backing away now too, tired of another day of watching him die, one last look, all four of them jostling at the door, waving good-bye so, for no reason, he picked a spoon off his tray and threw it at them, with his left hand, the last bouquet.

Thinking that spring night that he was thirty-three years old and still alive, healthy, already too old to be forced to war, even this war which they said was coming in Germany and France. Leaning on a rail gate and looking down into the small valley where the house and barns were cupped together, the lights on in the house and knowing Miranda would be wondering where he was. There was still enough light in the sky so that the house's fresh white paint glowed clean and new, painted last summer by him and Miranda, still believing that summer that she might get pregnant and that they could have children; and then turning and looking across the fields, they had fields in France too, wondering what this terrain would be like scarred by trenches and shells. America, they would come from the south and be unsure what to capture, what to do with it when it was theirs: the best tactic would be to draw them north into nowhere, a hundred miles north and let them freeze their asses off in the bush. Maybe they would just leave things as they were and be content to collect taxes and men, raising armies like Britain did for the Boer war and the Great War, whole generations of men taken off the land like so many feudal serfs, Richard S. Thomas the soldier stuck straight up for the Queen all his life, royal posture and rhyming Kipling dinosaurs. Thirty-three years old and the wind mixed cold and warm coming up from the west, blowing through his hair, thinner now, the first time he had felt it on his scalp that way. Thirty-three was the age when Christ had died; the poet had said in his diary that men who lived beyond the age of Christ's death were old enough to know better, whatever that was supposed to mean. Thirty-three the afternoon he came back from seeing Katherine, half-way through that year of his life. His birthday had fallen two days after Simon's death—and that day he had driven into town with Miranda to see the lawyer about the will. Everything in the office was leather: the black couch which Herman White had for his clients, the old harnesses and buggy whips he kept hanging from his walls, the desk top, and, of course, Herman White's shiny black shoes which he had polished every morning and every evening. Herman White made them listen to his interminably boring stories before he would get on with it, each story with its own little moral, his voice even more unctuous than Simon's, but without the bite—so that afterwards Richard couldn't help telling Miranda the rumour that Herman White the lawyer paid his cleaning woman ten dollars a week to come in every day at two o'clock and spank him with the buggy whips—sallow indoors skin and jet black hair, the hair on his head straight and oily, black hair coming out of his white shirt cuffs, his beard thick and bristly already at eleven o'clock in the morning, telling them his stories and then telling even more, and patently untrue stories about himself and Simon, whom he now made out to be his best friend even though it was common knowledge that Simon had claimed that once, while Herman White was in Kingston, his wife had invited him to tea. And when he went there she had propositioned him, saying that Herman White didn't know how to do anything any more. Simon had gone upstairs with her, but when they got into the bedroom and she took off her clothes, he saw that Herman White the lawyer's wife had hundreds of little red, blue and gold stars pasted over her body in an unprecedented milky way corset that extended from her shoulders to her knees, the stars arranged in horizontal colour bands, three rows thick, with little gold bursts at her nipples and navel—and the proof was that the stars were exactly the same as Herman White always used, in his appointment books and in his legal textbooks, marking off one paragraph from another. When they had been to the lawyer's office and the inheritance was transmitted in this official manner, they turned around and went home again, the deed in their hands, now owning the farm in some different way than previous; Simon having passed on to them not only the farm but the duty of finding someone else to give it to when they were finished. Thirty-three years old: four years older than Miranda who still looked like a young woman, but, trim and preserved already her body would soon begin to go its own way, without children, as if sterility were permissible on this farm. "He did his duty," Herman White had said of Simon, as if it were for him to say, and that now, unlikely at it was, Richard Thomas would have his turn to do his, it being left unclear whether there was any larger possible purpose or simply the holy mission of colonizing the earth: generations of men to be beaded out along the land like so many successive waves of trees and vegetation. There was some money too, so on their way home they went to the bank and then to the hotel to eat. When they were ready to leave it was already late in the afternoon, getting dark and the November sky grey and overcast, promising a bad winter. And remembering the poet's words as they drove the horses home, thought maybe they were true and that once again history would be repeated, and like Abraham and Sarah in their new possession of this land they would be able to have children. Or else be condemned to a purposeless self-preservation, to milk the land every year, enough to fill their bellies and their bank balance, nothing more, a straight trade, body for earth, three generations of bones to feed the land like so many fallen trees, animals. Knowing with Simon dead he owned the past now, his mind already turning to Katherine Malone and deciding to wait, one more winter, there was nothing but time.

"I'm sorry about yesterday," Erik was saying. Sitting beside him and drinking coffee out of a waxed paper cup. He was holding the cup near his face and Richard could see that his hands were getting marked with blisters and cuts. In the morning he had gotten up and shaved himself, standing in front of the mirror wearing his reading glasses and using the electric razor. After breakfast, he has walked with the nurse down the corridor to the lounge and back. His first time out of the room since he had come to the hospital. Still, the bed beside him was kept empty. And while they walked, the nurse had said that he should tidy things up now, when there was nothing to worry about.

"It's good to see you doing some work."

"Just shovelling shit," Erik said. He crossed the room to get an ashtray and Richard could see he was wearing sandals.

"You want to watch you don't get stepped on," Richard said, regretting it immediately, seeing Erik's head bob up and down, the same dipping motion that Simon used to make, but with Erik it was more elongated and hesitant, unaccompanied by the habitual reaching for the knife or cigar.

He watched Erik carefully opening his package of cigarettes, peeling off all the cellophane and then slitting the black government seal with his thumb-nail, neatly, along the edge of the cardboard.

"The others won't be here for a while," Erik said. He got up from his chair and went to stand beside the window where he lit his cigarette. "I'm supposed to talk to you about the farm and, before we get into a fight, I just want to say that I think you should leave it to Miranda and quit worrying about it."

"I'm not worried about it," Richard said. "I'm worried about you."

"I'm all right."

"So am I."

"You are looking pretty good," Erik said. Just like Simon, absolutely unselfconscious, flipping the cigarette about in his fingers, sitting on the windowsill now, knee bouncing with nervous energy.

"I should have beat you more when I was able," Richard said. Both his arms were working now and the flu was gone, but somehow he still felt sick, not cured or over the worst, but just at a new stage where the symptoms were more diffuse. He couldn't help staring at Erik, wondering if he would ever come alive, what would it take? And he was afraid of Brian too, keeping out of his way when Brian was in the room, not talking to Nancy at all, always deferring, waiting, Brian so dumb he didn't know anything at all; a man shouldn't hate his adopted son that way, Brian, the exact same age as Katherine's Richard, living where he had died, no reason—just fact. Herman White's nephew from Belleville was the lawyer now, keeping an office in each of three small towns and making his rounds, a secretary in each office and him now, they said, with a telephone in his car, making as much money as a doctor and living in a stone house with hardwood floors and two fireplaces. Erik, Miranda, Brian and Nancy: they would fill up the whole couch, and Leslie White, ten years out of law school and still wearing his uncle's gold cufflinks, would perform the reading of the will, in ignorance. Erik was looking back at him, as if he might have been speaking; maybe his sickness was only a mouth that swallowed up unattended moments, demanding more and more and, as it did, opening ever larger so finally it would turn itself inside out, like every other disease, and end up a floppy pink epiglottis and a long steaming throat. "Do you remember when you had your tonsils out?"

"Yes," Erik said. "It was the first time I got ice cream." Still looking at him and coming over to sit beside the bed. "You know," Erik said, "that just because I don't want to live on the farm, it doesn't mean I didn't learn anything from you."

"That's nice," Richard said.

"It's just that, well, there's a lot of important things going on in this country and so, you know, people have to be able to think clearly. And the university is the place where that happens."

"The rules ... " Richard said, remembering a previous argument when Erik had claimed that all logical thinking had rules.

"Yes."

"You teach people the rules," Richard said.

"Yes."

"What about life?"

"What about it?"

"Who teaches people how to live?"

"I don't know," Erik said. Richard could tell he was starting to lose his temper. He had just put out one cigarette and was now lighting another, forgetting even to go and smoke it by the window. "People have to teach themselves how to live."

"God help them," Richard said.

"He never has." Erik up on his feet, pacing back and forth from window to door. It was amazing, Richard thought, how easily he was baited, and wondered if Simon had found him that transparent, arranging the whole episode with Katherine out of his inexhaustible malice, God, Erik would never have stood up to that at all. "People think well, all right, all they have to do is tend their own garden as best they can, never look beyond it, as if the world has stopped so they can do whatever they want, but it's not true, things have changed, the whole world is connected together."

"It was always connected together," Richard said.

"Politically."

"That's what Hitler wanted."

"God." Erik had sat down now, giving up entirely, looking as if he had decided he would sit there without speaking until either someone else came or Richard died, whichever came first, it didn't matter.

"I'm sorry," Richard said. "I'm just an old man."

"It doesn't matter."

"But I've always thought that there was more to life than rules and logic."

"Of course," Erik said.

"A man has to know his own destiny."

"Oh Christ," Erik sighed, starting to get to his feet again and then slumping back into his chair. "No one has destinies any more," he said. "They live in apartments and breed goldfish." It was early afternoon, just after lunch. The courtyard was emptier than ever, mid-August doldrums, and the sun shone flat and hot on the black asphalt. Around the edges of the courtyard, and slowly encroaching on the middle, were crumpled-up chocolate bar wrappers, old newpapers, crushed milkshake cartons. There were only a few cars parked there, all of them seeming dusty and familiar.

"Hasn't rained for a while," Richard said. The patch of sky he could see was hazy blue. A few more days without rain and it would turn almost yellow-blue, mean and catty, Simon used to call those skies, hating cats himself, keeping two in the barn and none in the house, drowning any that ever came around, talking about Henry Beckwith's barn where you could count at least a hundred of them at any one time, so many cats that there wasn't room for them all to line up along the beams at once. Erik had composed himself again, was sitting with his cigarette by the window, where he was supposed to be, ready to be discovered by Miranda. In the middle of the morning the doctor had come, sat beside Richard Thomas's bed and told him that he could go home in a few days if he was still feeling well.

"But no work for at least six weeks," the doctor said. "No work, no sex, no liquor, no arguments, no spiced foods, no stairs." Every morning the doctor did his rounds at the same time, wearing a freshly starched linen coat and carrying a clipboard. "We used to keep people in the hospital much longer. But now." He shrugged his shoulders. His face was tanned and his hair wet, combed straight back. Whenever he saw a doctor Richard couldn't help inspecting him closely, looking for signs of disease and decay. He couldn't remember hearing of any doctors being patients in this hospital. His own doctor seemed not so young, maybe fifty: liver spots on the backs of his hands and on his face, the body unscarred by work, sedentary, the kind that would gradually get rounder and rounder.

"You should get more exercise," Richard said.

The doctor nodded. "No time." He stood up, patted Richard carelessly on the leg, as Richard would have patted a cow, in passing, and then left the room. Richard wondered if they were saving the bed for him. All day, making his rounds, fighting one losing battle after another. The feeling of fear again, this time sharper, in his throat; and it stayed with him, locked in his throat the whole morning, not moving when the nurses came in to see him or when he read his magazines, there all through lunch, making it hard for him to swallow and still, now, with Erik, it was in his throat and chest. He could ask for a tranquillizer. He wondered what would happen if he said to Erik that he was afraid to die, that he was so afraid to die that he had been hurting from it all day, that the fear was what had him that first day, bile and death, without knowing it, trying to fight it off by going out and then being caught anyway, that way, on his own beach which he had refused to sell because he believed in life, his life; and remembering again how it had locked him, kept him in the moment, tried to warn him that he was only struggling against his own life like an animal caught in a trap, twisting open its own arteries and bleeding to death. It would be better if the bed were cranked up more, if he could sit up straight and look at the wall or out the window, keep his eyes open. Now the room appeared to him as through a film, the innocuous blue plaster so successfully bland that it didn't seem to matter whether it was there, whether he saw it. Erik had gone and so Richard tried visualizing him in his empty chair, get the mind to concentrate on something else, remembered suddenly a book on self-hypnotism he had read fifty years ago, the rage of the school library, his brother Steven the best subject of all, passing out at the slightest command, crawling on the floor of the school house and barking like a dog, begging in the desert for water, until Henry Beckwith had caught them at it, and made the four main culprits stay after school, one standing in each corner, reciting all three verses to the national anthem fifty times each, in order. The centre of his vision was liquid pastel, blue, but the corners were filled, like the courtyard, with unaccountable rubbish, things he couldn't see when he swivelled his eyes, but were only visible indirectly, like dreams that are forgotten as quickly as they are recounted so in the end one feels only that something has passed. A hand on his arm and looking he could see Miranda had sat down in Erik's chair, second shift, was already emptying her handbag of special diabetic treats, mail for him, her white handkerchiefs to blot her lipstick on. What have you been doing? she was going to ask him, she asked him every afternoon and he thought he might say well, nothing, just dying. As if she herself would never die, neither with him or later; as if this was all right that he sit rolled up into a fat dying slug on this narrow bed, being cranked up and down three times a day and hoping to be well enough to take himself to the bathroom instead of using a bedpan, as if it was all right that he put himself and everyone else through his inch-by-inch drama because his death was absolutely unique and irreparable, the last mortal man being dragged off the stage, still singing, one hand over his heart and the other holding out his straw hat for applause, his pockets stuffed with pain tickets to be cashed in at heaven. Miranda had handed him a card: a cherubic angel wearing a pink shawl and a halo on the front and then inside, in raised gold lettering:

> In the fields the roses are red red red,
> And you can hear the tinkle of the cowbells;
> Today I hear that you are stuck in bed,
> I hope that tomorrow you will be well.

Beneath these engraved lines, Katherine Malone had signed her name, writing it carefully in her still perfect school teacher's-daughter hand, big round letters that might have been formed by a twelve-year-old, and surrounded her name with x's and o's; Katherine Malone now seventy-two years old, and when he had seen her recently, when they went to church at Christmas or Easter or to one of the socials that were more of a tourist attraction now than a community affair, she seemed older to him, indefinitely old, her body beyond everything except survival, fat, even fatter than him, soft, her face framed by curling grey hair, round face. Never far from Peter Malone, who was heavy too, heavier than either of them and looked like a bulldog with his huge jowls and lumpy flesh, hair still thick and black, parted down the middle and combed straight back so he looked severe and pocked, an old-world judge handing sentences of torture and death with complete assurance, or a missionary who didn't care about anything except keeping his feet clean, but he was still soft in his own way, giving Katherine flowers every year for their wedding anniversary and buying her nightgowns and négligées for her birthdays, every year the same, thirty-nine pink nightgowns all the same size, getting so monotonous with his gift that she retaliated by buying him scratchy long underwear every Christmas. Nine months after Simon Thomas's funeral, Katherine's baby was born. She called him Richard Malone, just like that. Miranda found out first, one day in town, and then came back and said to Richard how nice it was that Katherine Malone had remembered him that way, weren't they old flames? And that it was strange how birth and death were always mixed together, Richard's namesake being conceived at the very same time as his father was buried. And telling Richard how the day after the baby was born Peter Malone had gone to the General Store and handed out cigars, like he always did, only this time, of course he was only joking, he kept saying that he didn't mind being the one to hand them out so long as they were charged up to Richard Thomas's account, good old Richard Thomas, and wasn't it peculiar how he'd been keeping to himself these past few months, since the funeral, like all the Thomas men, playing his cards so close. The baby was born in mid-December and that year the snow was late coming, the ground frozen but bare until after Christmas, so Richard walked back the old way, to the Beckwith place, the afternoon of the winter solstice but then, in sight of the house but too embarrassed to go in, turned around and walked back. When he got home that day, running the last mile over the frozen fields, the furrows from the fall's ploughing all frozen into place, panicky, Miranda was upstairs packing, and said that she was going home to Winnipeg for Christmas and he could write her when he decided what he wanted. And if it was to include her, it had better include a child too, even if they had to go to the agency to adopt one.

"Maybe I could just get a scarecrow," Miranda said, "and sit it in the chair here."

"Sorry," Richard said, "I must have fallen asleep." She looked tired today, the lines on her face deeper than ever and her eyes looking as if they were propped open. "You should get more sleep." Miranda nodded. "I'm serious."

"So am I." She handed Richard another car, a thank-you note embroidered in buttercups and vines. "You should write something back to Katherine Malone," Miranda said. "She's always liked you."

"Sure," Richard said. He took the notepaper and envelope from Miranda and put it on top of the night-table, beside the diaries.

"You don't have the slightest intention now, do you?"

"You could tell her how much I appreciated it," Richard said, "next time you see her."

"You could tell her," Miranda said. "They said you can go home in a few days, and people will be able to come and visit you." So, good, they would prop him up in the living-room in a stuffed chair, under a blanket, yes, and he could have the Frank brothers and Katherine Malone over for tea, tea and sherry for the neighbours, though come to think of it none of those had ever been past the kitchen except maybe Katherine Malone once or twice for ladies meetings. "You'll want to get your eyes tested," Miranda said, "get new reading glasses so it's comfortable to read, you always said you wanted time to read. And Mark Frank is putting up a new TV aerial this afternoon, one of those kinds where you push the button and it rotates. Your arm *is* getting better, isn't it? Erik's laid a patio, out back near the tile bed, and mowed the grass so we have a yard, I always wanted one anyway. And he's getting one of those tables with an umbrella sticking through the centre so we can drink tea in the shade."

"To think I'm finally going to be a gentleman," Richard said. "I hope they let me smoke cigars; I can be like Simon and sit at the head of the table and tell stories." Looking up at Miranda and seeing the expression of absolute horror on her face. "I never knew you minded it that much."

"The insides of my cheeks were always cut," Miranda said, "from biting them to keep from giggling. Simon Thomas, Lord, I don't know if I would have married you if I would have met him first."

"He was an old man."

"He was so afraid of me," Miranda laughed, "and hated me too. Did you ever notice that he never once spoke directly to me, commented on anything at all, even thanked me for the supper? You would have thought I was your housekeeper, like his, Lord, he never let her out of the house with him unless he needed her to carry something."

"A person can't live past their time," Richard said.

"Your time, look at you, you're getting better and you don't even know it, and you'll be coming home too, you don't think I'd drive all this way to the hospital, every day for three weeks, just to watch you die, Richard Thomas." Leaning forward and laughing as she talked, establishing the new balance, making him feel caught out, sulking, as always knowing how to get by him in that way she seemed to have, almost magical, of knowing what was going on, seeing it as someone else might see an engine. Her eyes were open wide and her pupils green and almost sparkling, as they always were when she was in a good mood, delicate green-grey owl's eyes; she hunted that way too: sitting still and concealing her target until the last moment.

"I never thought I'd get old this way."

"Yes, well, me too," Miranda said. "It might not be too bad though."

"No."

"Lord, we could probably go on for twenty years like this, helping each other around the house, having our stupid fights, even last night I was mad at you when Katherine Malone came by with her card, seventy-two years old and fat as a cow but she was all dressed up and had her hair done all special just for you, hoping you'd be home, think, it took her more than thirty years to work up the nerve to come to see you at your house, I should have let her have you." Her hands and arms moving as she talked, still wearing the small diamond ring he had bought her two years after they were married, when they could afford it, in a jeweller's shop in Kingston. It seemed so long since he had seen her in a good mood, that morning he had pushed her away, asleep, now it would be six weeks.

"The doctor's afraid we'll kill ourselves fucking," Richard said, startled at how fast Miranda blushed, snapping red like a light.

"Go on."

"Well." Her hand on his leg; it would be possible to feel human again.

"Well," she said. She went to the door and locked it, and then came back and lay on the edge of Richard's bed, her head on his chest so he could put his arm around her.

"God," Richard said, "I've really hated this place."

"I know." So. He moved his hand on her back, trying to feel her skin through the cotton, encountering buckles and foundation garments. She had her head tucked into his shoulder and the heat of her breath came through there, scalding. "We should have a wider bed," Miranda said. And as she spoke, as if on a signal, someone came to the door and tried the handle. Then started knocking, sharp authoritative raps in bunches of three with a short pause in between. "All right," Miranda called. "I'm coming." Her lips had soaked through his pyjamas; she kissed him, bit through the wet spot. The knocking started again, continued until Miranda opened the door.

"It's all right," the nurse said. "It's time for his afternoon pills." She brought in a tray with two white paper cups: one large and filled with water, the other small, the size of a cream cup, filled with pills. She stood beside the bed and watched to make sure that Richard swallowed them all. "You don't want to worry about these things too much," the nurse said, and then left the room.

"We should spend the day together," Miranda said, "tell Erik to go home with Brian and Nancy; I could even stay at a hotel tonight, Lord, I'm sick of the drive." But he tired quickly, right after supper, and had to ask her to leave before visiting hours were over. And then, when she was gone, realizing that it was her presence that had been the strain: forced contact. He dozed off and woke up. It was still evening. The nurse had turned off the lights in his room, but the hall lights were on and he could see

other patients walking up and down. His window to the courtyard was open but there was no breeze, August heat, feeling close
to Miranda the way he used to sometimes when he would go to
bed with her after lunch and then wake up later in the afternoon,
alone, under the quilt in the middle of summer feeling absolutely
detached from all the work he was supposed to be doing and the
constant worry of getting the hay in before it was ruined. It was
amazing how easily his illness had pushed them apart. The only
other time they had really been separated by anything was the
winter Katherine had had her baby, Richard Malone, and
Miranda went home to Winnipeg for Christmas, making Richard
drive her to the train station over the bare frozen roads, saying
that if he wanted to walk all about the township, gloating over
his bastard child, he could do it without her having to watch. So
strange then to have the house to himself, something that had
never happened for more than a day. At first he just moped
around, had trouble sleeping, did the chores, felt silly for being
alone at Christmas. But soon he was enjoying it, rummaging
through the attic and the spare rooms, letting out the ghosts he
called it, beginning as soon as he came back from taking Miranda
to the station to talk to himself, walking back and forth from the
house to the barn remembering his mother Leah Thomas, the
invisible iron threads she had woven through the whole house
and farm, projecting her presence; and remembered how frightened he was the first few months after she died, so much so he
would go to Katherine, who was crazy about ghosts herself, for
consolation, thinking that somehow his mother would find a way
to take her revenge for his fear and meanness, Simon Thomas
drinking every night, released, while Steven, still sick with the
knife-wound and crying over his mother, stayed upstairs all the
time. Walking about the farm and unravelling the past, not even
thinking about why Miranda had left. Only waiting for Katherine Malone to hear that she was gone and come to see him,
wondering if she would travel so soon after the baby, sometimes
sitting in the kitchen and waiting for her but other times, disgusted with himself for wanting her so much, he would go for
walks into the bush, or pour his nervous energy into ridiculous
tasks, digging postholes in the frozen ground, spending days with
the horses and chains, pulling out stumps and junipers. Katherine

never showed, but on Christmas day Peter Malone came to get him for dinner, driving his new grey Percherons and with a flask of whiskey in his pocket. By the time they got to the Beckwith place, Peter Malone was laughing and slapping him on the shoulder, the flask empty, both of them smoking the special General Store cigars, embers flying back into their face and hair as the horses were galloped full-speed down the road. And after dinner Katherine finally brought him the baby to see, a long thin baby that looked sick already; she handed it to Peter Malone and he handed it to Richard, fat fertile Peter Malone who knew that any child of his would be healthier than this, held the baby out to Richard, as if it had been decided that he could have it, Merry Christmas, the three of them looking at this unattractive child and each other, the best a Thomas could do and lucky if it wasn't one of those idiot children like Frederick, Peter Malone drunk and with one hand still on the baby and one on Richard's shoulder looked sideways at his wife and then said he was sorry, passed out on his feet like a movie, swaying back and forth five times before someone finally thought to shove him backwards into a chair. Peter Malone started to snore right away so Richard, still standing with this baby in his arms, the other Malone children all excited now to see their father passed out, the first time in three months, thanked Katherine for the dinner, didn't know what else to say, walked home drunk in the cold. Then restless in his own house, pacing about the kitchen, drank half a bottle of wine that old Mark Frank had brought him and went outside and saddled up his own horse, a mare he had bought two summers ago for Miranda to ride, whipped it along the road to the Frank place, thinking they would still be up and that he would get drunk with them, but when he got there all the lights were out and he had to go straight home again. And when he got back he took another bottle of wine out to the barn and drank it while he rubbed down the horse, going outside twice to vomit and then coming back into the barn, drinking more, mumbling to himself the whole time, finishing the bottle and then going out into the barnyard, still on his feet, stretching out his arms and spinning around in the space between the barns, stopping dizzy and retching, going to the house for the last half-bottle and bringing it out; half a bottle half a moon, knowing that this would baptize him, reluctant father, there was nothing left except rubbing alcohol and he didn't want to have to drink that, walking from the house to the barn taking small sips, no hurry, knowing he was broken already, the last Thomas, they would find him and say that he was crazy anyway, small sips, each one a line from throat to stomach, bile and acid, vomiting it up as he drank it down, blood wine, blood child, and then the bottle was gone and he was sitting down, his back against the horse barn that Simon had given him, lying down on his side and bringing up frequently and casually as if he might have had the hiccups, lying on his side and realizing he was sober, his supper on the ground and on his face, getting up and walking to the well, taking off his jacket and his shirt and his undershirt and splashing the freezing water all over himself, numb sober, going into the house. The furnace and the stove were both out, he couldn't stop shivering; lit the kitchen stove and sat in front of it, unable to sleep, stunned, unable to walk, sitting and shivering in Simon's wicker chair waiting for time to pass and then, suddenly, his stomach contracting and cramping, pulling him to the floor, forcing him to shout, pounding the knotted muscles with his fists, what it must be like to have a baby, finally his throat opened and he vomited, vomiting again, a thin bloody stream shot right across the room. The alcohol rushed through his body in waves; he could feel it drenching his cells and then receding, each beat of his heart sending out a fresh supply. He knew he had to be outside, worked his way to his feet, and stumbled out the door, his stomach sore and aching, feeling a sudden affinity for the Frank men, knowing that this was the centre of their experience, drunk white witch doctors staggering around in the middle of winter passing through convulsions for this brief vision, the grey weatherbeaten barnboards pulsing in the winter dawn light, the cows moving slowly in their paddock, stretched out in a line on the hill behind the barn, each cow attended and sucked by its fall calf; the camping place of some nomadic tribe that had escaped the European forest for this new world and its instant hospitality and was strung out with their animals on the ancient glaciated shield of the continent, waiting for history to make them whole again.

Richard Thomas looked up to see Pat Frank sitting at the end of his bed, the chair pushed up against the wall and his feet on the aluminum bedstead. He had long bony legs and his shapeless grey-brown pants hung from them in wrinkles and folds. With one hand he steadied himself against the wall. The other was wrapped around a brown paper bag, tipping it back into his mouth. Pat Frank's head was large and fragile, the bald sunburned scalp framed by wisps of hair, entirely overwhelmed by the face, absolutely skeletal, flesh stripped away by years of drinking and eyes far apart and huge, only made bearable by the surrounding bone which somehow reduced them, made them just another extraordinary feature in this grotesque drunk's face. "My own stuff this time," Pat Frank said, offering the bottle to Richard.

"Jesus," Richard Thomas said, "a person would have thought you were trying to kill me with that other."

"I'm a failure," Pat Frank said. He spoke with that strange baritone rasp which seemed to stamp his family. His father, old Mark Frank, had put some clothesline in a glass of alcohol once to demonstrate the science of the conditioning of the vocal chords. His other son, and twin brother, also Mark Frank, spoke the exact same way. The only one of the three of them that could vary their own sound effect at all was, in fact, Pat Frank himself, who was able to rasp in his throat and whistle through his nose at the same time.

Richard looked at the clock beside his bed. Two o'clock in the morning. "Won't even let a man sleep," Richard Thomas said.

"Couldn't sleep myself," Pat Frank said. "So damned hot up there. Nothing to do but sit inside and listen to that damned brother of mine panting and sweating."

"A man is practically dead and his own neighbours come and wake him up in the middle of the night to measure him up for his coffin." He took a small drink from Pat Frank's bottle, made a face and passed it back. "Jesus," Richard said. "I'd sure like a cigarette."

"They say Erik has a job in Alberta."

"That's what they say."

"Not everyone is meant to live on a farm."

"Jesus," Richard Thomas said. And maybe it was true, if everyone at birth was issued little cards with their destiny written on in God's Own Indelible Hand.

"I guess I'm just an old drunk now," Pat Frank said.

"Yes," Richard said, "I guess you are." The bottle rose and fell, manoeuvered inexorably in Pat Frank's steady hand, waxing and waning like any other natural cycle.

"Old Simon was a stubborn bugger."

"I guess he was," Richard agreed.

"Two weeks after your mother died he came down to the house and got drunk. Then he offered us half the farm if we'd kill you."

"Old Simon Thomas," Richard said. "He always got his way."

"Not always."

"No."

"Whole family is dumb and stubborn," Pat Frank said. "All of you got heads like cedar posts. If Erik hadn't gone to the city the two of you would have been fighting like dogs the whole time. Worse than you and Simon." Those huge eyes swimming in alcohol and skin; and Richard could see passing across them the acknowledgement of the unsaid accusation, old Mark Frank who'd lost his farm because his sons were too busy drinking to make the farm go, the father and the two sons, each resenting the irresponsibility of the others, so that not one thing could be done on the farm without all three doing it at once, each watching the other to make sure that the work was meted out equally. And if one got angry he would begin to drink. Begin to drink in the morning or the afternoon or the evening or even the middle of the night when he woke up suddenly from a dream that told him that he was being exploited and he would drink everything that was in the first bottle that he happened to see and then he would drink the contents of every bottle he could find in or around the house, stopping only to pass out or eat a sandwich, keep drinking until the easy supply was gone and then hitch a ride to town where he would spend all the money he had and could find in the house on wine and drink that, and then go around to all the neighbours who might owe him money or a favour, or be willing to be owed money, and drink what might be procured there. The average drunk lasted therefore from a minimum of a couple of hours to a maximum of a month. By that time, having made himself entirely unbearable to live with, other members of the family would have begun to resent him, then mistreat him, and then, unable to change his course by any other means, joined him. Thus it happened that for ten years running no field was seeded on the Frank farm and for four of those years, the indiscretion that finally made it impossible to continue, the hay was never fully taken in, tempers flaring before it had even been brought to the barn or, sometimes, cut in the fields; and then, inevitably, the talents of the family were turned in a more profitable direction and they began manufacturing the wine in wooden kegs and eventually, at the height of their ambition, running a still in the back woods of the old farm that everyone knew about but wouldn't complain, even the police who visited once a year to pick up their supply of what passed for cherry brandy, *la crème de la crème,* old Mark Frank used to call it on the days that he could speak.

"Anyway," Richard Thomas said, "Erik wants me to give him the farm. He wants me to give him the farm so it will be his, and he can own it."

"Well," Pat Frank said.

"It's a good farm."

"You've got a nice piece along the lake there," Pat Frank said.

"The land is good."

"It is," Pat Frank said. "I hear Peter Malone say he might be going into sheep now. Says that he can't afford to keep improving the stock of his cows and that beef just isn't worth it."

"He'll make a living," Richard said. "And no one is going to tell him when to wake up in the morning."

"They say there's been more campers than groundhogs this summer."

"There's always someone to say that this land isn't meant for farming or that it should never have been cleared, or that the only future for it is some sort of park, for city people."

"Well," Pat said.

"Well goddamn well what?" Richard said loudly, almost shouting, slamming his palm against the mattress.

"Careful."

"Well *goddamn,*" Richard said. "The reason a person lives this way is, well, because this is the way a person lives. Dumb purpleassed baboon goes to the city and five years later he looks like some piece of shit should've been left in the old barn, not yet thirty years old and he can't hardly piss all the way to the ground. *Goddamn.* Simon was alive he'd die laughing to look at him."

"If I had children." Richard tried to imagine that: pink curtains in the windows of the old pig-barn and a woman, smiling and cheerful, standing at the door to welcome Pat home from his trip to the liquor store. "The widow thought she was pregnant once but it turned out she'd just misplaced something.

"A person might live in the city because they have to," Richard said. "Like say a person was dumb or crippled or something."

"Sometimes you're pretty dumb," Pat said.

"That's what they say," Richard said.

"Erik doesn't want the farm any more than I do. Not for the money either. Any time he gets within ten miles of the place he starts to twitch and shake."

"Takes some getting used to," Richard said.

"First time it happened I thought he'd bit a snake."

"Goddamn," Richard said. "And don't make me laugh or I'll come apart myself." And that's what it felt like too, muscles squeezing and contracting through his chest and stomach. The night nurse came and stood in the door, shook her head, declining, when Pat offered the bottle to her, and then came in the room and held his head in her hands, pressed against her stomach. Fingers lined up on forehead and scalp, still felt sensitive where the hair used to be. The warmth of her belly coming through the starched linen, pressing against the back of his skull and Richard Thomas shoves his head deeper into pillow, rubbing his scalp and flexing the muscles in his neck and back, blood brothers, the tiny crossed scar long since grown over, shallow white ridges.

"Mark's asleep in the lounge," Pat said. "I better wake him up to go home."

"Sure," Richard said, "anytime." His eyes closed as easily as they opened, sliding in and out of sleep expertly now, swiftly, each of them needing the other in quick succession. And when they got back to Richard's room the lights were off and they could see the nurse sitting beside the bed, resting her hand over Richard's wrist, pressing her case in long low whispers that followed them down the hall, past the empty wheelchair and into the fire exit; and again in the courtyard parking lot Pat Frank thought he could hear her through the open window—her voice, the lake, the hospital machines, all run together and muttering like a river of insects.

NINE

Now she is older. The child is older too: this year she is tall and skinny, hanging curiously in the doorways and the halls watching him with her mother; next year she will go to high school. Rose Garnett, polished and controlled, stalks the varnished floors of her expensive house, performs mysterious consultations. She is removed now; Erik can't believe the memory of her vulnerability. But still, she remembered him too, even the first time he was there, finally playing the game over his tea leaves and then inviting him back the next day for a late supper. Now that she had the child back, the truck was gone. Instead there was a red Italian sportscar. And after supper she said that they should go for a drive before coffee, and took him outside, making him climb into the passenger seat of her red car, driving slowly out of the city and then, on the back country roads, accelerated to ninety on the straightaways, screeching around the curves on two wheels. Slowing down again at the city, she took him inside for coffee and brandy. In her husband's absence she has become like his machine, the bones of her face narrow arched tubes, the skin stretched over them, smooth silk planes in repose. The hesitation has gone from her walk and there is only a polite and careless restraint. He supposes that her clothes must be expensive. They have their coffee and brandy in the living-room, sitting on a deep upholstered couch. From time to time, during supper, when they are walking back to the house from the car, later when they are sitting down and she is talking, she touches, casually, purposefully, giving him whatever warning is necessary. When he makes no objection, the omission is registered and she turns down the light. She asks him if he would like to come upstairs. In her bedroom she undresses him while he is standing up, taking her time with buttons and zippers, tiny kisses for his body as it is revealed. Then she takes off her own clothes and leads him to the bed. Her scar has faded and she is tanned with the exception of thin bikini stripes. Her body is now her most elaborate costume, her hair thick and curling from her shoulders, her eyes breaking the tension of her face, deep blue, round. She draws him inside her and he feels nothing more than a vague warmth and a small movement from before to after. They smoke cigarettes and she draws a bath for him. She gets into the bathtub with him, laughing, her breasts clapping together like small porpoises. Her daughter's name is Victoria. He knows that she is listening to this strange splashing, wondering why her mother and this guest have turned into fish. She wants to come and investigate but perhaps she is afraid of what she will find. Erik is sure that she is awake. Perhaps this happens all the time. Perhaps she has come before and discovered her mother in arcane positions with Kingston's most respected businessmen, stiff white historians from the university, psychiatrists who have decided to expand their horizons, visiting dignitaries from Mexico who would like to twin with a small Canadian city, a cosmetic salesman with a rare brand of bath oil. Perhaps there are hidden servants who make sure that such misunderstandings do not occur. Before he stepped into the bath they stood side by side in front of the full-length mirror, and she turned to kiss him, knowing he would see the reflection of her back, her calfs and thighs rounded with the effort of standing on her toes, her buttocks sectioned into different colours by the sun.

His existence has become simple and easy. In the mornings he wakes up and goes downstairs for breakfast. Everyone else is already eating. Sometimes after breakfast he helps Miranda with the dishes, tries to be useful around the house. But after they have talked about Richard and Miranda has drunk her two morning cups of coffee, she gets restless; he sees this, she is unaccustomed to having people in the house in the morning. He goes outside. At some point the farm grew away from him. Now he wishes it were a cottage on the lake. He hardly even talks to Brian except to ask, like a woman, what he has been doing today. For a few days he went out with Brian in the mornings, fixing the old cedar rail fences and replacing one section of that fencing with post and page-wire. But one morning Brian just walked from the house to the truck and left without him. Now in the mornings Erik works in the garden: weeding and harvesting. The soil is warm and spongy on his bare feet—curling around the edges, threatening to swallow them entirely. At first he felt out of place, wearing a faded, too tight pair of his old jeans that cut into his belly and made him feel suddenly middle-aged and paunchy. But he left his shirt and shoes off anyway, looking down at himself every few minutes to see if he had been transformed, wondering where his ribs have gone to, looking at what the shoes and the city have done to his feet, turning the toes red and blotchy, twisting the nails, the top of his feet now covered with a ridge of black hairs and mosquito bites. The first week he could only use the hoe for a few minutes at a time, his hands blistering and protesting immediately. Now the blisters are broken and bandaged. He can move up and down the rows of corn, chopping the hoe down into the soft earth, metal into earth, left hand, right hand, each cut bringing blades of pain into his shoulders and back. Periodically, when he straightens up, he looks over towards the trailer and sees that Nancy is looking at him. Sometimes she comes out for a minute to take something in for a salad. He has also become the guardian of the lawn: mowing it, building a patio out back, trimming the grass away from the stone foundations of the house, digging the weeds out from under the lilac bushes in the yard. He wears one of Richard's old straw hats when he is outside. He takes it off and rubs his arm across his forehead. There are random slapping motions to keep away the mosquitoes and black flies. At the end of each morning he washes himself at the well, splashing the cold water over himself, dissolving the film of soil and grass and insect bodies; and standing on the concrete well-casing, shivering, his skin contracted and purple, he feels it briefly, the body that has been violated by atrophy and smoke and time, that maybe is somnolent and in the process of being revived or maybe is just a corpse disturbed by all this unexpected activity.

A few days after he left Toronto, he phoned Valerie. He was standing in a pay booth at the edge of one of the shopping centres. It was only a hundred and sixty miles to Toronto but everything made it seem further. "You could come back for a weekend," Valerie said.

"No, I should stay until things are settled." Not being able to explain that if he was doing nothing else, he at least would do his duty and, if his father would accomodate the timing to the visiting hours, he would be a good son and go every afternoon for as long as necessary to watch him die.

"It must be awful there," Valerie said.

"It's boring." She didn't mention again that she might come to visit him. In order to place the call he had to explain things to the operator, have the bill charged to his Toronto phone number. Now for some reason he began to worry about how much this call was costing. After the initial exchanges neither of them were speaking. Behind their own silence and the buzzing static they could hear other voices, the words indistinguishable, but the rhythms clear, decisive murmurs of love and business.

"I guess I should go soon," Erik said.

"Okay." He could hear footsteps. One of the noises on the line disappeared and he realized it had been music in her apartment. "I don't even have your address there," Valerie said.

"I'll write you," Erik said. "Maybe I should get a postal box number in Kingston." More silence. Erik held the phone to his ear with his shoulder, was using his hands to get out a cigarette. He kept twisting around in the booth, trying to see if Brian and Nancy were finished getting the groceries yet. The booth was hot and airless. He pushed the door open with his foot, letting in the noise of cars wheeling around the parking lot, doors slamming rubber on metal. When the cigarette was lit, he threw the match out the door and closed it again. He couldn't remember if he was committed to marry her or not.

"Are you still there?"

"Oh yes, sorry," Erik said. "What was I saying?"

"Nothing."

"Oh." Her guest had turned over the record. "Well," Erik said, "I just thought I'd call and say hello."

"Okay," Valerie said. "Keep in touch."

"Well. All right. Good-bye." Stepping out of the booth, one hot ear, throwing out his cigarette and lighting another. Two o'clock in the afternoon and his throat was already dry and parched from smoking. The day he phoned Valerie: that was the day Brian had gone away for the morning without him. A week later, suddenly thinking of her, hardly even able to locate the time when he had spoken to her, he wrote her a letter, saying that his father was still hovering, Miranda needed him to be there, it might be some time. It all took less than half the page so he enclosed a key to his apartment and asked her to forward his mail. In due course he received it: a few university circulars and a dentist's bill.

In the mornings he worked in the garden. Then after lunch, they would drive to the hospital to see Richard Thomas. When he was very sick or unconscious, the four of them could all sit in the room at once, being very quiet, waiting. But when he was awake, all four were too much for him and each other. So they would visit him in platoons of two: Brian and Nancy, Erik and Miranda. After a while each of them developed their own small tasks and roles for the hospital. Miranda was mother: she brought him things to read and wear and eat. She talked to the nurses about his body functions. She bought him an electric razor and some spray-on deodorant. When he refused to be connected to this world, but wasn't too sick, she would sit beside him and read to him aloud, items out of the newspaper and a historical romance about the slaughter of the Indians in Huron County.

Brian was Richard's extension at the farm. When he was away from the hospital he did everything himself, shutting off the details of his day from Erik and Miranda, refusing even to talk about it while driving to and from the hospital. But once with Richard, he wanted to consult about everything: each cow's breeding and slaughter, the possibility that a certain calf might have pinkeye, the need to spend twelve dollars on some hardware and fencing, plans for which fields were to be ploughed in the fall. And when enough had been settled to get on to the next day, Brian would fall back on the old standard, the idea of getting the machinery for corn and building a silo. "It's the coming thing," Brian would say over and over, the exact words the milk inspector had used last time, looking reluctantly at Richard Thomas, both of them, wondering if it was worth the bother to farm this land with modern machinery, the fields so small that there would be hardly room for a tractor and combine to get going before it had to get turned around, the whole technology of modern farming designed for big flat fields with at least a few inches of soil uninterrupted by stones and bedrock. "Look at Peter Malone's farm," Brian would say. "Three silos now and he's never looked back. Course he's got more fields than us." And four sons on his farm and two adjoining farms so they could pool the machinery, but that didn't need to be said. Nor did they mention what they all knew, that the easiest way to make money from the farm would be to sell it to the real estate man for cottage lots and a trailer park, put the proceeds in the bank and live off the interest. The real estate man had come back after the first time. Brian had gone to meet him when he was still in the car, told him to go away.

During the hospital discussion Nancy would feed her husband the straight lines, sit with her legs crossed on the bed, stalk about the room in her new city wardrobe, obviously pleased to be spending this summer driving about and in a big cool building instead of being stuck in the trailer and Miranda's kitchen, doing the endless canning and preserving that was the usual summer occupation. When the men were dizzy with their circles and didn't know what to repeat next, Nancy would draw a deep breath and sigh. "Well," she would say, "at least we won't starve."

Erik stayed out of the way, sitting near the window and smoking. Twice a week, in the afternoon, he would stop the doctor in the corridor, try to intimidate him into revealing something. Twice a week the doctor would say that if things worked out Richard would be allowed to go home, mobile but unable to do heavy work, with a life expectancy, well, even a year is a long time in anyone's life and, besides, many people survive heart attacks perfectly well as long as they do something about the causes. The doctor never looked at Erik. He would only stare down at his feet or off to one side as he spoke. Sometimes he would pat Erik on the shoulder as he finished, as if to remind him not to take all this stuff so seriously. After all. And reminded Erik of the importance of getting his father to diet, to stay away from alcohol, tobacco and sex. Miranda was the timekeeper. On her signal Erik would go out to the lounge and tell Brian and Nancy that it was their turn to visit. Then he would sit in the lounge and stare out at the lake, read, talk to the patients.

Since he had begun coming to the hospital all the patients but the man with the small tumours had changed. The man with the tumours still stood at the window in his blue dressing gown, smoking his pipe and talking about his wife and summer cottage. Periodically he went away for weekends but he always came back. He said that he was under observation and suggested that perhaps he was already taking radiation treatment for his cancers. But then he had talked about x-rays in a very unusual way, hinting to Erik that they were extremely dangerous, not to be taken lightly, possibly something to be avoided at all costs, making Erik unclear whether the man's condition had even been diagnosed. After the first time he had met him, the time the man had said he needed a drink, Erik had bought him a pint of whiskey. Now the man always had whiskey in his room and sometimes Erik, if he didn't find him in the lounge, would go to visit him in his room, have a drink with him and look through what seemed to be a limitless supply of picture magazines. *Mr. N. Zeller* was typed on a piece of paper and stuck to the end of the man's bed, but Mr. Zeller never offered any verbal tag for himself, not even giving Erik a chance to confirm his speculation that his Christian name must be Norman. Or perhaps the anonymity was supposed to suggest that the name was more exotic, that in fact the man in the blue dressing gown was perhaps the well-known skipper of the *Nautilus,* obviously having been unexpectedly becalmed in Kingston and fallen on evil days. Nonetheless, Mr. Zeller, Norman Nemo, confided one day to Erik that he was no longer so fond of his wife, that his two blonde and healthy teenage daughters left him with a feeling of faint incestuous revulsion and that for his employer, a man whom he had not seen for many years, he had no feelings at all, not even gratitude. And after saying this, he had put his pipe in his mouth and in the same diffident tone with which he had originally announced to Erik the deplorable condition of his bladder, he had said that Erik was perhaps his only friend. This declared one evening, while he was in bed, wearing his gown and sipping at some cognac.

"Well," Erik said, embarrassed, looking away.

"No offense meant," Mr. Zeller added quickly.

"No, of course." Erik stood up. "I'm sorry, I promised I would make a phone call."

"Yes." Beside Norman Nemo's bed was a white telephone.

"I'll be back in a few minutes." Erik stalked out of the room, down the hall and past the nursing station and elevators to a small lounge where there was a pay telephone. Inserted his dime and dialed Rose Garnett's number. Over the telephone she sounded less removed, girlish. But when he arrived there, he had already lost hope again. She answered the door wearing paint-stained blue jeans and a man's shirt, several sizes too big for her, that had the sleeves ripped off at the elbows. She took him back through the living-room and kitchen to a room that faced into the back garden, with small French doors. The rocm was in a total shambles; recently an elaborately furnished study, it now had all its furniture pushed into its centre and covered by painter's linen. Off to one side was a pile of lumber and a table saw. A bookcase was rising up one wall and along the other some sort of bench was being built. Everything was covered with sawdust. Rose Garnett's eyes were grey in the bare light. The boards were all marked for their cuts, straight lines drawn by a lead pencil; she handed him one end of a board and turned on the saw–a brief sharp scream as it sliced through the wood and then she drew the board closer, for the next cut.

"You can change if you want," Rose Garnett said. "There's some men's clothes in the kitchen cupboard." And finding in the cupboard jeans and two shirts, the hunting jacket that had been in the school house–even the hat and rifle were still there, crammed into a corner, the muzzle of the rifle jammed into an old ruined pair of workboots. He put on the jeans. The husband had been shorter than him, stockier. He took a piece of twine and tied the pants on. The cuffs hung half-way down his socks. The shirt fitted well enough, the sleeves just a bit short so, feeling curious, he put on the hunting jacket and, extracting the rifle, the workboots. The boots were far too big for him, huge, must have been specially made for size fifteen feet. And the rifle. Automatically he had broken it open when he took it out of the boots and a shell had fallen out, .303–no safety catch. He put the shell into the pocket of the hunting jacket and went to the room where Rose Garnett was working. "You wind up in the small of the back," she said, looking at him. "The big feet are to keep you from falling over."

And later, when they were splayed out on her bed, Erik feeling scattered by her, taken apart, she rolled over and touched him gently with her index finger. "Touch," she said. "Touch. Touch." Not so gentle. "Touch. Touch." Moving her hands over his body, pressing, pinching lightly, drawing out pains in his back and stomach so he found himself humming as she touched him, curling up tightly with his knees pressed into his stomach, and then she began to rub her knuckles up and down his spine, circling them in the soft areas of his back, digging them in, making him feel like things were realigning in there somewhere, clouds of electricity moving sluggishly in the centre of his body, and at the same time a total exhaustion that seemed to blanket his nerves, something he couldn't move through to escape her or succumb to enough for sleep. Curled tightly, he locked his arms so that his knees were buried in his elbows; she rocked him back and forth on the bed, back and forth, seasick motion with her knuckles still digging and exploring, the sides of her hands chopping into his lungs and kidneys, the base of his spine. Slapping on the fresh garden sunburn, kneading his arms and shoulders and then back and forth once more, rolling him off the bed and onto the floor. "You're such a lump," she said. "What's wrong with you?"

"I don't know."

"Maybe you'd rather leave."

"No. I gave the car to my mother." And when she turned the lights off and shifted onto her side to sleep, Erik put one hand on her back, lay against her in the dark, unhappy and tense. Woke up in the middle of the night, dreaming he was the perfect man, floating through space in a glass ball.

One day when he went to the hospital, the wheelchair by the fire exit was empty. "They took her to a home," the nurse said. "We can't do anything for people like her. At the home she can have people like herself to talk to. She won't be so lonely."

"She never talked," Erik said. "The most she could do was rattle the arms of her chair."

"Well," the nurse said. She was one of what seemed to be an infinite number of student nurses who were assigned this ward on rotation. She was so much younger than Erik he felt awkward, almost fatherly with her. Near the end the old woman's skin had softened to resemble grey mucus. The nurse's skin was fresh and young, looked like it might glow in the dark. Her teeth still had tiny gaps between them that would grow together. "Well," the nurse said. "She wasn't sick. We couldn't do anything for her."

"She was just old."

"That's right." That was the day his father's fever had begun. They had put the sides of the bed up, like a great aluminum crib, in and out tubes snaking through the bars. Erik could lean over the bars and watch his father, the flesh gone suddenly grey and purposeless, like the old woman's. Or he could watch him on the machines, see him breathing on the dials of the respirator and the oxygen tank. A nurse was in the room at all times, sitting in a chair at the end of the bed, legs crossed, a clipboard resting on her upper thigh. Richard's chest moved up and down and each time his chest collapsed the machine hissed with it. The door to the room was closed now, with a NO ENTRY sign hung from it at eye level: NO ENTRY, lettered in red block capitals on white cardboard. A tube was inserted into the back of Richard's hand, to feed him. And they were ready to cut a hole in his throat to help him breathe more directly if necessary. The doctor said that they were trying to get his fever down, but they weren't worried about the possibility of another stroke. He said they might cut open his chest and insert an electronic gadget beside his heart, one that would tell it when to beat. Miranda seemed to have given up. She didn't like being in the room with Richard any more, so Erik took the longer shifts, safe now because Richard was beyond hearing or speaking. They said he was unconscious, but sometimes he would open his eyes. Flat and diffuse, the energy drained away by fever and pills, they presented no colour at all, tiny pupils bathed in a milky fluid. When he left them open for longer than a few seconds, the fluid would brim over the sockets, run like tears down his cheeks. He wasn't unconscious at all. Even if he remembered nothing at all afterwards, the doctor said they never did, as if he had gone through whole zoofulls of sick and dying animals and had all the possibilities charted out according to the best and most infallible method of modern science—even if he remembered nothing at all afterwards it didn't mean he wasn't conscious. The eyes would swivel towards him, waiting. And when Erik's eyes were lined up with them the messages would be sent. It was impossible that Richard would want to live this way very long. Erik could stand above the bed, looking down at the eyes, waiting for them to close and rest, willing the nurse to go away, wondering exactly when Richard would want him to do it, how. The possibility had occured to him once before, but then he had thought that it would simply be a matter of supplying the appropriate pills, after due consultation. But now pills would be impossible to ingest. He would have to grind them up, put the powder in the bottle that was suspended above Richard's head. Once he put his hand on Richard's. It was cold, white and cold, the muscles like liquid on the bone. He slid his fingers into the palm of the hand and it closed on them, like a baby's. Richard's hand so cold and Erik felt hot, flushed, waves of heat pounding out from the centre of his body, turned back at the edges, no way to escape, each reflected wave helping to wall in the next. He was swaying on his feet. The room was moving with his stomach, expanding and contracting, threatening to slip around. He looked over at the nurse. She had noticed nothing, was sitting half-asleep, her chin slumped down against her chest. Looked back at Richard and saw his eyes wide open, frantically signalling him, his mouth twitching. And then, with Erik locked into his vision, Richard's face relaxed, suddenly smooth and confident like the face of the hypnotist who has finally got his subject in the groove, all the lines and pockets in the skin filled with sweat and glistening but still in some way content, Erik's fingers held tight in his palm, eyes wide open and pupils dilated, beaming the coded signals direct. And Erik could feel the tension beginning to drain away from him, literally drain, down his legs and through the soles of his feet, which now seemed infinitely big, like Rose's husband's boots, so big it would be impossible to fall over, each cell grounded in Richard's universe, the hospital growing like some huge mutant flower out of the earth. Richard's eyes opening even wider, his mouth suggesting movements, words, asking the question and Erik, mesmerised, nodding his head up and down, yes—an image of himself as a baby lying in a crib and Richard standing above him, the same way, looking down, not just watching but willing the patterns right into him, picking the baby up and holding him to his chest, forcing his own heartbeat into him—all right, Erik thought, Richard's hand crushing his fingers, all right, and now for the pitch, he thought, breaking it.

But still he stood there, held him, other hand clenched around the aluminum rail, sweating, he slid his hand down the rail and it was shining and beaded where his palm had passed. He could still see Richard's eyes but his own were closed, closed tight, he was seeing everything through the lids of his eyes: the moist shiny rail that reflected nothing, the nurse who now stood beside him, waiting for him to notice her, Richard who now lay unmoving. Maybe she wanted to tell him that his father was dead. He opened his eyes. The nurse was sitting at the end of the bed, filing her nails. The machines were working: his father was still alive. Erik slid his fingers free and went out of the room, walking down the hall to get Brian and Nancy. His shirt was plastered to his back in a wide stripe.

From the lounge he could see the lake. But from the lake it was impossible to pick the lounge out from the midst of all the buildings, or even distinguish one building from another, all of them boxes of windows, shallow and glaring in the sun. The shoreline along the lake had been cultivated, a long grassed boulevard with trees and benches ran beside it. The lake itself was separated from the boulevard by a short cement wall and a rocky beach. Some of the rocks were huge, projected out into the water like glacial tanks. Erik found a place where he could sit, cupped by a warm hollow in a rock, his feet in the water, Richard's imprint still on him.

"Do you find the present so disgusting?" Valerie had asked him, as if he must be fixed on some other time, some immense single conglomerate complaint from his past that was supposed to be his excuse, and some equally compelling fantasy of the future in which everything would finally come right

　　　　　　Teeter Totter sliding way out onto the end, coming down hard and then pushing with his feet, springing, he and Brian trying to bounce each other off the wooden board Richard had laid across a sawhorse for them.

"Your parents must have been terrible to you. Don't you

remember anything?" Valerie had been to see a psychiatrist twice a week for three years. Before she went, she had gotten pregnant, had had an abortion. Then a month after the abortion she woke up in the middle of the night and swallowed all of the pills in the house. Now she didn't take any pills except for birth control pills. She wasn't afraid to look in the mirror. She liked her job. She only saw her psychiatrist occasionally and wouldn't talk to Erik about it. "Things come up," she said. She kept a black bound book beside her bed and recorded her dreams, drawing pictures in harsh magic-marker colours. He wondered if his leaving like this would make her start seeing him again. Perhaps the man in the apartment had been her psychiatrist, turning over the record while Erik was on the telephone. He had always suspected her of carrying his picture in her wallet. He had worn his farm jeans to the hospital and the lake water had soaked the cuffs, was working its way up towards his knees. He kicked his feet in the water, trying to watch the exact moment that his heels made contact, kicked harder, enjoying the twinges of the sharp stones against his skin, trying to anticipate the exact moment of impact, trying to find the exact border between sensation and pain. He looked back towards the hospital. The reflections on the windows had deepened from white-yellow to yellow-orange. He could see Miranda coming across from the hospital towards him, walking slowly on the grassed area that separated the hospital from the road, stopping and carefully checking the traffic, both ways, as if by instruction, then crossing the road quickly. She looked up and down the lakefront for him, found him. He waved at her, saw by the way she lifted her arm that she was tired but not devastated, nothing catastrophic, not coming to tell him that Richard was dead. Two or three days, maybe a week. Someone would have to distract the nurse while he put the powder into the bottle. Miranda was even smiling as she approached him, holding out her palms to feel the wind coming off the lake.

Standing in front of Rose's mirror they were colour-coordinated: Rose with her twin bikini stripes and Erik divided neatly in half, white from the waist down to his ankles. At night, the gap between the tanned skin and the white seemed absolutely irrevocable but the next day, in the bright light, they were not so far apart, the white beginning to flush pink and the brown transparent in the sun. They had gone down to Richard's beach to drink and swim. August, and there were still black flies in the maple bush, black flies and mosquitoes, and in the swampy places the bugs were even worse. "You can't run," Erik said. "If you start to sweat they're twice as bad." He couldn't remember the bugs being like this, or maybe he had known better than to go into the bush in the summer. The paths back to the lake were all used and kept clear by the cows; humans had to walk carefully, keeping their eyes to the ground. Rose carried a faded straw purse, the ends of two bottles of wine sticking out its open top. When they got to the beach, Erik found a shady spot and pushed one of the bottles into the sand, underwater, twisting it down in the white sand until only its neck showed. It had been almost eight years since that first argument with Richard, the night he had driven home from the school house in the snow. "You don't get much of a suntan in the city," Erik said. Sometimes in the summer he would lie out on a balcony or swim in a chlorinated pool. Twice he had taken a cottage with friends for Labour Day weekend. Now he was in the water, swimming slowly, his stroke awkward and unpractised, shoulders rolling from side to side, his timing off, so that when his head surfaced he was still breathing out, his lungs quickly tiring from the confusion. Rose was swimming lazily on her back, raising her arms high into the air, her breasts pointing white and absurd out of the water as she swam. When she got to the island, she simply stopped, stayed on her back, beached in the shallow water at the shore. Past the island, half a mile across the lake, was a rocky point where he and Brian used to swim in the summers, cord for bowstring wrapped around their waists and a small tin cannister full of matches. When he could touch the bottom with his toes, he began to walk in towards the island, still moving his arms in the water, the way he had cheated when he had first learned to swim. The air now felt cold, his genitals exposed and vulnerable. He knelt beside Rose, then lay down full length next to her in the water. He kissed her eyes, slid his hand from her neck to her belly, underwater.

She had become an acrobat. Every position she assumed was poised and accomplished. Now the back of her head was cradled in the sand and the water was breathing up and down her, licks across her neck. Her eyes were closed, the lids still streaked with make-up, the lashes rising curled and vulnerable. He moved his hand across her stomach, her hips. While he caressed her, he watched her face. Her face stayed still. The only change was when he shifted his weight, his shadow lurching across it, back and forth. The vein at the corner of one eye, beneath the top layer of the skin, began to vibrate quickly, out of control. She seemed oblivious to it, moved her legs so her knees broke the surface of the water. And then, drawing her knees up further, sat straight up. All afternoon they had been able to hear boats from across the lake, moving indistinct in the glare of the sun, but the sound sharp and definite, like a chainsaw. Now one of the boats was coming closer, its windshield a huge reflector in the sun, ribbons of white water peeling back from the prow. "You didn't tell me about this," Rose said. They could see the driver of the boat now, a white-haired man wearing sunglasses, standing up in the boat, hanging on to the wheel and saluting Erik and Rose.

"Go away," Erik shouted, not even able to hear himself over the roar of the motor, ridiculous to feel caught, naked on your own land. Rose was still lying in the water but Erik was getting up, waving them away. The driver was pointing to the channel, wanting to know if it was deep enough to go through. And then began to turn the boat, slipping it over on its side as it curved nearer to the island, a woman now visible, a woman who might have been his wife, her hair tied down by a silk handkerchief, steadying herself with her elbows on the gunwhale, fat arms shaking with the vibrations of the boat, binoculars held to her eyes, centering in on Erik's crotch, moving back and forth from Erik to Rose, the woman rotating as the boat turned, not missing anything, finally lined up with the back of the boat, staring down the trough of the wake. "Jesus," Erik said, as the noise of the motor receded, "they're getting worse every year." They could still see the boat, its motor idling now, turning in slow tight circles in the centre of the lake. And could see the two passengers moving, the man holding up a can of beer, walking away from the wheel. And the woman taking the wheel, turning the boat towards the island again, driving in slower now, the prow staying down in the water, no ribbons this time but the man now was leaning over the side of the boat, transformed into a Cyclops with a giant shining eye: the boat moved closer and they could see what the man had, a movie camera with a telescopic lens. His lips were drawn back with concentration, a thin curve of white teeth revealed; with one arm the man was trying to hold the camera steady, with the other, elbow sticking out horizontal to his head, he was pressing the button, the finger jabbing straight into the camera. The tip of his tongue protruded from his teeth as if they must be kept apart at all times or else, with their spring hinges, they would snap shut forever. The first time the boat had come in on them the engine had made a loud high whining sound. Now it was going slowly, a low hollow sound that was beginning to develop small breaks in it, as if a cylinder was missing, sputtering noises and coughing. The man still held the camera but was shouting instructions to the woman. She looked flustered, her head turning back and forth from Erik and Rose to the man, the boat now coming right into the narrow channel between the island and the shore. The motor coughed some more and went out entirely. The man was holding the camera to his eye, and now they could hear the waves from the boat slapping up against the beaches. The were sitting deeper in the water, to their bellies. Rose had her hands folded across her breasts, was looking curiously at the boat which was still drifting straight towards them.

"Shit," the man said, furiously adjusting the lens to keep Erik and Rose in focus, "will you start the boat will you?" Now the boat was only a few yards away from them. Erik had stood up and was walking towards it, to push it away before it grounded itself.

"*Harry*," the woman screamed. "We're going to *crash*." She pointed her finger at Erik walking towards them and then turned away. He could see her hair now, sticking out of her kerchief in tight blonde curls. Her face was covered with some sort of white cream for the sun. Erik was standing chest-deep in the water. The boat came in slowly and he caught its prow with his hands, fielding it like a huge impotent baseball. The man finally put down his camera. He was wearing a red-and-white-striped beanie and horn-rimmed glasses. Coming out from the temple pieces of his glasses were two small wires that dangled near his ears.

"Ran out of gas," the man shouted at Erik, gesticulating at the motor and a gas can beside it. "Don't go without gas," he shouted.

"*Harry,*" the woman shouted, "put in your plugs." The man moved towards the rear of the boat, began fiddling with the gas tank. The woman looked at Erik and shrugged. Her shoulders and neck were fat and powerful, like a bulldog's. She wore bright red lipstick and now was smoking a cigarette. The man had set up a funnel and was pouring the gas from the can to the tank.

"You shouldn't smoke when he's doing that," Erik said. He was still holding the boat.

"Ain't no use," the woman shouted, waving the cigarette, "Harry can't hear a thing with his plugs out." Rose was in the water, swimming swiftly on her side. She saw Erik looking at her and waved at him, her hand joggling happily in the air, the same way the man had waved when he first saw them. Erik reached over the side of the boat, took the cigarette out of the woman's hand and threw it in the water.

"The gas," Erik shouted, "you're going to explode the gas."

"*Harry.*"

Erik pushed the boat so it swung in an arc, pointing back towards the marina on the other side of the lake. Harry was chewing gum, trying to hold the gas can steady. The gas was slopping all over the place, in the hole, over the sides of the motor, down into the water where it spread in a thin blue film. "Smells terrible," the man shouted. He was wearing a short-sleeved shirt covered with palm trees and grass-skirted women. Rose had reached the shore and was sitting on the beach, a towel around her shoulders, drinking one of the bottles of wine. "She hates it when we run out of gas," the man shouted. Even while he worked the gum, he kept his tongue in sight. Erik was now surrounded by gas. When he lifted his arms out of the water he could see where it had ringed the flesh, tiny drops clinging to him, matting the hair and forming big oily bubbles on his skin. The man had finished. He screwed the tops back onto the can and the tank. "Thanks," he shouted. "See you again."

"*Hurry up, Harry.*" The man worked his way to the front of the boat, bermuda shorts and wide knotted calf muscles. Erik pushed the boat away, thinking of Norman Nemo and the submarine that took its revenge with the propeller, piercing through the hulls of wooden sailing ships in one last pointless gesture. There was a whirring sound, the motor caught, started, a deafening roar and the boat was off, the wash pushing Erik back in the water, swamping him in gas and bubbles. When he came up, his ears were splitting with the sound of the motor, the boat was already out of the channel, roaring towards the centre of the lake. The woman had the binoculars out again and the man had one arm extended high into the air, two fingers stretched apart in a V-peace sign.

The wine tasted flat and sour, seemed to belong to the world of gasoline and oil. He took mouthfuls of it, washed it around his teeth and tongue, spat it out in long pink arcs. The smell of the boat still lingered in the channel, a half-imagined grey haze of motor fumes hung over the water, folded in winding spirals, like the debris from an instant sunset kit. Rose had covered herself with suntan lotion and was lying face-down on a towel. Erik sat beside her, playing with his bottle of wine, smoking a cigarette. "If only my mother could see us," he said.

"She's a nice lady," Rose said. She pronounced this in a detached sleepy way, as if she had some secret knowledge of Miranda.

"Well, of course." He wondered what they talked about. Rose claimed that all she did was to look in people's teacups and tell stories. When she read Erik's leaves, she had told him that he would fall in love with a slim dark-haired woman. Valerie was slim with dark hair. Rose's hair wasn't dark yet, but it was getting there. He had been to see her a few times but it was as if they were old friends, had gotten to know each other well in the past and could now coast on whatever closeness had been achieved. Their intimacy seemed to take place in pantomine. Often he would catch her looking at him intently, as if he was on stage, about to perform his promised trick that was, in fact, so overdue that she knew he had forgotten what it was and that if she didn't remind him, he would just fade away in an inarticulate mumble. Her skin was smooth and slippery with the lotion. He slid his hand down her back, over her buttocks and legs. Whatever it was that had first made her seem so exotic had spread to her bones and muscles: now it was not only the way she held herself and dressed, but in every movement she made, like a fencer, parrying the world with swift invisible strokes, never straying from the tape. Where her spine had swung wildly askew it was now only slightly arched, flared in from her waist the way her hips flared out, fencer's costume, quick and sharp, no fat or extra targets. When he asked her about the changes she just laughed, said that he had never appreciated her, now the complete jungle cat, sensuous and without even the most momentary of debts. At the school house she had frightened him with her child who refused to speak, her sudden violence and her contempt for her husband. But all those things had been incidental, apart from her, like clothes. Now she had incorporated everything into her body and he could be frightened of her as she was, lying half-asleep and naked on the beach, bits of sand gradually finding their way to her oiled skin. He flicked away the grains of sand with his fingernail, crushed bugs on her when they landed, drank more of the wine, cold but still sour. The wine and the day sat uncomfortable in his stomach, so much ballast. He caressed her, but she didn't stir. He took his hand away and swallowed another mouthful of wine. Through his eyes the day looked blue and sparkling cool, the water riding to the shore in tiny sparkling wavelets, the sky clear except for a few high white clouds, small dense clouds that seemed miles away. He went into the lake trying to make it feel like it looked, but the water seemed cold, he couldn't get used to it. Somewhere he could still hear the echo of the motorboat. He decided he would just have to stay in longer, swam out to the island and back, swimming slowly, trying to put together the rhythm of his arms and lungs. When he got back to the beach, Rose was sitting up, dressed, waiting for him. He dried himself and put on his clothes. She waited for him, silently, inspecting some pebbles she had collected.

"You seem so removed," he finally said.

"That's what you want, isn't it?"

"I don't know."

"Maybe you'd better go back to your nice girl in Toronto. She can hold your hand and tell you that everything's all right."

"I'm not going to beg you," Erik said.

"Go ahead. Do something. Do *anything.*" Then she had spun away from him, laughing, not even holding herself where he had hit her. "I thought you were dead." She skipped towards him, one quick motion, flicking her hand out to Erik's face, dancing about like a boxer. "Come on," she said, "do it again."

"I'm sorry," Erik said.

"Don't be sorry."

"Well. You can't just go around hitting women."

"You can do anything. *Anything.* Did they stuff a set of rules in your ear when you were born?" She stopped in front of him, reached her hand into his trousers and pulled out his shirt. "Look," she said, "a trick I learned in the Navy." And taking one corner of the shirt in each hand, pulled it open with a snap, the buttons popping out serially, from bottom to top, dropping in a close pile on the sand.

"All right," Erik said. He felt numb and spoiled. He tucked his shirt back in, thinking that now he would be wide open to the bugs. It would be worse now too, because it was later in the day, darker. He wondered what was happening with Richard, whether the day had gone well. "This thing with my father is getting me down," Erik said. "I'll feel better when it's over."

"Over?"

"When he's home."

"Maybe he's going to die."

"I guess so."

"Did you ever see anyone die?"

"No."

"I saw my mother die," Rose said. "We were in a car accident. That's how I hurt my back."

"It must have been awful."

"Yes."

"I thought Richard had died once, when I was standing there."

"What did it feel like?"

"I don't know. Sad."

"What does it feel like when we have sex?"

"Nice. I like it." He looked at her as he said it, suddenly secretive, as if afraid the child for whom these rituals of death and sex were performed might have been revealed behind the adult shell.

"But it doesn't make you shout for joy?"

"Well. You can't start shouting when you're making love. It might scare you."

"You just get in there and pray for stormy weather. God, my husband was like that too. Scared all the time. You don't even feel it, do you?"

"What?" They were still standing near the lake, the basket and towels piled on the ground, waiting to be taken home. She was always this way, pushing, worse than the bugs. But the fear was there, part of his sensations, if not fear, at least discomfort, living somewhere in his bones where he couldn't get at it. Erik lit a cigarette. Maybe it had been Valerie in the train station, casually offering her life, like that, as if it was nothing. "Well," Erik said. "We better get going." He bent down and picked up the towels, wrapping them around the back of his neck, already thinking he could fold them into the front of his shirt when the mosquitoes got after him.

"So," Mr. Zeller said. Norman Nemo. The month in the hospital had melted him down, turning his greying hair completely white, taking twenty pounds away so that his muscular outdoors face had become hawk-like, his nose thin and curved now, bright red patches on his cheeks. "So," Mr. Zeller said. "The father is dying and the young son pines away, afraid to take what is his." They were in the lounge, Norman Zeller pacing back and forth, one hand inserted in his blue dressing gown to calm his bladder, the other waving the perpetual pipe. "Did I ever tell you about my career on the stage? Never mind." The lounge was dark, but with the light from the hall they could see each other, their reflections in the plate glass windows that faced out onto the lake. "Yes, so. We move into the third act. The father is afraid to die and the son is afraid to live." Norman Zeller gesticulated with his free hand as he talked. His voice had a surprising resonance. As if, Erik thought, it might even be true that he used to be a radio announcer, working New York music halls to finance his voyages. "Yes," Nemo said. "The whole family lives with this terrible curse of the future. All tremble at the sight of the iron fist of fate. Meanwhile I enter. I am Polonius, uncle of the bride. This robe is my curtain. And when I die the curtain falls."

"Good God," Erik said. "What about the doctor?"

"He is irrelevant," Nemo said. "A mere agent of the x-ray conspiracy, he symbolizes the false hope of the new world. For what can this doctor, this so-called medical madman do? He can put you in front of his machine, see through the very world of appearances to the real world. And what is his real world? A dried-up old skeleton. A few tumours. In the case of his religious patients it may include a St. Christopher's medal. The doctor marries Ophelia after she is dead." The lounge was filled with shiny leather furniture, couches and armchairs strung around the walls. Mr. Zeller preferred to pace as he talked. He had recently begun to favour a cane, a slim carved walking stick with a silver tip. He said it came from the coast of Africa, that it had been fashioned by a certain tribe of cannibalistic pygmies.

"Everyone knows that pygmies don't eat people," Erik had said.

"No one knows anything," Norman Nemo had pronounced. It was immediately elevated to his favourite line. He picked his walking stick off a chair and pointed it at the blank window. "No one knows anything," he said, not proudly but with a bad Shakespearean inflection, taking his own unfortunate condition as his best example. "To tell the truth, my wife won't let my children visit me any more. She says it's bad for them to see someone dying. She wants them to remember me as I was, in colour photographs." His wife only came to visit him in the mornings, when there were no other visitors, because she didn't want to be recognized. "Yes," Nemo said, "the stage is set. Man is only mortal. You are faced with the ultimate choice. On the horns of the final dilemma."

"To be or not to be," Erik said.

"To be or not to be *what*?"

"That is the question."

"Wrong character," Nemo said. "Your problem is that you're not allowed to kill yourself until you're alive."

"And how do you get to be alive?"

"*That* is the question."

"And the answer?"

"Well," Nemo said. "Who knows?" He walked back and forth across his tile parapets. "You know," Nemo said, "I like you. Here you are almost thirty years old; your father is dying, your women abuse you, your brother would like to kill you, you have no money and you hate your job before the first day of work. An ordinary man would be swamped by such a tide of bad luck. He would be rushing about, attempting to save something, patch up his life in any way he could. But you stay calm. These things happen but you are barely aware of them. The events are like undelivered mail. While your house burns down you are sitting in the basement, pricking yourself to see if you can bleed."

"All right," Erik said. "That's enough."

"I don't mean to insult you."

"Of course not." He tilted his watch towards the light: ten o'clock. "I'll see you tomorrow," Erik said. He walked down the hall to his father's room. The sign had been taken off the door and now it was left open at night, like the doors of the other patients. Miranda was still sitting in the dark room, beside Richard's bed. "It's time to go," Erik said. They stood in the hall before leaving. Mr. Zeller was sitting in the lounge, his legs crossed, holding his cane up in front of his nose. He signalled to Miranda and she waved back.

"He's a nice man," Miranda said.

"Yes," Erik said. "But he has a sharp tongue." Now that Richard was better they didn't all have to go to the hospital every day. Tonight they had the truck. It looked out of place in front of the hospital, old and unwieldy, sandwiched between two new cars, towering above them, covered with mud and manure. Erik had to climb in the passenger's side. The door on the driver's side didn't work any more, was wired shut, a temporary solution waiting for that mythical day when all these little things would be cleaned up. The odometer said only fifty-three thousand miles but the truck looked like it had lost a war. The dashboard was dusty and dented in over the glove compartment, which had then jammed shut so Brian had had to remove the door with a crowbar. The ashtray wouldn't close properly, was overflowing with cigarette butts and kleenex. Something had gone wrong with the original radio and it had been replaced by another, bigger model, one too large to fit into the radio hole so it was strapped under the dash with frayed binder twine and a big piece of old leather that had perhaps been stolen from the harness of a dead donkey. The windshield was pitted and cracked. Both outside mirrors had been sacrificed in forgotten battles. One front fender had grazed a gatepost and folded it in; so its headlamp was twisted off course, shone a firm beam across the front of the truck, illuminating the ditch on the passenger side as they went up the highway, wavering back and forth on the snow tires that should have been changed five months ago. For the steering wheel, Brian had bought a nylon fur cover and a knob with a tough two-breasted lady who had a whip wrapped round her waist.

"You should get married," Miranda said. "A person your age needs a wife."

TEN

The wind had started in the afternoon, circling in the courtyard, turning the blue sky grey and hazy. By evening it was stronger, a constant presence against the sides of the buildings, the closed-in court making it resonate in high whistling sounds. The yard trapped the wind; it had nowhere to go but round and round, circling like a tiny typhoon, filling the air of the yard with bits of dust and soot, slamming the empty cigarette packages and wadded-up tinfoil off the wall in an endless weather squash game. Sometimes there would be sharper sounds, small stones clicking against the windows. After supper, before they left, Erik and Miranda walked with him down to the lounge. August. The end of August and the sun was setting earlier. So it was almost dark now, grey-black at the top of the sky, red and uncertain around the rim. Beyond the lamps that lined the lakeshore road they could see the lake. The sound of the wind against the windows was not so loud here, in the open, and they could hear the roaring of the waves rolling into the shore. Mr. Zeller was in the lobby, blue and formal in his dressing gown, holding his pipe to his mouth and looking reflectively out at the lake, his shoulders slightly hunched, into the wind. He nodded at the Thomas family as they came in, gestured out towards the lake with the stem of his pipe. "Be rough out there tonight," he said.

"Yes," Richard said. "Wouldn't want to be spending the night on a boat." Or at the farmhouse, where wind always made him nervous, working the metal roofing in and out, squeaking against the stainless steel nails, shaking the windows in their frames. The rain was just beginning, each drop seconds apart, each drop leaving a long bubble streak as it was driven across the plate glass surface.

"It'll be a while yet," Norman Zeller said. Then, after turning back to the window for one more look, he pulled his gown tightly around him, bowed his head in Richard's direction, and made his way down the hall towards his room. He was much thinner now, his legs stick-like, far apart from each other where they emerged from the bottom of his gown, moving slowly, his slippers flopping up against his heels.

"Doesn't look too good tonight," Richard Thomas said.

"No," Miranda said, and then, with the easy false optimism of the relative of the patient who has been cured: "Well, he looked worse last night." Three days now and they would let Richard Thomas go home. He had already lost twenty pounds but, as he observed to Miranda when they weighed him, he didn't seem to miss it. Now his stomach was small enough to be contained within the edges of his vision. He would have to stay on his diet, lose twice as many pounds again. But everything had been decided. He would go home and he would be retired. In the mornings he would stay in bed late. Miranda would bring him his small breakfast and he would read. Then, in the summer, he could sit outside for a while. It would be permitted for him to walk, on the drive and on the road. Maybe next year they would let him chance the fields and the bush too, when he was strong enough to right himself if he lost his balance. They talked about getting a new dog, a puppy; Erik would pick one out for him at the Humane Society the day after he came home. If they ran out of money they could maybe sell some of the waterfront. But for now there was the disability pension, and the farm would still bring in something. After all. The rain had stopped temporarily; now the streaks were drying on the glass, long cloudy trails. All the cars had their lights on, were moving slowly back and forth along the lake. Through the wind Richard thought he could hear something like a foghorn.

"It's going to be bad tonight," he said, "driving. Maybe you should stay in town."

"Don't worry," Erik said. He was dark-tanned now, a thin line of sunburn running down the centre of his nose, like a child. But even with his tan and calloused hands he still seemed city to Richard, the way he avoided things with his body, wore his clothes as decoration, was always glancing nervously around himself, as if there was something about to bite. Simon Thomas would've drowned him, Richard thought. Would have drowned everyone if he could have gotten away with it. Simon Thomas would have made him fight it out with Brian, outside, no weapons, the way he had once tried to make him and Steven fight, Steven slow-moving and drunk, could have killed the two of them by sitting on them, didn't even get angry, just tuned Simon out, said he didn't want the farm and went upstairs to nurse his mother's memory. Sitting placidly in the dark as he did every night, crying but not desperate, just quiet and placid sitting in the chair he had taken from his mother's room and placed in his own, sitting until everyone else went to sleep and then getting into bed for the night.

"He's sick is what's wrong with him," Simon said once, "and he'll never get better. To see his own brother, like a tomcat, attack his father with a knife and almost murder him in cold blood, without provocation, as if God could forgive a man who attacked his own father who had conceived him and fed him and washed the shit from him when he didn't know enough to keep himself clean. What a man has to go through to keep order in his own family." Then grinning conspiratorially at Richard, slapping his shoulder and spitting all in one continuous motion. They had buried Leah Thomas in the cemetery but Simon never went back to see her grave, not once, not until the early spring day they took his pine-boxed body and stuck it in the ground beside her, lowered it with ropes while the housekeeper knelt and wailed and the minister earned his fee.

"Won't blow through these windows anyway," Miranda said, rapping the thick plate glass with her knuckles, moved away, startled when, as if called to life by her action, a sudden gust of wind rattled the glass in its metal frame.

"Well," Richard said. "You'd better get started." He was standing straighter these days, taller than Miranda again, walking more firmly, no longer looking just fat but also powerful, like he used to, his huge shoulders bulging out of the housecoat, anything he picked up transfomed into a delicate and fragile object inside those hands with their extraordinary wide palms and muscular sausage fingers. He could fix things, motors and machines, even clocks. Once Miranda had given him her broken watch and he had taken it apart, using a tiny jeweller's screwdriver he had found; but when he tried to pick up and manipulate the small pieces he had released, it was impossible, he could hardly feel the small brass workings on his fingers, couldn't turn or manipulate anything without using a pair of pliers to do it so finally, feeling useless and awkward, clearly having stumbled into a world where he was too gross to function, he had swept the pieces off the table with the side of his hand, off the edge of the table into a small cardboard box and taken it into the Kingston jeweller's where the man had long thin hands, wore wire-rimmed glasses and listened to classical music on the radio. Looked dispassionately at the remains and told Richard that he had ruined the watch and would have to buy another.

Richard stayed in the lounge while Erik and Miranda went down the hall. They both walked the same, loose-jointed and shuffling. But Miranda, crippled by her high-heeled shoes which were old and too small for her, walked with the dignity of a stoic, staying straight and erect, her head at Erik's shoulder. Erik's walk was more casual, dubious. At times it appeared that his knees or elbows would decide to go on their own private journeys. When he turned at the nursing station, to wave good-bye to Richard, he was so surprised by his own motion that he almost lost his balance and Miranda had to grab onto his arm. This would be the first rain for almost two weeks. It had calmed temporarily; the cars were moving more quickly along the lakeshore road. But the sky was ominous, grey-black and the wind still snapping at the building, waiting. It was the kind of weather that the cows wouldn't like. They would try to get into the barn. Or stand, head to head, in a circle in the cedar grove. Oats and hay from uncut fields would be flattened in this wind, pushed to the ground in all directions, impossible to harvest.

The lake was barely visible beyond the streetlamps and the headlights. There was something about this storm that made him uncomfortable, had kept him on edge all the afternoon and evening, constantly aware of the wind and looking out at the sky. Mark Frank had lost a barn once, twenty years ago, when the lightning had somehow travelled up a cable and set the hay on fire. That was late one fall, when it was already cold. The next summer the lightning rod salesman had come around, telling everyone, as if it was news, that one of their neighbours had had his barn burnt down. "You don't have to lose your barn to fire," the salesman said. "And you know, when the barn goes, you usually lose the animals too. Some animals will come from outside the barn just to get themselves trapped in the flames. Person wouldn't want to see that." What he had were little white glass balls, filled with copper, and with a copper finger sticking up into the sky. Soon there appeared, on top of every house and every barn in the township, little copper fingers, each mounted in its own white fist, three to a roof. They were connected to each other by metal cable and then a length of cable was secured to the ground, driven in with a five-foot-long copper stake. The salesman installed the whole apparatus himself, with the help, of course, of whoever was around, all the while congratulating the farmer on this wise investment, telling him how all the other houses looked so good with *their* lightning rods, but, well, not as good as *this* one. "It's something you owe to your family," the salesman would say, talking the same way as the insurance man who came around every time someone died. And when he was finished, they stood outside the house, walked around it, looked over at the barnyard, twelve white fists in all, each with its own wavy copper finger aimed straight at heaven. "There's absolutely no doubt," the salesman said, "absolutely no doubt at all that Mark Frank lost his barn absolutely needlessly. No it was not an act of God that he lost that barn, but a failure to apply the exact principles of science to his life." But when Miranda asked him if he could do something about the stove, because she didn't know if it was safe to stand near it during a storm, the salesman just tapped his fingers together, laughed, turned to Richard and shrugged his shoulders. "You don't have to worry about your stove," he said finally, "because it isn't attached to the *ground.*" Whereas, for example, Mark Frank's barn was entirely attached to the ground: a scattering of roofing nails and a rectangle of foundation stones.

The poet had died praying. This was Simon's favourite story, the final fantastic justice of the Reverend William C. Thomas, Englishman and poet, down on his knees at the grave of Elizabeth Thomas, wife of Richard Thomas and mother of Simon Thomas himself, the poet down on his knees on a summer's day when there were daisies and buttercups in the grass that grew on and between the graves, a warm yellow summer day early in July when there could be no danger from anything. In his last years the poet had grown disreputable. No longer attractive to the local women he had been forced to venture further and further for solace, always taking with him his motherless son, sometimes gone for weeks at a time. If he kept diaries for those last years, they had all been lost. "They say he even forgot how to talk," Simon Thomas exclaimed, slapping his knee, making it clear that he was the true keeper of the legend of this eccentric family member. But Herman White the lawyer had said the same thing, claimed he used to meet the poet occasionally in town, where he would wander about, going from house to house, asking for food in exchange for a brief visit with Eternity in the form of His Own Words. His son was always with him then, Frederick, a large quiet boy with a head so big it was out of proportion, shaped like a water-filled egg, quiet, never spoke at all until the poet got him going. Then, in the town, standing on someone's front steps or in their kitchen, the poet would start singing, stamping his foot and clapping his hands as he sung some bible marching hymn, emphasizing the vowels in the gutteral voice he had, English vowels heightened by some vague Scots inflection. And while the poet sang, softly at first, he would look at the boy, smiling and encouraging him as if he was a baby. And finally the boy would give some sort of smile back, the open infantile smile that everyone noticed, that the poet called God's Grace but the townspeople saw as proof of his innocence, though none was needed, and the boy Frederick Thomas would start to sing along, his mouth open all the time so he wasn't actually singing the words but only reproducing some aspect of their sound at a remove known only to himself. They said he had a high pure voice, no edge on it at all, open round, the kind of voice a baby would sing with if it wanted to. When they found the poet, dead on his knees, the boy was sitting beside him, undisturbed, singing in his way, shapeless tunes that were easily absorbed in the summer grass and clover.

"A man dies praying and it makes you wonder," Simon said, settled with his old man's stiffness into his wicker chair, Miranda's cooking tucked safely in his stomach which now, in his closing years, was beginning to bulge, sitting beneath his summer waistcoat like a ripening watermelon. He carried his knife with him all the time, to the end, always cleaning his nails or his pipe with it, holding it in his hand and looking guilelessly across the table at Richard, his eyes old and watery blue. Once the poet had his son singing, he himself would change tactics, following Frederick's example, grunting rhythmically so that his throat, stomach, hands and feet all became a percussive accompaniment to Frederick's angelic raptures. For these performances the poet would dress in his original red smoking jacket that he had brought from England—by now soiled and covered with patches which were themselves torn and mended again—a homespun shirt, and a few days growth of grey and dirty beard. "Drunk with God," Simon would say. But when Elizabeth Thomas died and was buried, the poet broke down at the funeral, threw himself in the open coffin and had to be pried away by the mourners. At that time nothing further was said. But the poet was punished when he died. They buried him away from the Thomas family plot, finally rid of him, off in a corner of the cemetery that was mostly weeds and rocks.

William C. Thomas
Father of Frederick Thomas

And when in his turn Frederick died, Simon wasn't going to pay to have his body transported from the asylum, said they could bury him right there. But finally he relented and had the coffin brought up in the train. It was just like after the war, when they used to bring the bodies from the hospital to the cemetery, the train tracks going right to the back edge. The whole town turned out to see it come, not so much for Frederick Thomas, whom few of them remembered, but because it was such an occasion to have the train at the cemetery again.

"He must have been really crazy," was all that they could say about Frederick Thomas, recalling stories their parents had told them about the poet and Elizabeth Thomas, the rumour that they had had a son, a half-brother to Simon, and that Simon visited him every week at the insane asylum in Brockville. "He must have been really crazy," they would say, accompanying the words with an underground giggle, half-laughing at the idea of someone being unable to keep up the necessary pretences, half-attracted to the possibility of letting oneself collapse into the landscape; and then trying to imagine how crazy it would be necessary to be, the exact details, the exact day-to-day, moment-to-moment details of being crazy enough so that they would have to be taken away—Frederick Thomas, solely distinguished by being the only person in the area who had ever achieved sufficient craziness to have been put in a special place. After Frederick Thomas was brought home in the train (the train making its special stop at the back of the cemetery so they could slide his body in its unvarnished pine casket out of the box car), they stood around the grave and gossiped about him, no one listening to the minister as he rattled through the abbreviated sermon, no one questioning the justice of the burial off to one side, his dead geography to be the same as his live geography, re-inventing the story of what had happened to him after the poet had died, in this same graveyard; because in between the time when the poet died and Frederick Thomas got sent to Brockville, a few years had passed, and in that time Frederick Thomas refused ever to go into the house, living in the barn at first, then finally roaming the fields and the township like any other animal, his hair growing thick and matted like fur, stealing food out of the fields and gardens in the summer and then foraging for berries and frozen potatoes in the winter, like a bear who couldn't hibernate. And after he had been brought up from the insane asylum to the cemetery, it was as if his exile was over. People began to talk about him, make him into part of their history, forgive him.

Richard Thomas pushed and twisted himself around in his bed, slid his feet down to the floor and into his slippers. He could stand up straight now, arch his back, stretch his hands high into the air and bend down again. His back felt thick and stiff, as if the bones were buried hopelessly in mounds of flesh and disused muscle. He tried to touch his toes but could only reach part way down, his fingers wrapping around his ankles. His robe had fallen open and he could see himself, a tangle of hair and fat, his pyjamas knotted around his stomach with a big bow. Looked again and saw that something was different, the bow of his pyjamas, realized he was actually seeing past his stomach, twenty pounds lighter they had said. Stood up and tried to believe he really would get better, thinner. Wondered about the exact measure of his sins, what his body represented in extra helpings of boiled new potatoes, pies with fillings of raspberries, blueberries, wild strawberries that Brian and Erik would spend a whole day collecting in quart baskets, the black thimbleberries that came after the others were over, long elongated berries that left dark purple stains on the hands and lips. "Open up," Miranda would call, throwing the berries at his mouth. They would walk to get them, in a stand of bushes that was near the house, taking Brian and Erik with them, carrying them at first, later walking them, then his hand, so wide, had enclosed Erik's entirely, his hand and half his arm so, Miranda said, when the two of them walked through the field together it looked as if Richard was eating Erik, had a big mouth at the end of his arm and had him half-swallowed already. Kissing Miranda and they would push the black pulp back and forth until finally one of them spat it out or ate it. The wind had come up again, steady now, not gusting. Now that he had noticed it, he would be unable to shut it out. He wondered how that worked, why it was that things swam in and out of focus that way, out of control; the magazine was lying open on the bed where he had dozed off reading it, he couldn't remember a word, might have been dead for all it mattered now. Miranda had said he should rent a television for his room but it was too late to bother. Erik and Miranda would be home, eating and planning the changes in the house. He could hear an elevator door opening, the squeaking wheels of the food cart. They would be bringing toast and beverages. They wouldn't let him have jam any more, it wasn't on his diet, but he was allowed marmalade. He hated the rinds: when only one arm worked he had to stare carefully at the plate and pick them out with his finger. Now he could use a plastic knife and fork, it was all right. They had told him not to use cream either; then they had put coffee on the forbidden list. The doctor had talked to him about diabetes but there were only pills, no needles. And there was something about blood sugar, eating more protein in the morning. With his meals, between them, in the morning when he woke up and at night before he went to sleep, there were pills, handfuls of pills, pills that came in slick candied tablets with their bright red and green surfaces and pills that were utterly serious, tasted awful, were covered with fine beige powder that stuck to the tongue and throat, pills that weren't tablets at all but multi-coloured capsules whose contents were designed to go off a bit at a time, like a continuous supply of seltzer, pills to do things and pills to undo the side effects.

"Oh these doctors," the night nurse would say. "They know what they're doing. My husband's brother studied to be a doctor for two years but he had to drop out. Too hard on his nerves." Richard fastened up his robe and went out into the hall. Mr. Zeller was already standing by the tray, nibbling the crusts off toast. It was a habit that didn't make him very popular. There were hardly any patients. It had been that way for weeks. The nurses said that it was strange, that it was the least business they had had for five years. Two women down the hall were getting varicose veins stripped. Every second morning, plastic vases filled with flowers were placed outside their door. There was a double room occupied by two patients overflowed from the eye section. One was getting cataracts removed. The other was having a cornea transplant. He spent all his time reading, a patch over the affected eye. Except for a man who was waiting for a kidney, Richard Thomas and Norman Zeller seemed to have the only serious illnesses.

While Richard Thomas was confined to his bed, Mr. Zeller had never actually stepped right inside the room and visited him. It was as if it would be an unnecessary indignity for Richard Thomas to be seen in the moment of his temporary inconvenience. He would stand in the door and say hello, exchange greetings with Richard Thomas's other visitors, move down the halls, exchange greetings and complaints with the conspiratorial intensity of the dying. The other patients all stayed in bed to eat their night-time snack. Richard and Mr. Zeller would often eat theirs together, in the lounge, staring out the plate glass window at the cars going up and down the lake, at the invisible water, at the occasional person who could be seen walking along the lake at night. "No one in this town walks," Mr. Zeller would say. "They would rather stand at the corner and die waiting for the bus."

While the courtyard was quiet, the wind was still strong, battering steadily against the big windows, whistling across the open area between the hospital and the lake. "There was a warning on the radio," Mr. Zeller said. Richard couldn't imagine where he had come from, this time, any time, with his faintly European accent, his secretive wife, his ornate and ridiculous walking stick that somehow reminded him of Simon Thomas, of something Simon Thomas would have wanted to have had if he had seen it. Maybe he would need one himself now, for getting around the farm. It would have to be stout: knotted and utilitarian. He had a sudden picture of his two hands, each one wrapped around a cane, his whole weight forward, the veins swelled out like bark. Mr. Zeller moved like Simon too, with that air of deception. But there was something he lacked, something vaguely turned in and unlived. He was standing beside Richard now, his pipe in his mouth and his shoulders hunched forward. "Quite a storm," Mr. Zeller said. "If we were at sea." He was sucking on his pipe, not noisy and greedy like Simon but still, the rattle was there, beneath everything. "If you don't mind me asking," Mr. Zeller said. "What were you thinking about just now, when that curious look passed across your face."

"I was thinking about my father," Richard said. "He smoked a pipe too."

"Ah yes," Mr. Zeller said. "You also remind me of my father. He was a big man, like yourself." Standing at the window they could see the revolving red light of an ambulance moving along the lakeshore, turning in at the hospital. At first the siren was muffled by the wind, but then it was carried to them, sharp and piercing. "Most likely indigestion," Mr. Zeller said. "Most people who die of indigestion do it after supper." He rapped his cane on the window. "My father was an interesting man," Mr. Zeller said. "He believed that he would be healthy forever if he drank two quarts of water first thing in the morning." The cart had arrived at the lounge. Mr. Zeller went and helped the nurse carry in the small trays of tea and toast. Richard was wondering what was happening with the person who had been brought to the hospital by the ambulance, whether it was some sort of indescribably hopeless and bloody mess or whether it was something simple, a broken leg or a lost toy. The rain burst suddenly, startling them all, exploding in a thick spray against the window, loud and heavy, overwhelming the conversation Mr. Zeller and the nurse were having, bringing them to the window to stand beside Richard. Now the lights of the cars were washed away, there was nothing visible except the layers of rain on the window, the reflection of the room. Mr. Zeller had one hand on the couch, gripping it like a rail, his face tense and worried, as if he really thought he might be swept to sea. A flash of lightning opened up the night: they could see the cars, the lake, the other buildings of the hospital turned a strange blue-grey colour. Then an explosion of thunder as the lightning flashed again, this time rising in long jagged streaks from the lake, lighting only itself and the large black-petalled clouds that answered it. The lights of the hospital flickered briefly.

"We've got our own generator," the nurse shouted. There had been no noise for her to compete with; her voice filled the lounge, an empty red balloon. "We've got our own generator," she repeated, quietly. The tail end of her sentence was wiped out by another thunderclap, more lightning from the lake, closer, near the shore, rising in a wide yellow sheet. The lights went out. The sheet stretched to fill their whole field of vision, a glowing supernatural wall. It made the night transparent; they could see the cars, lined up and stopped along the lakeshore, the lawn stretching a dull metallic green from the hospital to the road, the lake slate grey, splitting apart at the shore. Then it all slowly blackened, fading as if the world no longer existed but was only a retreating imprint on the eye. The lights went back on. The rain swept against the glass, soft and rushing, everything draining away. The nurse went to her cart, opened and closed the shiny drawers, put away the paper napkins, the left-over plastic-packaged marmalade and jam. Richard was sitting on a couch, the cup in his hand, his head bent over, letting the steam from the tea rise up into his face. For a moment, with the lightning, he had felt his body again, as if the energy was discharging into his bones, snapping him straight and young, felt his body as it had been forty years ago, bones, muscle and flesh, supple and fluid, showing Miranda the farm for the first time, his balance sure and poised, watching her try to adjust her feet to this uneven ground that slanted the body in a different direction with every step, the opposite of the prairies and the pavement of the city, seeing her assess all the impossible things that had already been done to this land, that would have to be done, the million-year-old rocks with their long deep splits, their cupped mossy areas, their immovable surfaces twice the area of a house. Yes, it must be an accomplishment to have made something out of this. But she said nothing about this gigantic conquest, only walked through the pasture with him, crouching to pick out weeds and wildflowers, bringing them back to Simon who didn't know what to do with them, finally laid them on the table so she had to find a jar for them herself. The bruises from the intravenous tube had spread and dissipated, covering the entire back of his hand, from knuckles to wrist, yellow with tinges of blue, a small red spot in the centre where the needle had been inserted. There was still thunder but it seemed further now, low rumbles that were felt as much as heard. The nurse walked up and down the hall, peering in the rooms to make sure none of the patients were frightened. There were no more hesitations in the electrical system and standing at the edge where the lounge and the hall joined, Richard could hear the sounds of television sets, of toilets flushing now that it was safe to get out of bed. Norman Zeller was still looking out the window, his face pressed to the glass, pipe put down or forgotten on the wooden sill, walking stick hooked beside it.

"Well," Richard said. They could hear another ambulance, moving slowly through the night. It wouldn't have been so bad up at the farm, away from the lake. The first couple of years after Brian had gotten back he had been afraid of storms, especially lightning; when it started he would come and stand at Richard and Miranda's door, waiting for Richard to come for him. If Richard didn't get up, they would find Brian there in the morning, sitting asleep by the door. But most of the time Richard would wake up too, and they would both go downstairs, light the kerosene lamps. In those days, even in the lamplight, Brian's scars still showed, flaming pink birthmarks. They would sit at the kitchen table, have something to eat and drink. Richard showed him how to play checkers and they would set up the board and make their moves while the house rattled and shook, the most noise of all being made by the rain on the tin roof, a thousand drops a second Richard would say, not knowing, wishing Brian would actually try to understand the rules and get on with the game. Brian would sit with his chin propped up in his fists, staring blankly at the board. With each series of lightning and thunder he would jolt awake, his body shaking in harmony with the sudden noise and light. His face would remain calm and immobile, as if the fear was a sensation which was out of control, but, fortunately, disconnected from any other part of his consciousness. Sometimes, unaccountably cruel, Richard Thomas would shake Brian's shoulder to wake him up, tell him it was his move. He would watch Brian's face as it moved from nightmare to checkerboard, the features thick and willing, uncomprehending, watch and be disgusted with the stupidity of this non-Thomas creature who was stronger and more capable than his own son, who had made friends with some strange boy and then almost burned to death with him, for something to do.

Mr. Zeller still stood at the window. The rain was gentler now, relaxed. "This reminds me of the tropics," Mr. Zeller said. He picked his pipe off the sill and re-lit it, blew a stream of thick white smoke from his mouth, waved the pipe in some vague gesture of palm trees and equatorial skies. He went and sat beside Richard on the couch, administered milk and sugar to his tea. "Cold tea," Mr. Zeller said. "It paralyzes the kidneys and strains the bladder. You know that when they take you apart, afterwards, your stomach is tanned like leather from all that tea. It's the tannin that does it, they say, tannin, you know, the same stuff they use for tanning leather." Mr. Zeller sighed, his mouth closed, smoke coming out of his nostrils in long delicate curls. "Yes," Mr. Zeller said, "I like your son very much. Perhaps that is because you remind me of my father. Were you ever psychoanalyzed?"

"No."

"Yes. Well. Perhaps it is not so common among farmers in this country."

"I don't think so," Richard said. "There was my father's half-brother who was in an asylum."

"Ah yes." Mr. Zeller had the bowl of his pipe cupped in the palms of his hands. He rubbed it meditatively, sighed again. "They say that some of the world's great geniuses can be found in institutions," Mr. Zeller said.

"Well," Richard said. "I never thought of it."

"Most people don't."

"No." Richard held his toast above his tea, hoping to warm it. The butter had soaked through, and the toast was congealed rather than dry. But the tea was cold too. He gave up and ate the toast as it was, hungry now, feeling that there should be something lying ahead, after the storm, some activity that would demand something from him.

"Well," Mr. Zeller said. "Your son will be successful. You will be proud of him." Mr. Zeller's words evoked in Richard a picture of Erik making his triumphant return to the farm, driving a huge black car, the body of the car festooned with ribbons and paper streamers, covered with trophies he had bought at some second-hand shop—old war medals, tails, stuffed mounted heads, whole carcasses thrown across the long black hood; Erik stepping out of the car and bowing, the cape and clothes too small for him, rented, his ankles and wrists showing bare, sticking out of the black silk cloth. The matador in the movie was absolutely graceful. It would never have to be said that his clothes were hand-sewn, that his victims lived their entire lives in anticipation of his final caress, achieved their own grace only at his pleasure, so, victor and victim they were joined for one brief moment. But only for that moment. Afterwards, in the scene at the café, there was no sign of the bodies of the dead, simply the young man surrounded by the beautiful women who wished to be near him. Perhaps he was secretly bothered by varicose veins and perspiration. When they moved in for the close-up at the end he seemed at first perfectly young and smooth, his black hair carefully sculpted to his tanned skin, his teeth white and even, smiling shyly at a lady who leaned close to him and whispered something, toying with his drink, like the bull, everything about to die for him the same way, over-ripe and waiting so that he needed only to apply the final touch, the coop de grass as old Mark Frank used to call it when they were killing chickens, then closer and it was possible to see the flash of gold in his smile, teeth that had already fallen, the nervous movements of his hands on the glass, waiting for the moment when he could go straight to the bottle, the sly way he ignored the ladies, not shy or bashful, but only reluctant to disclose that his whole act travelled with him all the time, lived with him in a covered wagon which he drove about the country all summer long, giving Sunday exhibitions of his talents.

"I made a decision last night," Mr. Zeller said. "I decided to donate my body to medical science." Mr. Zeller always wore red leather slippers. His first pair had been old and worn, caricatures of men's slippers that had been chewed by innumerable generations of dogs and children, turned maroon from age and sweat. But his new ones were suede, brought to him by his wife, discreetly packaged in a box covered with wrapping paper and bows. "My wife knows how to keep a secret," Mr. Zeller had said, when Richard had asked him once about the way his wife snuck up and down the stairs, never using the elevators, always coming at unpredictable early morning times, wearing outrageous hats and veils. "She's a television personality," he explained. "Out of work. She was a child star." His slippers were new, his hair silver-white and carefully cut. "My wife always said that my eyes were very beautiful," Mr. Zeller said. "I thought that someone might want my eyes. You know."

"Well."

"And my heart, " Mr. Zeller said. "I have a good heart. No offense, you understand. They don't use them for very long anyway, the second time around."

"It's all right," Richard said. "I never thought about it."

"Some people are very sensitive about their organs. My wife is like that. The very first time I met her, she bragged about her kidneys. She can still hold it for almost twenty-four hours. Remarkable in a woman her age. Even the doctor agrees." His pipe had gone out and Mr. Zeller took it from his mouth and tapped it in the ashtray. When that didn't work, he slapped it into the palm of his hands, the bowl making hollow sounds against his cupped skin, then pulled it away, a plug of ashes and tar having been yielded, complete, out of the pipe. He put the plug in the ashtray and pushed at it with his pipe. The outside layers were fine grey ash: inside the tobacco was sticky and wet, charred and only partially burned. "You understand," Mr. Zeller said, "I wouldn't want to be taken apart by some medical student who didn't know what he was doing. But I thought that someone might want my eyes." Mr. Zeller's eyes were blue. They matched his dressing gown. Sexless blue eyes that were undefined and liquid. Like the eyes of the matador, opened and indifferent to the camera. Like Simon's eyes had been when Richard returned with the doctor, Leah Thomas dead already, Steven Thomas passed out on his bed, Simon calm and covered with blood: his hands and arms, his neck and the whole front of his shirt, even his pants: eyes blue and blank that knew everything and nothing, could even ignore his broken leg swelled up inside his pantleg like a split sausage. Like Simon's eyes must have been a year later when he sat down and wrote Richard in Toronto, telling him that Katherine Beckwith was engaged to marry Peter Malone, the new hired man.

"Gentlemen." The voice of the night nurse startled Richard. It would be possible to die at home too. The next time he was in the hospital it would be more difficult. He would wake up and see the tubes leading to and from his body and that would be it, they would leave him there, locked into the jaws of their plastic and metal machines. The night nurse was pointing at her watch. They were supposed to be in bed by the time she came on duty. They went to the window for one last look at the sky. In the window he could see his reflection. Now it seemed as if his stroke had hardly happened. One eyelid was slightly drooped; it was imperceptible, he had already forgotten what it used to be like; and his arm did everything again, in every direction, but was somehow weaker, less in control, as if some nerves and connections had been burned out. The night nurse switched off the overhead light, letting them see outside. It was still raining, but the dense cloud cover had broken apart; there were fragments of open sky, signs that a moon would emerge into one of these gaps. The evening traffic was almost done. Cars moved sparsely along the lakeshore road, their lights white and steady in the easy rain.

"Well," Mr. Zeller said, turning from the window and walking to the door of the lounge where the nurse still stood, her hands on her hips and her head cocked to one side in the attitude of the indulgent television mother, "to sleep, perchance to dream. Goodnight sweet lady." And with his cane hooked over his arm, Mr. Zeller bent and took the nurse's hand in his own, kissed it. And with a nod to Richard, he was on his way down the hall, pipe in his mouth, carved walking stick tapping along the tile floor, thin chicken legs wide apart, spare hand in his dressing gown, calming the afflicted spot.

From his bed Richard Thomas could hear the night nurse making her rounds, whispering to the patients before coming in their doors, her rubber soles squeaking as she worked her way up and down the hall. He could hear the wind too, still moving briskly in the courtyard, but all the threat gone now. The rain had taken the temperature down and the breeze was sharp and cool through his window. He swung his feet out of bed and pushed the window so it was nearly closed. He liked the way these hospital windows worked, sliding up and down easily, to the touch, weights concealed in the sashes. The windows at the farm had to be pried open every spring, were put in their permanent summer positions with the first hot weather, screens propped under them. There was one beam in the basement that had rotted, chunks of dry wood and sawdust falling out every time it was touched. And one corner of the foundation that was beginning to crack. But it hadn't settled yet; the floors were warped but not tilted, and the doors still hung true. In the spring, sometimes, if there had been a lot of snow before the ground froze deep, there would be water in the basement, coming in the north wall, flowing through the mortared joints of the foundation stones, along a channel he had dug in the floor of the basement, out a pipe that had been jammed through the wall at ground level. The floor had always been dirt when Simon lived there, but Miranda hadn't liked it, had said she would be afraid to go down there unless there was a new floor. So he had had a cistern put in, a big one reinforced with iron rods, and covered the earth with a thin layer of concrete. Now the concrete was wearing away. They would have to do it again, properly. Erik was always saying that he would come home for the summer sometime, take out the old floor and put down gravel and then cement, surround the basement with drainage tile too, so that it wouldn't get wet in the spring. The house looked like it would stand forever, couldn't possibly fall down from its own weight or simply rot away like other houses did. The only thing that seemed to threaten it were the mice that ran incessantly in the walls and attic, eating away old wood, grout and twigs. Simon had hated cats, never had one in the house. But Miranda let them in sometimes and once or twice, without asking her, Richard had stuck a couple of cats up in the attic, intending to leave them there for a few days. But the noise always woke them in the night and Miranda would make him go and drag the cats away, put them outside. Mr. Zeller had shown Richard pictures of his house, a long low split-level home on the St. Lawrence River, twenty miles outside of Kingston. His daughters and wife were sitting on the front steps. In the background could be seen a flash of blue from the river, a corner of the boathouse roof. On one side of the house, in front of the picture window, was parked Mr. Zeller's car, long and low like the house, shining blue-black, its finish so highly polished that the sun glinted off the car's surface like gunmetal, too much for a mere camera to contain. Mr. Zeller had once pointed the car out to Richard when they were standing in the lounge. It had tinted glass and an air-conditioning unit. His wife wore her own sunglasses, drove with the windows sealed shut, slow and stately along the lake and then turned it, in the same dignified way, like a boat, a diplomatic envoy, going up the drive that led to the hospital parking lot. "That's my wife," Mr. Zeller had said, as if it was clear that this whole apparition, lacking only wreaths of white mums and marigolds, must surely belong to him and needed only the final detail to be clarified. As it turned out his wife grew orchids in the basement, raising them in hot glass boxes filled with water vapour and spiders. "This is an orchid," Mr. Zeller had announced, pointing to an incredibly bright and ugly plant that was on his bedside table. The next day it died.

His mattress was still up at an angle. Richard Thomas got up and out of his bed, cranked it down so it was level. Back under the covers, with his eyes closed, he stretched his legs and back, muscles tired from the day, feeling so much better tired than they did when he had just lain sick, doing nothing, only moving when he was exhausted from maintaining the same position. The sheets were crisp and fresh from the cool breeze. He pulled them around his shoulders, adjusting everything so the thin hospital blanket wasn't against his skin but contained by the sheet, pushed his toes down until they were at the end of the bed frame and then pushed against it, flexing his feet and calves, letting the blood and fatigue move up his body in waves, long sensuous waves like a child's night. He could smell the cool air. It would be fall soon, end of August approaching and in another couple of weeks the leaves would begin to turn. It would be a long season, he could feel it already, the days warm and crystal blue, the nights dipping below freezing at first, then the frosts extending straight through the dawn to the morning, lying thick and white on the grass like its own kind of foliage. In the afternoons he would sit outside on the new patio Erik had made. New boots and thick socks. There was something he wanted to do, a project, he would re-copy the poet's diaries before they faded beyond recognition. Maybe when he was better Brian could drive him to the back of the hayfield in the truck. He could walk back into the maple bush, find the log where he had tripped, swayed, decided to come up alive. The imprint of the bird's foot was still on his hand, stamped onto the nerves and small bones, thin spiny toes, ridged on the top but damp and slick underneath, live black needles, stamped on the same hand where they had inserted the intravenous, the bird's motion stopped only briefly then started again, showing Richard the hidden underfeathers of its wings, panic at discovering the animal was human. In the fall there would be time to walk and think. He would go back to the lake and sit on the beach again, maybe row out on the water with Brian, fishing. Walk along the old country road to the Beckwith place. Peter Malone was always saying they should go hunting together. Even in the fall the maple bush was like a jungle, vines and berries and different coloured maple leaves scattered everywhere in total profusion, layers thick on the ground, swept by the wind to hollows where they were as high as a boy's waist. When they used to tap the trees there, he would go back, every fall, with Brian and Erik, to cut the wood for the following spring, always trying to stay two years ahead, the cords stacked in long narrow rows leading away from the sugar house, like spokes. Erik and Brian, more trouble than help, Brian finally mastering the rhythms of the saw, pushing back and forth, not trying to do it all, Erik's body always working against itself, making things twice as hard as they had to be, taking only short turns at the cutting and then preferring to spend his time walking about dragging his feet through the sawdust and bark, kicking them, finally given the job of carrying and stacking the wood. Brian always taking things with complete seriousness, his scars pink oases in his summer-tanned skin, shoulders wide and square even as a boy, arms short and choppy, muscular, like a miniature replica of Richard, imitating everything he did. For sitting outside he would have a plaid flannel shirt, yellow and red, the kind the tourists wore with white buttons at the sleeves and a hem along the bottom, so it could be used as a jacket. Richard Thomas, farmer turned tourist, living off the farm run by his adopted son. Simon would never take a cent from him, not only refusing money but also vegetables or even wood for his stove. Richard would bring things in to him though, give them to the housekeeper. When Simon died she was left the house in town and the insurance policy. They had her out to dinner once but everyone was uncomfortable. And when Miranda went to town to see her, she stood at the door, asked her what she wanted and refused even to invite her in for tea.

Richard Thomas turned over in his bed, flapped the sheet around his shoulders so the air could get in, settle next to his body. Occasionally it was possible to hear a dog barking outside the hospital, or cats in heat. But the life with power here was microscopic, tiny germs and cancers that could only be seen through microscopes or deduced from the bodies where they had taken hold. But that wasn't his problem, the doctor had said. It was the parts that worked only sporadically, the pancreas that didn't quite know how to deal with sugar and the heart that was wearing out from having to supply such vast territories. Well. Medical science would have to progress without the remains. Or they could come and get him, dig him up from his corner of the cemetery, rebuild the tracks and take him away in a special railway car. In the lounge they had a library for the patients, a rack supplied with newspapers and magazines. *Mortality Is Just A Disease,* headlined one article, taken from a medical conference where doctors said that one day they would be able to re-supply people with a brand new version of their own bodies. And went on to describe how thousands of people believed in this, had themselves and their relatives frozen in anticipation of as yet undiscovered miracle cures. Maybe they would be able to resurrect logs into trees, marshes into lakes, cities into dark long-limbed forests veined by streams and rivers, all ages of animals brought back into simultaneous existence, dinosaurs living side-by-side with polar bears and deer, pterodactyls nesting in rusted Model T's. In the fall he would not feel so useless. All the crops would be in and he would be doing what was normal, walking around, making sure things were ready for the winter. They would let him help with the ploughing, that was nothing, sitting on a tractor pulling levers, turning the earth over in long black strips, always looking so fertile and promising when it was just newly ploughed and disced, hard to believe the crops would barely pay for the seed and gas. In the fall, the weather was always good. The rains were long and steady, destroying nothing, wetting the earth down for winter, pushing up the levels of the lakes and creeks so the fish could survive, so nothing would freeze right through. In the fall, the summer swarms of bugs that surrounded and tormented the cows in clusters about the eyes and nose and mouth thinned out, disappeared with the cold. The animals' coats thickened and they were sleek and contented with themselves, happy to spend the afternoons lying on hills and taking in the last days of warm sun, filing lazily to the back of the farm to drink from the lake, beginning to hang around the barn in the evenings, get accustomed to humans again, their constant touch, vague memories of snow and grain.

"Where was I?" was what the night nurse asked him, sitting down by the bed. Even now that he was better she followed the familiar nightly rituals, taking his temperature, wrapping his arm with her inflatable tube and testing his blood pressure. Miranda would have to do this too, check on him every night, take his temperature, count the pills to make sure the right amounts were there and gone. She would watch over his diet, regulating sugar and checking things off on the big mimeographed sheets they had already given her to paste up in the kitchen. The metal of the thermometer under his tongue was becoming the most familiar taste of all, sharper and more disagreeable every day as the anaesthetic of nicotine and tar wore away. The desire to smoke was occasional but not bothersome. The nurse said it was usually like that with the good patients, not much trouble, and besides, there were all the other drugs to adapt to, substitute. The air hissed out of the tube and she took it off his arm. "Soon you'll be normal," she said. "Just like anyone else." More figures were entered into her book, would later be put on the big chart at the nursing station. There was an intern who came up twice a week and copied the numbers from the chart, drew them into graphs. He had a part-time job working for a drug company and one day all these averages and trends would appear in a medical magazine, part of an advertisement for heart drugs. Richard could remember reading one of these magazines in a waiting room: most of the advertisements were taken up with possible side effects and, with every drug, they seemed to be the same, ranging from dizziness to nausea to sudden death. The nurse extracted the thermometer from his mouth, the metal clicking against his bottom teeth, faint twinge of an old filling, metal on metal. "There," she said, "that's enough." She put her notebook away, sliding it into a pocket of her starched white dress. She had a vast supply of these dresses, all exactly the same, and cardigan sweaters she wore over them, different colours. In the pockets of her uniform dresses she kept the equipment that was part of her job: notebooks and thermometers, pills and candies for recalcitrant patients. In her sweater she kept her personal items: a pocket-size packet of Kleenex, a cigarette case and matching lighter, a tube of lipstick. Richard could never remember what colour it was but she put in on constantly, even in the dark, puckering her words as she rubbed it on, sliding her lips against each other in a motion Richard took to be common to all women, characteristic, like the grimaces that accompanied each plucked hair. The wind still rose in occasional spurts, scattering bits of water against the glass, whistling high and hollow through the narrow gap between the window and the ledge.

"It could rain again," the nurse said. "Mr. Zeller said he's often seen weather like this, nights that it rains and clears every few hours. He's used to the weather I guess." The nurse had begun to shift her attentions, moving to the centre of the more obvious need. When he was home he would remember her, waking up early in the winter mornings, the light grey and blue through the frosted panes; he would see her silhouette there, in the frost, recall her constant movements, straightening and comforting herself in the chair beside his bed, always touching him, talking. Maybe when he came back he would ask for her again, special, he wondered if people did that, requested to receive the final comforts from their favourite nurse. By then he would have become part of the story, one of the few who had resurrected themselves from serious illness to return to, well, non-hospital life, whatever that meant to her, standing up instead of lying down, living in suspended animation between bouts of being born, being sick and dying.

"Tired tonight," Richard Thomas said. He stretched again, careful and slow, still hesitating to move quickly in any direction, afraid something might pop or strain. The nurse put her hand on his shoulder and stood up. He liked the way that felt, a woman's hand now, not just a blanket. Her fingers were long and capable, strong, always *there,* through all the distractions.

"I'll see you later," she said.

"Later," Richard Thomas said, adjusting the sheets and blanket around his shoulders again, enjoying the summer luxury of settling down to sleep with cool rain-fresh air. He woke up as the night was ending, the light a delicate pink, like a rare flower, pink, turning his room into a large still painting, the bricks and windows in the courtyard pink and blue and purple, the colours soft at first and then flowing together, deeper, the air warm and heavy, carrying the scent of this remarkable morning. He sat up slowly in his bed, letting the day possess his body, swung his feet to the floor, through a moment of pain in his groin and stomach, gone as quickly as it came, stood up to open the window and as he lifted it, felt it again, this time across his chest, like a bar, knocked him back onto the bed, but it was all right, he wasn't even breathing hard, there was no residue, the window open wide now and the air seemed a presence, everything connected by the warmth and the colour—his blood, the bricks, the glass, the planet turning slowly into the sun. This time the pain took him to the floor, exploding in the centre of his chest and shooting out his neck and head; even as he fell he knew that part of him must fight it, reached up with his arms so that when he was down he could start to drag himself up again, from his knees, his hands on the sill, the pull of his body through his shoulders and back, couldn't lift his own weight, saw himself wrestling cows and bulls in the barn, easily pushing them into stalls and bales, animals ten times his size, the pain now intense heat, still in the same place, pulsing in the centre of his chest, filling his body with blood. And again, hammer and anvil: in the echo Simon moved, skinny and clothed in preacher's black, walking slowly towards him in his polished black shoes, contented and complacent, smoking his pipe, pointing it at him, shaking it like a long righteous finger, turning away. Richard Thomas coughed. There was blood, thick and red, catching on his lower lip and hanging down like an extra last limb. Coughed again, *goddamn,* would a person have to drown in it? His hands were on the window ledge, hooked over it, holding himself up to the pink morning light, still trying to get onto the bed. He got his elbows up on the ledge, tried to pull. He could feel his back bumping into the mattress, pushing it away. A car drove into the courtyard, stopped. A door slammed. Something moved in the corner of his eye. Richard Thomas coughed again. It tore apart his throat; he gagged and tried to spit the blood. The pressure built up but didn't hold. It rose and then relaxed, slashed open, coughed free a long red waterfall. Footsteps. A sudden gust of wind brings tiny noises from the courtyard, birds' claws against the metal car roof, damp black toes like needles in his veins, stones and sand colliding, the sound of a wine glass being set on polished wood. Falling. The forest rising all around, swallowing the light. Leaves and earth.

ELEVEN

In Toronto at night, shuttled from the train to the subway and then disgorged by the subway onto Bloor Street, Erik finds himself an alien again, the lights and faces jumble together into tangles of features and eyes. He stops on the street. A man in a short-sleeved shirt pushes against him, shoving him to the edge of the sidewalk so that his back is against a building. He can feel the rough brick through his shirt, catching on the wounds he has brought with him. He feels like it is the first time in the city but not that he is young. And now that he has made his second landing in Toronto and is of the city, not just a visitor, it is immediately a ghetto for him; there is nowhere left to go except other cities which would all be the same city. Bloor Street is forgotten but already familiar, as familiar as all of its possibilities, the cabs double-parked at the tavern across the street, the woman who has stopped and is staring into the window beside him, the ten-year-old boy trying to ride his bicycle through the sidewalk traffic wearing his cowboy hat and with a baseball mitt dangling from the handlebars. Erik begins walking again and goes to a corner where there is a phone booth. Inside the booth the walls are decorated with various offers of insertion, short poems and flights of fancy. The telephone books were once placed between hard covers and hung from counters beneath the telephones. Only the covers and small bits of pages remain. Erik dials the operator and asks for Valerie's number. While he is waiting for the operator to look it up, he thinks that he must know it, that it will come to him just as he is told. In the adjoining booth a man is shouting into the telephone. Even though it is summer and night-time, the man is wearing a heavy black wool coat and sunglasses. The operator gives Erik the number and as she speaks he remembers it. The man has oily black hair and hasn't shaved for days. "I'm not paranoid," he is shouting. "Look." His voice drops. "A man has to have friends. I have friends. I don't have to put up with this." He pauses to let the inevitable logic seep through to the listener. "Please," he says. "I won't bother you. I just want to come over and see your cat." Erik walks out of the phone booth. The crowds are moving in both directions on the sidewalk, pushing him into a decision, demanding that he somehow organize an entire life, a destination, at least an attempt at appearances. All the faces are different. He doesn't look away as people approach him and they look back at him, as if he might be someone they know. He goes into a restaurant and sits at the counter. The waitress is Chinese and very young. As more people come into the restaurant she nods at them, saying hello to each one as they push past the counter to the booths at the back. Erik realizes that he should have sat in a booth too, only bums sit at the counter. He sees one with a newspaper on the seat and slides into it, the red vinyl upholstery immediately sticking to his shirt. There is a strange smell in the air, a smell of combined foods and spices and grease that adds up to nothing at all except dirt. He flips through the menu. There is no item on the menu that resembles anything he has been eating. He orders a cheeseburger from the beautiful young waitress and lights a cigarette. The neon lamps in the restaurant are tinted blue and pink. He has to go to the washroom. To get there he must descend a flight of steps, make innumerable turns in the damp restaurant basement, following signs and arrows. Finally he has arrived: a long trickle of urine has reached out from under the door. Inside the bathroom there is a toilet and a sink. Both are filled with wadded-up paper towels. On the walls of the toilet are written more offers and a few modest verses: all traditional and rhymed, some illustrated. He pees holding his breath and then goes back quickly, following the backwards arrows and running up the stairs. In his booth the cheeseburger is waiting for him. A glass of water and a napkin. It looks good; he realizes he is hungry. There is a bottle of ketchup beside the napkin dispenser and he lifts the top bun off the cheeseburger. A slice of pre-cut cheese is partly melted onto a bumpy hamburger patty. The corners of the cheese have dripped all the way down to the bottom of the bun, pinned over the meat like a tarpaulin. On top of the cheese is some green relish and a small mound of chopped onions. Erik picks up his knife and spreads this all out evenly, adding ketchup and spreads that too. He takes a sip of water. It tastes flat and stagnant, laced with chlorine. He bites into the cheeseburger and through the bun and relish he can taste the hot lumps of meat, fried to black charcoal and grease. The salt and spices cut through the food and burn against his tongue and the roof of his mouth. To finish he has to light a cigarette and smoke it while eating.

The waitress takes his money at the counter. While looking out the window she punches a button and the change comes whirling down into a metal tray. Then Erik is back on the street again, still undecided, the food intact and foreign in his stomach. He begins walking one way, stops, turns around. His feet get tangled with the wheels of a baby carriage and he hurriedly extricates himself, pushes to the inside of the sidewalk. He finds himself pressed against the glass window of the restaurant, looking in, looking at the waitress who is again operating the cash register and now smiles at him. Erik decides he will walk for one mile and then turn around, come back and ask the waitress what she is doing when the restaurant closes. He steps into the sidewalk traffic again, this time confident, purposeful, thinking that now, with Richard dead and the farm sealed off from him, he is truly marooned in the city, that the other years were only time passed waiting for this. He has lost the habit of averting his eyes. The faces, each one framed and clear like the figure of Rose Garnett stepping through the school house door, the wild curving of her spine already evident in the way she bends towards her child, the faces snap by, one by one, each time the eyes surprised as his own, hold for a moment, stick and solidify in apparent recognition and then slide around in hesitation before coming back to ask the question; and each set of eyes carries its own hallucination, stamping its exist-ence on the city as if truly believing it was something more than one of the millions of peripheral existences that the city pulls into its edges, make-believe destinies that it uses to fuel itself. The eyes stop and then move on, the lives briefly displayed and then

212

buried again beneath the summer clothes and tanned faces. He has the image of thousands of bowls of jello, overturned and running together in the heat. He is walking awkwardly, stopping and starting with every person that passes him, his stomach now knotting around the ground meat and spices, sending out warnings, a fine layer of sweat that seems to have clogged all his pores, is choking his lungs and sealing his body like a small building closed down with a fatal disease. He wonders if the school house has been boarded up, if Rose Garnett drives there on weekends in her red Italian car.

"Do you have a cigarette sir?" A girl stops him. She smiles and curtsies, eager to please at this distance. Erik reaches into his pockets and shakes his head. She is attentive, smiling he thinks because she has finally in the middle of the night run into someone even more disoriented than herself, this thirty-first of August night that is already midnight and turning into a September morning, that soon will be getting too cold for shirtsleeves and will eventually demand some combination of shelter and stamina. Their hesitation is suddenly so gigantic that they are both embarrassed, reach for each other and turn away at the same time, finally are standing on the street gripping each other's arms, looking sideways. They are standing beside a movie marquee: naked figures sprawled huge and sexless across a poster, gaping mouths: SEX IS FUN stamped across their genitals in red ink, an irrevocable promise that makes the movie obsolete.

"No," Erik says. "I was just going to get some." She looks at him, looks away, already forgiving him and starting to move on. He slides his hand down her arm and turns her elbow, feeling twice her age (later he finds out she is seventeen and four months pregnant, possessed, therefore, by his estimate, of several times the life he is), feeling that by turning her so they face in the same direction he is making some kind of commitment, obscure but definite, and can sense in her the expectations she must have of his mastery, at least age and money must make him a protector, and then walks with her to a new restaurant, taking his hand away again so she may have her choice. When they are finally sitting down and he has bought the cigarettes, he tears off the cellophane and opens the package expertly, crisply, passing them to her as a matter of great urgency. And she accepts it in the same way, withdrawing one of the cigarettes and then, after ritually tapping its end on the table, inserting it in her mouth like a cork plug. Her hand goes below the table and reappears with a lighter. She proffers the flame and Erik, alerted by something which has cut through the cacophony of restaurant stimuli and people, is aware of the presence in her of death, with the same certainty it had existed in Richard Thomas, but in her it is a weapon and not a fate, a weapon she wears without knowledge or care. Her hair is thick and tawny, her smile wide. In this moment she is confident, pulled out of the street and into a series of gestures and rituals she knows well, turning the cigarette in the ashtray so the ash falls off neat and whole: in a few minutes it is dotted with these small circumcisions. They drink their coffee and talk about the weather. "You'll want to stay with me tonight," she says, looking confidently at Erik and then averting her eyes, afraid.

"All right." They finish their coffee and she leads him back onto the street, down along Bloor Street until the taverns and stores thin out to a smaller, quiet street that runs off it, like a tributary. The halls of her house smell vaguely of antiseptic. She lives in the attic.

"This is my room," she says, and signals towards the bed. "I'll make some tea." Already early morning and cool, her room seems damp and low-ceilinged. His legs ache ache from the unaccustomed pavement so he sits down on the bed and lights another cigarette. The floor of the room is littered with discarded jeans and shirts, record jackets, half-read magazines and empty incense boxes. These objects of the generation that is not yet her own stop at the wall where there is oddly a crucifix hanging, a brass crucifix hung from an adhesive picture hook. And below the crucifix is a long shelf with a matching brass incense burner and a small leatherbound Gideon Bible. Automatically he picks up the Bible and begins leafing through it, unable to read because the print is so small and the room is lit only by a painted lightbulb suspended from the centre of the ceiling. "It's a good book," she says. She kneels beside him on the floor and puts down a tray with tea and thin biscuits. He feels there is no way at all he can connect with her except to drink the tea she has brought and so he does, finishing it in long burning gulps before she even has a chance to offer him a biscuit. "Lie down," she says. "When you're tired you have to rest." He knows that this is just an opening and that later she will demand stone mansions and limousines. He lies on his back and with his head on the pillow is instantly hospitalized. "Have some tea," she says.

He woke up knowing where he was, as if he had been waking and falling back to sleep all morning, his arm stretched out across the bed remembering that the girl had been there and gone, gone hours ago. The low hum of an electric alarm clock. He looked at it and saw that it was two o'clock in the afternoon, that it had been set for eight. The time made him nervous, set him in motion, crossing the room and finding the sink, splashing water on his face and using his finger and her toothpaste to try to take the night away from his mouth. His baggage was where he had left it, one suitcase in a locker at the train station. He went to make the bed and saw that she had left a note and a key for him, on her pillow. Without thinking he put the key in his pocket: the key, the piece of paper, and a short pencil stub that he found on the shelf below the crucifix. The teapot and plate of biscuits were still beside the bed. He decided against eating, put the tray near the sink and lit a cigarette. When he went outside, he wrote down the number of the house and the name of the street. Walking along Bloor Street again, walking east towards the train station. Bloor Street is the place where all the smaller streets are leading to. Lined with shops and movies and taverns and hardware stores, each of these masked with people standing in front of them, talking to each other, doing nothing, smoking cigarettes and drinking coffee and pop out of styrofoam containers and tin cans, brushing real and imaginary ashes and dust off their wide-cuffed checked trousers, loud patterned suits and jackets that have come out of these same windows, whispering and cementing endless unknown deals. Erik was walking again towards the centre of the city, past the restaurant where he went with the girl, past the subway stop where he had emerged from his train journey. He could see his own apartment building, the tip only, a high-rise that was only a few hundred yards away. He stopped, trying to decide which way to go. But there were too many people on the sidewalks for him to stand still; and he was pushed with the crowd until finally he resumed walking with them, east along Bloor Street towards Yonge, the summer afternoon grey and humid with the sky a grey dome hubbed over the city. The stream of people on the sidewalk grew denser, bunched up and then curved out on both sides like a swollen human pore to enclose the ambulance that was parked at the curb, outside an apartment building; the doors of the building opened and a stretcher appeared. Several men were leaning over the side holding down a woman who was thrashing and kicking. "Life is a tragedy which no one understands," she was declaiming in a theatrical Louisiana accent. She bit the arms of one of the men who held her, and momentarily her upper body was freed and she could reach over the stretcher trying to grab at the wheels and pull herself onto the ground. She was naked and as she swung towards the ground one of the men hastily covered her with a sheet, standing between her and the crowd with a look of extreme embarrassment. Then the woman got hold of the sheet and pulled it away from the man. In the scramble other arms let go of her and suddenly she was off the stretcher and running. "Let the fucking bastards see me," she yelled–then stopped at the door of the building and turned towards the ambulance, her arms outstretched, laughing. More people were coming out of the building, grabbed her and began pushing her towards the ambulance. The man with the sheet rushed up and wrapped it around her, putting his hand to her mouth so that she was reduced to muffled grunts and curses. Finally they had her in the ambulance and it began to move down Bloor Street, its siren slow and high-pitched, like the mating call of an hysterical streetcar. The man with the sheet still stood on the sidewalk. The sheet was now wrapped around the man's wrist and arm: with the ambulance gone he was the centre of attention. The heel of his hand was bleeding profusely. "She bit me," the man said to Erik. "The bitch bit me like a goddamn dog."

After two months in the country carrying no keys at all, Erik's pockets seemed to be bulging with them: the keys to his apartment, to his office at the university, to the girl's apartment, even a big key, thick and light with a dull aluminum surface, for the train station locker. And when he had finally walked there and gotten his suitcase, he was inexplicably exhausted again, too tired to eat, and he took a taxi back to his apartment. It was as he had left it. There were clothes strewn all over the floor from his hasty packing, the mail Valerie stopped forwarding, dirty cups and saucers in the sink. He paced about his apartment, felt ill at ease, put on a record. He had sent post-dated cheques to the landlord but he hadn't bothered with the telephone bill. Now the phone was disconnected. Good. He stripped off his clothes, kicked them in the direction of his dresser and went to take his shower. He stood in the tub facing the water, gingerly soaping the cuts on his back, then put his head directly in the stream of water, letting it spray against his eyes and scalp. He shaved without drying himself, letting the water drip onto the tiny red tiles that were supposed to be the touch of luxury distinguishing this particular high-rise, making it desirable above all others. In this fluorescent bathroom light the whites of his eyes seemed enormously young, unwilling to concede anything, as white as the lather against his sunburned skin. When he was finished shaving he went into the living-room and turned the record over: classical music, woodwinds and strings that marched in long melodies and counterpoints, music that Valerie had given him. Now she would be making her careful gifts to her psychiatrist, long wide ties with harmless animals frolicking on a pastoral background. The apartment seemed to belong to a previous existence. He felt uncomfortable in it, didn't want to stay. There was a lawnchair on the balcony, toppled over by some wind, rusting from the whole summer's rain. He unlocked the glass doors and retrieved it. Then didn't know where to put it and shoved it outside again. His suitcase was open in the middle of the floor. He found clean underwear and put on his jeans again, liking the feel of the denim against his bare feet, jeans and an old cotton shirt from the farm. In the suitcase were the three diaries Miranda had given him, the ones he had seen Richard reading in the hospital. They were leatherbound, with ribbons attached to the binding for keeping the place. One of the ribbons had a ring knotted to it, a small gold ring with a nondescript stone: it was blackened and lumpy, looked as if it had had an accident in a fire. Dressed now, he turned off the record; without the noise and the excuse of getting clean he felt trapped in his own space. He nervously sorted through the diaries, trying to decide what to take, chose the diary with the ring, Volume One, and then immediately walked out of his apartment, before he had time to think about it, out into the hall and pushed the door closed behind him. Outside again, he felt foolish and panicky, looked up at his window and wondered if he would have jumped. As he stood in front of his building, people walked in and out of the lobby, neighbours, people he had never spoken to. They paid no attention to him or to each other: the only necessary politeness was the ritual holding open of the unlocked door. Perhaps they assessed each other, estimating the chances that this one or that one might really be a thief, might try to climb in balconies at night or steal chained furniture from the lobby. He began to walk quickly, came to the corner and didn't know where he was going, turned automatically towards the girl's apartment. The sky was clearing but it was still hot; his hand was already sweating against the leather binding of the diary. Erik Thomas, he said to himself, my name is Erik Thomas. He let his lips move over his name, pronouncing the words out loud. Erik Thomas, only son of Richard Thomas, who was the only son to survive his own father, Simon Thomas. He had half-suggested to Rose Garnett that they live together but she had ignored it, as if it was clear that he couldn't possibly mean such a thing, that he was obviously incapable of letting anything pass in or out of his own boundaries, that he was simply saying it out of boredom. He was stopped again, standing still and looking down, his socks and sandals dusty from the street, the sidewalk marked with cracks and coloured crayon outlines for hopscotch, paper garbage lining the gutters and spilling out onto the street. He was standing beside a nursing home, the kind they had gotten for the old woman in Kingston. A garage adjoined the house and there was a door leading out onto its roof. There was a wrought-iron fence and plants along the perimeter. All the patients were white-haired and in wheelchairs, blankets draped over their knees and transistor radios blaring different stations into the sun. He could smell the heat rising from the streets, tons of uncollected garbage, food decaying in plastic cans behind restaurants. He was sweating. There was no one he wanted to see, nowhere he wanted to go. His stomach felt ill-at-ease, unsettled. A police car passed by slowly, two uniformed men inside. Erik began walking, irrationally afraid that he would be questioned and asked for papers; he walked quickly, holding firmly onto the diary, walking west towards the girl's apartment, late afternoon, watching the sun bob in and out of trees and buildings. And when he was finally there, he lay down on the bed and opened the diary, surprised to see that it was written in pen and ink, the unfamiliar writing faint and difficult to decipher, then seeming like Richard's hand, large and square and careful.

After they arrested me in London they took me to the prison. At the end of a week, they threw me out on the streets again. Then I went towards the river thinking I might find a place to sit with my wounds immersed in the water. There was a girl who saw me & the blood that was caked on my clothes & skin. She took pity on me & took me to where she lived. She was very young & not yet a woman nor could she speak or hear. I would not have gone with her but for her touch which was light & shy like a child. Her mother told me that this girl was unable to be employed in the factories because she was too frail & too stupid even to work in a house & so they let her do as she pleased. & her mother (who was not old but might have passed for twice my age & had two more daughters) washed me & let me lie in her bed for three days. The girl stayed constantly with me & though she could not hear me she wanted me to talk all the time; because she could put her hand or her head on my chest & feel the rumbling of the words which passed through me to her like a train.

One morning her mother woke her up & said to prepare herself in her best clothes; & she gave her a small linen bag to pack. Because it had been spoken in that part of the city that there would be given £10 King's Dowry to any woman who would sail to the colony of Canada & was legally single. & the girl's mother had seen one of the men who advertised this; & had arranged to take the money for herself though later she agreed she would share half of it with her daughter. So this girl who could not speak or hear & did not have a name was taken to the boat & I went with her hoping the Captain might take me in her place, as minister & deckhand. Where I found him was on a long wooden dock which jutted out from the land into the river; the boat was moored to this dock and seemed a small ship to weather the famous gales of the Atlantic. Beside the boat were lined up barrels of different goods for the colony & provisions for ourselves; &

the Captain showed me a beaver fur hat & said that on the return voyage, the vessel would be filled with these furs. Also on the platform were all the women who had signed to go. They were surrounded by the sailors & the crew who were joking with them & telling superstitious tales about the sea. I made my offer to the Captain but he only laughed & asked what kind of minister would want to sail with a boat-load of women. & I said,

"God knows all flesh was one & that it was therefore fit that a man should want to surround himself in such a way."

& the Captain laughed again & said I could dine at his table for he would take me aboard as his clown & then, giving a signal, the crew pushed us all, the girl included, up a wooden ramp to the ship; & once we were there the ropes that moored us to the dock were loosed right away & I did not see the Captain again for some long time.

Our ship was one of twelve & when we came across the ocean in this apostolic convoy we were like an army of the dispossessed. We had thought ourselves better than our nomad ancestors who had wandered to Europe from Mesopotamia & Africa, but now we too were disinherited & forced to seek out a new world; & so we closed the circle on our past.

They kept us in the hold like cattle not knowing that we were pressed body to body in God's way. The sweat ran from flesh to flesh like a river & the river of our common sweat was our love of God & He knew that & caused it to pass through us & through the wooden membrane of the ship to the ocean. & so it was that even though some ate more than others we were all nourished, even after the storms which ruined most of the food. But the officers of the ship mistook their own privilege to keep each his body to himself as if it was a jewel being hoarded by a miser; & after the storm they stole food from the crew & from the passengers but still they fell ill and starving & then hearing that I was a minister of God they called me up to them & begged me to save them & I said,

"If you desire to be saved then you must first believe & therefore get you up from your bed & walk out upon the decks of the ship where you can receive the sun & be seen by God & show Him that you receive Him & his creations by standing naked in His World."

& after I said that I walked down between the rows of hammocks. I came to a man whose face was the face of a dead man with white skin exuding a week's growth of beard; & on his face & throat though the skin was dead white there were red blotches. I opened up his linen shirt & there were more red blotches all over the surface of his body, especially the places where the flesh beneath the skin had been starved away & the skin lay mottled like a watery hide directly on top of his bones. & seeing he would be the first to die I lay down beside him to whisper further things to him, but he turned away from me & asked that I be taken from the room. His voice was unclear & hoarse & though his sickness made him look peaceful, his countenance changed with speech so that it was greedy & sullen. I got up out of his bed & I said,

"God promised Canaan to the Jews. He promised it to Abraham not because Abraham was special among men or privileged among men but because he saw God. & so he left the land where he had been living & journeyed to Canaan with his barren wife. & when they arrived she was no longer barren & she had a son. & then God came to Abraham & asked him for his son. Because with man there is life & there is death & there are things which are alive & things which are dead & man has divided the whole world into what is alive & what is dead & says that what is alive may rule over what is dead & that what is alive and more powerful may rule over what is alive & less powerful. God promised Canaan to the Jews & Moses led them back from Egypt because he struck a stick against a rock saying this & this are dead, even though God had taught him nothing was greater than any other thing, Moses was not allowed to enter the land of Israel & died only seeing it. Because man without God is mortal he takes his life to himself & says that his life is his own & is different from other lives. & one man says that I am one man & not another man because I have my nose & he has his nose. Each man therefore owns himself & sets himself a place in this mortal world of life & death saying I have so much life & therefore can cause so much death as if there were no other way. With man there is life & there is death but with God there is only life because that is all He knows."

Again I walked between the rows of hammocks until I came to the man who had denied me. & this man, still wearing the shards of his white linen uniform, lay now stiff on his back, wretchedly at attention thinking I was the Captain. & again I lay beside him in his bed & before he could speak against me put my hand beneath his open shirt so he could feel my flesh against his flesh, flesh against flesh as it is written, & I said gently,

"Why are you living like a fool & dying like a fool? Why must you be blind when it is easier to see the truth than to be ignorant? This is God's universe & man is meant to walk upon the land & breathe the air & join his flesh with others so he may be with God. This is God's universe & I am Abraham being sent into Canaan to father a new race of men. I say that in your ignorance you are more stupid than the insects you thoughtlessly crush; you are more depraved than the slugs that inhabit your stolen meat & now live in your body, which is eaten already as if it had been ten years in the grave & smells more like a corpse than like a man."

& as I spoke I rubbed his chest & stomach with my hand to make his own body feel the blood beating through my own body; & to make the rhythms of our blood mesh & harmonize & come together because though we were in man's way sailing upon a ship upon an ocean we were in God's knowledge pulses in the aether; & as I rubbed my hand against him I could feel his stomach rise & fall with his breath which grew deeper now & I whispered to him that he should sleep & then when he woke he should eat nothing but take only a small drink of water. After this I climbed down from the canvas hammock & I took off all his clothes while he slept & covered him with a light blanket.

All the while I was with the sick man, the captain had been watching me. Also standing in the doorway with him were two men who followed him everywhere to protect him from the crew—who were said to desire to make a mutiny & sail the ship up the St. Lawrence River past its destination until they came to a place where they could settle on the shores of one of the Great Lakes. & they would take with them the women who were being sent across to the colony to be wives for the men who lived in Montreal & Kingston.

As I came to the doorway the Captain & his men stood without moving. Then the two men came forward &, one to each side of me, took hold of my arms & led me out onto the deck. There they led me to one of the lifeboats & passed my arms over its top & lashed my wrists together so I was stretched & suspended with only my toes on the deck. All this happened in silence; & then the Captain stepped up to me & tore off my shirt; & saw then that my back was already covered with scars, scars up & down the length of my back that were old & black & scars that were new criss-crossed with my ribs from my shoulders to my waist. He slapped his hand against my back & said that a minister who buggered a dying man was no minister at all & that it was only out of pity for the women on the boat that he was not drowning me. & then he slapped me again on the back with his hand, so hard that it drew blood from the unhealed wounds. & he said that if the man lived he would spare me too but if he died he would have me whipped until I died. & then he threw the shirt over my back & left me there, hanging by my wrists from the keel of the lifeboat. & he said that any person who was seen to bring me food or water would also suffer the same fate. But God did not betray me here for soon, even though the water stayed calm, I could see a cloud, soft and grey, drifting across the sky towards us. It came & hung above the ship & loosed a gentle rain that soothed my back & ran down the boat where my cheek was pressed against the wood & ran in little streams in the grooves where the wood was pressed together & so I could put my tongue in a groove & shape it like a V-trough so the water ran straight into my mouth & slaked my thirst. & after the rain, the clouds stayed but were diffused so that the sun could shine through them & make a rainbow stretching to the New World.

When the sun set it was without show because of the

clouds which were on the horizon, but the stars near the dome of the heavens were able to shine through the whispy clouds that veiled them without hiding them & by that time, because of the rain which soaked and stretched my ropes I was able to rest almost comfortably, my feet full on the deck. That night was almost warm & I thought of crossing the tropics where one sailor I knew in London had gone. He had sailed on a ship that crossed the centre of the earth & then went South round the Cape to India. & when they were there, he said, they traded what they had for tea & spices & then when they ran out of things to trade they stole the rest & he himself had killed two men who were small & brown & too weak to fight. & he said that before he killed them he saw into their eyes which were large & with the pupils dilated with fright; & he said this is what the European nations are: countries which build vessels to sail about the oceans & bring back luxuries so that someone may sit in their wig & their powder & hold something to their lips & say a few words to their servant who lives like an animal—like the sailor who is pressed from the street to serve in the marine, like the men he killed, swinging an iron bar he said, & the first did not understand what was going to happen but the second, having seen the first die did not go down on his knees for mercy like a Christian but stood as the sailor swung the bar, stood rigid even though his eyes were loosed with fear, & as the bar descended towards his head he waited as if he had the timing of a god & spit in the sailor's face just before it crushed his skull. & all the time he was speaking to me of this the sailor held one of my hands between his hands and rubbed them back & forth frantically. He told me of the women that had been promised to them & of nights spent under the strange tropical constellations & of the long white sand beaches where the sun reigned pagan & supreme bringing forth trees & fruits from the land. He said that they had stopped at one of these islands where there were men & women who were dark like Indians but who were taller & stronger & paddled from one island to the next in canoes which they fashioned from burnt out trees. & he said that some of the sailors on the ship had been so long without a woman that they went ashore one night & stole some of these women because they wore no clothes & were gentle. He said that he had seen too much to live & it was true that one of his eyes was now permanently round & open whereas the other was closed & shrunk away from everything & the skin around it was folded & old as if it was the eye of an elephant. & he said that the eye that was round & open was as it was because of all the places it had been but the eye that was closed had seen truly only one moment: the thin brown lips open in derision & then pain & death.

The evening passed & the watch changed. The clouds moved thin & fast across the sky snapped trim now by the wind which filled and spread the sails so the ship gained speed too & the water could be heard spraying steadily off the hull back into the ocean.

At the beginning of the first morning watch they came to wake me up & undid the ropes which held my wrists saying that the sailor had survived the night & was better. They gave me a small piece of hard bread & put me down with the women. There, hardly able to walk because my legs had cramped & finally gone to sleep, I pushed my way along the wall until I came to the place where the girl would be waiting for me—in a back corner of the hold where we slept every night. It was so crowded in that boat that even in a few hours absence the carpeting of flesh had spread to fill this small corner & the girl was herself crushed up against the wall without even enough room to lie flat. But then we pushed and made ourselves a small opening & lay down; & her touch was as it had been in London, light & hesitant but knowing what it desires & she moved her hands over me to see that they had not hurt me & then she drew me down in the dark & we were together as God had willed it.

Erik turned the diary over, his eyes and back sore from reading on the bed, in the half-light of the setting sun. Looking east out of the girl's window he could see the glow that was now given to the houses. In this neighbourhood they had all been adorned with aluminum siding: pink and blue and white and red. The houses were lined up in long receding rows, looking like toys with their doll-house colours and their aluminum windows which shone brightest of all, reflecting long chrome streaks into the pools of water that lay on the gravel roofs of the garages that separated one row of houses from the next and were themselves garishly painted, each one marked with its own red sign lettered in solid black capitals: PARKING SPACE FOR RENT, NO TRESPASSING, BEWARE OF THE DOG; each one lettered according to the fancy of the owner and the limitations of the single Bloor Street Hardware Store which supplied these announcements, three for a dollar, along with signs to rent any conceivable proportion of the houses which had been chopped up and redivided with plasterboard and plywood to yield the requisite visual privacies so that each might live out his own metropolitan fantasy, restricted only by the limits of imagination and the infinite surface of the city which shone now at this hour in absolute imitation of the revolving neon lights which would soon replace the sun and reveal the city as it was intended; but for these few moments there was at least a series of objects: the gravel roofs of the garages and their pools of water which anticipated the bright rows of houses and now, the sun having moved lower, their new grey concrete chimneys, and behind them the trees which masked but did not hide the encroaching downtown which was visible in the shape of two office buildings towering high, even in their miles-away-perspective, above the houses—their vertical rows of window turned pink and shiny by the sun as if they were not steel and sand and portland cement, but a new kind of flesh, babyish and hesitant, that required love and compassion like a rare and delicate desert flower with its exquisite brief petals and quick poison.

Now it is the first day of September, five days since the death of Richard Thomas, and the time since the funeral is still whole to Erik, unbroken and continuous with his dreams unlocked and vivid every night dealing out the past and the scene at the cemetery, Brian springing at him with a broken bottle and then the two of them rolling on the grass, down the hill and away from everyone, back where the railroad tracks had rusted and died but near enough the grave so Erik could sense his father's presence, still there in his body only forty-eight hours dead and still live to the touch and look, coffin open, dead man looking up seeing all with eyes closed, Katherine Malone the old woman now in her black coat with a Persian collar she got in anticipation of her own funeral, bending over the body and kissing Richard on the lips before he was lowered into the grave, kissing him on the lips and turning to Miranda as if to say, "there, now I've done it and I dare you to undo it." His father's presence was still alive in these mourners—who knew what had died with him, knew it in their bodies that had bent and been broken by machines which already lay rusting and obsolete—who had tested and made their muscles, fighting against the weight of a horse dragging a plough through ground so rocky that the wrenches of metal against stone were not occasional but rhythmic and unceasing, marking the beginning of the morning and carrying the muscles past exhaustion, arms that had swung scythes now sold as curiosities at country auctions; but it had taken a family a day to cut a field a man could now mow on his tractor in a couple of hours, a day to cut it and then it needed to be turned and dried, piled and tied into stooks until finally it was dragged on wagons to the barn where it was swung into baskets which were pulled, block and tackle, up to the long metal track that ran under the peak of the barn roof; they mourned him—the women fat from the endless winters of potatoes and bread, and the men, some of them fat too, but others skinny like Pat Frank, young and thin looking from the front in their baggy dark suits but from behind, looking like turkeys, with their stringy necks wrinkled and wattled from the sun and their hands always turned out, the muscles of the forearms continuously enlarged now and and the hands too, all of them frozen and broken and pounded into huge floppy masses of calluses and scars and half-fused bones that had settled into some intermediate territory between their owners, cows' teats and machinery. They mourned him without particular grief or feeling but as a necessary marking of their own passing and stood shuffling their feet and gossiping while the minister droned out his sermon in his young and unconvinced voice that had lost interest in these old people who attended their church with such dull regularity and forced him to drive especially to them, every Sunday, from his other, better parishes, and recite the exact same sermons and lead them in the exact same hymns that they were used to. And when he was finished what he had to say, he gave his signal and the coffin was closed and the two men who were employed by the cemetery and the monument works began to throw shovelfuls of dirt into the grave, the earth sounds being absorbed by the wood and the occasional stone bouncing off the iron trim that went around the coffin—two bands, top and bottom. The minister left first, saying something to Miranda and then walking quickly to the car. The others were slower, stopping at the graves of their relatives on their way to the road, still gossiping, comparing this funeral to others and asking each other what there would be to eat at the Thomas house. The men automatically segregated themselves from the women and children. A bottle was passed around. Erik stayed standing by the grave, watching it being filled. He saw his mother surrounded by women, they closed about her, Katherine Malone right at her side, her arm hooked in Miranda's, gradually walking her to the road. They would be with her all day, always by her in the kitchen and the living-room, knowing she would do the same for them, helping her serve the food they had all made, do the dishes; and, without being asked, someone would stay with her in the house, all next week when Erik was gone. The men stayed near the grave, waiting for Erik. He saw them but didn't know what to say, how to receive their offer. They were men from the town, nearby farms, Peter Malone who was his godfather and Leslie White the lawyer he had met yesterday; some of them he had hardly spoken to in his life, the others he hadn't seen for years, since he went to college, encountering them only briefly when he was on vacation, shopping in town for Christmas presents. "Still going to college?" they would say, slap him on the arm, ask after Richard. Or, later, they would only nod, wish him a good Christmas. When the grave was finally filled, they patted the earth down on top with the backs of their shovels, inserted a small wooden cross at the head of the grave for a marker. In a year there would be a tombstone to be unveiled, with Richard's name blasted into the marble veneer. Now they raked the earth smooth, threw grass seed on top. All this was done without talking, the two gravediggers clearly resenting Erik standing there, watching them, as if they somehow still held something of value to do with the man they were burying. With Erik there they had to be careful not to step on the grave, work quickly and with their faces turned away.

When they were finished, they took their shovels and ropes and threw them in the back of the truck that was parked near the grave. As they drove away Erik could see the mourners starting to move away too. The men had given up on him. But they still hesitated, not wanting to leave without him. Erik lit another cigarette, turned his back firmly on these black-coated mourners who only made him feel uncomfortable. His throat hurt from the cigarettes and his own inability to cry. The will had been long and complicated. Now Miranda owned the farm. Brian could live there and work it as long as he wanted. It was a victory of sorts; when the lawyer had explained what this meant Brian had not been able to keep from smiling. Afterwards Nancy had announced that now it would be possible for them to have children, as if Erik's existence had previously rendered them sterile.

Except for the lawyer and the preacher, both of whom owned city leather shoes, the men all wore thick black shoes that were heavily coated with polish and bulged with creases. Even the Frank brothers had shoes like these, bought decades ago, shoes for going to church and funerals and the hospital. "You want a drink?" In his black suit and starched white shirt Pat Frank looked like he should have been the minister, tall and burned, the minister or the undertaker; the other men had moved away so Erik took the bottle and drank some, for no reason except to wet his throat against the hot afternoon and the cigarettes. "They say you're leaving tomorrow," Pat Frank said.

"On the train."

"Well," Pat Frank said. Come over and have a drink with your brother." He put his hand on Erik's arm and turned him so he could see Brian, sitting and waiting for him on a stone at the corner of the cemetery, talking to Mark Frank, a long brown paper bag in his hand. "You don't have to," Pat Frank said.

"It's all right." They walked over to Brian and sat down on the grass beside him. The stone was the last in that section of the cemetery. Beside it was a hill that sloped down to the railway tracks, now torn up and rusted, the cinder bed still half-visible through the weeds and grass. "I hear they're thinking of using the railway again," Erik said. "For tourists."

"Come up from Brockville like it used to," Mark Frank said. Brian had his tie undone. He laughed when Mark Frank spoke, tipped the bottle back again.

"Fucking tourists," Brian said. "Couldn't move their arse from the chair to the shithouse."

"Don't be dumb," Erik said, reaching towards Brian to take the paper-wrapped bottle from him, to have a drink, but Brian pulled it away sharply, his arm swinging behind him, shattering the bottle on the gravestone and then bringing it forward all in one motion, jagged neck and paper with wine still dripping from it. Closer and he saw Brian wasn't going to stop, Erik ducked and could feel the glass pushing and tearing against his suit jacket, then it was through and digging into his back and shoulder like giant cat's claws. Rolled away, from Brian, down the hill, and Brian was trying to stay on top of him, free the bottle from his coat so he could swing it again. Stopped at the bottom and somehow he was on top, legs straddling Brian and his hands around his throat, squeezing, didn't know what to do and saw the two Frank brothers walking slowly down the hill towards them, pausing when they saw him look, saying nothing. Brian wasn't resisting at all; his arms were flapped out at his sides, motionless, the bottle gone and his hands empty. Erik let go of Brian's neck, saw the red marks where his fingers and thumbs had pressed into the skin, his hands now feeling cold and weak, useless. Brian's eyes were closed. The scar on his cheek formed a smooth dull triangle. He was smiling. Erik stood up and took his coat off. It was torn in the back, there was some blood on it. One of the knees of his pants was torn out too, both legs grass-stained.

"Take off your shirt," Pat Frank said. He ripped a length from the bottom and soaked it in wine, wiping Erik's cuts with it. Mark Frank and Brian stood in front of Erik, watching him undress and be cleaned. Mark Frank took out a package of cigarettes, offered them to Erik and Brian, lit matches for them. Brian's neck was fading to its normal colour. It had felt strong and muscular, invulnerable to anything Erik might do. Brian coughed and turned his head to spit. "All right," Pat Frank said, "you're not bleeding too bad." Erik put on his shirt again. The back was bloody and there was a piece missing from the bottom; but from the front it looked normal. He put on his jacket too and started walking up the hill. He thought he could feel the bleeding begin again with the effort of climbing. Everyone else was gone. He walked over to his father's grave and stood above the wooden marker. The lump in his throat was gone but he still hadn't cried. The grass would grow where they had thrown the seed and the mound would settle flat with time and rain. One day he would take his own children to see this grave and they would wonder how someone related to them had come to be buried here, whether this meant it was true that their father had been born on a farm.

The next morning he woke up and felt sore and swollen; his eyes were closed and tired and didn't want to open. He went to move the blankets and when he tried to lift his arms he could feel the cuts along his back and shoulders, see where the skin had been turned away from itself, like riverbanks, peeling away and thickening at the edges, leaving new unprotected snakes of blood. The house was absolutely still. The sounds he could hear were wind and birds. He opened his eyes and it was warm and blue, the sky soft like a May morning, an invisible haze that melted and absorbed the clouds at their edges. The click of a cup and saucer from the kitchen and then the sound of a chair being pushed back, scraping along the floor. He looked out the window and saw the trees' shadows had foreshortened; it was almost noon. When these leaves turned they didn't go red but gold, wide lime-golden sprays of leaves that hung above the ground and fluttered tenuously, like aspen leaves, like courtiers; the cuts he could see weren't so bad, smeared over with patches of yellow disinfectant. Water pouring from the kitchen taps. A kettle being set on top of the stove. Clothes to wear back to the city. "They'll think you're a hippie," Rose Garnett told him later, standing outside at the train station. His suitcase had pushed him from the garden to the city; now in his jeans and sandals he looked like a student coming back from his summer in the country, tanned and long-haired, clean, saying good-bye to a woman in a sports car.

First they went to the hospital to see Mr. Zeller. He was in the lounge, in his blue gown, staring out at the lake. When he was introduced to Rose Garnett he bent briefly over her hand, as if he were about to kiss it, then straightened up again and turned back to the window. The lake held the sun in a wide yellow saucer, tipped it up with the waves so they were blinded, turned it into millions of white drops and then released it. "My wife is out there," Mr. Zeller said. "She said she'd be sailing in front of the hospital today." It was impossible to see anything in this light. Norman Zeller was hunched forward, his eyes squinted, wrinkles curving out gently from the corners of his eyes. He was smoking his pipe and had his walking stick hooked over the ledge. The hair on his head was completely white now. His eyebrows were beginning to turn too, the tips first, like cat's fur. "Well," Mr. Zeller said, not looking at Erik, "soon you will make up your mind."

"I'm going to Toronto this afternoon," Erik said.

"Ah yes, well. The play is over. Now we all go home and darn our socks." He turned from the window and extended his hand. His face was still evolving with his death, thinning, sliding from square to hawk-like and now to a ferret, the nose even more prominent, long and pointed, his chin beginning to recede, cheeks sunken narrow triangles.

Now Erik imagines that perhaps the poet and Mr. Zeller are somehow the same, that the poet too had this cruel pointed face, but without the formality, simply moral and clear, like the man who gives back what he has received. Looking out the girl's window he could see that people had begun to turn their lights on. Where they hadn't, the sun left only a dull yellow reflection, rays of yellow and red barely visible against the evening sky. There was a visual transition from day to night in the city but the sounds were the same, the traffic never seemed to vary, a continuous stream of cars and trucks with faulty mufflers and loud horns. The girl's apartment was a big room with a cupboard converted into a bathroom. There was a sink in the room, a sink with a small counter and a door underneath to get at the plumbing. Above the sink were some shelves. All the girl's food seemed inedible: Mexican spices, dried soups, a giant can of corn oil, canned Portuguese fish, ten pounds of sugar, ten pounds of whole wheat flour, three cans of cubed carrots. There was a box of crackers on the counter; he began to eat these, eating them and drinking water. He looked under the sink and found a pot and a can opener. When he was finished eating, he took off his shirt and inspected his wounds in the mirror. The poet's words had transformed them into martyr's welts. The antiseptic had washed away with the shower and Erik could see that the skin was growing scabs, bulging half-cylinders that were healing quick and confident, despite everything. He found a hot-plate for the soup and while it was cooking the girl came in, knocking first, as if this guest required everything that was possible. She had two salmon sandwiches with her, salmon on brown bread with thin slices of cucumber. She reminded him of a picture of Mr. Zeller's teenage daughters, of Rose Garnett when he first met her. While they ate, she cleared away the mess in the apartment, stacking objects on her shelf, putting clothes in a cardboard box. She did all this briskly, making it clear that the routine was entirely normal, the way things were meant to be. She had brought a candle with her too. She lit it, lit a stick of incense with the same match, put a record on. The overhead light shone into all the corners of the room. With everything ready she made a pot of tea and then brought out a deck of cards. According to the alarm it was now ten o'clock. "Do you want to play cards?" she asked.

"Sure," Erik said. He was sitting cross-legged, opposite her. While she spread all the cards out on the floor he straightened his legs, rubbed his knees, wondered if she would think that he was impossibly old, already arthritic. They had told each other their names. She said that it was the first time she had lived away from home. She took special vitamins and food pills for her baby. Now she pulled some knitting out of her purse, something blue with three needles sticking out of it: it was going to be a boy.

"The idea is to get pairs," she said. "You get to turn up two cards each time." She poured the tea, for both of them, and passed the sugar bowl to Erik. "You have to try to remember the cards," she said. "That's why they call it concentration." She beat him easily, several games in a row. While they played, she knitted. When it was eleven o'clock she yawned and put away her wool and her needles. Erik stood up and took the dishes to the sink. "You don't have to wash them."

"That's okay," Erik said. "You bought the sandwiches." He wondered who he was saying this to. While he washed the cups and plates she went into the bathroom. She came out carrying her clothes over her arm. She was wearing a pink nightgown. She got into bed, the same side she had slept on the previous night, and curled into the pillow. It was possible that her parents had given her the nightgown for Christmas, that they didn't know where she was.

"Don't forget the lights," she said.

"All right." She closed her eyes. Erik tiptoed around the apartment, rescuing the diary from the bedspread, emptying the ashtray, planning to go back to his apartment but not wanting to leave.

"Don't go," the girl said. "Come and say good-night to me." Erik went to the bed and kneeled down beside her. She put her arms around his neck, pushing the flannel up against his face, kissed him chastely on the cheek. "Don't leave me alone tonight," she said. "You can read and listen to my records. You like reading, don't you?" She spoke with her face in front of Erik's, her nose touching his.

"All right," Erik said. "That would be nice."

"All right," the girl said, enlarging the tones of his voice. She was holding Erik's hand. She slid down under the covers. Then she closed her eyes, kissed each of his fingers. His hand beside her face now seemed gigantic, overwhelming, as if she was a child that he could hurt through mere carelessness. But she already carried more life within her: his hands had created nothing at all: their greatest achievement was that they were too weak or faint-hearted to kill. Erik moved away from the bed and sat beside the girl's shelf, beneath the crucifix. He put the diary on the shelf, found an ashtray and put it there too. Perhaps tomorrow he would make another light for the room, hang it from the ceiling over this place like an altar, somewhere he could sit and read while the girl slept. It was hot in this attic, no floors over it to keep away the heat. It was necessary to leave the windows open so all the sounds of traffic came right into the room, the sounds of traffic and of people in the street, talking and arguing in foreign languages, endlessly climbing in and out of cars, sitting on the street playing radios and waiting for the heat to dissipate, walking up and down from house to house, street to street, waiting for something to happen, trying to justify another day gone by, have something happen to make it worth going through again. The girl's breath rattled in her sleep. She shifted and was silent. Erik opened the diary where he had marked the place with the ribbon, let the ribbon hang free, watching the ring swing on this short pendulum.

The week after my punishment the Captain sent for me &

asked me to come up to the bridge with him. From there the other ships were visible & counting them I saw that there were now only ten other than ourselves & I asked the Captain what had happened. & he said that ship had been lost in the storm; but that some of the men had been saved. The day was clear & we looked always towards the horizon in the hope of land; & the captain said that earlier in the day one of the sailors had reported seeing certain birds which indicated we might be only three days away from Newfoundland. & there, the Captain said, we might stop; for although the island had rocky shores & was covered with forest so dense it was difficult to walk in, there it would be possible to get fresh water. All the while he talked to me in this most unusual civilized & kind way as if we were gentry & seated in his parlour. As he spoke he gripped the railing with his hands which were thick & muscular with the little finger on each hand stumped & nail-less & missing one knuckle. He was not a tall man but thick-set & strong with a paunch that hung jauntily over his wide belt. His face was no mask at all but cruel & rough-skinned, with the appearance of muscles working beneath the surface in continuous rhythms of rage. He had not yet actually used it but he always carried with him, in one of those four-and-a-half fingered hands, an oiled leather whip which he said had been bequeathed to him by his great-grandfather, along with the antique silver pistol in his belt. That man, he said, had been a pirate & a Spaniard & had bought his peerage with Aztec gold. & in his unusual & soft voice which seemed to betray his own cruelty by its very lowness & the look of him as he spoke–the look of those men who in the name of their false religion attempted to destroy me & have killed so many others in the exercise of their power which is only death & has destroyed Europe & made it reach for the New World as a drowning man–he told me that if I liked he would tell me the story of his hands. He said that it had happened to him fifteen years ago when he was twenty-seven years of age & in charge of his first ship. He had been taking on cargo in Morocco & one night he had gone to a place to drink & have a woman. & the woman he had chosen had taken him to a room & given him some food

& some drink which had loosened something in him & made the time flow as if it was a river. He had wanted the woman very much but she would not have him; so he said he would give anything for her because by this time he was so weak he was unable to take her by force. & she said that if he wanted her he must walk over to a place in the wall that she showed him & put his finger through a small hole that was there. He did as she asked & then felt a terrible pain & when he drew his hand back it was as it is. & then, he said, she made a great fuss over his wound & wiped away the blood with a white bandage & put a poultice on his wound. She commended him & agreed that he was a brave man to trust her & that she would offer herself to him gladly if he would trust her once more. & he said that she was of great beauty & that her eyes glittered & that she had a power that was unlike any other woman's for as she spoke & gazed at him he felt himself become an instrument of her will & felt her will overcome his own so that despite himself she pulled his body up with the force of her mind & made him walk to the wall again. & he said that he was still able to speak to her but despite his words he once more trusted her for she said she would not hurt him twice. & she said that she had been with no man for many months & that he would not regret this night for she knew already that she loved him with great passion. He told her that he believed her but that she should show her love by releasing her power over him & letting him come to her in his own way as it was meant to be. Then she laughed at him & said that in truth she cared for him not at all & that he was free to go. He felt her power leave him; & though he could not move his body towards her he could walk towards the door. Then, he said, he walked from the wall to the door & the door to the wall, back and forth several times, mapping out his exact freedom. & then she said to him again that she would offer herself to him if he would trust her & that it was not asking more of him than he had already asked of her. & he wanted to know what she felt for him; & she said that she did not know or care. He walked to the door & knew she had no power over him. He opened the door to step outside but on the other side there was nothing at all, not even air as if they were floating in the sky, nothing at all, neither light nor darkness nor emptiness nor fullness. He closed the door & came back into the room & she was still sitting where she had been, on a long curved couch that had a Persian cloth thrown over it. & he noted that the area of his freedom was as it had been & that he could not approach her. She began to sing & not in words but humming & short cries & words that were no words but nonsense. Again he felt her power overtake his will but this time it was different because there was nothing it would make him do; so he sat down on a pillow near the door. After a time he rose & opened the door again & through the door he saw nothing at all; & if he stepped out the door he would fall into an endless abyss; & he closed the door & walked towards her & this time she let him approach her & she told him to put his hand on the table which was in front of her & he did & she drew out a sharp knife & quickly cut the other finger, with a single fast stroke, & again, like the first, washed & cared for the wound. She showed him the ring that was on her hand & it was silver with a mysterious green translucent stone unlike any he had ever seen. She held the stone near to him so he could see the light of the lamp in it & he felt her power in him again & the stone was the source of the power; & it made him bend closer & closer to it until the light had the brilliance of a sun & it shone from the stone with this deep & penetrating brightness which was absolutely round & surrounded by a halo of exquisite violet of such colour it was of a living flower; & the brilliance of the light entered not only his eyes but seemed to have filaments stretching to the severed stumps of his fingers which now throbbed & bled. She leaned forward with the ring until it was touching the floor & he followed it with his eyes & with his hands & then he was lying on the floor too with the ring in front of him & she said she had been a fool because she had thought that an Englishman would be able to resist the power of a pagan ring & that it was foolish to waste it & she drew the ring into the shadows again so it seemed only dull green & unremarkable & he felt the power of it leave him & was again passive & she told him to come & lie beside her on the couch

& he did & she said that he had fulfilled his part of the bargain & that now she must fulfill hers & she took off her clothes & he saw that she was only a whore, fat & used; & she laughed & held out to him her own hands which were whole & perfect.

While the Captain spoke he looked out at the sea & had his hands grasping the rail, squeezing it the whole time & by the end of his story there were flecks of blood forced out onto the stumps of his little fingers. & he said that every time he told the story or dreamed about her the blood appeared that way though the skin was never broken & had healed without even leaving a scar. He showed me his fingers closely & I could see that the skin was all connected without line or seam as if he had been born like that—for the skin had grown about the tips of the bone & had even formed its surface in curves & whorls; so whole was the skin that it seemed these little fingers were as they were meant to be—small parodies following the hand in impotent mime. Then he drew a ring out of his pocket & he showed it to me. It was a small ring, gold, with fine engravings of snakes in its arch. He said that she had told him to take this ring to remind him of his dreams; & that if we reached land he would give it to me because all the crew said I had saved them & the ship. Four days later we were in sight of the forests of Newfoundland & the following morning, when a boat was sent ashore, the Captain made me his present of the ring, as he had promised.

The ring was knotted to the ribbon, blackened and deformed, as if it had been held briefly in a fire. Erik worked the knot free with his nails, took the ring and tried it on his little finger. It was small, barely fitting the first joint. The girl's hand was stretched out on the pillow. In sleep her face was pale and child-like. He took her hand and held the ring beside it, put it on the second-last finger of her left hand, wedding band, wondered if this was the poet's intention, to have the ring passed through the family this way, as a sign. The girl sighed and turned over in her sleep, took her hand away and slid it under the covers, between her knees. Miranda would be asleep now. She had told him that Katherine

Malone would be staying there with her, the two of them together, they had lots to talk about, Miranda said. Erik switched off the light and got into bed with the girl, leaving his underwear on, careful not to touch her. But as he settled in she moved against him, her back against his back, the soles of her feet flat against his calves. Her breathing was still slow and regular. He tried to breath with her, adjust his body to hers, convince himself he was sleepy even though it was less than twelve hours since he had woken up. With his eyes closed he could see the cemetery, Brian's face as he held him round the throat. If Richard had left him the farm it would have only been a problem. His body was still and his breathing was slow but something inside him fought this, was still high-pitched and alarmed. He could take care of this girl, take her out to Edmonton with him and help her have her baby. Every night they would sit cross-legged in his new apartment, all the cards face-down, picking them up in pairs. He was drifting in and out of sleep, dreaming that the land would finally rebel, rise up and out from under the concrete, toppling buildings and smashing apart roads and factories as thoughtlessly as an animal shrugging off flies. The girl had turned and put her hand on his belly, moved down and tugged at his underpants. He pulled them off and rolled on top of her. She had her hands on his hips, belly pushed against his, her hands on his hips pulling him inside of her, her head arched back on the pillow, mouth open and smiling. Slipped her hands up his sides and onto his back and shoulders; he could feel the ring catching on his back, it was harmless, he would leave this girl to live her life without him; her fingers soothed where the ring disturbed, played up and down his spine. The tension in him faded and inverted, everything was dulled, hardly awake. He tried to sense the body in her, this life she carried which he had mistaken for death, as if either extreme was equally dangerous, to feel the extra heartbeat of this hidden child, to feel something for this girl who moved beneath him in harmony with Richard's death, finally drawing the tears out of him, opening his throat and his belly but knowing nothing of what she was doing, living out her own fate in this one night they borrowed from each other; and the girl's mouth was open, neither smiling nor frowning and the moon shining through the window caught her teeth like a row of gravestones, a row of grey-green gravestones, a row of grinning masks of the poet; and at the end of the row, identical to all the others but cut off from them was his own face, transparent and desperate that there would be something to forgive him, swallow and forgive like a mother who has only imagined her children; and then the girl made small noises, her body fluttering, her mouth closed and turned into itself, its own release which was absolutely private and removed from him, this new beginning.

Matt Cohen

The Colours of War

The second of Matt Cohen's Salem novels, *The Colours of War* is set some time in the near future, when both Canada and the United States are in a state of civil disorder, with food and fuel shortages, corrupt government and armed forces patrolling the streets.

In the centre of this world of unpredictable violence is Theodore Beam, journeying by train from Vancouver to the small Ontario town of Salem. His mind flooded with childhood memories and experiences, Theodore wavers between past and present, fantasy and reality, innocence and corruption.

The Colours of War is at once science fiction, political fantasy and an unforgettable story of alienation, loyalty and love.

"...a technical *tour de force* for Cohen, a real virtuoso performance."

The Globe and Mail

Matt Cohen

The Sweet Second Summer of Kitty Malone

This is the story of two lives inextricably intertwined. After twenty years of loving each other, hating each other and ignoring each other's existence, Kitty Malone and Pat Frank have reached the point of no return.

"The people in this book are all striving to come of age the second time around and the story of their struggles is both intriguing and marvellously told."

Timothy Findley

"A violent and tender story of love... human and triumphant in spirit... splendid writing."

George Woodcock

"Funny, potent, bittersweet... a work of joy and mastery."

Dennis Lee

Matt Cohen

Flowers of Darkness

Looking for an escape from their life in Ottawa, Annabelle and Allen Jamieson move to an old stone house in the sleepy town of Salem. There, Annabelle begins to adjust to the muted rhythms of a town dominated at one end by the brooding Presbyterian church and at the other by a smoky tavern.

Annabelle, an artist, starts work on a mosaic depicting the people of Salem. As autumn gives way to winter, and then to spring, they step one by one out of the mosaic and into her life.

Flowers of Darkness tears away the serene façade of a small town to reveal undercurrents of passion and hatred. Alive with the spirit of a man and two women and their haunting and unforgettable story, it is a stunning achievement by one of Canada's finest novelists.

"*Flowers of Darkness* is a strong, deeply felt, adult work of fiction... Cohen writes lyrical, wide-open, yet masterfully sure and skilful prose."

Maclean's